THE LODGE

OTHER NOVELS BY PAUL FINCH

Detective Sergeant Mark Heckenburg

Stalkers

Sacrifice

The Killing Club

Dead Man Walking

Hunted

Ashes to Ashes

Kiss of Death

Rogue

No Quarter

Detective Constable Lucy Clayburn

Strangers

Shadows

Stolen

Standalones

Crime/Thriller

One Eye Open

Never Seen Again

The Island

Fantasy

Stronghold

Dark North

Writing as PW Finch

Historical/Adventure

Usurper

Battle Lord

The Devil's Knight

THE LODGE

PAUL FINCH

THOMAS & MERCER

This is a work of fiction. Names, characters, organizations, places, events, and incidents are either products of the author's imagination or are used fictitiously. Any resemblance to actual persons, living or dead, or actual events is purely coincidental.

Published by Thomas & Mercer, Seattle

www.apub.com

EU Product Safety contact:
Amazon Media EU S. à r.l.
38, avenue John F. Kennedy, L-1855 Luxembourg
amazonpublishing-gpsr@amazon.com

ISBN-13: 9781662526343
eISBN: 9781662526350

Cover design by Dominic Forbes
Cover image: © Marko Aliaksandr © blackboard1965
© Angela N Perryman / Shutterstock

Printed in the United States of America

For my mum, Margaret,
who was always there for all of us

Prologue

Harry was prone to walking out on his wife. Not in a permanent way, and not even spectacularly. There was never any door slamming, no throwing of ornaments. Not any more. These days, when things got to be too much, Millie becoming unbearable, their financial woes stacking up like millstones on top of him, the easiest option was to get up from his living-room chair, pull on whichever coat or jacket was closest, walk into the hall, grab his car keys, and drive.

Just that, drive. Whatever time of day or night it was. Drive.

He was aware that this wasn't a manly response to abject despair. But screaming arguments rarely resolved anything; he and Millie had had plenty of those and probably weren't much the worse for them in truth, though it was dispiriting in the long term and both physically and emotionally exhausting, plus there was never a constructive outcome.

No, it was better just to vacate the premises for a short cooling-off period.

On occasion, when it was especially bad, he tended to find himself behind the steering wheel with tunnel vision, literally not knowing where he was or where he was heading for. And being honest, it was easily done. He and Millie had lived in central Lancashire for the last thirty years, but it was still a landscape of villages and small towns, extensive farmland and hilly, wooded countryside, so, once darkness fell, it was easy to find yourself navigating solely by your own headlamps, following unmarked, unlit lanes and seeing only the dark humps of nameless hillsides where the horizon should be.

On this occasion – an uneventful midweek night in late September – he'd travelled a significant distance from home before his nerves had settled sufficiently for him to try and work out where he was. He must have taken half a dozen turns at random and had been on the road a good forty minutes before he reached a small crossroads, a single signpost on the grassy hummock in the middle pointing one way to Claughton and the other to Inglewhite. Even Harry was surprised by that. It meant that he'd been motoring along obliviously for five miles or more. Still, at least he now had his bearings, and happy ones they were, seeing that the Coach and Horses pub was located on the other side of the crossroads.

He drove around to the pub's rear, finding room in the car park, and entered through the back door into a traditional interior – horse brasses, gnarly beams and the like – where various small groups and couples were dotted around at different tables.

Harry didn't hold with drinking and driving. But on this occasion he needed something a bit stronger than a diet cola.

He waited at the bar for a couple of minutes, enjoying the friendly atmosphere, made fleeting small talk with a nice-looking blonde lady, and when it was his turn to be served, ordered a single measure of Chivas Regal.

It wasn't that Millie was obstreperous by nature, he told himself, making his way to a seat close to the fire, but she had to understand that the economic chaos into which their life together had descended was not purely down to him. Okay, she never actually said it was, but he was certain she believed it.

So many years ago, when he'd left that secure job to start his own business, things had never looked brighter. But the perks of being his own boss, working his own hours, he and Millie able to take holidays whenever they chose rather than having to bow and scrape for permission, had paled as the many stresses of life as a one-man band set in. Millie, formerly a teacher, though she'd left that profession long ago to raise their family, had gone the whole distance with him. And she'd been supportive. She'd taken various part-time jobs, sometimes several at once, to see them through sticky patches, but ultimately, they'd never made it to those sunlit uplands where life, if not prosperous, was at least comfortable. And he was sixty next year, so what chance of anything changing now?

He sipped morosely by the pub fire.

Maybe he was projecting his own sense of guilty inadequacy on to his wife? He'd wondered about that several times. She'd stuck with him, which surely indicated that she believed in him, or had believed in him once. But there was no disguising the disappointment in her eyes whenever they went over their accounts together, the heartfelt sighs when she thought he wasn't listening (or perhaps when she thought he was), her failure to laugh or even smile when he tried to make light-hearted comments.

It couldn't be easy hiding it, of course, when your partner had proved himself a loser time and again. 'But perhaps,' he muttered, 'you could try a bit harder.'

He glanced at the clock over the fireplace, seeing that it was almost ten-thirty.

Even if he'd been inclined to have another one, which he wasn't, he'd have recognised that it was time to head for home. They wouldn't be able to patch things up tonight. Millie would be in bed when he got back; it was early for that, but she'd need a sulk of her own to get the latest row out of her system. Hopefully, they could talk over breakfast. But in the meantime, he didn't want to frighten her by making her think something bad had happened to him. Before finishing his drink, he went out to the rear of the pub, where he popped into the Gents. When he returned, he tugged his coat on, threw down the last of his whisky, took the tumbler to the bar, thanked the barmaid, and breezed out to his car.

He was halfway home, on another of those lengthy, unlit stretches, when he began to feel odd. Initially, it was as if the vehicle's interior, even with its air conditioning blasting, had turned stuffy; breathing had become a chore. He tried to power his driver's window down, but his fingers felt heavy and clunky, and he couldn't find the switch. Attempting to turn the internal light on, he almost veered off the road.

Perspiring hard, Harry tugged open the collar of his shirt, yanking the V-neck of his sweater down. Try as he may, he couldn't seem to get enough oxygen into his chest. In fact, he was turning dizzy, his vision blurring, the road twisting and turning. The next thing, his car had mounted the kerb and plunged deep into the luxuriant mass of leafage on the left, where it stalled.

Thankfully, he was uninjured. At least, he presumed he was. He'd been securely belted in, and the Volvo hadn't collided with anything heavy. But it was still a struggle to breathe, especially as he swam in and out of consciousness, unable to focus his thoughts.

It took far more effort than it should to fight his way out into the fresh air, shoving his shoulder against the driver's door, pushing it through leafy twigs. With senses fogged, he stumbled along the Volvo's bodywork towards the road. Another vehicle cruised past but made no effort to stop and offer assistance.

At the car's rear end, he lacked even the awareness to distinguish how much of the vehicle was buried in the undergrowth and how much still on the carriageway. The only light to discern anything by was the blood-red glow from his taillights. With legs like rubber, he slipped down from the kerb. Only toppling backward against his car kept him upright.

'You all right, mate? Had a bump?'

Harry had no idea who the man was, or where he'd come from.

One minute there'd been no one there, and the next someone was holding his arm. Even then, his impression of the man was misty and undefined. A huge wedge of a body, big strong arms. A hard-angled face shimmering with crimson light.

Spittle bubbled from Harry's puckered lips.

'Hell, you're in a state.' The man grinned. His eyes seemed huge. 'Good job it's me who's come along and not some copper, eh? You hurt?'

No reply was possible. Harry's neck gave out, his chin hitting his chest.

'Whoooaaa!' the man said, catching Harry under his armpits. 'Bleeding hell, mate. How much you had? Listen . . . don't worry.' Gloved hands gripping him firmly, Harry was eased back against the Volvo's boot. 'Here you go, mate.'

There was something about his voice. His accent, maybe? It wasn't local. But his tone too. Did he find this funny? Harry didn't, but he couldn't indicate that. It was like being dead-drunk, only minus the enjoyable process of having got there.

'In you get . . .' the man said.

He lowered Harry backward on to some kind of flat, yielding surface. Harry tried to resist. But it was futile, his thought processes too muddled . . . it seemed an age before he realised that he was inside his own car. That was all right, then. Wasn't it?

'Drive you home, mate, don't worry. Let me check the damage first.'

Harry realised that he was lying on the back seat. His thoughts drifted sluggishly. Until, with an echoing *thud*, the driver's door closed.

'All good,' the man said from the front. The engine growled to life, the car reverberating. 'Think I can get us out of this mess easy enough. Where do you live, mate?'

Harry tried to reply that he didn't want this, that he wasn't drunk, that he needed an ambulance rather than a Good Samaritan, but none of it came out coherently.

'Don't worry,' the man said. 'Tell me on the way. Be there in a jiff.' Harry sensed motion. Initially, they'd reversed, but now they were travelling forward. 'Park in your drive, if you've got one . . . have a word with your missus, Bob's your uncle . . .'

For countless minutes, the world passed Harry by in a dance of flickery shadow.

'Tell you what, mate,' the driver said over his shoulder. 'Going to take a shortcut I know. That all right with you? Course, no need me asking really. Because that's where we're going. Whether you like it or not.' He chuckled. 'Nothing to say about that? Funny . . . I reckon you'll have plenty to say in a few minutes. Though no one'll hear you.' He chuckled again. 'No one who cares.'

One

'Harry Anderton was the Night Monster's fourth victim,' Nick said, steadying himself in the bus's central aisle. 'And the first who was male. Harry was a struggling small businessman whose financial affairs were going off the rails. That was typical of the sort of person the Night Monster preyed on. Who else would be out and about, worried, weary, travelling aimlessly so late at night? Only people with problems . . . folk who were beaten down by life. His other eight victims were much the same. But all of these troubled existences came to a very brutal end right . . . *here*.'

On cue, Clara swung the bus to a halt, and applied the handbrake.

Liz stood up from the front passenger seat. 'Okay, everyone. Hope you're ready for this.'

The six passengers stirred, checking they had their phones, cameras and such. Outside, though cool, it was bright and clear for mid-November, the mellow sun embossing the remaining scraps of leaves with gold.

'Again, you can leave your valuables on the bus,' Liz said. 'Clara will stay with it.'

One by one, the passengers disembarked via the vehicle's front and rear nearside doors.

There was a faintly detectable air of nervousness about them, as if what they were about to witness here would challenge even their resistance to true-life horror. In so many ways, they were hardened to this sort of thing; they'd even paid for it. This was the Murder Tour, after all. That was its actual name, and it did exactly what it said on the tin: took in one site after another where terrible acts of inhumanity had been performed, not just in the distant past but relatively recently, and in this case, *very* recently. Though perhaps that was the reason why this particular spot, the location of the Night Monster's torture chamber, was already getting under their skin. The past was a distant country, but the present was reality.

Their hosts on the tour, screenwriter Nick Thornwood and his rather lovely girlfriend and business partner, Liz O'Hara, were in a buoyant mood, as they had been throughout, remaining cool and unaffected at every stop. They were even more used to real-life ghastliness than their passengers, of course. Despite their wholesome, youthful appearance, they'd already made quite a name for themselves guiding eager-beaver sightseers along this grim and ghoulish trail of *cause-célèbre* unpleasantness.

'This is the closest we could get in the bus,' Nick explained. 'As you can see, the landowner's bollarded off the actual entrance to the site.'

There was a break in the hedgerow at the back of the lay-by, which might once have been broad enough for a vehicle to pass through, though now it was blocked by a single concrete post.

'If the building's not here any more, what's the site used for now?' asked Roy Southerby, a guy in his late forties with a hulking physique and dense black beard.

'Nothing,' Nick replied. 'It's not like they can build on it again. No one's going to buy a house here and, having already got rid of one unsightly industrial unit, the owner doesn't want another.'

Roy Southerby looked sceptical. 'So, he prefers a patch of wasteland?'

'Given what happened,' Liz said, 'I think he'd just prefer that everyone forgot this place even exists.'

'There's nothing left of the original building at all then?' asked an elderly, white-bearded gent, whose name was Darius Brant.

'Nothing whatsoever,' Nick said. 'It got demolished after the trial. But you can tell where it once stood, because the grass doesn't grow there.'

'Is that true?' the youngest of the guests enquired. His name was Jordan Pugmire, and he was somewhere in his early twenties, his youth evidenced by the black T-shirt he wore, which carried an image of Freddy Krueger grinning behind his splayed, knife-like fingers. 'I thought it was a myth.'

'I'm sure there'll be a scientific explanation,' Freya Swanson replied. She was a slim, pretty woman in her mid-thirties. She had short, very blonde hair – there was something Twiggy-like about her – yet her humourless manner and rather severe outfit of black jeans and black leather jacket suggested that she liked to distance herself from the herd.

Nick, meanwhile, glanced at the bus and received a thumbs-up from Clara Kershaw in the driving seat, which meant that everyone had got off. He strolled past the bollard into the narrow lane beyond. It was made from packed dirt, but deep in brown weeds, as if no one ever came here. It veered leftward as he roved along it, thick autumnal foliage on either side. The tour party scurried in pursuit.

'Most likely, nothing grows here because the topsoil was so badly damaged,' Liz said, walking at the rear. 'You'll remember that before Travis Monkton, the Night Monster, started making use of the building, it was a storage facility for farm chemicals. All sorts of nasty stuff.'

The lane veered right again, the entrance to the wasteland appearing fifty yards ahead, delineated by two mossy gateposts standing one to either side. They could already see that the barren earth beyond was grey rather than that rich black-brown you normally found in this part of the world. The few straggles of vegetation poking through it were wiry and desiccated.

'Goodness me,' Darius Brant said, half to himself. Approximately seventy, but sprightly, and something of a stand-out figure in his flamboyant flowered jacket, pink shirt and tie and broad-brimmed sunhat, he'd proved himself good company on the weekend thus far. He was an affable chap and clearly well educated. But suddenly he seemed subdued. 'There's already an ugliness to this place.'

The others were muted in their response, Nick noted. Even Roy Southerby, who had the look of someone who'd never been frightened of anything.

At many stops on the Murder Tour, the grim realities of history were now masked by an environment that had changed, or at least where nature had concealed everything in greenery. That especially applied in this corner of north-west England, the ceremonial county of Lancashire. Famous as a keystone of the industrial north, because there were still many grimy mill-towns here, this particular part of the county, Pendle Forest, was mostly agricultural. It was difficult to associate death and tragedy with such pleasing scenery – but perhaps not impossible, as they'd shortly see.

'Seems wrong there was any kind of industrial unit in a lovely, leafy place like this,' a plump, showy woman whose name was Charlotte Gray, opined. 'It wouldn't have needed any murders there to already look horribly out of place.'

'Even in paradise you can find a little corner of hell,' said the one member of the tour party who hadn't expressed a view since they'd arrived here.

Nick and Liz swapped curious glances.

The commentator was Martha Lloyd, who was somewhere in her early fifties. In truth, she'd caught Nick's eye the previous day, when he, Liz and Clara had collected everyone at Manchester's Piccadilly Station. Firstly because she was shapely and good-looking, but also because she was the first non-white person they'd ever had on the Murder Tour. Not that she seemed to be having fun. She'd shown minor interest in some sites they'd visited but had mostly remained stern with disapproval.

And now she came out with a comment like 'a little corner of hell'.

'You studied up on this place, Martha?' Nick asked.

'As if,' she said disdainfully.

'Okay, fair enough . . . fair enough.' He halted between the gateposts, turning to face the others. 'Well, welcome everyone. To use the name it's known by hereabouts . . . welcome to Satan's Meadow.'

Two

'As I say, there's nothing left of the building itself,' Nick said. 'But this is where it once stood.'

The waste-ground was perhaps a couple of hundred yards squared and hemmed in on four sides by trees and undergrowth. Evidently, it wasn't a natural gap in the woodland, having been cleared at some time in the past, probably so the chemical store could be constructed, but it was curious to see almost nothing growing there. The ground itself, dry and firm as there hadn't been rain for several days, was gritty and littered with leaves, but also cans, bottles and the tattered remains of fast-food cartons.

'The building itself was never much to look at even before people learned that Monkton had been using it as a death house,' Nick added. 'Nothing more than a faceless concrete bunker. Of course, by the time Monkton arrived, it was long derelict . . . so it suited his purposes perfectly.'

'A lot of people are still baffled the Night Monster ever came hunting round a remote area like this,' Freya Swanson said.

'I think it's that business we touched on earlier,' Nick replied. 'All the Night Monster's victims were targets of convenience. People he encountered by pure luck while driving around late at night. The fact it's so rural, that there'd be so few witnesses . . . that made it easier for him. At least, that was the police hypothesis.'

'Never seemed like a surefire way to stalk prey to me,' Roy Southerby remarked. 'You could drive around rural Lancs all night and never see anyone.'

'Well, he didn't commit murder every night,' Nick said.

'It was nine victims in six years,' Freya Swanson added.

'That we know about,' Jordan Pugmire said.

Freya shot him an irritated side look, which Nick thought curious.

'The thing to consider,' he said, 'is that, though this was twenty years ago, and number plate recognition technology was unknown, Monkton already had half an eye on the traceability of whatever vehicle or vehicles he used on these hunting trips. I mean, he chose an area like this, which wasn't a hundred per cent ideal for him, him not being a native – he came from south Manchester, remember – because he'd scoped it out in advance. Outside the major towns up here, there's very little conurbation, next to no streetlighting, and almost no roadside cameras at all.'

'Must've been one or two cameras.' Charlotte Gray sounded surprised. 'I mean, this was the 2000s. It wasn't *that* long ago.'

'When Monkton was arrested for the Night Monster crimes,' Freya said, 'the police found a map he'd made, on which he'd clearly marked the few working cameras there were. This had enabled him to drive around freely and yet leave no trace of his presence on any surveillance footage.'

'Correct,' Nick confirmed, no longer surprised that the Murder Tour guests nearly always seemed to know more about *this* case than any of the others, though Freya appeared to be especially knowledgeable.

'My God, what's that?' Charlotte suddenly blurted, pointing.

On the north side of the barren patch, some comedians, presumably the same ones who'd been partying here, had erected a bizarre, totem-like structure, though closer inspection would reveal that it was actually an old coat-stand, with various oddments like rusty watches, fragments of broken jewellery, a single high-heeled shoe, a man's belt and the like, dangling from its arms. At roughly head height, a rotted horror mask was suspended. It was crimson in colour, with horns, bared fangs and skullish cavities for eyes.

'My God,' Charlotte said again.

'Tatty bit of street art,' Nick said with a shrug. 'Not everyone shuns this place, as you can see.'

'Those things hanging there. Are they supposed to be trophies? I mean from the victims?'

'Supposed to be, I imagine. Nothing to do with the real victims, though. The people who stuck that thing up are most likely teenagers.'

Nick was playing it all down, but there was no denying the oppressive atmosphere here. The weird, spindly mannequin with its hoard of dangling trophies; the foul, poisoned ground; a silence that was all-enveloping – it was late autumn, so there shouldn't be an echoing chorus of birdsong, but again, this was rural England, so there ought to have been something.

Slowly, they advanced into the middle of the dead ground.

'If nothing bad had ever happened here, you'd have to make something up,' Jordan said.

Darius nodded, thoughtfully. 'That's rather an astute observation.'

'Can you take a photo of me, Mr Brant?' the youngster asked. 'I mean next to that sculpture thing?'

'Erm . . . certainly, my boy. Lead the way.'

The twosome, who throughout the tour thus far had shown an inclination to be friends, odd couple though they doubtless were, now veered away together, Jordan handing over his phone. Equally fascinated, most of the rest of the group slowly dispersed, Martha drifting aimlessly, Roy prowling what looked like the original building's outer perimeter, and dictating into a hand-held device.

Charlotte hugged herself as though cold. 'Satan's Meadow, eh? It's well named. Feels like we're a long way from anywhere, here.'

'As I say, suited Monkton,' Nick replied. 'Such isolation would suit any killer whose preferred means of murder was power tools.'

She shuddered all the more. Even Freya – who'd entered the site in businesslike mode, and even now was taking photographs with what looked like a top-of-the-range camera – overheard this and flinched at the thought.

If he was honest, it amused Nick in a strange, humourless sort of way.

He and Liz held the Murder Tour every Saturday between February and November. Each time, they picked up a brand-new batch of gore hounds at ten sharp outside Piccadilly Station before heading out of Manchester in Clara's clapped-out old Toyota Coaster mini-coach, and proceeding to tour the north-west, but visiting only those points on the map where murders, massacres and other horrors had occurred. Among them, for example, the Georgian-era cellar in the heart of Liverpool, still accessible, where in 1826 a kind of resurrectionist wholesaler had stocked hundreds of body-snatched corpses in barrels of brine ('the Pickled Persons Pitstop', as Clara referred to it); or the isolated millpond on the outskirts of Bolton, where in 1751, fifteen years *after* the abolition of the death penalty for witchcraft, a local cobbler led an angry mob in the 'swimming' and beating of an elderly couple suspected of being 'conjurors', from which brutality both of them expired (a weathered post nearby was all that remained of the original gibbet where the cobbler's executed corpse hung rotting until the birds pecked it to shreds).

Yet, this last-but-one port of call, way up in the Lancashire hills – the Night Monster's Lair, Satan's Meadow – was always the one that seemed to disquiet people the most. And highly likely it wasn't just because the Night Monster's murders were the most recent atrocities on the itinerary. Even by the normal standards of serial killers, there'd been something uniquely horrible about Travis Monkton's one-man crimewave.

The 'Night Monster'. What a name the press had dubbed him with.

You didn't get much more on point than that. And of course, it hadn't made things easier for the general public that, throughout his spree, no actual murder scenes were discovered, only the deposition sites where the dismembered remnants of his victims were left neatly packaged in bin liners. The mere concept was appalling: innocent citizens vanishing without trace – one minute there, the next gone – snatched from various corners of rural Lancashire, and only turning up again having been sawn into pieces and wrapped in black plastic. When the maniac was finally arrested, and the truth came out that all the victims had been killed and butchered in the same place – an abandoned chemical store now turned torture-and-dissection chamber sitting right in the heart of scenic Pendle Forest – it struck the entire country with a sense of appalled horror.

The Night Monster's victims had been chosen randomly, with no distinction made between the sexes. Likewise, there didn't seem to be any age restriction: the youngest was seventeen, the eldest sixty-four. It certainly wasn't the case that Monkton only abducted sex workers, so there was no comfort to be found in some fantasy that 'good' girls and boys would be spared. Most likely though, it was the extreme torture and mutilation Monkton had subjected them to in the privacy of that dank little bunker that had made the most lasting impact. As Nick had already mentioned, he'd used electrical tools, which he'd powered up with a portable generator.

Such a beast had even lived up to his reputation in the dock, cutting an indifferent, ice-cold figure, tall, powerfully built, with stony yet handsome features under his neatly cut straw-blond hair, his cerulean gaze fixed on some point in the near-distance, responding neither to questions from the judge nor insults from the public gallery. 'An aloof, blue-eyed devil', as one of the nationals had described him. After all that, the ten life sentences Monkton had received, to be served without possibility of remission or parole in Gull Rock, Britain's most infamous high-security prison, had barely seemed adequate.

In truth, it was little wonder that this was always the most sensational stop-off on the tour. Though thus far at least, Charlotte Gray had shown no inclination to wander around, remaining steadfastly close to her two hosts.

'What gave you the idea for the Long, Dark Weekend?' she asked.

Nick shrugged. 'It was mainly Liz. We were chatting and she just came up with it. I mean, it's mid-November now and we're approaching the end of our first season, so we thought it'd be nice to mark it in some way . . .'

'The one-day tours are fine,' Liz added. 'As you probably know from the website, Ms Gray . . .'

'Call me Lottie, please. All my friends do.'

Liz smiled. 'Lottie . . . as you know, the normal form is we pick people up at Piccadilly on Saturday mornings, and drop them off there again, mid-evening. But we're only able to cover a small part of the region when we do that. So, one week we do the lower half . . . you know, Cheshire, Merseyside, Manchester, and the next week we do the upper half . . . Lancashire and parts of Cumbria. But with the Long, Dark Weekend, we're able to cover the whole area. The lower half on the Friday, the upper half on the Saturday.'

Lottie nodded as she watched the rest of the group. 'Including two atmospheric stay-overs.'

Nick half-smiled. 'You didn't find last night too distressing, I trust?'

'Well . . .' The woman's thoughtful silence on the matter kind of suggested she had, but then The Eye of Horus Inn – where in Tudor times a maniac landlord had installed a trapdoor in a bedroom, from where he pitched over sixty guests into a cauldron of boiling tallow – didn't just boast an alarming history; it stood on a bleak, windswept point off the Ribble Estuary, and hadn't been too salubrious to look at, either inside or out.

Liz smiled again. 'You'll be more comfortable tonight, I assure you.'

'That's a relief,' Martha muttered, roaming past. 'Tonight being the much-touted big surprise, I was wondering if we were going to find ourselves sleeping in the same damp cell where the Pendle Witches were kept the night before they were hanged.'

Nick and Liz made brief eye contact again, baffled that the woman was even here. She was clearly hating every minute of it.

'So, how come a film writer like you spends his spare time running this tour?' Lottie asked Nick.

He shrugged, pondering the best way to answer. 'Well . . . it's fun, and it allows me to research true crimes. The more barbarous the better, of course.'

'Of course,' Lottie agreed. 'Non-barbarous murders are far too boring.'

'Gives me ideas for movie projects and that.'

Lottie turned to Liz. 'And how did he drag you into this strange, dark world, my dear?'

Liz smiled, amused that Lottie, like so many other ladies of a certain age and culture, assumed a young woman like her wouldn't have got into the horror scene unless some brutish bloke had coerced her.

'I enjoy it too,' she said. 'Nick and I first met at Manchester Uni.'

'Ah.' Lottie tapped the side of her nose. 'I detected from your accent that you at least aren't a local girl.'

'I'm a Manc,' Nick said. 'But Liz is posh. Comes from the south coast.'

'We studied different courses but got to know each other at the Horror Club,' Liz added. 'That was just a fun thing too. We all used to meet to discuss books and watch movies . . . Nick was studying English lit, specialising in Gothic fiction, and I was doing business and commerce. So, we'd probably never have met otherwise.'

'The Horror Club?' Lottie pondered, looking bemused. She too, it occurred to Nick, was a bit of a conundrum by normal Murder Tour standards. Heavily made up, dripping with jewellery, wearing high-heeled leather boots and an insulated silver mac over a colourful Phase Eight day-dress, she definitely wasn't the sort, at least from appearances, who you'd normally find immersing herself in true crime gruesomeness.

'Well, I suppose it takes all sorts,' she said, nodding at the others: Freya standing deep in thought; Roy still absorbed in his Dictaphone; Darius taking another photo of young Jordan, who posed with thumbs up alongside the totem pole. 'You have quite a range of customers here, and we're all engrossed.'

'You're not unusual, don't worry,' Nick replied. 'A lot of people these days are happy to pay for what they call "experiences". Dark tourism's a growing industry.'

'Dark tourism?' Lottie mused.

'Should please you, shouldn't it?' Martha said, strolling past again. 'Knowing that you're not alone in getting a kick out of human depravity.'

◆ ◆ ◆

Nick stood by the bollard, watching as the tour party straggled back up the lane into the lay-by, and filed on to the bus. Most were now keeping their own counsel.

'A tatty piece of street art, I believed you called it?' Darius said, stopping alongside him. 'Drunken teenagers responsible?'

'Oh, that weird statue,' Nick said. 'Yeah.'

Darius tilted his hat upward as he glanced back along the lane. 'I'd describe it more as a kind of artistic interpretation of Travis Monkton, myself.'

Nick, who knew Darius to be an art dealer, shrugged. 'I guess that's what it's supposed to be, but to me it's tat. I've always had a problem giving credit to something that looks as if it only took two or three minutes to put together, you know?'

'Oh yes, I'd agree. I'm a fan of modern art, but not when it's taking the mickey. I can't see that figure back there ever appearing in the Tate. But for all that it's crude, it somehow adds meaning to that terrible place.'

'I saw you taking a couple of pics of your own once you'd sorted Jordan out.'

Darius nodded. 'Young Pugmire and I come from different backgrounds, but I think there's something about that dreadful site and its ghoulish guardian that affected both of us in similar ways.'

'You seemed to be having fun.'

'Sort of, but there's no denying that it felt . . .' Darius paused, searching for a word.

'Eerie?' Nick suggested.

'"Eerie", yes. Puts the case succinctly.'

'I'm just glad we're leaving before it gets dark,' Lottie added, strolling past.

Nick grinned. 'Won't be properly dark for another three hours.'

She headed towards the coach. 'I'm still glad we're leaving.'

'Allow me to help you aboard, Miss Gray.' Darius hurried in pursuit. 'For what it's worth, I wouldn't like to spend time here after sundown either.'

'Satisfied customers?' Liz said, bringing up the rear.

Nick pondered. 'They're not the chatty gaggle they were when we arrived.'

She nodded. 'Another lot mulling over the real meaning of inhumanity, eh?'

Clara now appeared in the bus's front door. 'Think that's everyone,' she called. 'Ready to take a headcount?'

'Sure am.' Liz clambered aboard.

Nick glanced back once before going after her.

It was now almost two-fifteen. In normal times their next port of call would be scheduled for later in the day, because it would be the grand finale of the tour. But this being a Long, Dark Weekend rather than a Saturday day trip, the big climax would come this evening, and that visit would be something very special indeed, though this next stop would still serve nicely as a prelude to it – as the aperitif, so to speak.

Nick indicated to Clara that they could set off. The tour party might well traverse the next set of country lanes in pensive mood, thinking gravely on the cruelties they'd spent the weekend wallowing in, pondering some of the most evil deeds men are capable of.

But just wait till they reached the small, rundown cottage on the outskirts of Longridge. When they finally got the chance to put faces to that evil. When they found themselves standing eyeball to eyeball with some of the worst monsters in human history.

Three

If anywhere resembled the environment where you'd expect to find a very strange man, it was Michael Caruso's cottage. Externally, it was a standard, rundown affair: misaligned brickwork, a sagging roof, a jungle of decaying vegetation on all sides. Internally, it was a warren of crooked passageways. The place was clearly aged, but there was nothing quaint here. It had stone-flagged floors and low beams, but everything was dingy and drab; those parts of the plaster walls not covered by paintings had cracked or were flaking. But it was the paintings that were its most bizarre aspect.

They came in various sizes, and hung on every side, corridor and reception room alike, no attempt having been made to affect symmetry or order; they'd simply been positioned wherever the householder had found adequate space.

The images themselves were spookily lifelike.

'Like looking at a photograph,' Lottie said, staring at a depiction of Ted Bundy.

They knew it was him because a caption located above the portrait named him. However, there was no possibility of failing to recognise him here given the quality of the painting, the handsome maniac grinning hungrily as if he were sizing them up through an open window.

'Creepy, eh?' Roy said, genuinely meaning it.

'Remarkable,' Darius agreed.

'What's this, do you think?'

Like many painters, Caruso had signed the canvas in its bottom right-hand corner, but in the bottom left-hand, also in scribbled handwriting, there was a Latin inscription.

'That's the painting's title, I believe,' Darius said, adjusting his glasses. 'He always does them in Latin. Possibly a bit pretentious.'

'"*Pessimus omnium,*"' Lottie read aloud.

'"The worst of them all,"' Darius translated, his gaze narrowing as he moved on. The next portrait displayed a rather mournful-looking man with a receding hairline, whom the stencilled panel above named as *Danny Rolling, the Gainesville Ripper.* Again, a shortish Latin script sat in the bottom left-hand corner: *Culter eius acutissimus erat.*

'"His knife was very sharp,"' Darius translated.

Nick supposed that Darius ought to know. The guy was already in 'quiet appraisal' mode, no doubt assessing everything with a professional eye. By all accounts, Caruso's original paintings, most of which were here on display, were priced at between £600 and £2,000 each.

'So, all these paintings are for sale?' Lottie asked, moving on next to the image of a particularly brutish-looking man whom the panel above said was *Earle Nelson, the Gorilla Murderer.*

'Good God, what else?' Martha replied. In keeping with her attitude all along, Martha appeared to be more disgusted than most.

'But does anyone buy?' Lottie wondered.

'Oh, they buy,' Liz confirmed. 'On our one-day tours, this is usually the grand finale, and they come cashed-up accordingly.'

'What an unedifying spectacle,' Martha muttered. 'Ordinary, everyday citizens pouring money into the pockets of a convicted murderer.'

Roy chuckled. 'Caruso's fully rehabilitated now, haven't you heard?'

'Yes, of course.' Martha indicated the face of Clyde Barrow, *the Texas Rattlesnake*, whose youthful features were streaked with blood and punctured by multiple bullet holes, as they had been on that day in 1934 when law enforcement had put his freshly machine-gunned corpse on public display. 'On this evidence, there's nothing wrong with him at all.'

'Who did he murder?' Lottie asked quietly. 'Caruso, I mean.'

'Some poor lass who lived next door to his family home in Preston,' Roy replied, lowering his voice. 'He was only eighteen at the time, and she was twenty-one. He reckoned she'd been taunting him. You know, sunbathing in her backyard in a bikini and all that.'

'Of course,' Martha chipped in. 'Obviously, it was the girl's fault.'

'So . . . what happened?' Lottie asked, looking in equal parts horrified and intrigued.

Roy shrugged. 'Broke in one night when her family were out and strangled her. Raped her first, obviously.'

'Obviously,' Martha said. 'If you're going to do a job, might as well do it properly.'

'Why did he get released so early?'

'Why do they all get released early?' Martha said. 'Because the Parole Board are a set of ivory-tower-dwelling dickheads.'

Lottie looked worried. 'I hope they didn't make a mistake.' She glanced at Roy. 'If they did, I'm glad we've got you with us.'

'Worry not, Miss Gray.' He balled his big fist. 'There's no man alive I can't deal with.'

Martha snorted. 'I'm so glad you people are finding this funny.'

'Oh, come on, Martha,' Lottie said, but before Martha could reply, an odd nasal voice intruded on them.

'Come through, ladies and gents.' It was Michael Caruso himself. 'Please come through.' He'd greeted them at the cottage's front door, and had admitted them enthusiastically, but had then withdrawn into the interior as they'd milled about in the entrance passage. Now he'd reappeared in the doorway to a well-lit room at the far end.

Caruso was somewhere in his late forties, tallish – about six-two – and of lean build. His appearance was unkempt, with a scruffy grey fuzz of a beard and long, straggling grey hair. His eyes, which were pale green, twinkled eerily.

'Come along, come along please.' He beckoned them into a room at the end of the passage. 'I'm sure we've all got things we need to be doing.'

'I wonder who it is in your case?' Martha asked no one in particular.

'For God's sake,' Lottie hissed. 'He might hear you.'

Caruso ushered them through into what it became apparent was his studio, bright daylight shafting in from two large arched windows, the floorboards stained over and over with paint, a range of canvases and easels propped against the walls. The air was pungent with turpentine and spirits.

'Check that out.' Roy nudged Jordan and indicated a small, L-shaped counter, on top of which several neat piles of signed prints, all enclosed in plastic sleeves, sat alongside a small electrical device. 'Bastard's even got a card machine.'

'Good,' Jordan said. 'I don't carry cash any more.'

'You're here to buy?' Roy asked.

'Only the right picture.' Jordan, a pale young chap, who, with his smooth black hair and widow's peak looked vaguely vampirish now that Roy thought about it, remained po-faced despite the older man's obvious surprise.

'Just don't hang it in your bedroom,' Roy said. 'Give you nightmares.'

'Only movie killers in my bedroom,' Jordan replied. 'The real ones go in the spare room.'

'Believe in making your guests feel welcome, eh?'

'I don't get too many.'

'Can't imagine why.'

'Welcome to my Gallery of Infamy!' Caruso's voice cut across them. 'Apologies if at first glance it seems a bit chaotic, but then' – his wolfish smile broadened – 'we're all children of chaos, are we not?'

'There's no doubt of that,' Martha mumbled.

'Believe it or not, we have endeavoured to bring some rhyme and reason to the utter madness you see around you.'

No one responded to that. Not even Martha.

'As you'll have noticed,' Caruso said proudly, 'the corridors and passages are dedicated to our American cousins. They've certainly elevated serial killing to an art form in the good ol' US of A. Even though many states maintain capital punishment as the ultimate deterrent, America's most murderous are seemingly still as eager to do their work as ever. Of course, a humble art institute like this, try as it may, can never be comprehensive. We've only scratched the surface of America's most evil . . .'

Not for the first time – and he'd heard this spiel on several occasions now – Nick wondered if Caruso's use of the 'royal we' was an affectation or a genuine reference to both the showman and salesman performing in front of them now and the darker other self that he'd supposedly kept at bay ever since his early prison release.

'Rest assured though . . .' Caruso cracked a toothy grin, 'we have many more canvases yet, and we are doing our damnedest to fill them all.' The ex-con took a breath. 'The vast land of Russia, one of the USA's few challengers when it comes to serial murder, can be found in the gallery just left of the front entrance. Be sure to call in. Experience for yourself the cold-eyed gaze of such embodiments of Eurasian nightmare as Mikhail Popkov, Andrei Chikatilo and Alexander Busheyev. Meanwhile, students of Western European mass murder should attend the ground floor gallery to the right. There'll be many familiar faces in there. Joseph Vacher, anyone? Henri Landru?' He grinned again. 'More exciting still, our Hall of the Grandmasters is located upstairs . . .'

'Grandmasters?' Martha couldn't keep the disbelief from her voice.

Caruso adopted a sober expression. 'It's not a title we bestow easily. It isn't for example awarded simply for quantity. If it were, Ted Bundy would surely be in there. He confessed to thirty murders, but his true estimate is likely over a hundred. Likewise, Gary Ridgway with ninety, Pedro López with three hundred. But these were just crude men. Brutes who struck at easy victims with minimal planning and next to no finesse . . .'

'Finesse, I see,' Martha said. 'So, in the grandmasters' case, it's all about *quality*?'

Caruso clearly heard her scathing tone but didn't rise to it. 'Not a term we'd use, dear lady. No, the Grandmasters are those who've made an especially huge impact. The world's most mightily empowered lunatics. Jean-Bédel Bokassa, for example, president of the Central African Republic, who not only ordered the clubbing to death of hundreds of political prisoners, but participated himself and even dined on the remains . . .'

'He'd be in the right company with this guy,' Clara mumbled into Nick's ear.

Nick nodded, amused, but couldn't help wondering at her presence.

Clara was as down-to-Earth and blue-collar as they came, regarding her part-time bus-driving gig with him and Liz purely as a job. She only wore the sweater and anorak with the *Murder Tour* logo on the front and back because they'd asked her to, and rarely partook of the attractions. That was partly because, going by their long chats with her, she'd led something of a lived-in life, herself. The marks of it were even visible on her body. An old V-shaped scar on the back of her left hand was inflicted when an ex-boyfriend had taken umbrage to being shown the door and attacked her with a broken bottle. Once a handsome woman, she now affected a vaguely curious look, one eye brown and the other green, the result of being punched by a late-night bus passenger who was too drunk to want to pay.

After all that, there wasn't a lot you could teach Clara about the wild animal that lurked within Man, and as such, she generally preferred to sit on the bus when they visited the murder sites, playing *Candy Crush Saga*. All that said, it was no surprise to Nick that if she was ever to pop in on one of them, it would be Michael Caruso's house. Such perhaps was the temptation of genuine twistedness.

This place was a freakshow, of course. The whole of the Murder Tour was a freakshow, but the set-up here, in this damp, dilapidated cottage on the edge of the Lancashire moors, was a masterly inclusion. However creeped-out the tourists were by the weird, demented faces adorning its interior walls, or by Caruso's thinly relished glee as he articulated some of the worst atrocities in mankind's history, many guests invariably acquired paintings or prints from his shop, or at least took photographs as mementos of their visit.

'Where are the English murderers?' Jordan asked loudly. 'You must have a room just for the English?'

'But of course.' Caruso seemed pleased by the question. 'Our Hall of Great Britons can also be found upstairs.'

'*Great* Britons?' Martha said.

Caruso's eyes glinted as he appraised her.

'For so small an island nation,' he said, 'and for a land which to many across the world still stands as a beacon of prosperity and civilisation, Great Britain has made a remarkable contribution to the annals of cold-hearted slaughter.'

Martha shook her head again, but this time said nothing.

'Martha's not appreciating this at all,' Liz muttered.

'Each to their own,' Nick replied, quietly.

'Should've known what she was getting into, shouldn't she?' Clara said. 'But at least that little fella seems keen.' She nodded at Jordan, who was bouncing from foot to foot like a hyperactive child.

'I assume Travis Monkton's in the Hall of Great Britons?' Jordan said. 'He *is*, isn't he? I read somewhere that Monkton's is the only portrait you painted from real life . . . as in, the man himself actually sat for you. They're all saying it's the one painting you never wanted to sell, but that now you've changed your mind?'

Caruso smiled fondly.

They trooped upstairs in single file.

'I'm fascinated by the oft-aired belief,' Caruso said, leading them into the Hall of Great Britons, 'that national characteristics are detectable within murder sprees. For example, I've heard criminologists opine that German serial killers are distinctive for their sadistic, sexual crimes – that would certainly be true of the likes of Kürten, Haarmann and Grossmann. Likewise, the Americans are more notorious for their so-called thrill-killings. We've already discussed how Ted Bundy, though a successful predator, was little more than a brute, a wolf in sheep's clothing admittedly, but a fellow at least as addicted to the opportunist stalk as he was to the actual slash. We British on the other hand seem to be more about the planning.'

The tour party listened, seemingly rapt, but whether from fascination or horror, it was difficult to be sure. More deranged faces glared on all sides of them.

'John George Haigh.' Caruso tapped the frame, within which the well-groomed Haigh, wearing his rubber apron, posed alongside the acid drum in which he'd melted nine persons into human sludge. 'Few killers in history have as carefully selected, groomed and then disposed of their victims.' He moved on. 'Take Christie. Though a sex fiend by any standards, he developed a number of skilful strategies by which to ensnare the young women he murdered, including posing as a doctor or abortionist, offering quack cures for everyday ailments . . .'

Lottie looked as though she wanted to speak but instead stared glassy-eyed at the painting of John Christie, the familiar bald head and bespectacled face leering back at her.

'We know all about Christie and Haigh,' Jordan cut in. 'It's Monkton I'm interested in. Is it true that you're finally ready to sell it?'

Caruso regarded him with affection. 'You're very keen, young man. In that case . . .'

A single painting, not yet hung, stood separate from the others on an upright frame, covered by a loose cloth. When Caruso whipped the cloth away, the Night Monster was revealed. Nick barely even glanced at it. He'd seen plenty of images of Travis Monkton already. Mostly mugshots, when he'd been researching the case. But even a quick glance was sufficient to indicate that the legendary killer, whose fair hair had thinned and receded by the time of this sitting, and whose famously impressive physique had shrivelled considerably, suddenly looked like an ordinary mortal. It appeared that Caruso had perched his shorts-and-T-shirt-wearing subject on a stool in their shared cell at Gull Rock, though from the painted figure's stiff posture and tightly folded arms, the one-time blue-eyed devil of murder and mayhem was finding the whole experience uncomfortable. Behind him, whatever light source the artist had used cast his shadow on a brick wall of gunmetal grey.

'Doesn't look like a mass murderer, does he?' Freya commented.

'Half of them don't,' Roy replied. 'That's why they clocked up numbers. Only an idiot would let a drooling gargoyle get close to them.'

'How much do you want for it?' Darius cut in, his tone suddenly sharp and businesslike.

'Ahhh . . .' Caruso seemed unsurprised. 'We get straight to it. Excellent . . . well, as the most valuable painting I possess, this particular piece is selling for £4,500.'

Jordan looked startled. 'I was told nothing was on sale here for more than £2,000.'

'That may have been the case before today,' Caruso replied.

Jordan reddened. 'You're trying to con us.'

'Con you?' The artist put a hand to his chest. 'I'm the owner, therefore I set the price.'

'That may be,' Darius said, dismissively, 'but your valuation is far too high. I'll give you £800 in cash now.' He dug a roll of notes from his jacket pocket. 'And you and I both know that's more than it's worth.'

Caruso smiled thinly. 'The price is £4,500.'

'I'll give you £900!' Jordan piped up, reaching into his pocket.

The rest of the tour party watched, intrigued. Darius glared at the younger guy; in the blink of an eye, it seemed, the genial grandfather figure had vanished. 'Are you out of your tiny mind?' he hissed.

Jordan looked a little thrown to have found himself bidding against Darius, but now steeled himself and persisted, waving his wallet around like a winning lottery ticket. 'One thousand, Mr

Caruso. I'll give you £1,000 right now. You take cards, I've seen the machine downstairs . . . so I can pay you straight away.'

'You're a little fool!' Darius snapped at him. 'All you'll do is inflate the price even more.'

'I want it,' Jordan reiterated, 'and I'm prepared to pay for it.' He slipped a credit card from his wallet. '£2,000.'

Caruso's eyebrows arched. 'A generous offer, but the price is still—'

'For God's sake, Caruso!' Darius sounded exasperated. 'You know you're going to sell it to one of the two of us. Who else is coming here today with a pocket full of cash?'

Caruso gave a sly smile. 'You'd be surprised.'

'Face facts, man. You're a skilled painter, but you'll only ever really be known for that ghastly crime you committed.'

'So why are *you* so keen to buy from him?' Martha wondered. 'You're a professional, that's evident. So, there must be some interest out there.'

Darius glanced irritably round at her, before realising that the others were watching him too, at which point he reddened.

'Come now . . .' Caruso walked around the easel. 'This painting is one of a kind. Be honest, sir . . . with yourself if no one else. You're plainly under instructions not to leave this place without Travis Monkton under your arm. That much is obvious.'

'All right . . . all right.' Darius looked resigned but now began peeling notes from the roll in his hand. 'I'll give you £2,500 for it, and that's my absolute limit.'

Jordan, meanwhile, though he looked anguished, stepped forward again. '£2,550.'

Darius rounded on him, all pretence that he was some benign mentor now dispensed with entirely. 'You little toad!'

'I've as much right to buy it as you have.'

'You wouldn't know quality artwork if I hit you over the head with it . . . Either that, or you're just a bloody little weirdo.'

'Says you,' Jordan retorted, finally recognising his 'friend' for the fraud that he clearly was. 'Look at you . . . dressed like a fucking paedophile.'

To Nick's relief, because he'd increasingly been feeling that he ought to step in, it was Michael Caruso who did the honours.

'Now, gentlemen,' he said. 'There's no sense falling out over something like this . . . Let's see. You're both prepared to pay . . . shall we say £2,500? It's less than I'd hoped for, but I can tell when there are people in the room who really want something. How about this? I'll let the Travis Monkton go for two-five . . .' he cocked an inquisitive eye first to Darius, then to Jordan, 'to whichever one of you two is able to persuade me that he deserves it most.'

There was a brief, startled silence.

'What kind of asinine game is this?' Darius hissed.

'It *is* a game of sorts,' Caruso conceded. 'There's a prize at the end, after all.'

'What the devil are we supposed to do?'

'Persuade him,' Martha said.

Darius glanced helplessly at the faces around him, then made an exasperated but resigned gesture. 'My name is Darius Brant. I'm co-owner of the Ludgate Gallery in London, and senior partner in the Brant & Denton Dealership. I'm here today on behalf of a valued client, who – and I'm being completely honest with you here – as well as having amassed an astonishing collection of fine art, has an avid interest in, well . . . *murderabilia* . . .'

He let the word hang.

'True crime collectables,' Freya said.

Fleetingly, Darius seemed sheepish. 'Not everyone considers it a tasteful endeavour . . . and I'm one of them. But my client's main interest is not so much gruesome trinkets – hangman's nooses and the like – but artworks created by the criminals. It's about as "outsider" as any artform can get, and much of the market for it exists underground, but it *is* a market, and my client has been dipping in and out of it for quite some time. The works themselves aren't always worth much in quality terms, but it's the notorious names attached. For example, he owns original paintings by John Wayne Gacy, Henry Lee Lucas and Ronnie Kray . . . he even has a couple by Adolf Hitler. It's a niche interest in the art world, to say the least, but such pieces are hugely resaleable.'

Caruso pursed his lips. 'If I'd known this from the start, Mr Brant, I'd have put a valuation of £20,000 on my painting of Travis Monkton. But if nothing else, I'm a man of my word. The price stands at £2,500. But Mr Brant, you haven't yet persuaded me why *you* should be the beneficiary.'

Darius looked astonished. 'Isn't it obvious? Sell your picture to me and it will be exhibited in a museum. A private museum, admittedly, but the art world's great and good will still get to see it . . . and admire it. And there's a *lot* to admire. In fact, your very obvious talent will likely drive more business your way.'

Caruso glanced at Jordan. 'And you, young sir?'

After the art dealer's articulate pitch, the younger contender seemed a little wild-eyed. 'My name's Jordan Pugmire, and I . . . oh shit, I just *want* it. I mean, I really want it. I have a lifelong interest in the dark side of humanity.'

'That doesn't make you unusual,' Caruso replied. 'The average thriller writer would say the same.'

'Well . . .' Jordan struggled to add more, until, rather unexpectedly, he spun round and pointed an accusing finger at Freya. 'My sister wouldn't let me into their group. They said my interest was childish, puerile.'

The rest of the tour party exchanged glances, Nick and Liz included. None of them had known that Jordan and Freya were siblings. Not only had it never been mentioned; they didn't look remotely like each other.

Freya rolled her eyes, but Michael Caruso seemed intrigued.

'Their group?' he said.

'We're the north-west branch of the Murder Resolution Society,' Freya said, in a tone implying that she was only explaining this under sufferance.

'Ahhh.' A light of understanding came into the ex-con's face. 'You're a private investigator.'

'Not quite. We're strictly non-profit.'

'But you enquire into unsolved murders, do you not? Make efforts to link them together. And then present the police with dossiers on cases that you believe represent unidentified serial killers.'

'We're serious about what we do,' she said. She glanced at Jordan. 'Unlike *him*. He's just into this stuff to get his rocks off.'

'That's not true!' Jordan blurted. 'My interest is at least as legitimate as yours.'

'Are you for real?' she said. 'We've got former murder detectives and retired forensic scientists in our group—'

'So, Mr Pugmire,' Caruso interrupted. 'You are the oik of the tour party?'

'Excuse me?' Jordan replied.

'You're only involved in this because you like nasty stories?'

'No . . . I want to investigate. I want to help catch these madmen . . .' Abruptly, the youngster broke off, wondering if he'd said the wrong thing. 'Look, that's why I want the Travis Monkton painting. I mean . . . I've read online that there are supposed to be secrets concealed in it. Secrets about those murders, which have never yet been revealed. I want to be the one who uncovers them.'

'And you think that'll mean the Murder Resolution Society just throws its door open for you?' Freya said scornfully.

Caruso considered. 'If they don't, I'm sure that will be the Murder Resolution Society's loss . . . and the madmen of the world's gain. *Your* gain, however, Mr Pugmire, is this painting of Travis Monkton. For the bargain basement sum of £2,500 of course.'

Jordan looked both astonished and elated.

At the same time, Darius's jaw dropped. Deep crimson blots appeared on his cheeks. 'Caruso, you can't be serious!'

'Apologies, Mr Brant, but my mind is made up.' Caruso lowered the cloth over the painting and turned to Jordan. 'Young man, the *machine*, as you call it, awaits us downstairs.'

In a daze, Jordan followed his host out of the room. Darius stumbled after them. 'In God's name, why? At least tell me that.'

Most of the others, still fascinated by what they'd just witnessed, went with them. Only Nick and Liz were left behind.

'Did you know that Freya Swanson was part of this Murder Resolution Society?' Liz said.

'You know I do due diligence on them all before accepting their bookings,' Nick replied.

'So?'

'Well, yeah . . . course. She made no effort to hide it.'

'And do we really want to be associated with that group?'

'Probably the real question is do they want to be associated with us?'

But Liz was uneasy. 'Haven't they run into legal issues now and then? I seem to remember some news story about them being warned off by the police . . . for pestering bereaved families, harassing suspects, that sort of thing.'

'Liz, we take everyone and anyone on the Murder Tour. It's not like we occupy some kind of moral high ground.'

She pondered. 'I wonder what Freya thought she'd get from it? All our cases are closed.'

‘Well, there’re rumours about Monkton, aren’t there? That the full story hasn’t been nailed down yet.’

She lifted the cloth. ‘If that’s it, she didn’t show much interest in this.’

‘Like she said, they’re serious people. They’re not looking for – what was it Darius called them? – gruesome trinkets.’

Liz glanced again at the various faces ranged around them, the mad, the bad, the twisted and the insane. ‘It’s never entered your head we might be tempting fate with all this stuff?’

Nick chuckled. ‘Tempting fate?’

‘I mean, we do so much promotion on these guys’ behalf. Wouldn’t be much fun, though, if we actually met one.’

‘That won’t happen.’

She eyed him. ‘You got a crystal ball, or something?’

‘No. But they’re few and far between. That’s why the Murder Tour’s so popular. You don’t run into killers like this every day.’

‘To be fair, you don’t need to,’ Liz said. ‘You only need to run into them once.’

Four

Compared to the damned souls whose corrupt and destructive lives they would always deny they were celebrating, Nick and Liz were something of a picture postcard couple. She was a green-eyed redhead, 'fetchingly freckled', as Nick had once described her, and of slender, athletic build. He meanwhile was tall, lean and dark-haired, 'good-looking in a conventional, boyish sort of way' (Liz's words).

They were never what their clients expected when they rolled up to collect everyone on Saturday mornings, though the bus itself probably was, the way it came chugging and juddering on to the station forecourt. The Toyota Coaster was a fine old make, but this one had seen better days, its ancient bodywork beaten and badly resprayed. A relic from the golden age of British film, one might say, something you'd expect St Trinian's to go on holiday in, or the *Carry On* team to pile into for a saucy weekend. Clara herself, at first glance, seemed a grouchy sort, with her odd eyes and her long grey hair always tied in a severe bun, but the happy-go-lucky couple who were hosting the tour, invariably looking smart and snug in their black *Murder Tour* sweaters and anoraks, seemed the epitome of middle England, at odds with the horrors they'd shortly be entertaining their guests with.

In truth, the dead-body wholesaler and the gibbet where the rabble-rousing cobbler had hung in chains were only the tip of the iceberg. Other similar attractions on the schedule were legion. There was the lonely Pennine farmhouse, where in the 1870s a deranged vagrant had sledgehammered to death an entire family for having refused him a berth in their barn. Then there'd been the Lovers' Lane Murders in Cheshire in 1954, where over the course of two weeks two courting couples had been shot dead while canoodling in their parked cars, a case still unsolved, the road where it had happened now a busy part of a built-up neighbourhood on the outskirts of Knutsford.

But like Liz and Nick themselves, the Murder Tour – the Long, Dark Weekend in particular – hid the majority of its darkness behind a pleasingly pretty facade. Because, from Michael Caruso's house, the bus had initially headed west but soon cut north into the vast realm of high, rolling grassland and thickly wooded hills known as the Forest of Bowland.

Now that they'd left the main network, the roads became narrower, all signs of habitation falling behind them. At this point in November, of course, the hour had gone back, so though it was only just past three in the afternoon, daylight wouldn't linger for much longer than an hour or so. It was progressively cooler and greyer out there, blankets of mist rising in the lower valleys. All very scenic, but when it came to downright eeriness, the scene was setting nicely for the big reveal.

All along, Nick and Liz had sought to fuel interest in the Long, Dark Weekend by keeping their final stopover secret. A big surprise that was guaranteed to be worth the price of the tour in itself. According to the promos they'd put out, it would be even more interesting to horror hounds than Michael Caruso's gallery of the disturbed. But they would only divulge it when the time was absolutely right.

Initially, of course, there were other distractions. The majority of the tour party were busy feasting their eyes on the glorious landscape outside, but young Jordan, who'd positioned himself at the very back of the bus, hadn't been able to resist opening the box and bubble-wrap that Michael Caruso had provided and taking out his new acquisition. The portrait of Travis Monkton, framed in carved walnut, was rectangular and about two feet by three, so he could only appraise it fully by propping it up on his knees and leaning its back against the seat in front. It just so happened that Darius had chosen that seat for himself.

'I don't understand why you even want it,' the dealer said, now in a more conciliatory tone. 'It's well known that even Caruso didn't like it much, didn't think he'd caught the essence of his subject . . . that's why it took him so long to put it up for sale.'

'It's the hidden messages I'm interested in,' Jordan replied.

'Oh, that's piffle . . .'

Eventually, even Freya, who'd initially also been at the back of the bus, now came down to the front, where the rest were gathered.

'What're the scores on the doors?' Nick asked.

'Oh, if only it was that simple,' she replied. 'Jordan keeps insisting there're all kinds of revelations concealed in there. Says that because Monkton and Caruso bunked together for several months in Gull Rock, Monkton almost certainly talked, and now Caruso is letting the secrets slip. But all Darius is interested in is buying the wretched thing. Every couple of minutes or so, he offers another hundred quid. By my estimation, it's now worth a good two thousand more than Jordan paid.'

'Any reason you didn't mention that Jordan's your kid-brother?' Nick enquired.

'You mean apart from the acute embarrassment?'

Nick shrugged. 'He seems to know his true crime.'

Freya looked dismissive. 'Jordan's just a horror freak. Any kind of horror. Look, we're step-siblings. We're not the real thing. When my dad hooked up with his mum, Jordan thought he'd found a kindred spirit in me, but in the Murder Resolution Society we take this stuff seriously. When we discuss killers, we're not talking about Freddy Krueger or Hannibal Lecter.'

Nick glanced back along the bus. 'I suppose Travis Monkton's the closest thing the real world's ever offered to that.'

'Maybe,' Freya said, 'but the Monkton case still requires proper analysis.'

'You were able to prevent Jordan joining this Murder Resolution Society on your own?' Lottie asked, applying mini squirts of Chanel No 5.

Briefly, Freya looked awkward. 'I . . . I persuaded the rest of the team.'

'Seems a bit mean,' Martha said, sounding unsurprised.

'It's only until he's older and wiser.'

'What is he, twenty?' Nick asked.

'Twenty-one.'

Roy looked impressed. 'He's cashed up for twenty-one.'

'Inheritance from his father,' Freya explained.

'You sure he's spending it wisely?' Lottie asked, still applying scent.

'I'm not his keeper.' Freya's tone was final on that matter at least.

'You trying to perfume away the atmosphere of Michael Caruso's cottage?' Roy asked Lottie, jokily.

'I'd be so lucky,' she replied. 'This is good stuff, but that place was odious.'

'Well . . .' Now, Liz turned to face them. '"Odious" is a word that no one would associate with our next port of call.' She glanced at Nick, adding pointedly: 'What do *you* think, my love?'

'Now?' Nick asked her.

'As good a time as any.'

He nodded and stood up in the aisle, steadying himself again by gripping the backrests of the two nearest seats.

'Ladeeez and gentlemen.' He raised his voice, intentionally sounding like the MC at a prize-fight. 'Maaaay I have your attentiiiooon?'

Even the bickering twosome at the back fell quiet.

Nick beamed. 'I trust you're all enjoying this specially extended Murder Tour?'

There was only a muted response, primarily because they were all suddenly listening. Here at last was the big surprise, the highlight of the trip, something thus far kept from them.

'Only one stop remains,' Nick said, 'and we'll be there in roughly twenty minutes' time. Before then, I have a couple of questions for you.'

The tour party waited, the only sounds the scraping of cardboard at the back, where Jordan was reinserting his prize into its box.

'"I'll run the rivers red with your blood."' Nick said it aloud, ultra dramatically, clearly quoting some famous snippet of speech. '"I'll hang your skins as far as the eye can see. The forest vermin will play amid your bones."'

'So . . . is that like a threat?' Roy chuckled. 'Is that the big surprise? We're all going to be sacrificed in some woodland ritual?'

Nick grinned again. 'You're closer than you may think.'

'That's encouraging.'

'How about this one?' Nick quoted again. '"There are deeper, darker places than hell, my friend. Beyond this world lies madness and chaos. My advice: prepare for the worst . . ."'

A range of nonplussed expressions greeted this. Nick feigned a look of disappointment.

'That's from *House of Torment*,' a voice said. '1960.' It was Jordan. He swayed along the aisle towards them. 'And that first one was from *Reign of Blood*, 1968. Two classic horror movies.' Silence followed. 'Am I right?' he asked eagerly.

'You *are* indeed,' Nick said. 'I'm impressed.'

'Which, seeing as we're all the way up here in Bowland Forest, can only mean one thing,' Jordan said, now talking very quickly and very excitedly. 'Black Tarn Lodge?'

Again, the rest of the party glanced at each other, perplexed.

'*Is* that it?' Jordan asked again. 'Are we visiting Black Tarn Lodge?'

'We're not just visiting it,' Nick replied. 'We're staying there overnight.'

The youngster gaped. 'For real?'

'What's all this about?' Roy asked.

Liz stood up. 'You haven't heard of Black Tarn Lodge?'

Lottie frowned. 'It rings a bell . . .' Then her mouth dropped open. 'God forgive sin . . .' She clutched her hands together as though praying, her gold and silver bracelets rattling. 'Wasn't that the home of Eric Helgoland?'

Nick grinned and nodded. 'Got it in one.'

'Who was an associate of Aleister Crowley?' It was a question rather than a statement, though Lottie looked nowhere near as enamoured by the idea as young Jordan.

Now Freya had become interested. 'Crowley the occultist?'

'"Black magician" would be a better description,' Lottie said in a tone of disapproval. 'The man sold his soul for forbidden knowledge, and Eric Helgoland was no better . . .'

'Helgoland died in 1930,' Jordan said irritably. 'More interesting to us is Black Tarn Lodge's most recent owner.' He glanced round at them. 'You must've heard of Edgar Karnwood?'

Yes, they'd all heard of Edgar Karnwood.

'One of Britain's most famous and prolific horror film actors,' the young guy added, thrusting his phone at them, its screen depicting the head and upper body of a suave-looking chap, probably in his early sixties, with well-defined features and salt-and-pepper hair and moustache, elegantly clad in a ruffled shirt, bowtie and pale blue smoking jacket. 'Came from factory-working Lancashire stock but grew up to be Mr Debonair. And a terrific actor. Easily on a par with Cushing and Lee.'

'If you say so,' Freya replied.

'You should be honoured,' Jordan lectured her, and the rest of them in general. 'Edgar Karnwood's one of the greatest actors this country's ever produced.'

'Yeah,' she said. 'I'm sure Dick Burton and Larry Olivier would vouch for that.'

'And for clarity, this is where we're spending the night?' Roy asked, looking bemused rather than excited. 'At this guy's house? I mean, does the poor bloke know?'

'For Christ's sake,' Jordan retorted. 'Edgar Karnwood died in 2012.'

'That's correct,' Nick said. 'At the ripe old age of 101. Allow me to give you some context. Black Tarn Lodge was the perfect English residence for Edgar Karnwood, real name Herman Matlock. For various reasons. It didn't just have an esoteric history, which suited his image; its isolation provided an ideal escape for him from the chaotic world of movie-making and the huge public interest that swarmed around him during his heyday in the '50s, '60s and '70s. Of course, he had to imprint it with his own personality and interests too, and so in certain circles, the house became a legend.'

'Sorry, but I've never heard of it,' Roy said.

'As I say,' Nick continued. 'In *certain* circles. Edgar Karnwood made his last movie when he was eighty years old. That was in

1991, so it's probably true to say that his star has faded over recent decades.'

'I always heard that he was a very nice man,' Lottie added. 'I mean, given that he starred in so many horrific films.'

'They were perfectly in keeping with the other horror films being churned out at the time,' Jordan said.

'They were X-rated, I know that,' she said. 'And I'm not saying that's a bad thing, but why on earth would he choose to live in such an awful place as Black Tarn Lodge?'

'Why, what's wrong with it?' Martha asked. She'd set herself aside from any conversation since they'd left Michael Caruso's house, but now couldn't seem to resist asking at least a couple of questions.

'Eric Helgoland,' Lottie said. 'He held orgies there, black masses . . .'

'I think some of that's been overstated,' Liz replied. 'Helgoland was a transgressive by the standards of his time. But he was also an intellectual, an author, a lecturer . . .'

Lottie still looked troubled. 'I think there's more to it than that.'

'You seem to know quite a bit about it?' Roy asked her.

'I'm sure I only know half of it,' she replied. 'If that.'

'Look, Black Tarn Lodge has a Gothic vibe, I won't deny it,' Nick said. 'That's why we've chosen it. But it's been beautifully refurbished inside. Plus it's got its place in history. Originally built in the seventeenth century as a hunting lodge for the Marquess of Ribblesdale, it hosted a number of famous people who stayed there as guests. Oliver Cromwell, Charles II, Dr Johnson, Prince Albert.'

'There you go,' Roy said to Lottie. 'Dr Johnson, Prince Albert . . . must be respectable.'

'That was in the past,' she replied, still sounding dubious.

Nick forged on. 'It was purchased by Eric Helgoland in 1900. Whatever else the guy was, he was reclusive . . . and a house like this, located literally in the middle of nowhere, was the perfect spot for him. His hiding place from the prying eyes of the world, you see. But it was thirty-five years after Helgoland's death, 1965, when Edgar Karnwood acquired it. During the interim period it had stood completely empty, and obviously it deteriorated a little . . .'

'But Edgar Karnwood brought it back to life,' Liz said.

'Correct,' Nick added. 'He valued his privacy, but once he'd renovated the place, he often entertained guests there. He was also an ardent collector of mementoes from his many horror films – props, costumes, you name it – with which he completely filled the place.'

'This is so cool,' Jordan said. 'Are they all still there?'

'Very much so,' Nick replied. 'Because after a lot of legal wrangling, Karnwood's grandson, Simon Matlock, has now taken ownership of the Lodge and is planning to start renting it out complete with all its original contents. He's thinking Halloween parties, whodunnit weekends . . . even a writing retreat for authors specialising in dark fiction.'

Roy frowned. 'So . . . we're all going to write a novel then?'

'No,' Nick replied. 'With luck, you'll all be too busy soaking up the atmosphere and enjoying the slap-up meal that Simon Matlock's laying on for you as part of this deal.'

Again, glances were exchanged. They hadn't eaten badly on the tour thus far. The cover price was all-inclusive of lunch and dinner on the Friday, breakfast, lunch and dinner on the Saturday, and breakfast and lunch on the Sunday, but nothing had been said about a banquet in a stately home.

'There's another treat too,' Liz said.

'Sure is.' Nick grinned at them, a proverbial Cheshire Cat. 'Black Tarn Lodge also has its own Movie Room, where Edgar Karnwood treated special guests to pre-launch viewings of his latest films. Though there is one Karnwood movie that no one ever saw—'

'Not *Malifique*?' Jordan interrupted, eyes bugging.

Roy glanced at him. 'Walking encyclopaedia, you, aren't you?'

'It's the only Edgar Karnwood film that ever got banned,' the younger man said eagerly.

'I heard about that too.' Lottie frowned again. 'Wasn't it supposed to be absolutely revolting?'

'I wouldn't go that far,' Liz said. 'And it wasn't actually banned.'

'It was withdrawn, though, wasn't it?' Jordan said. 'Too controversial even for 1976?'

'Edgar Karnwood himself withdrew it,' Nick explained. 'On viewing the film after it was completed, he insisted on buying all existing copies because he was so appalled by its lurid content. He destroyed all but one, which he kept purely for academic interest.'

Roy looked puzzled. 'So, why did he ever make it?'

'The story was that he was overworked at the time, very tired, and he'd, well . . .'

'Lost the plot,' Jordan cut in. 'Wasn't thinking clearly, all that stuff.'

'Whatever, it cost him a fortune to suppress the film,' Nick said. 'But he succeeded. *Malifique* has never been seen by the viewing public.'

'And that's tonight's real treat, is it?' Martha sounded even less enthusiastic than Lottie.

Nick eyed them appraisingly. 'As the final part of this weekend's Murder Tour, this first-ever of our Long, Dark Weekends, tonight . . . once we've dined, you'll have the option, if you wish it, to take your seats in the Movie Room, where Simon Matlock will play the only copy of *Malifique* remaining in existence.'

Jordan looked faint. 'I thought this weekend couldn't get any better . . .'

The young horror buff might have been bowled over, but the reaction from the others was more subdued. It wasn't true that they were indifferent, but they didn't look inspired either. A few mutters of 'great', 'cool', 'interesting' were not exactly how Nick had hoped they'd respond. He put a brave face on it as he slid back on to his seat.

'Well, we had to stay somewhere tonight. But I thought they'd be a bit keener than this.'

'They'll be fine,' Liz said, next to him.

He huffed. 'Perhaps from now on we should reserve Black Tarn Lodge for if we ever do a horror movies tour.'

'Nah, Liz is right,' Clara opined from across the aisle. She drove on with her usual steady competence. 'Half the places you've called at, you don't know whether it happened for sure, do you? Was there really a maniac landlord in The Eye of Horus? What was that place we visited in Moston? Boggart Bridge? Are boggarts a real thing?'

'It's supposed to be the ghost of a girl who was thrown off the bridge by her lover,' Nick said.

Clara grinned. 'Must be real then—'

'Check that out!' Roy interrupted, pointing.

Without warning, the road had become a narrow bridge crossing a deep but natural valley, the lower reaches of which were filled with autumn gloom, though several hundred yards further along it, a Victorian-era viaduct spanned the same gulf on towering brick arches.

'The old Skipton-to-Lancaster line,' Nick said. They reached the other side, plunging back beneath the orange-yellow canopy of the autumn woods, the distant, classical structure lost to sight. 'Ceased to operate in 1922. There are no railway lines up here at all now. Lancashire's famous for its industrial landscapes, but this is the Forest of Bowland. England's forgotten wilderness.'

'And yet we still have bus stops?' Freya nodded through her window.

They'd just swung back into the open, passing through an unmarked crossroads, and were now heading uphill again, even thicker ranks of semi-naked trees enclosing them from either side, but further down they had indeed just sighted a lonesome bus stop sign.

'We're not completely isolated up here,' Liz said. 'There are outlying farms and shepherd huts, the odd remote settlement . . .'

'And then of course,' Nick added, 'there's the Lodge.'

'How long before we get there?' Freya asked.

'Five to ten minutes, depending on how rough the road surface gets.'

Predictably, the road surface *did* get rough. It had once been a real road, but now was broken, potholed, adrift with autumn leaves, and of course from here, it was all uphill, not steeply but continuously. Thankfully, Clara, who might have been middle-aged, and though tall and spare of frame, was a rangy individual possessed of a wiry strength, steered them on determinedly, showing all the skill and stamina she'd picked up as a professional bus driver in Trafford Park, Longsight and Salford, so it wasn't quite ten minutes before the land levelled off again and the woodland thinned out. Suddenly they were back on open moorland, rolling, hummocky peat undulating off towards a distant, barren ridge, though well before then, on the far side of a glittery sheet of night-black water, stood the unmistakable outline of Black Tarn Lodge.

The tour party got to their feet, leaning against their windows to stare at it.

At first glance it was a mass of turrets, towers and battlements, a small castle rather than a traditional country house. But then the various tall windows became visible, behind which firelight shimmered, along with gutters, pipework and on the other side of the battlements, slanted sections of modern slate roof. Even from this distance, a good half mile at least, they could see that it had been built from heavy black stone, which rendered it a stark, bleak structure, especially when framed against the emptiness of the rising moors.

'Wow!' was all Roy could say. 'I mean . . . *wow*!'

'That could be a movie set,' Freya said.

'It may be yet,' Nick replied. 'Mostly restored by Karnwood's grandson, it's a lot more luxurious on the inside.'

'It's perfect,' Lottie said. 'I mean as a place where the UK's number-one portrayer of murderers and madmen once lived.'

'You a fan, Miss Gray?' Roy asked with mock suspicion.

'Not exactly,' she replied primly. 'But I've been around longer than most of the rest of you, so I probably remember him better. Anyway, I keep telling you, it's "Lottie".'

'I've got nearly all his films on Blu-ray,' Jordan said. 'Karnwood might've been old school, but some of the characters he played were evil personified.'

'There you go,' Nick muttered. 'New bit of promo. "Visit the House where Evil Dwelled."'

Liz frowned. 'I don't know. We don't want to start attracting total loonies.'

Clara threw her a sidelong smirk. 'You sure you haven't already?'

'I think our current lot are pretty sane.'

'Still waters, Liz,' Clara snickered. 'Still waters.'

Five

In modern times, Black Tarn, a famously deep, dark body of water, was known as Black Tarn Reservoir. Though of natural origin, fed by various upland streams, it was now used to provide water for the townships of Preston and Blackburn. Black Tarn Lodge – whether the tarn had been named after the house or the house after the tarn, Nick was unsure – sat on its east shore, with outbuildings on either side and a mosaic of gardens at the rear. The main house faced directly on to the water, only a driveway of hardpacked grit, about twenty metres in breadth, separating the two of them. The drive itself ended in a circular turning area about fifty yards south of the front entrance, where what looked like a black Jaguar XJ was parked.

Now that they were closer, it was evident that what had at first appeared to be a grim, gaunt structure, a semi-ruined relic of the past, had for the most part been lovingly restored. Though built from heavy black stone, that was mostly for Gothic effect: the brickwork was neat and clean, the windows fitted with stained glass, which mostly looked new, especially as it sparkled with firelight. Any dense vegetation growing along the side of the tarn had been cleared away, leaving a gentle, pebbly slope leading down to the surface, while the building's pipes and gutters had also been freed of moss and lichen.

As the bus arrived, the passengers' attention was divided between the building itself and the tarn, which as evening descended was slowly disappearing under a layer of pale, grey mist.

Meanwhile, a tall figure had appeared in the main entrance.

'Lord help us,' Clara said, as she eased them to a halt, the tyres crackling on grit. 'Is that Matlock?'

'That's *Simon* Matlock,' Nick replied. 'Not Herman, obviously.'

The similarities were undeniable, though Herman Matlock, aka Edgar Karnwood, had famously stood at six-foot-six, while his grandson was slightly shorter at around six-foot-three. At the same time, while Edgar Karnwood had been famously affable and charismatic, his descendant had an air of gloomy despondency. He was clean-shaven, but his short, neat hair was white rather than salt-and-pepper grey, while in contrast to the fashionable 'country gent' styles his grandparent had always favoured, he wore a solemn black suit and black tie, which would have been more fitting for an undertaker.

'Looks like he's going to give you a right royal welcome,' Clara said, applying the handbrake.

'He needs this thing to work as much as we do,' Nick replied. 'Apparently, he put a lot of money into the renovation, so he needs a good launch. That's why we got such a great deal. He wants it to go viral afterwards about what a smashing time we all had.'

'In which case, he needs to work on his smile.'

'Not like you, Clara,' Liz tittered, 'being all judgemental.'

There was more than a hint of sarcasm there. Clara was a working-class woman of good old Manchester stock. She didn't suffer fools.

'Good evening,' Simon Matlock said, when they stepped out of the bus on to the drive. 'Mr Thornwood? Miss O'Hara?' For such a physically large chap – like his grandfather, he was no beanpole despite his height – he seemed hesitant and uneasy.

'Yeah,' Nick said, offering a hand. 'We met in Manchester, very briefly.'

'I remember.' Matlock shook with him. 'This is all of you?'

'As I said,' Nick confirmed. 'Six guests in total. With ourselves, eight.'

Matlock attempted a half-smile, then lurched back towards the open front door, which in itself was quite impressive: tall, arched and reached by three broad steps. 'Allow me to show you around.'

'I'll stay out here for a minute or two, and supervise,' Nick said. 'We'll all be coming in in a sec.' He nudged Liz to go with their host, then went over to where Clara had just opened the luggage compartment in the side of the bus.

Darius, meanwhile, stood watching as the large, white-haired man in the sober black suit made hunched, clumsy efforts to escort Liz through the house's main entrance. 'Not exactly Bela Lugosi,' he commented.

Roy, who'd appeared alongside him, looked puzzled. 'Sorry, what?'

Darius put on a faux-Eastern European accent. '"I am Dracula . . . I bid you welcome" and all that.'

'Jesus,' Jordan muttered as he headed up the steps, rucksack at his shoulder, the boxed painting tight under his arm. 'It's a horror classic. Surely everyone knows that one?'

'Oh, that . . . yeah.' A light of understanding came into Roy's face. 'The old, crackly *Dracula*. Didn't think it was that scary, to be honest with you.'

'The point I'm making,' Darius said, 'is that on the evidence so far, the apple seems to have fallen a long way from the tree.'

Roy frowned again. 'Sorry . . . I'm not getting you.'

'It doesn't matter.' Darius patted his arm, hefted his holdall and went indoors.

Roy turned away to the luggage compartment, where Clara was helping the rest of them reclaim their bags. 'Cheers,' he said, reaching past her and lifting out his sports bag, then spying that Lottie was struggling with a large holdall and a small suitcase. 'Lot?'

Gratefully, she handed him the case.

He shouldered his own sports bag before glancing up the great baroque facade. 'Does this look like the sort of place your diabolist would hang out in? I don't mean the actor, I mean Helgoland.'

'You surely don't need to ask that, Roy?'

'He's been dead a long time, you know. I mean . . . 1930. Unless it's his ghost you're worried about?'

Rather to his surprise, Lottie took that seriously. 'I don't believe spirits can harm us. If they exist at all, they're incorporeal. But . . . *evil.* I *do* believe there's a power of evil in the world, and when it gets you in its grip . . . oh, sorry.' She realised that he was looking at her strangely. 'You must think I'm a complete lunatic.'

'Not at all.' He chuckled, ushering her up the steps, adding: 'Not a complete one.'

Nick hadn't needed to supervise very much, but he hung on while Clara, for all her fifty-odd years, clambered lithely into the compartment to reach his and Liz's two haversacks, which were the only ones left. Nearby, Martha, the sole remaining guest, stood in her poncho with her own bag in hand, regarding the venerable old building that would be their home until this time tomorrow.

'What do you think, Martha?' he asked.

She glanced at him. 'Excuse me?'

'Well, you've been quite critical so far. Of everything and everyone. I'm just wondering how you think the tour's going? I mean, from a purely objective point of view.'

He was aware that he was being cheeky; it was self-evident the woman didn't want to be here, so there was an element of provocation in his enquiry, but he was intrigued too. He genuinely didn't know why someone who felt as Martha did would even come on a one-day Murder Tour, let alone a Long, Dark Weekend.

'Being objective . . .' She seemed to give genuine thought to it. 'I think that bringing everyone here, to a place that looks perfect for seeing us all murdered in our beds, is the ideal way to round things off.'

'Well . . . if that's a compliment, I suppose I'm grateful.'

'You shouldn't be, Mr Thornwood. Because murder really isn't a form of entertainment.'

He was taken aback a little by the earnestness with which she said this to him.

As Martha went inside, Liz came out. 'Everything okay?' she asked.

'Erm . . . yeah,' he said. 'Except Martha's scared we're all going to get murdered in our beds.'

'Well, if we are' – Liz glanced across the lake, scarcely a ripple breaking its black, mist-covered surface – 'it'd be a long time before anyone found us out here.'

Six

The first thing that struck them on entry was the life-size waxwork of Edgar Karnwood, which, on its six-inch marble pedestal, stood at nearly seven feet in height. It was located in the main hall, about twenty yards in from the door, but positioned on the left. It didn't directly face any new arrivals when they first came in, but was impossible to miss. It was perfect down to the smallest detail, the famous old horror star captured sometime in his late thirties or early forties, because his hair and moustache were darker. The striking figure wore a grey, double-breasted 1950s suit, the jacket partly fastened, but had struck a casual pose, one hand in his trouser pocket, the other holding a half-smoked cigarette. He might have been a famous charmer, but this version of him wasn't smiling; rather, he was smirking, as though at some secret knowledge.

'A gift from Madame Tussauds,' Simon Matlock said, coming to join Nick and Liz. 'In 1965 my grandfather had a place in London, in Belgravia, and a similar-sized pad in the Hollywood Hills.' He spoke with a heavy, near-ponderous tone, as if articulating thoughts was a chore for him. 'He commuted between the two regularly but rarely got back up to his native Lancashire. However, when it was announced that he was buying the Lodge, Tussauds were glad to oblige. It seemed they'd already updated the facsimile they currently had of him. By this time, he was in his mid-fifties, and the older one, this one, was standing in a cupboard somewhere.'

'Wouldn't have done to leave Edgar Karnwood in a cupboard,' Liz observed.

'No, indeed,' Matlock replied, missing the humour.

They proceeded into the hall itself, around which the rest of the tour party were now wandering with an air of fascination. It was a reception area but had clearly once been the main living room of the great baronial hall, where the Marquess of Ribblesdale and his lackeys had feasted each night after their hunting escapades.

Something of that aura certainly remained.

It was a huge, vaulted chamber, the apex of its hammer-beamed ceiling soaring to maybe sixty feet or so, its vast floor smoothly paved, though laid with rugs here and there. On the left side, at the north end of the hall, a richly carved timber staircase, newel posted in stone, with sculptures of heraldic animals atop each one, ran upward to a minstrels' gallery, which circled the open space on three sides. At ground level, its wainscoted walls were hung with grand old paintings but also shields, banners, and square glass cases in which various oddments were displayed. Flames already roared in a huge fireplace on the south side, with carvings depicting mysterious runic symbols on the stone hood over the top of it. Towering potted plants, and several suits of armour, flickering with firelight, added further regal touches, while an arrangement of modern but comfortable, flower-patterned furniture, armchairs, sofas and the like, plus several convenient coffee tables, occupied the central area, the way one saw in the lobbies of corporate buildings or London hotels.

It was all in keeping with the grandly Gothic exterior, redolent both of wilderness lodge and border stronghold, but at the same time it felt warm, welcoming, everything spotlessly clean, without a hint of real-life wear and tear. It was a reconstruction of that era rather than a remnant, Nick realised, a high-spec country retreat that was rich in historical atmosphere.

'What are these curios?' Lottie wondered, moving from one glass case to the next. The first one she saw contained a jewel-hilted dagger, the blade curved into a near-crescent, the next a crusty green bottle with a stopper in it and a skull and crossbones stencilled on the glass. 'Memorabilia from Mr Karnwood's many movies, I imagine . . .' She stopped suddenly. 'What in God's name . . . ?' She indicated a leopard-spotted, five-clawed glove.

'*Last of the Leopard Men* . . . 1959,' Jordan said. 'That's the weapon the witchdoctor used to kill his victims. Usually while they were tied to a wooden frame. Modern-day wokies would hate that movie. They'd call it colonial, imperialist trash, but I still think it holds up. Wasn't really filmed in Africa, of course. They used existing footage of the savannah for linking material, but the actors were only ever on studio sets. Lots of fake greenery.'

'For God's sake, boy, give it a rest,' Darius groaned.

'I don't think my grandfather was especially proud of that one,' Matlock said, hovering in the background.

'Don't see why,' Jordan retorted. 'For 1959 it had some very gory kills in it. All done in Eastmancolor too, so the blood was as red as it gets.'

Clara meanwhile had sidled up to Nick and Liz. 'If that's all, I'm thinking . . . ?'

'No worries,' Nick said, clutching her by the hand. 'I know you need to get away.'

It had already been agreed that Clara, who had family duties that evening, would leave them at the Lodge once she'd dropped the tour party off, and return to collect them the following afternoon.

'Back tomorrow, four-ish?' Clara said.

'Perfect,' Liz replied.

Clara eyed the looming, motionless shape of the Edgar Karnwood waxwork. 'A good night should be had by all in here.'

Nick grinned. 'Not creeping you out, this place, is it, Clara?'

She gave him a withering look. 'Nicky, I used to drive the late bus in Salford and Trafford. It's going to take more than a stately home with five-star accommodation to spook me.'

'Only kidding.'

'Bloody better be, young man.' She winked before heading outside, zipping her *Murder Tour* anorak.

'If I might have your attention, ladies and gentlemen!' Matlock said loudly.

No one had strayed too far, but all of them now huddled closer.

He regarded them warily, as if he'd suddenly realised that he didn't know them, and they might transpire to be hostile. 'I . . . erm, I promise I'll be brief. You're most welcome here at the Lodge. I imagine that by now you've all been advised about the house's history. It only falls to me to add that you have the entire run of the premises, save those parts of it that are already locked. There aren't many of those, I'm sure you'll be glad to know, but those that are, are mainly storage areas or unfinished sections of the property as yet unsuitable for the presence of guests . . .'

Despite having promised to be brief and having acknowledged that they were already well-informed about Black Tarn Lodge, he went on at some length and with laborious slowness, describing the house's past and in particular the role his grandfather had played in reviving it after the many years during which it stood empty following Eric Helgoland's death.

'Did Helgoland die here?' Freya asked. 'At the Lodge?'

'Alas, no.' Matlock looked solemn. 'He'd left these premises several years prior to that. He was in his seventies by then, suffering from pleurisy and increasingly frail. He died in a care home on the east coast, somewhere near Whitby, I believe.'

'Is it true that he died begging for the presence of a Catholic priest and raving for God's forgiveness?' Lottie asked.

'As to that, dear lady, I have no information.'

It would have been an interesting addition to the story, if he had, Nick thought to himself. In fact, Matlock was probably missing a trick there. In Nick's version of events, Helgoland would have died right here, in one of the rooms upstairs, and would most certainly have expired while pleading with God to spare his soul.

'You'll notice we have no staff as yet,' Matlock continued. 'We are not currently classified as a hotel or inn. At present, you are simply guests in my private home. However, my housekeeper, who is only on site during the day . . .'

Who won't stay here after dark, Nick thought. *Because no one in their right mind will!*

'. . . has prepared a cold buffet, which awaits us in the dining room, where I recommend we reconvene at seven this evening, though cocktails and other drinks – all on the house of course – will be available in here from six. In the meantime, you'll notice that an envelope addressed to each one of you waits on the sideboard cabinet over there. In it, you'll find your room key and an introductory letter, containing any additional details you may require. I keep a master key of course, which will open any bedrooms in the event of an emergency.'

They shuffled over to the hall's north side, where, just below the staircase, an extensive sideboard set with bright green cloth – three ornate candelabra burning on it, one at either end and one in the middle – was laid with a row of eight sealed envelopes, one for each guest.

'Personalised envelopes are a nice touch,' Nick muttered, 'but they're a bit basic. Plus, they've all been typed.'

'Maybe he's got crappy handwriting,' Liz said.

'In which case he should've got someone else to do it. In a spooky scrawl. Blood-red ink.'

'You've been watching too many horror films, Mr Thornwood,' Lottie said with a chuckle.

'That's a point,' Nick said. He turned to Matlock, who again was hovering around in the background like a pale-faced ghost. '*Malifique?*'

'Ah, yes . . .' Matlock raised his voice. 'Tonight's film show, ladies and gentlemen, commences at nine o'clock. You may take drinks into the Movie Room, though I'd rather that plates of food and the like were confined to the dining area.'

'No popcorn?' Roy said, looking dismayed.

'I . . . erm . . .' Matlock regarded him mournfully, as if this were something he ought to have considered but hadn't.

Roy grinned. 'It's a joke, mate, don't worry.'

Matlock seemed nonplussed.

'So, everyone!' Nick said loudly. 'It's nearly four o'clock now and we only dine at seven, so we've got plenty of time. But pre-drinks at six, yeah?'

There were mumbles of agreement.

They trooped upstairs in their ones and twos, bags in hand. Liz found herself at the rear, Darius just in front of her, and then Jordan. They halted almost immediately, the younger guest having seen something he liked.

'Wow!' He indicated a series of five paintings on the wall alongside the central section of staircase. 'Are these the originals from *House of Torment*?' He didn't wait for anyone to give him an answer. 'Bet these'd be worth a bob or two, Mr Brant. There'll be collectors all over the world looking to get hold of these.'

Darius, just below him and now impeded, looked grumpy simply to have been addressed by the youngster, but he still put his glasses on, interest visibly sparking.

'We know that Edgar Karnwood was an eager collector of props from his movies,' Liz replied to Jordan. 'So I assume they're the originals.'

Intrigued, Darius glanced more closely at the painting to his immediate left. 'They do seem vaguely familiar.'

'They're from *House of Torment*?' Jordan said again.

'Perhaps you could refresh my memory?'

'A lot of Karnwood's films were B movies,' Liz said. 'But some of them were a little bit better than that. I mean, all Edgar Karnwood's movies are outdated now. But one or two are still regarded as classics. I mean, *House of Torment* . . . early '60s, I think . . .'

'1960,' Jordan corrected her.

'1960,' she said. 'It's really a very good film. Based on a classic Gothic novel. Karnwood played the patriarch of a wealthy but degenerate New England family, who gathers them all together at their ancestral home because a fortune teller has predicted they'll all die at the hands of a supernatural being, but in reality of course he's totally insane and planning to kill them himself . . .'

'And these paintings?' Darius said. 'They play a role in the plot?'

'Not exactly,' Liz admitted. 'But there's a famous scene where Karnwood's character escorts his youngest son's innocent fiancée up the staircase and they pass one painting after another, and as they all portray his ancestors, he describes each one and the terrible things they did.'

Darius went on up the stair to the second painting, and then the third. Like the first, they depicted individuals with more similarities to animals than human beings.

In truth, he was vaguely familiar with the movie they were talking about. He hadn't cared for it much, but if he recollected properly, there'd been a higher level of artistry in that particular film compared to Karnwood's others. In particular, because of his normal pursuits, Darius remembered the portrait sequence. It was certainly interesting to see the original images up close and in the flesh. They were crudely done, of course. They'd probably been splashed on to canvas by some moderately talented studio hand who'd had nothing else to do for half an hour. Their memorabilia value would clearly be high, though they weren't pleasant to look at. There was something more than unsettling about the strange, malformed faces. Their goat-like, ape-like and even reptilian features were all the more disturbing when you considered that *House of Torment* had ended in an absolute welter of blood, death and torture.

He glanced down at the vast hall with its ancient fittings and eerie, towering figure near the front door. It now lay empty, flickering with fiery shadows.

'Everything all right, Darius?' Liz wondered.

'Sorry,' he laughed. 'Letting my imagination run away with me.'

'Know what you mean. I'm glad these paintings are on the stairs and not in the bedrooms.'

'Indeed.' He glanced at the next portrait up. It depicted a near-hybrid between man and hog. In fact, the only discernible human features were the eyes – and they were the eyes of a madman.

Seven

'So, how do we think it's going?' Nick wondered, coming out from the bathroom in his underpants.

Liz was on the bed, wrapped in a towel. She glanced round from her phone. 'The Long, Dark Weekend overall or *this* part of it?'

'Both.'

She mused. 'I think that on the whole people have enjoyed themselves enough to put the word out. We're only going to do these Long, Dark Weekends now and then, anyway, aren't we?'

Nick wiped a blob of shaving cream away. 'So . . . we think it's a goer?'

'I think it's a goer enough to do another one. This place has been the crowning glory, but whether Matlock will let us have it as cheaply next time is another question.'

'I'm guessing there'll be no chance. Not when this place is up and running properly.' Nick went back into the en-suite to start running her bath. On returning, he rooted in his bag for some canvas slacks and a clean polo shirt. 'Though, by all accounts, when he first came up with this idea, he couldn't find any potential business partners. They all thought this place was too far from anywhere.'

'I'd have been wary of that too, but . . .' Liz pushed back a coppery-red lock and studied the plush bedroom: another huge fireplace, rich hangings, more antique furniture, a four-poster bed. 'He's done a bang-up job. I mean, which London hotel would offer this level of comfort without charging an arm and a leg?'

As usual, she sounded pleased rather than excited, but that was Liz all over. She couldn't help but be analytical, sometimes to the point where Nick was frustrated. Like when she insisted on going through restaurant bills with a fine-tooth comb, or when she turned her nose up at amazing-looking holidays even if, in her view, they were only a teensy bit overpriced. Of course, it was better to have someone like that with you than against you.

She got up and went to the window, opening the curtain.

Below them lay the reservoir, though its surface was hidden by mist. The far shore had a semi-mystical aura, huge boulders arrayed along its waterline, trees ranked thickly behind them, their autumn canopies glinting orange. Beyond that, the rolling, empty landscape was no more than a haze.

'When I first came up here from the south,' Liz said, 'I assumed all of Lancashire would be just like Greater Manchester. You know, factories, terraced houses.'

'Lots of people think that.' Nick climbed into his clothes.

'Can't believe how beautiful this place is. Even at this time of year.'

She was still gazing outside. He came over and joined her. The fast-approaching sunset had deepened the dusk to purple-black, and at the same time set fire to the trees on the far shore.

'To think that Matlock *inherited* all this,' she said.

'I know.' He kissed her bare shoulder. 'Lucky bugger, eh?'

'He's sitting on a goldmine.' She glanced around at him. 'And he might not be the only one.'

Nick frowned. 'What're you looking at me for?'

'This place doesn't inspire you? Make you want to get back behind your keyboard?'

Frustrated, Nick moved away. 'I've told you. I'm done with all that.'

'I sincerely hope not. Not when it's billed all over the Murder Tour website that you're a movie writer.'

'That wasn't my idea.'

'We *both* agreed it would help drum up custom.'

'Yes, but it's a lie.'

'No, it's not. Nick, you're a very talented writer.'

He sat on the bed, pulling on his socks. 'If I was talented, I'd have made it by now.'

'At thirty? You realise how young that actually is?'

'It's just . . .' He shrugged. 'All the rejections, you know . . . all the knock-backs.'

'I'm not saying it's not hard. But doesn't this place inspire you? I mean, look at it. It's gorgeous and Gothic and scary all at the same time. You could set an Edgar Karnwood movie here, but you could set an Agatha Christie here too. It must be open season for ideas in that head of yours.'

Nick glanced at her, but didn't immediately reply. It wasn't the shortage of ideas that was the problem, more the shortage of sales. And that was a subject he didn't even like to broach in conversation, not with anyone, but especially not with Liz. She was his life-partner. They'd been a firm fixture in each other's lives since the start of their respective university courses, and all these years later, none of that had changed. They were soulmates, pure and simple. But that was all the more reason why the subject of his writing career embarrassed him.

This was a woman he loved and had always wanted to provide for – or at least impress that he could be an equal partner in their relationship. But in reality, it was Liz who'd done all the providing thus far. Yes, it had been a collective decision that she would get the 'proper job' – i.e. admin work – while he chased the dream. And yes,

Liz was correct: he *was* a dab hand when it came to script writing, and he knew his horror inside out. But for all that horror was the low-budget film market that endured, the genre that churned out ticket sales, that bucked every Hollywood crisis because it would always find an eager young audience, each one of his forty or so scripts to date had been rejected. Even the handful that *had* been optioned had returned to him in due course, all interest having lapsed (and usually after the 'production companies' involved had demanded endless senseless rewrites, which had finally ruined the product anyway). Given the amount of work that went into writing scripts, it was heartbreaking, soul-destroying, utterly exhausting.

'If only these guys could articulate what it is they want,' he'd once complained to her, citing the many so-called film producers (usually one-man bands equipped more with enthusiasm than capability) who, despite being unagented, he'd still managed to get his scripts in front of. 'But all they ever seem to know is what they *don't* want.'

'All the more reason to keep trying,' Liz had replied.

He'd exploded in response. 'Have you any idea how fucking draining it is, conceiving something that might just work! Storylining it! Filling it with believable characters! Adding subtext! And then knocking all that complex crap into a meaningful, workable narrative that can work cinematically? Only to then have it bounced back with scarcely a word! And for this to happen again and again! And you just blithely respond with "you have to keep trying"!'

He'd apologised later, of course, as he always apologised. Liz was only trying to be encouraging. For the sake of his mental health as well as their mutual prosperity. In the meantime, she was endlessly prepared, or so it seemed, to keep doing the day job, shuffling paper, opening and closing filing cabinets, making cups of coffee for managers, just so that he could take another shot and another shot after that.

'I just don't think it's fair,' he said, slipping his feet into a pair of tennis shoes. 'You doing the nine-till-five slog, while I faff about.'

'Faff about?' She arched an eyebrow. 'First time I've heard you call it that.'

'You know what I mean.'

'Nick . . . it was your idea to create the Murder Tour. That's paid a few bills.'

'Yeah, but only a few. It's hardly the making of us.'

'No, but it'll serve in the meantime.'

He stood up. 'You mean till I get my big break in the movies?'

'Why not? Let this place seep into you. One kingpin of the horror world did. Why not you as well?'

He smiled, crossed the room and pecked her on the lips. 'You're too kind, hon. As always.'

'Hey, I've got an interest in this too. If I didn't think you were good enough, I wouldn't keep nagging at you. Those scripts won't write themselves.'

'Well . . .' He backed to the door. 'This place is about as atmospheric as they come, I suppose. Wouldn't be a bad title actually . . . *The Lodge*.'

'There you go. You've only been here forty minutes and you're cooking with gas already.'

He gestured, genuinely warmed by her words. 'What would I do without you?'

'Heaven only knows.' She turned to the bathroom.

'But we need more than this, Liz.' She glanced back. 'I mean, you're right . . . the Murder Tour's doing better than we expected. But it's not wonderful, and you need a better life.'

'"We", Nick, not "you".'

'You can't drudge away in that bloody office forever. You deserve some excitement.'

'You never know . . .' She went through into the bathroom. 'We might find some of that here.'

◆ ◆ ◆

Nick halted on the minstrels' gallery, surveying the hall's vast, fire-lit interior, though now that it was dark outside, various discreet side-lamps had also been switched on, adding to the overall homeliness of the scene.

From what Nick had seen online, like many antique buildings constructed with half an eye on defence, Black Tarn Lodge was in essence a solid square block. It faced westward across the tarn, its back to the eastern hills, and though it covered nearly fifteen thousand square feet, there was no courtyard, and no extensive north or south wings. It was a huge, all-in-one structure, built for the most part around its main feature, which was the great hall, though there were many other rooms, suites of rooms and corridors leading off from this. While the property fronted directly on to the tarn, the gardens, which as far as Nick knew had first been laid out and cultivated in Victorian times, were located entirely at its rear. He'd only seen them in map form on the website, but as far as he recalled, they ascended eastward towards the moors, and so were actually a series of stepped terrace gardens, each on different levels, but all of them extensive and comprising complexities of interlocking lawns, arboured walks, orchards and the like. Though they'd been in their full glory during Edgar Karnwood's tenure, they'd apparently been neglected in the years since, and were now wild, overgrown and badly in need of some TLC, which Simon Matlock had been planning to provide in the spring.

So, while the place was already in guest-ready condition, certainly in terms of its accommodation, there was a little more work to do. When it was finished all over, renting it out for Halloween parties and as a writers' retreat would be a criminal underuse of such a facility. Like Liz had said, Black Tarn Lodge could sit in the front rank of Britain's most lavish country hotels.

Again, he could only marvel at the younger Matlock's good fortune.

Just then, movement caught his eye. Leaning over the banister, Nick, who'd expected to be the first to come down, saw that Roy had beaten him to it. Hurriedly, he descended the ornate staircase to join him.

The big man had scrubbed up and put a clean roll-neck sweater on under his denim jacket. He'd also partaken of the various bottles of booze which, during their absence, had appeared along the sideboard where the envelopes had been. He currently sipped from a crystal tumbler, the amber fluid inside it suggesting a generous tot of whisky, and stood assessing a free-standing display case on a table, a particularly large one.

As Nick ambled over, Roy nodded at the object of his interest. 'Thought Christmas was supposed to be a fun thing.'

Inside the case was what at first appeared to be a wooden doll's house, though on closer inspection it was sculpted into the shape of a castle covered in snow, and set with many small doors, each of them numbered, a few standing open, revealing the miniature carved figures of goblins, ghosts and in one case a fierce, horned figure with a bulging sack on his shoulder, miniature human hands and feet protruding through the neck of it.

'The advent calendar from *The Christmas You Deserve*,' Nick said. 'Came out December '72. Karnwood played a deranged toy-maker who sent killer toys to all his enemies.'

Roy considered. 'Be a novel way to punch some tickets. Good job it's not real, eh?'

'Christmas would never be the same again,' Nick agreed.

'And that waxwork's bloody creepy too. Talk about lifelike.'

They wandered over to the figure near the entrance. The tall, motionless form regarded them in silence.

'Madame Tussauds prided themselves on making lifelike duplicates,' Nick commented. 'The original Madame Tussaud was a wax sculptress who found employment during the French Revolution making models of all the famous heads that came bouncing down the guillotine steps. Keeping a record, I suppose. Guess it was ultra important she got the details right.'

Roy grimaced. 'Imagine getting that CV: "I'm not good for much, but I don't mind sitting next to a river of blood and I can work wonders with chopped-off heads."' He blew out a long, unsteady breath. 'No wonder people like horror movies. At least they didn't really happen.'

'Speaking of which, you visited the Costume Vault downstairs yet?'

Roy glanced at him. 'Downstairs?'

Nick nodded across the hall to its north-west corner, where a closed doorway stood alone, a majestic antlered skull on a shield above it. 'Apparently, most of the great man's outfits are on display down there.'

'And we can just walk down and check them out?'

'Like Simon Matlock said, we can go anywhere that's not locked.'

'I can see a key in the door from here.'

'I know,' Nick said. 'I tried it earlier. Seems Matlock's left it open.'

'Very trusting, isn't he?' Roy said, as they wandered over.

'I've vouched for you all,' Nick replied.

'In that case, *you're* very trusting.'

◆ ◆ ◆

Liz hadn't felt that it would be quite right to dress up this evening. At least, she didn't fancy adorning herself in some glamorous evening gown, or spending ages on her hair and make-up and jewellery. Instead, she'd gone for 'casual but alluring': heeled boots, tight jeans and a loose-fitting blouse, her hair tied in a girlish ponytail.

She came out on to the gallery overlooking the hall at roughly quarter to six, having expected to see the rest of the tour party milling about downstairs, but surprisingly, no one was there, the only movement the rippling firelight playing across the antique fittings and sumptuous old furniture. She descended, spotting the various bottles and trays of glasses set out along the sideboard, but immediately decided that it wouldn't be the best look for *Murder Tour Ltd* if one of its directors was the first on the booze.

Which was when she spotted the front door standing open. Only an inch or two, but clearly indicative that someone had gone outside.

That wasn't surprising. It should be pretty spooky out there in the misty darkness. Precisely what this tour was all about. Liz went out as well.

But there was no sign of anyone, and the silence was absolute.

The mist didn't just swamp the reservoir now. It had stolen up onshore. Thankfully, the exterior lights, which seemed to be located all along the front of the building, did much to penetrate it, but it still hung in semi-opaque drapes all the way between here and about a hundred and fifty yards away, a good sixty past the end of the house, where what looked like a timber jetty projected outward into the murk.

She hadn't noticed this on first arriving, all their attention riveted on the Lodge itself. She thus strolled along the drive in that direction, arms folded, heels crunching grit. Clearly there was someone outside, otherwise why had the front door been left open?

'Hello?' she called. 'Someone out here?'

If there was, they didn't reply.

Eight

The entrance that led down to the Costume Vault might have been impressive, but the stairs were less so, comprising two flights of narrow, grubby steps made from bare concrete. The cellars themselves were quite extensive, literally a network of rooms and passages expanding as far out in every direction as the property above ground did. They had been laid with new cement and their brick walls whitewashed, but the electric lighting in the corridors, due to a rickety-looking installation just inside the cellar door, was poor, and this added to the lower level's dim, labyrinthine aura.

On one hand that worked well, Nick thought, as he and Roy ventured through it. After all, this place was all about scaring folks – or at least, the Long, Dark Weekends were about that – so it certainly suited *their* purposes, though he suspected it actually stemmed from Simon Matlock not yet having a real handle on what he wanted to do here, or at least misunderstanding the level of panache required. This was a special part of the house, so it ought to have a special atmosphere, rather than feel like a run-of-the-mill basement.

At least the rooms themselves were worth visiting. The first one they stumbled into had nothing really to do with Edgar Karnwood. It was done up as a kind of private chapel, with several pews made from black wood facing a crude-looking altar. On the surrounding walls, where the Stations of the Cross would normally be, there were blow-ups of black-and-white photographs, several featuring a gaunt, bald-headed man, sometimes wearing dark robes, though in some of them he was naked and performing what appeared to be a complex and painful form of yoga, while in others he was standing amid circles of cross-legged acolytes, men and women, also nude.

'Well . . . we knew there was an Eric Helgoland room,' Nick said.

'Yeah.' Roy sounded wary. 'The black magician.'

Nick walked past the pews towards the altar. The lighting in here was better, though again he couldn't help feeling that a showman might have tinged it red. 'I wonder if this was where Helgoland held his rituals.'

'Looks like it,' Roy said.

Behind the altar a black cloth hung on the wall with a white pentacle painted on it, zodiac-type symbols at each of its five points.

'Matlock got this part of the place right, at least.' Nick surveyed the altar table, in the middle of which there was a human skull with a black chalice to the left of it, a wavy-bladed sacrificial dagger to the right, and outside of those, a pair of black candles.

'It's all phoney, though . . . yeah?' Roy said. 'I mean, this guy, Helgoland . . . he didn't really worship the Devil?'

Nick pondered. 'Helgoland would probably say he didn't. He was an occultist for sure, but he'd argue that he was a student of mysticism, alternative religions and so on. But to everyone else . . . well, black magic's black magic, isn't it? But now you mention it' – he glanced at the pentacle on the cloth – 'this is definitely a Satanic altar, which probably means it's a mock-up. Matlock likely got the idea from one of his grandpa's films. I doubt Eric Helgoland owned any of this stuff. It all looks too new.'

'Lottie won't be keen. She's a bit nice for all this, to be honest. Mind you . . .' Roy pondered. 'She says she believes in spirits and that, so you never know.'

'Each to their own.' Nick walked back towards the door.

At which point, a voice sounded from somewhere out in that maze of brick corridors. It was deep, harsh, and yet echoey and dissonant.

'Rise!' it said. 'Rise . . . you night things, you spawn of desolation . . .'

Nick gazed at Roy, startled. His hair even prickled.

'. . . go forth, wander the darkness . . . and bring me blood!'

◆ ◆ ◆

They'd arranged for the tour party to stay over one night at Black Tarn Lodge mostly via a series of Zoom meetings. Neither Liz nor Nick had actually been here before. So, aside from what they'd already seen of the place, neither of them knew much about it.

Liz hadn't expected that it would be so far from anywhere else, nor that, magnificent as the house was, it would be perched on the edge of a body of water that was just about as forbidding as anything she'd ever seen. It was only when you were standing looking at it, especially with mist wreathed around you, that you understood what it meant when a reservoir or tarn was so deep; rumour held that it descended to seven hundred feet. She also realised that she knew equally little about any of the actual facilities the house offered. What were the gardens like? She was aware they hadn't been attended to yet by Matlock or his property restorers and so were pretty unkempt. But how extensive were they? Was there anything to be gained by wandering around them tomorrow during daylight, or were those unattended sections so excessively unkempt that they were impassable, maybe even dangerous?

And what of this now in front of her?

She was sixty-odd yards past the house, the great angular structure having receded almost completely into vapour, but ahead, the jetty had come fully into view. A causeway of clean-cut timber, it led out over the water for seventy or eighty yards. On the other side of it, a small, roofed structure, a boathouse presumably, fronted on to the waterline, and now that she was close, she could even see two boats tethered side by side about halfway along, which was encouraging. A boat ride across the surface of Black Tarn would be an interesting experience the following day.

As Liz strode out, the only sound the lapping of water against the pilings and the clicking of her heels on woodwork, she became aware that about forty yards to her right a headland jutted out almost as far as the jetty itself. This was just at the point where the shoreline became wooded, so the small promontory was dense with trees and other vegetation.

She reached the two boats, which sat on her right, tilting and jostling each other. They were four-man motorboats, each with an outboard engine tilted upward at the back, their propellors clear of the water. That was good news too, because she doubted anyone would fancy *rowing* around the reservoir, not if they'd be making a night of it tonight.

It was colder out here than on the shore, and Liz, with no coat on, was feeling it already. She hugged herself as she strode on, finally reaching the jetty's far end, which was marked by two mooring posts that were taller than she was.

The mist rolling over the silky black surface was semi-hypnotic. It was easy to imagine the gloomy abyss below, though it was harder to picture the far shore, which she couldn't even see, not to mention any other solid ground, because when she glanced over her shoulder, the landward end of the jetty was also concealed, the house itself only visible as several equidistant blobs of barely discernible light.

Fleetingly, nothing else seem to exist in this void of shifting greyness.

And that was when she sensed movement somewhere to the right.

She turned, and momentarily, a break in the vapour revealed the extreme end of the headland, which was roughly level with her. It also revealed a figure. A tall figure, standing very still, wearing dark clothing, its head turned in her direction.

◆ ◆ ◆

'What's occurring?' Roy demanded.

'What?' Jordan swung around, startled.

It was one of the larger cellar rooms, perhaps fifty yards in length, thirty wide, and brightly lit. At first glance when they'd barged in, it had appeared to be crammed with garishly clad but motionless people. Only at second glance did it become plain that these were department-store-type mannequins, each one on its own plinth, various pathways winding between them. Jordan was in the very middle, planted in front of a tall shape in an evening suit, a Masonic-style cloak and a straggling white wig.

'That voice you just made!' Roy said, pink-faced.

Jordan still looked surprised. It seemed he'd been talking aloud into a kind of segmented tube, about two feet long, put together from various pieces of carved but hollow wood and flaring broadly at its lower end like some kind of latter-day didgeridoo. He offered it to them as if this explained everything. 'This is how he gave them their instructions.'

Nick chuckled with relief. 'You scared the crap out of us.'

'What am I missing here?' Roy asked.

Nick took charge of the instrument. 'It's the voice manipulator from *The Evil of Dr Caligari*.'

'1958,' Jordan added eagerly.

'Basically a remake,' Nick said. 'Karnwood played a mad hypnotist, who sent sleepwalkers out to kill off his academic rivals.'

'And it still works.' Jordan took the instrument back, placing it next to the caped, white-wigged figure. He looked slyly amused. 'So I scared you, did I?'

'Not me,' Roy answered quickly, puffing his chest out. 'Just made us think there was someone here who shouldn't be.'

The younger guy shrugged, his enthusiasm for the Costume Vault taking over again. He ranged about between the silent effigies. 'This place is amazing.'

He stopped in front of another besuited mannequin, blank-faced and rather ordinary, the three-piece outfit distinctly dating from the late 1970s, though it was stained all down the front by what looked like a hardened olive-green syrup.

'What was that one about?' Roy wondered. 'A bloke who throws up after he's had too much pea soup?'

'*Metamorphoid,*' Nick replied, equally impressed by the tainted suit. '1977.'

'One of Karnwood's goriest films,' Jordan added. 'He plays a moonbase scientist, who when he comes back to Earth has been infested by an alien parasite and his outer form starts disintegrating while he's still alive so that the real creature inside can get out. First though, he tries to cover it up with an ultra-realistic mask. There's this classic scene, when he's addressing Congress . . . and he just starts coming apart, all this green goo running all over him.'

'Sorry I missed that one,' Roy mused.

'If that doesn't take your fancy, look at the rest. There're two or three more rooms of this stuff. Total treasure trove.'

Nick nodded. 'As I told you.'

'Played Sherlock Holmes, did he?' Roy asked, noting a featureless figure wearing a Victorian tweed cape and deerstalker.

'Only once,' Nick said. '*Hound of Hell*, 1966.'

Roy frowned. 'Think I remember that one.'

They moved on among the silent, watchful forms. Nick had never been down here before either, and though he'd heard about it, he'd never expected to see so much that he actually recognised: the scarlet plate armour and chainmail of the crazed Prince Archaeon, the Vlad Ţepeş-type despot of the 1968 hell-fest, *Reign of Blood*, was unmistakable.

'Karnwood was in a Bond film?' Roy asked, stopping next to one particular wall display: what looked like a dark-blue, adult-sized Kevlar vest spread out against a larger-than-life 007 gun-barrel motif.

'*Do or Die*,' Nick reminded him. '1975. He played the corrupt MI6 chief who was later executed by a death squad sent by SPECTRE. Karnwood's character was gunned down, so he wore the exploding squibs in his own clothes, but needed some protection underneath, just in case any fragments went the wrong way. It was near enough his only non-horror film.'

Roy nodded to himself, as if this were one starring role that he approved of. Jordan, meanwhile, was totally blown away, taking yet more selfies, shooting video footage, giving a running commentary as he roved around.

'Certainly got a happy customer in *him*,' Roy observed.

'I'm hoping you'll all feel you've got your money's worth by the end,' Nick replied.

'Can't speak for the others, but my area of interest is still the real thing.'

'Maybe we'll get some of that too.'

'Eh?'

Nick grinned. 'Only joking. Big spooky house and all that.'

Roy looked doubtful. 'Don't think I've ever heard of a real murder occurring in a place like this. They're usually in town centres, on the backstreets of sink estates . . . rarely in stately homes.'

'You're not telling me the world's crime writers have been getting it wrong all these years?'

'Well, no . . . there's a first time for everything.'

◆ ◆ ◆

Liz blinked hard, but the unmoving shape on the headland remained in place. She edged forward, bewildered, eventually reaching the point where another inch or so and she'd topple into the water. She reached out unconsciously, one hand clasping the mooring post, shamelessly staring.

That face. She knew it . . . she *recognised* it.

It was ridiculous. How could that be? How could she even distinguish it on this misty night, from over forty yards away? And yet there was no doubt in her mind: she knew him.

And perhaps he realised this. Perhaps he suddenly understood that he'd not only been spotted, but identified, for as the swirls of mist closed in again, he burst into motion, swinging around and charging into the undergrowth, running with heavy, crunching footfalls back toward the shore. No doubt to divert along the waterline.

And cut her off.

Nine

If running in high-heeled boots wasn't hard enough, running along a jetty made from thick planks with inch-wide gaps in between them made it harder still. A couple of times as Liz thudded back towards land, she caught a toe in one of those gaps, half-tripping, and once almost pitching into the reservoir. And all the way of course she glanced sideways at the headland, what she could see of it in the mist, as if that huge shape would be visible plunging through the undergrowth, staying parallel with her, or maybe now ahead of her, determined to get into her path.

Liz gasped hard in the cold air as she reached the end of the structure and descended the two crude steps on to dry ground, glancing leftward again, certain he'd be barrelling towards her through the gloom. He wasn't, but she could hear a rustling and thrashing of vegetation on the other side of the boathouse.

She stumbled in the direction of the main building. Surely, she'd make it? Its front door was only a hundred and fifty yards away. Meanwhile, water splashed behind her. She imagined a heavy stone accidentally kicked by a pursuer coming at pace. He'd been tall. Much taller than she was. He'd have a longer stride and would effortlessly close the distance between them. In fact, was that the impact of his feet she could now hear?

'My God!' she whimpered.

Less than a hundred yards remained and yet that seemed an impossible distance to cover. She almost tripped again, tottering to the waterline. *Good Christ, not that!* Even if she only blundered into the shallows, she'd never get out again in time.

She corrected her direction, thrusting forward again.

The castle-like edifice towered. Lights were visible from its front windows, even from the open front door, which still seemed too far away. Her booted toe again struck something, kicking a divot out of the grit. This time she *did* fall, landing on her left knee. It jolted horribly but the adrenaline was pumping. She scrambled upright, only to find a manlike shape directly in front of her.

A piercing scream might have ripped from Liz's chest, had Nick not spoken first.

'Whoa, whoa, whoa . . .'

She grabbed him, fingers sinking like claws into his arms. 'Nick . . . there's a . . . look out, there's a—'

She glanced behind them . . . and saw nothing but curling mist.

He hugged her to him, clearly seeing how distraught she was. 'What's the matter?'

'There was a man. He was . . .' Already Liz's certainty was faltering. 'He was chasing me.'

'A man? Who?'

'I don't know. I . . .' She shook her head, bewildered, still clinging on to him as he gently set her aside so that he could investigate. 'I went to the end of the jetty and . . .' She fought to recall the exact details, now wondering wildly how much she'd actually seen and how much she'd imagined. It could *not* have been Edgar Karnwood. Surely it couldn't? 'He was on the next headland along. He ran back to shore. I thought he was trying to cut me off . . .'

Nick regarded her uncomprehendingly. He surely could see how alarmed she was. She was breathing fast and drenched with sweat. But when they gazed together along the drive towards the jetty, they saw nothing but vapour. Fleetingly, the jetty itself was visible, but there was no one there. 'Liz, I . . .'

She saw the doubt in his eyes, and it steeled her. '*I'm telling you I saw him!*'

'And he saw you . . . while you were on the jetty? And he chased you?'

'He ran towards the lakeside . . .'

'Okay.' He took her hand. 'Let's walk back along the lakeside and see.'

She resisted. 'Nick, did you not hear what I just told you?'

'Whoa, keep it down, eh? Everyone's gathered for drinks. I came out to see where you were because the door was open. It's wide open still and they're just the other side of it. They might hear.'

She wanted to retort with heartfelt bitterness: *Like I fucking care!*

But Nick was right. Panicking was no solution, much less *spreading* panic. And especially not when Liz had always prided herself on being the level head of the partnership. Instead, though with some reluctance, she let him lead her back towards the jetty.

'You don't believe me, do you?' she said.

'Course I do. I believe you saw something. But it was probably just a groundsman.'

'A groundsman? At this hour?'

'It's only just after six.'

'But Matlock said there were no other staff on site.'

'Well, I don't know . . .' Nick shrugged. 'A tramp maybe?'

'All the way out here?'

'They have to get from town to town somehow,' he joked.

'Nick, there was something else too!'

He stopped and looked at her.

She hesitated, suddenly feeling shamefaced. 'I . . . I recognised him. At least, I thought I did.'

'Okay . . . who was it?'

Again, she hesitated. 'Nick . . . it was Edgar Karnwood.'

A long, long silence pulled slowly taut between them. Finally, Nick shook his head. 'Hon, you can't go saying things like that. At least not in front of the others. They'll think you've gone barmy.'

'But what do *you* think?' She grabbed his hands.

'There must be an explanation. Maybe it was Simon Matlock. I haven't seen him since we all went to get freshened up, and when I left the hall, he still wasn't—'

'It wasn't Matlock,' she said sternly. 'It was his grandfather. I've watched enough of his movies to know him when I see him.'

'His grandfather? Who's been dead since 2012?'

'I know how it sounds.'

'It'll sound even worse to the others. They'll assume we're trying to put the frighteners on them. And you've seen this lot . . . they're not easily scared, so they'll probably take the piss, say we're trying too hard. Liz, it could spoil everything.'

'So . . . what? We just ignore it?'

Nick shrugged. 'I'd rather you tried to rationalise it.'

'Rationalise it?'

'Come with me.' He tightened his grip on her hand and walked on to the jetty. They mounted the steps and set out along it side by side. Again, the only sounds were their footfalls and the water gurgling under the timbers. When they reached the far end, the headland was only partly visible, more veils of mist drifting landward.

'I don't know how you could have seen anything over there,' Nick said.

'There was a break in the fog.'

'Like in the movies, you mean? You know, when it always happens at the most dramatic moment . . .'

She yanked her hand free. 'What're you trying to say?'

'I just think you might be mistaken.'

'Is there anything over there that even half looks like a man, which might have fooled me?'

'Well, no . . .'

'So, I imagined it?'

'Well, what do *you* think you saw?' He was starting to sound exasperated. 'A guy who even if he'd faked his own death would now be one hundred and thirteen years old? So maybe it was his ghost who ran after you. But if it was his ghost, why was it out here and not inside, where there'd be more opportunity to scare people?'

There was logic in this, of course. What Liz thought she'd seen was impossible.

'Isn't it at least a chance there was *someone* there?' she said.

'Yes.' He took her arm and steered her towards the shore. 'And because of that, we're going back inside now, closing the front door behind us and barring it.'

It sounded like a precaution, but he exuded no air of genuine concern that Liz could detect.

'Nick,' she said, 'there must be half a dozen ways to access that house that we don't know about.'

'There'll be nine of us in there, Liz. Even if it's the worst-case scenario, and there *is* some homeless guy hanging around, how deadly would he need to be to pose a threat to a group of that size?' They reached the shore and walked towards the building. 'And let's not say anything about Edgar Karnwood's ghost, eh? They'll roll on the floor laughing.'

'All right,' she agreed. 'But make *sure* we lock the door behind us.'

'We will. And we keep schtum, yeah?' He eyed her as though looking for reassurance. 'About the whole thing?'

She stopped in her tracks. 'So, not only do you want to pretend there's no one here who wishes us ill – you don't even want to warn the others that there might be?'

'Liz, what do you mean "wishes us ill"?'

'*Nick!*' The anger was growing in her again. *'He chased me!'*

He regarded her long and hard. It must be plain that she wasn't putting on an act here. That she was genuinely frightened. He glanced again into the mist. It was so thick out over the lake that it could literally have concealed anything. On land it was shifting and breaking, but equally impenetrable.

'We can warn the others if you want,' he finally said, sounding defeated. 'But ten to one they'll assume it's a put-on.'

'If so, that'll be *their* judgement call.'

'Liz . . .' He put his hands on her shoulders. 'Are you sure you're not just letting this whole thing get to you? I mean, we've been discussing murderers and madmen all weekend. And now we're spending the night here, where the trappings of lunacy are hanging on every wall . . .'

'You think I'm losing it, Nick? Like, all of a sudden, the Murder Tour's got too much for me?'

'I'm just saying we should think twice before causing any kind of scene. You've surely noticed that this thing's going very well? Our first Long, Dark Weekend's been a success. Everyone's had a good time, and now they're going to have a few drinks and a good dinner. They'll watch the horror movie, and then they'll go to bed feeling they've had a completely satisfying Tour.'

'Martha won't think that.'

'Martha's just weird,' he said, trying to shrug off the frustration he clearly felt about that. 'I'm not sure what she's even doing here.

But the rest will, and that's all we can ask for. Do you really want to throw a cat among the pigeons now?' He watched her earnestly.

Liz knew what she'd seen, but she understood his position. 'I suppose it depends what kind of cat it is.' She glanced again into the mist before heading up the steps to the front door. 'Let's hope it's not a deadly dangerous one.'

Ten

Once they were back inside, Nick and Liz closed and bolted the heavy front door. The rest of the tour party, meanwhile, had assembled by the sideboard, where they were helping themselves to drinks. Liz needed a minute or two before going over to join them.

The others, it seemed, had mostly bought into the occasion and tidied themselves up for dinner. None had come equipped with actual evening dress, with the exception of Freya, who looked ravishing in a figure-hugging, slit-skirted scarlet frock; Lottie, who'd donned a knee-length sparkly number and seemed to have added yet more bangles to her wrists and rings to her fingers; and Simon Matlock himself, who stood to one side, again more like a spare part than the owner of this extravagant property, but wearing a tuxedo and bowtie. Darius hadn't been able to dandify himself any more than he already was, while Jordan had made a minor adjustment to his day wear, dispensing with his Freddy Krueger T-shirt for one depicting the cruel, bloody-mouthed features of Christopher Lee as Dracula. Martha had gone to the least trouble, donning the same drab cardigan and jeans she'd worn earlier.

For the most part, they exchanged pleasantries as they were led into the dining area, which was off the main hall in its north-east corner.

The waiting banquet, unveiled from beneath sheets of foil, was to be served cold but consisted of luxurious and exotic fare: various charcuterie platters, savoury croissants with cheese-and-herb toppings, mini quiches, lamb and chicken skewers. At the heart of it all sat four sumptuous dishes: a glistening glazed ham, an enormous smoked salmon dressed with prawns and devilled eggs, a beef joint ready for slicing, and a huge bowl of Greek salad filled with olives and feta. For afters, there was a range of fruit tarts, cream cakes, meringues and gateaux, and several wooden boards layered with biscuits, crackers, cheese wedges and grapes.

It was all laid out amid glinting crockery and glassware in another elegant room, ancient masters on the walls, interspersed with heraldic banners and framed stills from Edgar Karnwood's movies. Handsome wooden chairs and side-tables were set around the walls, enabling the guests to sit comfortably once they'd loaded their plates.

'Those paintings on the staircase, Mr Matlock,' Darius said as he picked at his fare. 'I understand they have significant value in the world of the horror film?'

Matlock, again standing to one side like a servant awaiting instructions, came swiftly to attention. 'That is correct, sir. Indeed, that's correct.'

Darius made a casual gesture, as if it were only of minor interest. 'I don't suppose you could put a price on them? Both individually and as a set?'

'A price?' Matlock seemed surprised. 'I'd need to consult the documentation for that, sir, which is all stored in my private office. I can do that later, if you wish.'

'No, no.' Darius made light of it. 'A rough idea will do.'

'I honestly wouldn't like to guess. But I'll check the details for you at the end of the evening.'

Darius nodded and smiled.

'He's wondering if they're for sale,' Martha said, sipping her glass of Chardonnay.

Darius stared daggers at her. 'I never said any such thing.'

'For sale?' Matlock seemed shocked. 'Good heavens, no. They're *not* for sale. That would mean breaking up the Karnwood Collection, and that can never happen.'

Martha gave Darius a wry smile. 'Looks like you've reached another dead end, Mr Brant.'

Matlock glanced from one to the other. 'I'm afraid I don't understand?'

'Nothing to concern yourself with, Simon,' Nick said amiably.

'Mr Brant here is an art dealer,' Martha explained. 'He came on the Long, Dark Weekend under false pretences.'

Darius visibly reddened. 'My interests go far beyond the purely commercial, Ms Lloyd, I assure you—'

'Well, it's not like there hasn't been lots of interesting artwork to look at on this tour,' Liz interrupted, seeking to defuse the situation.

'That's one way of putting it.' Martha sipped more wine.

'It's quite simple,' Darius said stiffly. 'The art world's always been interested in the macabre. Goya's *Saturn Devouring His Son* must be one of the most grotesque images ever committed to canvas. It's disagreeable to some perhaps, but an important work nevertheless.'

'Devouring his son?' Roy looked both astonished and repulsed. 'Sometimes I'm glad I never had a classical education.'

'I don't think you need an education to appreciate the finer things,' Lottie said. 'Even if they are of the darker variety.'

Martha nodded sagely. 'That is definitely a fact.'

'Horror movies are popular at all levels of society,' Jordan chirped up.

'I wonder why?' Lottie replied.

Roy shrugged. 'Folks just like a good old scare, don't they?'

She looked thoughtful. 'A *safe* scare maybe. I mean, monsters are frightening. But they're not real.'

'Killers *are*, though,' Martha cut in. 'And that makes events like this one rather harder to understand.'

'Excuse me, Martha,' Freya said. 'But I'm confused. Didn't *you* pay to come on this trip? Aren't *you* just like the rest of us?'

'Ahh.' Martha smiled. 'Our resident private detective joins the debate. Feel free to come in on this all confident and gorgeous, Freya, but let me tell you . . . this Murder Resolution Society of yours counts for very little. You're just as bad as all these others. You're playing at it, having fun with other people's misery . . .'

Freya remained cool. 'I'm still interested as to why *you're* here?'

Even over so short a period as a single weekend, the majority of them had now become used to Martha's acerbic personality, and so paid it no attention, though Simon Matlock looked mortified, as if an argument between guests was the last thing he wanted.

'Perhaps we can lighten the tone a little?' Liz suggested. 'What do you say, Mr Matlock? What was it like when your grandfather was alive? How did he manage to collect all these artefacts, and how were you persuaded to maintain the collection after he'd died?'

'Erm, yes, well . . .' Matlock cleared his throat before commencing a rambling, monotonous monologue, which went on at tedious length, during the course of which the guests treated themselves to another helping of mouth-watering savouries, and then moved on to the desserts. Even then he droned on, and eventually, with everyone looking wearied by it, Nick decided to intervene.

'This is all fascinating,' he jumped in, 'but I do believe we have a movie to watch?'

He was greeted by mumbles of relief, even from those who hadn't been so openly keen to attend the forthcoming screening.

When the alternative was Simon Matlock's not-so-potted history of his grandfather and the great man's many achievements, only Lottie seemed to lack enthusiasm for *Malifique*.

'Why don't you all go and settle down for the film,' she said pleasantly. 'I'll join you when I've done these dishes.'

She was already busying herself along the length of the table, stacking used crockery and gathering up cutlery, which certainly looked odd given her obvious penchant for fine clothes and chunky jewellery. Simon Matlock for one clearly considered her a woman of breeding.

'Please don't concern yourself.' He hurried across the room, almost as if ready to remove her physically from the task. 'I shall attend to the table later on, and my housekeeper will be in on Monday to take care of everything else. She'll be positively livid if she comes all this way and finds someone else has done the job for her.'

'Oh, well in that case . . .' Lottie looked sheepish as she backed away. Even when Matlock advised everyone to follow him to the Movie Room, she seemed disinclined to go along.

'Lottie?' Nick asked when the others had left.

'This *Malifique*?' she said. 'Isn't it supposed to be rather horrible?'

'Lottie . . . all weekend, you've been visiting the scenes of real murders and massacres, where genuinely sickening deeds were done.'

'Yes, but none of them right in front of me.'

'Well . . .' Nick was a little surprised. Only slowly was he learning that gore hounds came in all shapes and sizes – some, it seemed, who weren't even keen on the sight of blood. 'Look . . . even if Edgar Karnwood didn't like the end product, *Malifique*'s only a film.'

'But isn't it supposed to be very realistic?' She sounded genuinely concerned.

He shrugged. 'It was made in the seventies, so it's probably not *that* realistic.'

'Perhaps "realistic" is the wrong word. *Nihilistic* maybe? What I mean is . . . Mr Karnwood's other films were rather camp and costumey. This one, though . . . wasn't it supposed to be a real shocker? About a mentally ill man who revels in committing horrible acts of cruelty against helpless victims? It sounds so awful.'

Nick thought again about Karnwood's own objections to the finished movie on the grounds of taste and decency, and how, according to him, it was too grim even by horror movie standards. He'd given an interview at the time, in which he'd said something like: 'Ultimately, my pictures are all about entertainment. But there's nothing of that here. There's no light at all in *Malifique's* darkness.'

'It's still just a film,' he said again.

Lottie remained unconvinced. 'It'll be easy to imagine that it's not. I mean, all the rest of this tour we've been told stories and visited the sites where terrible things happened. None of it felt real. But this time we'll actually be *seeing* it . . .'

'Well, we can't force you to watch it, Lottie.' Nick shrugged again. 'There's no harm in you sitting the film out and taking the opportunity to enjoy the rest of the house, check out the props, costumes and such.'

'I suppose I could . . . but I'd have to do that on my own, wouldn't I?' She bit on her bottom lip, clearly not liking that prospect either.

'I don't know what else to suggest,' Nick replied. Rather reluctantly, he added: 'I suppose I could sit out here with you . . . ?'

'Oh, no, no. I know you're really keen to see this film. It's a missing gem, isn't it?'

'It's only so I can say I've seen it. It's not that I'm turned on by the violence.'

Strange argument to try and make, he reflected. *That you desperately want to see this notoriously violent movie, even though it isn't the violence you're interested in. Supposedly.*

'It's okay,' Lottie said decidedly. 'I'll come into the Movie Room with the rest of you. I can always cover my eyes and block my ears.'

Nick felt relief as he showed her out of the dining area.

He'd have been loath to sit the movie out, having been looking forward so much to finally getting to see it, but he wouldn't have been comfortable leaving Lottie out here either. He told himself that he was being daft and shouldn't read anything into it, but Liz, one of the most stable people he knew, *had* said that she'd seen someone outside.

'Nonsense,' he muttered, escorting Lottie back across the hall.

'Sorry?' she asked brightly, clearly putting a brave face on the coming ordeal.

'Nothing . . . nothing.'

Absolutely nothing, he told himself. He refused to dwell on the emptiness and silence that now would fill the rest of this vast, multi-roomed mansion, or the eerie masks and costumes, or the hideous fire-lit faces on those paintings on the staircase.

Liz got it wrong and there's no one outside. Or in here. Just us.

But even so, he was glad that Lottie was coming with them.

Eleven

The Movie Room was located on a lower level, just below the ground floor. Not in the cellar as such, but it was accessible by a narrow passage on the east side of the main hall, which was decked with yet more stills from Edgar Karnwood's many films. First, they came to a room on the right, though this, Simon Matlock said, was his private office and always kept locked. Ten yards further along, on the left, stood a door that was partly open. Glancing through it, Nick glimpsed a large, heavy projector, its lens positioned against a small square aperture. Another few yards on, the passage ended at a single swing-door upholstered with red leather, its pull-bar handle made from polished brass.

Before they went through, Matlock turned to face them, his saturnine features even more solemn than previously. He took what looked like a roll of white cloth from his tuxedo pocket and shook it out into a sack. 'Ladies and gentlemen, at this point I wonder if you might permit me to collect all your phones, cameras and other electrical devices?'

The party shunted to a halt with mumbles of low consternation.

'I sincerely apologise,' Matlock said. 'I'm sure you understand, however, that the presence at the Lodge of *Malifique* is of key importance to the economy of the estate. We can't run any risk of video or photographic piracy.'

'I think that's a reasonable request, don't you?' Nick said, addressing the others.

The majority seemed less convinced, but Roy was the first to shrug, dig his phone and his Dictaphone from his denim jacket and drop them both into the sack. Matlock nodded graciously. Nick and Liz followed, as did the others, though in a vaguely disgruntled fashion.

'I guarantee they'll be stored in a very safe place,' Matlock assured them.

With the phones handed over, they proceeded through into the Movie Room, though Matlock himself went into the projector room, closing the door behind him.

The mini theatre was the last word in comfort: a small, vault-like chamber, but warm and cosy, with fabric soundproofing on the walls, and four rows of six plush armchairs, complete with drinks holders, facing down a gentle slope towards an enormous viewing screen. As soon as everyone was comfortable, Matlock, presumably watching from the square projection port on the wall behind them, hit the lights, plunging them into blackness.

Bang on nine o'clock, the movie began to roll.

While Nick had no doubt that *Malifique* would be a draw for any hardcore horror fan, he wasn't overly impressed with it himself, and soon felt he understood why the grand old movie star had disowned it afterwards. Karnwood played a top psychiatrist, whose wife went insane and murdered their children, and who, when he tried to treat her with experimental techniques in his private asylum, committed suicide. Sent mad himself, he embarked on a new hobby, posing as an everyday GP to lure scantily clad young women back to his now spookily derelict hospital, where he strangled them into unconsciousness and then performed unnecessary and horrific operations on them. In itself, the concept wasn't un-Edgar Karnwood-like: a weird madman stalking his nubile prey and luring them to ghastly fates, but in nearly all of Karnwood's previous outings there'd been a distinct aura of tongue-in-cheek. Yes, they'd been lurid and bloody, but they'd been pantomime-ish too. Rarely had they been as grimy and gritty as this. For decades, cinema audiences had *oohed* and *aahed* at crazy Edgar Karnwood creations like Prince Archaeon, Ron Hobart, the parasite-riddled space scientist, and his uniquely OTT versions of Baron Frankenstein, Mr Hyde and the Phantom of the Opera. This role was very different, and perhaps more in keeping with the Murder Tour concept overall. Here was Edgar Karnwood showing you what real maniacs are like. Here was the face of true homicidal insanity.

'Well, that was edifying,' Martha said when the end credits cut off, and they were plunged into blackness again.

'Didn't make sense,' Roy grunted. 'Three or four times, the cops could have caught him there. Even in the seventies, SOCOs would've been all over that.'

'You could say the same about some Hitchcock films,' Jordan argued. 'You seen *Frenzy*?'

'Good God, boy,' Darius snorted. 'You're putting what we've just seen on the same level as Alfred Hitchcock?'

'No, but it gave me the shudders . . . which is what it was supposed to.'

'Just another misogynist fantasy,' Freya said dismissively. 'I mean, I know you men hate women, but I'll never understand why you actually get off on seeing us killed.'

'Are we supposed to be sitting here in the dark?' Lottie asked, cutting across them.

'That's what I was wondering,' Liz mumbled to Nick.

He stood up and turned around. No light was visible through the projection port. Likewise, there was no sound of anyone moving around in there.

'Can we have some lights down here, Simon?' he shouted.

There was no response. No lights came on.

He called out again. 'Simon! You in there, mate?'

'Maybe there's been a power cut?' Lottie suggested.

'That wouldn't stop him replying to us,' Roy said.

'Health and safety nightmare, this place.' Darius sounded strangely pleased by that. 'Accessible only by God knows how many miles of cart track. The Fire Brigade will love that bit on its own. Enough flames in the hearth, meanwhile, to burn down London Bridge. Only one member of staff here to deal with any emergencies. And now we're expected to travel around in the pitch-dark.'

Nick ignored him. 'Simon! Everything okay?'

The silence from the darkened projection room was total.

'We'd better go and look, eh?' Roy said.

'Yeah.' Nick sidled out from his and Liz's row on to the shallow stairway. 'Sure he'll be all right. Probably fallen asleep.'

While the others remained in their chairs, Nick and Roy headed up the steps. It was so dark, they had to fumble their way to the swing-door. Beyond that, the lights in the passage had also been extinguished, though a faint illumination shone along it from the main body of the house. Nick kicked the wedge into place to keep the swing-door open, so the others could find their way out, and then went through the side door into the projection room, slapping the wall as he did, and activating the light switch.

Simon Matlock wasn't in there.

The heavy, old-fashioned projector was in place against the aperture, a sizeable reel of film still on the spindle, but the machine had been switched off, while the stool behind it had been shoved to one side. The rest of the room, which comprised almost nothing – a few shelves, a couple of empty cardboard boxes – stood deserted.

'Like there was no one even in here,' Nick said.

'Except for that,' Roy said, coming in behind him.

Nick glanced round to see him pointing at the section of bare plaster wall just under the projection port. The plasterwork was white, which made it much easier to see the trail of tiny red droplets. Nick was inexperienced in these things, but even he recognised blood spatter when he saw it.

◆ ◆ ◆

'I'm sure it's nothing,' Nick told them all. 'He'll have cut himself on something. Minor thing. Accident.'

The guests faced him sceptically across the central block of furniture in the main hall, where they'd all gathered.

'Operating an old projector?' Martha said.

Nick shrugged. 'Anyone can trap a finger.'

They didn't need to answer that. The response was written in their fire-lit faces.

'He's not in his room,' Liz said, coming down the stairs. 'It's locked and there's no light on.'

'Seriously, guys?' Roy said. 'What's going on?'

'I'm sure it's nothing,' Nick said again.

'That's not what we're reading from your body language,' Freya said.

'Maybe they're just good actors,' Martha suggested.

It took a moment for that penny to drop.

'Is that what this is?' Lottie said. 'Some kind of set-up?'

'Christ help us!' Darius blurted. 'Please spare us that. We've had to sit through that appalling film and now we're capping the whole thing off with a game of whodunnit?'

'If that's it, I'd rather we'd done it *before* dinner,' Lottie said. 'It's quarter to eleven, and all I want now is to sit down with a coffee.'

Liz approached Nick, speaking quietly. 'You don't think Matlock misunderstood what we wanted, do you?'

He frowned. 'You mean set up a murder mystery game without telling us?'

It didn't seem likely, but the truth was that Nick didn't know. From the moment they'd met him, Matlock had struck them both as affable but awkward, stolid but unimaginative. For the most part, he'd done a good job here at the Lodge, but how much of that was down to him and how much to the interior designers and other artistic types he'd hired? It didn't seem possible that he'd even have thought to add an extra something to the itinerary without discussing it with the tour organisers first, let alone had the wherewithal to set one up.

'Don't you think we're owed an answer?' Freya said loudly.

'Look.' Nick waved a placating hand. 'I'm sure everything's all right.'

'You keep saying that as if there's a reason to think it isn't,' Roy replied.

'What's going on here, Nick?' Martha asked, for the first time using his first name. 'Where's Matlock?'

'I'm sorry . . .' Nick shrugged. 'We don't know. So . . .' He set off walking, veering across the huge room to the array of bottles and glasses on the sideboard. 'Why don't we have a drink, eh? Simon'll show up. I mean, he's got to . . . it's *his* house. Honestly guys, there's absolutely nothing to be worried about.'

'Except that our host is missing and there's blood on the wall,' Martha said.

'The blood's easily explained . . .'

'Yes, it's a trapped finger.' She chuckled without humour. 'You ever tried pulling the other one?'

'Well, he's not bailed on us, if that's what you're worried about,' came Jordan's voice, accompanied by a sharp blast of cold air. 'His car's still outside.'

They turned to see that he'd opened the front door, which now stood ajar.

'No, no!' Liz jolted into action. 'Close that door!' Though she didn't actually give him a chance, dashing over there herself, shoving the massive slab of timber back into its frame, the *boom* thundering through the building as she rammed its bolts home.

Only on looking back at the others did she realise she'd made a minor spectacle of herself. Even Nick seemed startled.

'It's just that . . . it's dark,' she said awkwardly. 'And cold.'

She glanced at Nick again, who struggled to say anything.

With increasing speed, it was dawning on him how shaken up she'd been by her experience out on the jetty. He'd hoped she'd have dismissed it by now as an optical illusion brought on by the darkness and mist, but apparently not.

'Okay, guys,' Roy said slowly. 'Okay . . . either this *is* a put-on, and if it is, it's very well done, I'll grant you that – you're a decent pair of actors. Or it's actually real.'

'Surely nothing could have happened to Mr Matlock here?' Lottie said. 'Not in his own home?'

'Perhaps we'd better look around, eh?' Martha said, watching Nick and Liz with keen interest. 'Just to make sure.'

'Can't hurt,' Freya agreed.

As the others fanned out to search, Nick led Liz to one side. 'Whatever's happening here,' he said, 'and I'm sure it's nothing . . . you've got to keep it together. These people are our responsibility, remember.'

'Yes!' she hissed. 'So don't you think we should warn them that we may not be alone?'

'Liz, come on . . .'

'I know you think I was hallucinating out there . . .'

'I just don't see who it could be. For God's sake, hon, let's not raise a panic when we don't necessarily need to. How stupid will we look?'

'Better looking stupid than being found liable for taking risks with people's lives.'

Nick shook his head. 'There's one other thing you've probably not considered.' He hadn't really wanted to mention this, though it was bugging him. 'If everyone decides this place is too dangerous, where else do they go?'

'Well . . . I mean . . .' Liz frowned as she struggled to find an adequate answer.

'Exactly,' he said. 'Clara's not coming back with the bus until tomorrow afternoon.'

'Matlock's car.'

'You're suggesting we steal it? That's assuming we can find his keys.'

'Okay, we call for help.'

'Matlock took our phones.'

'They must be lying round here somewhere.'

'Yeah? I don't see them.'

She pivoted, scanning the hall. 'Nick, this is ridiculous.'

'He said he'd put them in a safe place. An actual safe perhaps? And before you ask, there's no sign of one of those either.'

She glanced at him, increasingly shocked. 'Are you saying we're stuck here?'

'Finishing the tour in the middle of nowhere seemed like a great idea when we planned it, didn't it?' he replied. 'It doesn't now.'

Twelve

No one was actually saying they thought something bad had happened to Simon Matlock, but from Jordan Pugmire's perspective, the atmosphere in this place was suddenly tense, and his smug confidence that he'd got something good out of this weekend as well as having enjoyed himself had taken a knock.

Surely, there wasn't any *danger*? They weren't under actual threat, were they?

It had to be some kind of complex ploy on the tour organisers' part. Nick and Liz had already pulled two amazing rabbits out of their hats in bringing everyone up here in the first place and then in the screening of *Malifique*. But if there was something happening here that shouldn't be, Jordan's next instinct was to look to his own. He wasn't frightened for himself, he thought, as he scampered up the staircase, but if nothing else, he was going to check that his room was locked, and his new acquisition, the Travis Monkton painting, was exactly where he'd left it.

As he hurried along the minstrels' gallery, the activity below, while not panic-stricken, was animated, people moving from room to room calling out Matlock's name.

He turned left from the gallery into the second of the bedroom corridors. His own room was the third one along. When he reached the door, he found that it was still locked, and relaxed a little.

At which point, a flutter of motion caught his attention.

He glanced down to the left end of the corridor, which was a T-junction, certain that a figure had just walked past it.

'Mr Matlock?' he said. 'That you?'

No one responded.

'Mr Matlock?' Jordan walked a little way down. 'Mr Matlock!' Louder this time, but still there was no reply. He wasn't really sure who it was that he'd seen. He'd barely glimpsed them, but he had an idea that they'd been tall. And Simon Matlock was tall.

He walked the rest of the way to the end, turned right and found himself facing another long corridor. There were more rooms off this one, though he doubted any of these were being used. Not that this mattered, because the person he'd seen was visible again, albeit about forty yards off. As before, Jordan only glimpsed him: a tall figure in dark clothing, who promptly turned right and vanished.

'Hey . . . yo!' Jordan hurried forward. The guy was either deaf or a bit ignorant; more likely the latter. Now that he thought about it, Jordan couldn't help resenting the disrespect he'd recently been shown. Others in the tour party clearly hadn't appreciated his various recitations, though he suspected that owed more to the youthfulness and energy he'd brought to them. Just because all the others were fucking has-beens. But Darius Brant for one had shown his true ugly self in that row over the painting. Young people having money didn't compute in the minds of some tetchy old wankers.

And now *this* weird bugger was being cocky with him.

'Matlock!' He raised his voice. 'People want to get on with the evening. They're wondering where you are!'

He reached the point where the figure had disappeared. The corridor ended at a bare wall, though a black curtain hung on his right. When he drew it aside, another staircase ascended.

'Matlock!' he shouted up. No one answered, but light shimmered down.

Jordan went up. The corridor one floor above was more or less a carbon copy of the one below, though the doors to the rooms here had no numbers on them, and were for the most part shabby, badly in need of a lick of varnish. The lightbulbs overhead were unshaded and there was a smell of dust. Clearly, this was one of those parts of the house that wasn't yet fully renovated. As before, Jordan saw someone turn a corner about forty yards ahead.

Christ's sake! 'Hey, Matlock!'

Jordan broke into a run. When he reached the corner, he found another side entrance, though this one had neither a door nor a curtain covering it. The staircase that led up from here was basic and utilitarian: hard wooden treads, the plaster on the walls yellowed and scabby. Again, there was light from above, but this time it was weak, flickery.

He ascended anyway, stamping loudly.

'Mr Matlock, you're neglecting your guests . . .'

The place this staircase brought him up into had the atmosphere of a tower room. It was smaller than any room here that he'd seen previously, and circular in shape, its floor composed of bare boards. Cobwebs fluttered from the ceiling, and there were items of discarded furniture, along with boxes spilling dust-coated bric-a-brac. There was no window, but the light, which came from a single candle on a shelf, was just strong enough to show the ladder in the corner slanting up to an open hatch in the ceiling.

'Mr Matlock?' Jordan weaved his way amid the junk. He stared up through the square hole into darkness. 'You up there?'

Still, no one replied, which was odd. And also a bit spooky.

It was the only place the guy could be.

Jordan decided that he was too peeved to investigate any further, but then it occurred to him that all this would make a great post for his social media. Talk about a neat way to personalise the experience of having visited the scariest house in northern England. Though not if he'd come all this way on his own and then chickened out when it suddenly got dicey. Not that he was scared, as he'd now prove.

'Yo, Matlock!' he called, ascending the ladder. When he poked his head through the hatch, he was in an even smaller room than below. Nothing more than a narrow loft space. It surprised him a little; he'd assumed it would be cavernous under the Lodge's steeply pitched roof, which, from what he'd seen, was quite extensive, running from one end of the main building to the next. But then he remembered the small room below, the tower room maybe. So, perhaps this was the interior to a turret or something similar. Either way, there was no sign of his quarry.

'Mr Matlock?' he said, puzzled.

He clambered up properly, squatting on a slimy joist.

The place was dingy as hell. It was also musty, like a cage or hutch. He pivoted around. Even with the light filtering up from below, it was too dark to see anything.

'Mr Matlock?'

Movement rustled overhead. Jordan glanced up. Again, nothing was visible, but fragments of grot spiralled down. One landed in his open mouth. He gagged and spat it out, wiping frantically at his lips. And then sensed heavier movement just to his left.

'Matlock?'

Was that a figure . . . very close by? Crouching like some animal.

'Mr Matlock?'

Jordan squinted, now able to see better because additional light was suddenly seeping in. A cloud must have cleared outside, slices of moonlight penetrating a rotted timber grille.

'Mat . . .'

The crouched shape came at him.

Jordan barely had time to scream.

The last thing he knew was an explosion of violent feathery movement all around.

The last thing he saw was the face of a thousand horror films.

Thirteen

They'd all heard the noise outside, so even though Liz was still hesitant about opening the front door, there was no question that someone needed to, and it was Nick who did the honours, hurriedly withdrawing the bolts.

'Sounded like a scream,' Freya said, as the rest of them stood waiting.

The door swung open. Outside, the mist rolled and wreathed, but thanks to the exterior lights, the body lying face down on the drive, just left of the front steps, was clearly visible. Fleetingly, Nick was too stunned to speak.

In the first instance, he wondered if they'd finally found Simon Matlock, but then it struck him that, whoever this was, he was wearing a T-shirt.

'Is . . . is that Jordan?' Roy said, appearing at his shoulder.

No one responded, though all of them had now crowded into the doorway.

'Hey, Jordan!' Roy said, shoving through and descending the steps. 'Lying down on the job for any particular reason?'

Jordan remained unresponsive.

'Is . . . he all right?' Lottie asked querulously.

Roy approached the stationary form before slowly sinking to one knee. Liz also pushed past and went down to join him

– at which point, she froze, hands wrapped together in front of her mouth.

Nick now went down as well. 'Shit,' he breathed, firstly when he saw the bug-eyed expression on Jordan's twisted, rigid face, then much louder, 'SHIT!' when he spied the angle at which the young man's head was lying. 'He's . . . he's . . .'

'He's dead,' Roy replied, grimly calm. 'Dead as the proverbial.' He rose back to his feet. 'Broken neck, I'd say.'

The rest of them had also now part-descended the steps, but none came any closer.

'He . . . he can't be dead,' Lottie stuttered. 'He's probably just stunned.'

'I'm afraid it's a bit more than that,' Roy replied.

'Roy, you must be mistaken!' Her voice had turned shrill, frantic.

'I assure you I'm not.'

'How . . . ?' came a wavering voice. It was Freya. Previously she had stayed at the top of the steps, but now she tottered all the way down. She'd visibly turned pale, and her large brown eyes were bright with tears. 'He's . . . I mean . . . seriously, he's *dead*?'

Roy stood awkwardly, remembering that they were siblings. 'I'm very sorry.' When she lurched forward, he made a move to stop her. 'It's best if you don't touch him.'

She complied with that, holding herself back, but gazed down at the body with lingering shock. 'How is this poss . . . what happened?'

'I can't pronounce on that, but there's no question he's passed on.'

She glanced at him. 'You're sure?'

Roy nodded. 'I am. I'm sorry.'

'We have to get everyone away from here,' Liz muttered into Nick's ear. 'Something's very wrong.'

He glanced at her, distracted. 'Obviously something's wrong. We've got a dead guy at our feet . . .'

'But how can . . . who could have attacked him out here?' Freya asked.

'I doubt it was that.' Roy indicated several fragments of slate and broken guttering lying scattered across the driveway. Then he glanced upward. 'I think he fell.'

Freya gazed upward too. They all did.

'From the roof?' she asked incredulously.

'How the hell could he have got on the roof?' Martha said.

Roy shrugged.

'Wait, look . . .' Nick pointed up. 'There's a kind of boarded-over window, or air vent or something. In that turret, just to the right. It's broken open.'

They strained to see through the eddying mist, but just above the level of the outdoor lights, some ninety feet up, they were able to distinguish the shapes of two twin turrets. In the middle of each one there was a squarish vent. On the left, what looked like a wooden grille was fixed there, but on the right, it was a square black hole.

'What in God's name was he doing up there?' Darius wondered.

Nick was as shaken as the rest of them, but was already feeling a twinge of responsibility. 'I suppose I should go up and check. See what's what.'

'I'll come with you,' Roy replied.

'I should come too,' Freya said. Her tears had dried, but she suddenly seemed urgent and animated, all her normal cool reserve deserting her. 'It's the least I can . . .'

'Oh no, my dear.' Lottie put an arm around her. 'You should come and sit down.'

'I . . .' Freya glanced from one to the other.

'I think you should,' Liz said. 'Seriously. You've just had a terrible shock.'

'I'm not . . . I . . .' Freya struggled to explain. 'He wasn't my real brother, remember. I . . .'

'Real brother or not,' Martha said. 'You need to come inside and sit down.' For once, her tone wasn't scathing, though neither was it overly sympathetic.

Freya glanced at Nick, who nodded encouragingly. Finally, she nodded too, and with Lottie and Martha's assistance, ascended the steps.

'In the meantime, we need to find something to cover the body,' Liz said.

'No,' Roy replied. The man who had a quip for every occasion now spoke with grave authority. 'No one touch him.'

Freya glanced sharply down from the top of the steps. 'I thought you said this was an accident?'

'I'm sorry, Freya, but even if it is, that doesn't mean one of us won't have a case to answer.'

As gently as they could, the two older women steered her inside.

'So what do we do?' Darius said. 'Surely, we're not just leaving him lying here.'

'Someone can stay with him, if they want to,' Roy replied. 'So long as they don't touch him.'

'I don't think any of us should stay out here,' Liz said, glancing around. 'I think we should all go indoors.'

Darius looked even more shocked. 'Leave him out here alone?'

'Whether we leave him alone or not, we'll have to call the police,' Nick said. 'And they won't want anyone touching anything.'

'So definitely no blanket to cover him with,' Roy added. 'That's TV stuff.'

'Good God in the highest,' Darius said slowly. 'And we thought all these murderers we've been talking about were inhuman.'

'It's purely a practical measure,' Roy said.

'Call it what you want, Southerby. It's still inhuman.'

When the art dealer had also gone indoors, Nick turned to Roy. 'It doesn't feel great, I'll admit.'

'How about we save the value judgements till we find out what's going on here?'

Liz approached him. 'You think there's a problem?'

Roy shrugged. 'Guys, we've got one man missing and one man dead. What do you think?'

◆ ◆ ◆

It wasn't easy for Nick and Roy to find their way up to the turret in question. There was still no sign of Simon Matlock, and neither of them had a clear mental picture of the mansion's upper floor layout. All they could initially do was be guided by instinct.

The turret containing the shattered air vent had looked to be located almost directly above the front door, but that didn't make it easy to find. As well as the first floor, which was on a level with the minstrels' gallery, where all their rooms were located, the house had a second floor above that. This was higher up than the great hall's ceiling, and comprised a maze of corridors and rooms still awaiting refurbishment. Eventually though, just after eleven-thirty, they found a side staircase which took them up from the second floor to a candle-lit attic crammed with abandoned, dust-shrouded furniture. At one side of its ceiling there was an open hatchway.

'Think that could be it?' Nick said.

'Well, it's open,' Roy replied. 'Which suggests someone's been up there recently.'

They accessed the hatch by use of a ladder which they found lying on its side amid the junk, finally entering a narrow, circular loft-space.

'Feels like the inside of the turret to me,' Roy muttered.

As their eyes adjusted, they saw pigeons roosting in the conical space overhead, all of them astir, fluttering from nest to nest, dust and feathers drifting downward. The joists on which the men found themselves perched were thick and slippery with bird filth, much of which had been smeared, as though some previous investigator had been moving about forcefully. Meanwhile, the square air vent just to the right of them, which had shattered outward and was clearly the one they'd seen from below, was easily large enough for a man to fall through.

'Wouldn't even have needed to lean on it hard,' Nick said, gingerly probing the fragments around its rim, all of them wet with rot. Roy hung back, again reluctant to touch anything. 'Penny for your thoughts?' Nick asked.

Roy considered. 'It's not impossible he slid on this shite, lost his balance, fell against the vent. But more likely, if he'd done that, he'd just have put his foot through the plaster ceiling underneath us. Don't you think?'

Nick glanced cautiously out through the ragged aperture. 'Do you reckon that's enough of a drop to guarantee death?'

'You can fall six feet and die, if you land awkwardly enough. But the chances of surviving that out there? Nine times out of ten, death'd be certain. Why, you wondering if he did it deliberately?'

Nick withdrew inside again. 'If I was looking to kill myself, nine times out of ten wouldn't be good enough. I'd need a cast-iron one hundred per cent guarantee.'

'Plus, wasn't he chuffed because he'd just bought that painting? One minute he's acting like the cat who's got the cream, the next he goes and tops himself? Doesn't ring true to me.'

They glanced at each other uneasily.

'So, what are we saying exactly?' Nick asked.

'This guy, Simon Matlock . . . is he on the level?'

'What do you mean?'

'What I mean is . . . could he have a screw loose?'

'Well, I don't really know him. Tonight's the first time I've properly met him.'

'Okay.' Roy looked increasingly troubled.

'But, I mean . . . his efforts to restore his grandfather's estate are well documented,' Nick said. 'He's super-rich, of course.'

'Yeah, well . . . you'd better trust me, that's no guarantee of sanity.'

Fourteen

'You really are talking out of your backside, Mr Brant, if you don't mind me saying,' Liz said heatedly.

Darius, standing by the fire, responded with a self-satisfied smile. 'I've already mentioned it once. This place is a health and safety disaster. It looked that way the moment we arrived, and now we've had proof of it.'

'So, you're planning to sue us? Is that right?'

'I don't think he'll need to,' Martha replied from a nearby armchair. 'It's more than likely the authorities will prosecute.'

'And if they don't,' Darius added, 'I'm sure Mr Pugmire's family will have something to say.'

'Oh yeah?' Nick chipped in, he and Roy coming down the staircase. 'The same Mr Pugmire you got on so well with, Darius?'

The art dealer affected an unapologetic air. 'Young Jordan and I were quite friendly. We only fell out over his foolish approach to that ridiculous impromptu art auction. Hardly means I'd wish death on him.'

Lottie hurried over to the staircase. 'What did you find up there?'

'That turret was deffo the place the lad fell from,' Nick said.

He looked to Roy for confirmation, but the bearded big guy went straight to the sideboard and poured himself a large, neat Scotch.

'This a good time to get soused?' Freya wondered. Her tears had dried properly since earlier, but her tone was sharp and irascible.

'When isn't it?' Roy said over his shoulder.

'The ventilation grille was broken outward,' Nick explained. 'Rotten all the way through. Might as well have been made from balsa wood.'

'There you have it,' Darius said, triumphant. He glanced at Liz. 'You two are in trouble, I'm afraid to say.'

Roy swung round to face them. 'They might not be the only ones.'

Darius mused on this. 'The ultimate responsibility will obviously lie with Simon Matlock.'

'And maybe the person who *pushed* young Jordan,' Roy shot back.

Lottie looked stunned. 'You said it was an accident.'

He sipped his malt. 'I said no such thing.'

'You're saying it was murder?' Freya whispered.

'I'm saying we shouldn't make any assumptions. And that includes assuming it was an accident.'

'But someone *could* have pushed him?' Freya sought to confirm.

Roy sipped again. 'It's not impossible.'

Nick glanced at Liz. She seemed paler than he'd ever seen her before.

'None of *us*, surely?' Lottie said. 'We were all down here.'

'Maybe, but we were all spread out,' Martha countered, getting to her feet. 'I mean, we were all in different rooms . . .'

'Martha, don't be ridiculous,' Lottie said.

'I'm not. *I* didn't notice that Jordan had gone upstairs. Did any of the rest of you?' She glanced at them one by one, receiving no reply. 'There you go. That shows how much attention we were paying to each other.'

'So . . .' Lottie stuttered, 'we're saying one of *us* is a murderer?'

'No,' Roy replied. 'But we can't discount it.'

'But none of us even knew him,' she protested. 'Let alone had reason to kill him.'

Martha half-smiled. 'I'd hardly say he was well-loved in this little group. Would you?'

Inevitably, unavoidably, they all turned and looked at Darius, whose shoulders stiffened and eyes immediately narrowed.

'I've already told you,' he said. 'Jordan and I—'

'Jordan the "little toad"?' Freya cut in. 'The "little weirdo".'

'I've already made clear—'

'All you've made clear is that you really wanted that painting.'

'Look, I was down here with the rest of you!' Darius's cheeks were tinging pink.

'We've covered that too. We don't know who was down here and who wasn't.'

'All right, everyone, come on . . .' Nick glanced from face to face, each one of them tense and fearful. 'Let's be sensible. Especially you, Freya. I know you've suffered a loss, but we shouldn't get carried away. How could shoving the kid through that vent have secured Darius the painting? Besides, what was it worth . . . a few thou? Who's going to kill over that?'

'Nick's right.' Roy threw his whisky down. 'It's not our place to be spreading suspicion. We'll all have to account for our movements when the cops get here.' He glanced round. 'I presume someone's called them?'

Only blank expressions greeted this.

'With what?' Freya asked.

'Shit,' the big guy replied, only now remembering that Matlock had taken their phones.

'What about *this*?' He crossed the hall to an antique desk and grabbed up an ornate Edwardian-looking telephone receiver. However, there was no sound from it. When he lifted the rest of the device, it wasn't even connected.

'Ornamentation, I'm afraid,' Liz said. 'Part of the decor.'

'There's no landline at all?' Nick asked.

'Doesn't seem to be,' Freya replied.

He shrugged. 'In that case we're just going to have to search hard for our own phones. They can't have vanished into thin air. If we all of us make a kind of pattern search . . . you know, cover the whole premises section by section, and at the same time look for Matlock too . . .'

'All of us, Thornwood?' a caustic voice wondered. '*All* of us. Are you quite serious, you insufferable little prat!'

Nick glanced round, startled. Darius stood frowning at them, his lips tight and quivering, the teeth bared amid his white whiskers. 'How dare you! I mean, how bloody dare you! Seriously . . . the sheer gall of it. How dare a bunch of weirdoes like *you* accuse someone like *me* of a crime like this. And then calmly tell me that you now need *my* assistance? The absolute affrontery . . .'

'Why?' Freya asked. 'Are you some paragon of virtue?'

'I was lured here against my will!' he snapped.

'What are you talking about?' Liz retorted. 'You came on this tour for your own reasons. To buy a painting. You failed, and that's the long and short of it.'

'No one mentioned anything to me about staying overnight in a crumbling old mausoleum which clearly isn't safe for rats to live in.'

'Don't be ridiculous. This place is top-notch. The only parts that are unsafe are out of bounds.'

'No one told me I'd be expected to participate in some juvenile game of whodunnit. And then, when we have the inevitable fatal accident, which I could have warned you about in advance, a bunch of people like *you*' – his gaze roved the entire group – 'a gaggle of bottom-feeding, mouth-breathing ghouls, have the absolute cheek to point the finger at me—'

'Hey, pal,' Roy cut in. 'I've just explained that no one's getting blamed for anything at the moment.'

'Even if you had,' Darius retorted, 'why would I listen to *you*? Who made *you* an expert? On anything?'

Roy looked as if he wanted to reply harshly but checked himself.

'If you're insisting on getting to the crux of it,' Nick countered, 'what do you think the cops are going to say? You think they won't at least be a little bit interested in that argument you and Jordan had?'

Darius grinned as if it were all too ridiculous. 'Nice try, Thornwood. But you're still going to be sued.' He grabbed his hat and headed for the staircase, turning once again at the foot of it. 'I'm going up to my room now. I'm locking myself in and I don't expect to be disturbed for the rest of the night. By all means, play your silly little game . . .'

'Are you mad!' Lottie half-shrieked. 'Someone's just died!'

'In which case cobble your excuses together.' Darius spoke airily, as if it were no longer any concern of his. 'Get your stories straight, whatever's required . . . but don't bother me until morning.' He glanced at Nick again. 'At which point I expect that ridiculous jalopy of a minibus to be waiting at the front door. I have no intention whatever of hanging around here until tomorrow afternoon.'

They watched gloomily as he turned and headed upstairs. Liz seemed about to say something else, but Nick motioned at her to keep it in check.

A long, tense silence followed, which Lottie finally broke.

'So, we're searching this place top to bottom.' She sounded distinctly unexcited by the prospect.

Nick understood why. It wasn't far off midnight now, and while no one was exactly sleepy – they were too wired – the prospect of going shelf by shelf, drawer by drawer through this immense country seat was truly daunting.

'How about we start in Matlock's private office?' Liz suggested. 'Even if our phones aren't there, or even if they're locked in a safe, that could be where he keeps his landline.'

'Good idea,' Roy said.

'Except the office is locked,' Nick reminded them.

'So?' Roy replied. 'We force the door. I think we've got cause enough for that?'

Again, Nick was reminded that he and Liz only had token command here. It hardly extended to their authorising what would amount to criminal damage. The situation was fast becoming desperate, but seriously? To start smashing things up?

'Why don't we just look round the house again first?' Lottie said, seemingly as discomforted by the idea as Nick. 'Matlock might just have collapsed somewhere. You know, had a funny turn or something.'

'Have we forgotten that we saw blood in the projection room?' Freya said.

'You never know, the two might be connected,' Martha replied. 'Matlock traps his finger and it's so painful that he has a . . . what did you call it, Lottie? Oh yeah, "a funny turn" in some distant part of the house.'

Lottie gave her a reproachful stare. 'You seriously think this is amusing?'

'What's amusing,' Martha replied, 'is how you're now hoping against hope that nothing nefarious is going on here. And this after spending an entire weekend lapping up the murder and mutilation of others.'

'In my case, it's not that at all . . .'

'No time for excuses, Lottie.' Martha became energised. 'Let's hope you're right and all we're dealing with here are unfortunate accidents. And who knows, maybe we are. But just in case, when we split up and go searching, let's make sure we do it in pairs, eh? Not singles.'

Fifteen

Darius might have put a calm face on it as he ascended the staircase, blithely dismissing the rabble below, but in truth he was seething.

The brazenness of their accusing him of murdering that puerile maggot, Jordan, had raised things to a whole different level. Wasn't it enough that, having spent all weekend being dragged across the depressing north-west of England, with its grimy towns and derelict factories, putting up with those awful real-life murder scenes, watching the rest of these drooling idiots get excited about the cruelties of killers and sadists from history, he'd then seen the sole object of his interest – the Travis Monkton painting – pass, through the most ridiculous turn of fate, into the hands of a pimply-faced child? And yet now, after this whole abysmally planned adventure had gone completely haywire, they had the unmitigated temerity to eye *him* with suspicion.

To seek to lay the blame for it entirely at *his* door.

In reality, it wasn't enough to simply storm off. Not even as grandly as he'd done it.

They wouldn't be impressed by that. They might briefly be miffed that someone had finally told them to their faces exactly what they were, but there were enough narcissists among them who genuinely believed they were in the right. On top of that, despite his ordering them to leave him be from this moment on, there was little real chance of his evading any further repercussions that might occur this night.

For one thing, there *had* been a suspicious death, so the police would be summoned. Whether they actually got here before dawn was another matter. This was the British police of the twenty-first century, after all. Three times now Darius had been a victim of crime in London, and the cases hadn't even been investigated, never mind solved. The Keystone Cops had nothing on this shower. But they *might* get here, and then he'd be roused from his sleep and required to answer questions. Even if the law was not successfully summoned, the hullaballoo the rest of the tour party were now creating would keep sleep at bay. Already he could hear them shouting for Simon Matlock again as they wandered this ridiculous, rambling house. On which matter, he doubted he'd be able to sleep in this bedroom anyway.

He glanced around him as he sat at the end of his four-poster bed.

It was superficially luxurious: crushed-velvet drapes, tapestries, period furniture. But doubtless it was supposed to evoke memories of some long and rightly forgotten Gothic romp featuring that overpaid, overhyped ham, Edgar Karnwood.

Darius had seen only a few of his movies in truth. Many years ago, when he was young. He'd paid them no mind then, and he paid them no mind now, though he had to admit that the one he'd seen tonight had had a different effect on him. Darius disliked hospitals. In fact, he had a phobia-like terror of them: needles, surgical gowns, unblinking surgeons' eyes staring over the tops of their masks. This was probably down to his less than healthy childhood, but it had been bad enough with those hospitals modern and fully functioning, whereas in the movie they'd seen tonight, the horrendous place had been abandoned: filthy, rat-infested, dank corridors, rusted wheelchairs, blood smeared on the walls.

And there'd been blood on the walls here too.

Yet more reason not to stay, he told himself as he packed his few belongings into his holdall, pulled on his fur-collared coat, and opened his bedroom door a couple of inches.

The real reason of course was the business around the Travis Monkton painting. It wasn't as if he'd done anything to hurt that stupid young Pugmire, and as Thornwood had said in a rare moment of insight, what would he have gained from that if he had? The painting wouldn't have automatically transferred into his ownership. No, the police would definitely clear him. Darius was certain of it. But he was equally certain that they'd ask some searching questions. He might even be taken into custody. Word would get out and this whole unsavoury business would be exposed – the Ludgate Gallery, and Darius Brant in particular, irrevocably connected to the acquisition of artworks by murderers, a scandal that would be gossiped about across all the dinner parties of north London.

And if that wasn't bad enough, of course, his special client would be displeased.

As he stood by his narrowly open door, listening to the shouts of the other guests, that latter possibility chilled him more than anything else. Because certain people, when they were upset, were capable of anything.

Literally *anything*.

Being honest with himself, Darius wasn't sure that, even if he left the premises now and succeeded in getting back to civilisation by morning, it would make a whole lot of difference. The truth would still come out about what he'd been doing here, and there might even be a price to pay for his leaving the scene so abruptly; in some quarters it could be deemed an admission of guilt. But remaining here was not an option.

If there was absolutely nothing else for it, at least if he could return to the real world, he could make a phone call and prepare his client in advance for the bad news. Perhaps his client might be able to advise him or even offer some form of protection.

Who knew?

He closed the door to a crack as Lottie and Freya trudged past, tiredly calling out Simon Matlock's name. Brain-dead hooligans, all of them. Did they seriously think that, wherever Matlock was, he wouldn't have heard them by now? Did they genuinely not consider it possible that he was concealing himself from them because he wanted to? It was all part of this ridiculous game, and he probably hadn't yet learned that someone had died for real. How stupid were they?

Though in actual fact, the stupider the better.

Because in the next few minutes, Darius would be out of here.

He waited until Lottie and Freya's voices had diminished, and then let himself out from his room, locked the door behind him, and with bag in hand, and coat fastened up to the throat, went quickly along the passage and on to the minstrels' gallery, peering down into the hall. As he did, Nick sloped out into the middle of it, where he stood disconsolately, hands on hips. He looked worried.

You've got good reason to be, Darius thought smugly.

Slowly, wearily, Nick wandered off, and Darius took his chance, scampering down the staircase. The fact that he had white hair and a white beard often deceived people into thinking that he'd likely be encumbered in some way, perhaps by age or arthritis. But in fact, Darius was sprightly for a septuagenarian. For one thing, he had no doubt whatsoever that he'd be able to walk the full distance down to the bus stop he'd seen en route here. By his estimation, it was about a mile and a half, but it was mostly downhill. He waited at the bottom of the stairs, glancing across the hall again. The fire in the massive hearth was finally burning low, the room's low-key sidelights providing somewhat dimmer illumination.

All the better.

He set off towards the front door. As he did, he passed the towering facsimile of Edgar Karnwood, its glassy eyes seeming to follow him.

Good God. This place.

Just before the door, he spotted something else of interest. On the right-hand side of it stood a wickerwork umbrella stand containing a couple of old and rather ragged-looking brollies, but also a hefty walking stick with a curved handle. Darius didn't need a stick, but on a night like this, it might be useful to have one. He glanced around again, and then took charge of it.

Doing his best to be quiet, he drew the bolts back on the front door. None of them was stiff thankfully, while the heavy key, which still sat in the lock, also turned easily. He eased the door open, stepped outside and closed it behind him with a *click*. Ignoring the outline of Jordan's broken form, he glanced out over the reservoir, though it still lay hidden under a foggy pall so thick now that even the mansion's exterior lights couldn't pierce it deeply.

It didn't matter. He knew where he was going. There was only one road away from here. Its surface was rugged, and he didn't have a torch, but he could manage it if he was careful.

But as he headed north, the Lodge falling behind, soon lost in gloom, he began to wonder just how wise a move this had actually been. Even though he was gloved and coated and of course had now jammed his hat tightly on top of his straggling white locks, it was suddenly very cold. It was also quiet, the only sound the clumping of his feet. There was scarcely a ripple from the reservoir.

He passed something on his left that was faintly visible. It looked like a set of steps leading up on to a wooden causeway. Alongside that was the vague, boxy outline of a small structure.

At first, he was bemused, but then recalled glimpsing a jetty, or something similar, when they'd first arrived here.

He strode on determinedly, but twice half-stumbled on the increasingly rutted footing. For the first time, perhaps belatedly, it occurred to him that maybe his expensive, lace-up leather brogues had been an unwise choice for a long-distance hike.

'Long distance?' he muttered contemptuously. 'A mile and a half?'

He could do that in his sleep. Although, an inner voice responded that he'd only guesstimated a mile and a half, and it might be significantly further than that.

Well . . . it still didn't matter. He was in good shape. He'd have no problem getting as far as the bus stop, and after that it would all be easy. At which point, he again stumbled. He cursed loudly as he slumped down on to one knee, only the stick preventing him going full length.

Grunting, he heaved himself upright.

And thought he heard a faint snicker somewhere in the shifting gloom.

He stared around, unable to distinguish anything.

Of course, it was nonsense to think he wouldn't hear odd things out here. He walked on, his holdall weighing heavily in his right hand, his right shoulder already aching. He had the stick in any case, so he didn't need to worry about someone trying to sneak up on him. He'd give them a damn good clobbering.

Even so, he tried to walk faster. And again, half-tripped. He had some idea that the roadway had now taken him away from the reservoir. In which case he was making progress. Right on cue, the road tilted downward.

'Thank God,' he breathed. It wouldn't exactly be easy from here – he'd be walking harder and faster than he'd been used to – but it would be easier.

And indeed, though the road descended at a shallow gradient, gravity assisted him, his breathing softening, though it didn't help his nerves that even in the thickness of this vapour, he didn't just sense but now saw the phantom shapes of semi-skeletal trees and bushes along the verges. Obviously, they were scary to look at. What else would they be? When November came to the English woodlands, death came too, and quickly. There was a dampness, a smell of fungus. Everything was drab, wet and decayed. But it was perfectly normal. A part of the natural cycle. Close by him, something rustled.

Darius glanced left. Then right. Then behind.

He saw nothing untoward. There was no further sound either, though he had an impression that someone had come slinking out of the bushes on to the road at his rear.

It could have been an animal, he supposed.

An animal? Seriously?

The thundering silence persisted as he strode on. How far was it to the bus stop now? Probably no more than half a mile. Ten minutes' walk.

Half a mile? Are you kidding?

He glanced over his shoulder, seeing thick, curling mist shot through with glimmers of moonlight. He increased his pace, and yet at the same time did his level best to walk quietly. Absurdly, he realised, this was an effort to prevent whoever was on the road behind him knowing that he was here.

For God's sake, there's no one on the road behind you!

And yet, he'd heard them.

There was a chance they hadn't seen him, whoever they were. In conditions like these, everyone was blinded.

He glanced over his shoulder again, and because he was descending away from that dark, cold water, which doubtless was the source of the pea-souper up at the Lodge, it appeared to be thinning a little. But the road was still mostly obscured. To right and left, the mist flowed between the black, twisted trees.

'Bloody ridiculous,' he muttered. In a moment of angry defiance, he stopped, pivoted around and shouted at the top of his voice: 'It's bloody ridiculous! Do you hear?'

The only response was a distant echo. And then a faint snicker.

He went on down the road. It steepened again, which must have meant that he was approaching the bus stop. Though probably not, because the stop he'd seen had been on flatter ground, at a crossroads, and there'd been no immediate tree cover around it, only open fields. The tree cover here meanwhile seemed to be closing overhead like a roof, blotting out those few rays of moonlight.

Darius half-stumbled again . . . and heard the sound of other footfalls not far behind him.

He whirled round, still seeing nothing.

Yet he could hear those feet. Or could he? Was it the thudding of his own heart?

That snicker again . . . cruel, guttural.

He lurched off the road and into the undergrowth, chopping with his stick as he fought his way through. It didn't matter that it whipped his face or plucked at his expensive coat.

His only hope now was to hide. Good God, he had to find somewhere to hide!

Sixteen

Immediately beyond the kitchen's outer door – the tradesman's entrance, as it would once have been called – there was a small kitchen yard, most of it paved, with a woodpile in one corner and a small stack of tools in another. Beyond that, accessible by a single, broad opening with a rusted iron trellis arching over the top, lay the infinitely more expansive and yet completely dark and mist-covered terraced gardens. Could Simon Matlock be out there somewhere?

Nick peered through the arch into a wall of blank nothingness. It was bitterly cold, which, on top of any potential hazards owing to the gardens' untended state, was another reason why neither he nor any of the others were willing to go and look. Eventually, he and Roy took a side path which led around the exterior of the house, passing a built-on annex or conservatory, and then along a narrower passage leading between a couple of freestanding outbuildings, and finally through a side gate on to the front drive, where Matlock's gleaming black Jaguar XJ was parked.

'Before you ask, I don't know anything about hot-wiring cars,' Roy said. 'Not that you can hot-wire a motor like this anyway.'

'It would lock itself down, yeah?' Nick said.

'Be totally immobilised.'

Nick pondered. In the absence of Simon Matlock – and it was now twenty past midnight – Liz's solution of earlier had finally presented itself again: if they could somehow get their host's car to start, they could drive to the nearest farmhouse to summon help by telephone. It would be a crime of sorts, but at present who knew where they stood with regard to the law? Up towards the front of the house, the crumpled form of Jordan Pugmire still lay unattended.

'Don't even think about going and interfering with that crime scene,' Roy said, noticing that Nick was staring that way.

'Shouldn't we at least cover him?'

'No. Look . . . I know it's hard to deal with, but under normal circumstances they'd put a cordon around the body, a forensics tent over the top. But we haven't got any of that stuff.'

Nick glanced sidelong at him. 'I normally make checks on everyone who wants to join the Murder Tour. All I gleaned from your socials was that you're a security guard. But actually . . . you're a cop, aren't you?'

Roy looked as if he didn't really want to answer. '*Was*, yeah.'

Nick nodded. On reflection, everything had pointed to it. The irreverent sense of humour; the increasing air of authority as the crisis had evolved.

'Any particular reason why you've kept it quiet?' he asked.

'It's a long story, which I'd rather not go into. In fact, I'd appreciate it if you'd keep it under wraps. At least for the time being.'

'Murder tourism not the kind of hobby ex-officers boast about?'

'It's a bit more complicated than that.'

Nick could sense that the big guy genuinely didn't want to discuss it, which possibly implied that he'd left the police under a cloud. 'Well, seeing as I'm already uncomfortable about having forced entry to Matlock's private office . . .'

'I think we were justified under the circs.'

'. . . I certainly don't want to cause damage to his luxury car as well.'

They regarded the vehicle glumly. It hadn't been difficult breaking into Matlock's office, though they'd found nothing in there of interest. There'd been a wall of books, many referencing horror films and the golden age of the movies, others connected to more genteel pursuits like landscaping and country house architecture. There'd also been a table with a desktop computer on it, and a leather swivel chair pulled underneath. They'd tried to access the computer, only to find it encrypted. There'd been nothing else useful, such as a set of keys for the car, or a bag containing their phones, tablets and iPads. There hadn't even, as far as they could see, been a safe.

'I don't understand why he'd do a runner and leave his car,' Roy said.

'Look,' Nick said. 'You're an ex-cop . . . do you really think we're looking at foul play here? We've had one death, which could have been an accident. And one disappearance, which we've no explanation for, but which also might be innocent. Couldn't it just be a coincidence they both happened tonight?'

Roy shrugged again. 'Coincidences happen. Unconnected bad things sometimes come in twos.' He frowned. 'Though never in my experience.'

◆ ◆ ◆

Now that he was thrashing his way through foliage, even desiccated autumn foliage, Darius was less able to detect whether he was being followed. In fact, driving headlong in a blind panic was doubly problematic. It wasn't just masking the sound of someone else; it was pinpointing his own location for them.

Unless there was no one there at all.

Which he wouldn't know unless he brought himself to a halt and listened.

He blundered on another hundred yards before stopping, only managing this by looping one arm around a tree. He peered back, breath wheezing, his now hatless hair a sweat-soaked mass.

His eyes strained into the mist.

The nearest trees were black pillars in grey. He dug into his inside pocket and put his glasses on. Still nothing. All he could initially hear was the horse-gallop thumping of his own heart, though after a time even that began to subside.

He listened on.

There were drippings galore. But no footfalls, no noisy rustling.

The sweat slowly chilled on his face and down his back, the seconds elongating into minutes.

Finally, tightening his grip on his holdall handle, wielding his stick like a sword, he recommenced walking, again taking the downhill route. There was nothing he could do about the crunching of his footfalls, but he winced at each impact, a sensation growing again that someone was close behind.

As before, the bushes and thickets crowded in. More snagging, more plucking, Darius moving faster and faster as the slope steepened.

Whispers of moving leaves sounded on his left.

Fresh sweat spangling his eyebrows, he darted to the right, battling his way through further reams of wet, meshed vegetation. Ten yards, twenty yards, thirty, forty, fifty, and then suddenly the woods seemed to open and he blundered out on to the road again, continuing to run, still heading downhill. And now hope surged in his chest, because the mist ahead was ebbing, and suddenly he could see the crossroads. A hundred yards further on, his heart heaving like a lump of raw, sore muscle, Darius decelerated from a run to a jog. He scarcely believed it when he found himself on flatter ground. The tree cover fell behind as he wobbled across the middle of the empty crossroads.

There were still some traces of mist around. On three sides of him the fields were only partially visible, but at least he could see the sky with its scattering of stars and its slice of moon.

Brandishing his stick – if anyone was watching they'd now see that he had a weapon – he walked determinedly towards the bus stop sign, and there . . . waited.

Except, waited for what exactly?

It only took a few more seconds for Darius Brant to start feeling foolish.

Who knew how long it would be before a bus came? Or even if one would come at all?

He looked to the sign near the top of the pole. It was just about readable in the moonlight and clearly carried the numbers of several different bus services. If nothing else, they indicated that this stop was still operational. But now his eyes had alighted on something else.

Halfway down the pole, at head height, was a clear plastic plate, behind which was some paperwork; a timetable. The plastic was old and grubby, but he rubbed at it with his elbow, scanning the fading print underneath.

The last bus to call here on a Saturday night arrived at 21.05 hours and departed at 21.10.

Darius had no idea what time it was exactly. Like the others, his phone hadn't been returned to him, and he didn't keep a watch these days. But, at a guess, it was approaching half-past midnight. To make things worse, the first bus due the following morning was at 07.05.

Darius wanted to laugh. Without humour. In dry mockery of himself for such stupidity. But really, it was no laughing matter. With all the huffing and puffing of the downhill chase completed, he was feeling the cold again. His coat was no protection because he was damp with sweat. So, any crazy thoughts about hanging around here until morning were out of the question. The problem though, was what else could he do?

There was one solution, but it would be unbearable swallowing his pride and returning to the Lodge. Though even then, humiliation in front of all the others would be the least of it. He was tired to his bones, his limbs leaden. He didn't even know if he had the lung capacity to make that journey again (ascending this time, of course, rather than descending), and when he looked over that way, the uphill road awaited him like a black, mist-filled tunnel.

Was he still up there, whoever Darius suspected had followed him?

Wait here a little while first, he told himself. *Just to regain your strength.*

But the cold was intensifying, his toes and fingers aching. And where would he gain that new strength from? He'd brought no water, no food. His eyes roved the open fields again, hoping against hope that he might spy the glimmer of a distant farmhouse.

Which was when he spotted the figure.

Sixty yards back in the field directly opposite.

Standing half-concealed in mist, motionless as it watched him.

When he'd thought he was being chased, Darius would have been stricken with terror to see anyone. But how quickly his priorities had changed. He'd wanted a farm, but here was something potentially better. A farmer. Or at least a farm worker. That latter seemed quite possible, actually. Didn't these chaps work all kinds of godforsaken hours? Fellow might even have a tractor nearby, with room on it for a passenger.

With all other options spent, Darius ambled over the crossroads, still watching the figure, which remained perfectly still. A mesh fence bordered the field. It came to about chest height and there was barbed wire along the top, but only a few yards to his right, there was a stile. That was fortuitous too.

He climbed into it but then halted again. The watching figure hadn't moved an inch. To be fair, he wouldn't have needed to be some brainless bumpkin to be surprised by Darius's presence here. Any normal person would be startled to see a townie all the way out in the boondocks at this time of night.

'I assure you I'm quite sane,' Darius called out.

The figure still didn't move.

Was that sinister? Was this the character who had followed him down the wooded lane?

If so, now that he'd been seen, he apparently didn't wish to come any closer. That was probably the good news. The bad might be that he was some local village idiot who took to wandering these empty rural roads all night on his own. But even someone like that might still lead Darius to safety.

The art dealer stepped through on to the field, put his bag down and, after a brief afterthought, placed his stick alongside it. No sense in looking threatening. He advanced with arms outspread, stumbling once or twice amid piles of hay.

'I wonder if you can help me? I've no transport and no phone.'

No movement whatsoever.

They were only about twenty yards apart, but more mist was rolling down from the woods. It drifted past the unmoving shape in sluggish, milky skeins, but not so thick that it concealed the pitchfork Darius suddenly noticed the figure was holding at its side.

'Whoa!' he said. 'I say, old man. You're putting the wind up me rather. At least speak.' The figure remained silent.

Darius halted. The last few yards had seen autumn clouds scudding across the moon, blotting everything out, plunging the waiting shape into blackness. But just as quickly, the clouds cleared again, and the farmer's face was at last revealed.

His hideous patchwork face, which was made from scraps of cloth sewn crudely together, a sickle of jagged stitching where his mouth should be, and worst of all, his eyes: two bright but soulless buttons, which regarded the art dealer with utter and alien indifference.

Seventeen

'Where is everyone?' Liz wondered, coming into the dining room and finding Nick sitting alone, picking in desultory fashion at what remained of the food.

'Gone to bed.'

'Bed?' For some reason that surprised her even though, as the night had worn on, the remaining guests had turned progressively grouchier.

'What else is there to do?' he replied. He sounded defeated, beaten, maybe understandably, but she wasn't sure that simply being dejected was a solution. 'We should do the same.'

'Go to bed?' she said. 'With Jordan still lying outside?'

'He's not coming to any worse harm now, is he?'

'For Christ's sake.'

Nick sighed. 'Hon . . . we can't find our phones and there's no vehicle we can use to get away from here. So everyone going upstairs and locking themselves in is probably the next best thing.'

Liz pondered. There was undoubtedly some truth in that, but to her mind at least it felt like a surrender: to respond to a possible threat with simple inertia. 'Matlock's clearly the key to all this, wouldn't you say?'

'Of course, but he's missing too.'

'Could that blood on the projection room wall have been a diversion? To make it look as if he's a victim as well?'

Nick shrugged. 'I suppose.'

'This place is probably riddled with secret passages. I bet he can move around undetected.'

'What would be the point?'

'That's a good question,' she said. 'But let's look at what we know. That figure on the headland—'

He pulled a face. 'You mean Edgar Karnwood?'

'Look, I've already admitted I could have been mistaken. It was a big guy, and my head was full of Karnwood's face because of all the pictures in here . . . not to mention that nightmare-fuel mannequin in the hall. But I *saw* someone. We can't just dismiss that.'

Nick knuckled at his forehead. Torpor hadn't overwhelmed him yet, but he was clearly flagging. 'Maybe it *was* Simon. He's tall, and there's a faint family resemblance.'

'I agree. The problem is that Simon was already inside when we got back to the house.'

Nick thought. 'Maybe he got back inside before we did? We delayed a couple of minutes before coming in because we were chatting. We even went back to the jetty first.'

'Wouldn't he have passed us going to the front door?'

'He might have circled round to another part of the house under cover of the mist. Like you just said, secret doors.'

'So, you admit it,' she said, 'Matlock could be playing some kind of game here?'

Nick frowned. 'And chucking Jordan Pugmire to his death was part of it?'

'Listen,' she replied. 'If we've learned one thing from all these killers we've been studying, they don't always need motives that sane people like us would understand.'

'In which case' – he laid his cutlery down – 'you and me should definitely go back upstairs. The sooner it's morning, the sooner we get out of here.'

'Unfortunately, and like we keep on reminding ourselves, Clara's only bringing the bus back tomorrow *afternoon*.'

Nick got to his feet. 'At least we'll have daylight.'

'Don't hold your breath for that, either,' she said. 'It's only quarter to one.'

◆ ◆ ◆

It only occurred to Darius when he was several hundred yards up the road that he'd left both his bag and the stick behind at the stile. But he never contemplated going back for them.

'A scarecrow!' he chunnered to himself. '*A scarecrow!*' The only reason it had been standing upright was because they'd tied it against a sturdy iron post.

But good God! On top of everything else, that had been the limit.

That awful face, sagging and stitched, stuffed with straw.

And those eyes, those piercing yet lifeless eyes . . .

'Fucking scarecrow,' he wheezed as he hobbled uphill.

Only a scarecrow. But it had still been a no-brainer that he'd veered away from it across the field, tripping and falling in the stubble and hay, but always getting up again, clambering hurriedly through the boundary fence regardless that its barbs slashed his palms and tore at the fabric of his coat. He could have run the other way of course. Back to the stile, back to the crossroads, but then what? He'd still be in the middle of nowhere. There was still no bus coming. And he had no clue where any of those other roads led to. Except that it would be far, far away. Much farther away than he could possibly walk to in his current state.

In all honesty, he wondered how he was going to manage it up this road, though at present he was relying on pure adrenaline, most likely the product of raw fear.

He was about halfway up when he was re-enveloped by mist. Even that didn't matter.

'Just . . . a scarecrow,' he said again, ascending in long, wobbling strides.

A dummy made from old clothes and straw. Tied there so it wouldn't flop over. Even the pitchfork they'd put into its glove-for-a-hand had needed to be tied in place too.

And yet the horrible thing had encapsulated just about everything he'd done wrong these last few hours. What had he been thinking, going down to the crossroads? How had he thought it would make him any safer? How had it ever entered his head that he'd somehow be getting one up on the rest of them?

Invisible foliage rustled on his left.

Darius ploughed stubbornly on, eyes spearing the gloom, but increasing his pace, drawing on his deepest reserves. Whatever he'd heard, it didn't make itself known again for another three or four hundred yards, another rattle of twigs and leaves from somewhere he couldn't see.

'My God,' he sobbed, legs now throbbing.

When the road levelled out again, the woods receding to his rear, he drew no comfort from it. Up here, the mist swamped him like grey, turgid liquid. He could barely see his hand in front of his face. But hope encouraged him. When he passed the jetty on his right, the high, angular outline of the Lodge emerged ahead, still lit along its frontal eaves.

With a loud splash, something landed in the water perhaps only twenty yards to the right. He still didn't look. 'Fish!' he said loudly and frothily. 'Reservoirs have fish, don't they? It was a tarn once. A real tarn. It must have fish.'

Only when he passed the end of the house and, one by one, the darkened windows slid by, did he risk glancing behind. It seemed miraculous that no one was there. Just ahead meanwhile, in front of the main entrance, Jordan's body lay where it had before.

Again, Darius avoided looking at it. Shoulders heaving, he toppled up the steps, falling once on to his hands, before righting himself and blundering to the heavy door. This would be a terrible moment if for no other reason than sheer embarrassment. Perhaps this was why, though it was a faint hope, he tried the heavy handle before knocking, turning it until it *clunked* – and to his amazement and delight, the door swung inward.

They hadn't locked it. Most likely because they hadn't realised that he'd gone out and left it unlocked.

Thanking God, he slipped inside, closing the door behind him as quietly as he could, easing the bolts home. There was no sign of anyone in the great hall, which now, lit only by the lamps, was filled with shadows. Darius waited there a moment, panting like a racehorse, letting the warmth embrace his shivering, sweat-soaked form. It was tempting just to throw himself into one of the armchairs in the centre of the room. He was worn out, but he was also spitting feathers, and all there was to drink in his bedroom was cold water from the tap in the en-suite.

He walked unsteadily towards the sideboard, where various bottles were still available, only to come in line with the door to the dining room, where movement flickered.

He glanced over there, seeing Liz and Nick standing together, talking.

They hadn't yet spotted him, so he backtracked until he was out of sight and close to the foot of the stairs. He plodded hurriedly up, hoping that he wouldn't see or be seen by anyone else. He hadn't looked in a mirror yet but had no doubt he was in a torn, filthy state. His hands were bleeding, which would be something he'd struggle to explain in the morning. But he certainly couldn't face any awkward conversations now.

Thankful to make it to his room without encountering anyone, he unfastened his coat, took his room key from his jacket pocket, turned the lock and slid inside.

The light was still on, and the room was exactly as he'd left it. He yanked his clothes off, throwing them on to the floor. He'd brought some additional gear, but it was packed in his bag down near the bus stop, so at breakfast time he'd need to wear the same grubby garments that now lay in a crumpled heap, but again, he'd worry about that after he'd slept.

He swayed into the en-suite, where he ran himself a hot shower, paying special attention to his lacerated palms. After that, because he had no pyjamas, he climbed back into his underpants and then under the duck-down quilt, which was luxuriously soft on his bruised and aching limbs. He reached out and hit the bedside switch, plunging himself into darkness. And heard a faint rustle. Like cloth or fabric.

Darius sat bolt upright.

Just in time for the noose to drop cleanly over his head.

Before he could shout or even gag, someone threw their weight on the other end of it, the noose cinching tightly at the nape of his neck, the rest of the rope creaking audibly as it was drawn swiftly over the top of the four-poster's bedframe.

Eighteen

'It'll be no comfort being in our bedrooms,' Liz said, as she and Nick ascended to the minstrels' gallery. She stopped at the top and gazed down into the shadowy emptiness of the hall. 'Even behind a locked door . . . if some killer's got the freedom of the rest of the house.'

'I still think it's the safest option,' Nick replied, as they turned down the corridor to their room. 'Like we've said, if it's Matlock, he'll know every nook and cranny.'

She didn't initially answer, because something had distracted her.

One of the bedroom doors they'd just passed stood ajar by a couple of inches. Suddenly scared again, she lurched towards it and pushed it wide open.

And couldn't suppress a scream at the sight within.

◆ ◆ ◆

Roy was the first of the others to get there. He'd clambered into jeans and a T-shirt but stood barefoot in the doorway to Darius's lamp-lit bedroom, peering dumbfounded at the sight of a limp, half-naked body dangling by the neck from the upper section of the bedframe. Nick, red-faced and frantic, had already taken hold of the hanging shape around its knees in an effort to provide support.

Liz, meanwhile, was several yards away, wildly trying to untangle the knot where the rope, which was pulled taut across the room, had been attached to a pipe on the side of the radiator.

'Get a knife or something!' Nick yelled.

'A knife?' Roy stuttered. 'I've no knife. What the hell happened?'

'I don't know . . .'

Before they could say more, Liz loosened the rope and it went slack, the body slumping down on top of Nick. Darius hadn't been a big man, but a lifeless body is all weight, and it bore him heavily to the carpet. Roy scampered forward, dropping to his knees. As he did, others arrived in the doorway in the shape of Freya and Lottie, the pair of them exclaiming loudly in horror and disbelief.

'No!' Roy shouted over his shoulder, as he fingered the noose open and felt for vital signs. 'No one come in, no one . . .'

Martha had also now arrived outside the room. 'What do you mean, no one come in?' she demanded, sounding slighted.

'Stay outside. All of you.'

'Do as Roy says!' Nick got to his feet. 'He's a cop.'

'Christ, what a mess,' Roy groaned.

Darius's face had turned purple. The eyes had swollen in their sockets until fit to burst, and were now tinged with crimson, the mouth agape but thickly coated in saliva.

'Dead?' Nick asked, already knowing the answer.

Roy nodded. 'I'm no doctor, but I'd say so, yeah.'

Nick glanced up the rope, which still hung over the top of the bedframe. 'Suicide?'

Roy indicated the bed; not only had the quilt and coverlet been yanked away, but the entire mattress had been pushed right across and out of reach of Darius's dangling feet. 'I suppose he could have kicked that thing away before he jumped. You know, just to make sure he couldn't change his mind.'

'Jesus,' Nick breathed.

'I'm not being serious, you dickhead.' Roy shuffled backward on his knees, leaning down to examine Darius's left hand, which he then offered up for inspection. 'See this. Fingernails are torn and bloody, as if he was struggling with the noose. There are also lacerations on the palm. They look recent.' The ex-cop shook his head. 'One unexplained death could be an accident, but then you have an apparent suicide too, in the same place on the same night? Forget it.'

◆ ◆ ◆

'Has it occurred to anyone that auto-erotic asphyxiation is one of the best ways to disguise murder?' Roy said in response to Lottie's question.

There was a contemplative silence in the main hall. It was now two o'clock in the morning, but the fire crackled brightly again because Nick had thrown some additional logs on to the embers. What remained of them were all present, though having initially rushed to the fatal bedroom in variations of nightwear, all were now fully dressed in outdoor clothing and coats as the obvious next step was headlong flight. Lottie in particular had gone through a remarkable transformation, stripped of all jewellery, her face scrubbed clean of make-up, wearing everyday jeans and a jumper. She currently sat tearfully in one of the armchairs, arms folded tightly around her scrunched-up silver mac.

'You presumably know all this because you're a cop,' Martha said. It wasn't really a question.

'Yeah.' Roy glanced at Nick. 'Thanks for that, buddy.'

'For Christ's sake, Roy!' Nick retorted. 'We can't sit on this. We need some expertise in the room, and there's only you can provide it.'

Roy mopped a big hand through his dark hair. In truth, he looked as worried as the rest.

'And just to be clear,' Freya said, 'this expertise of yours means you're dead sure Darius didn't hang himself?'

'I didn't say that,' Roy replied, 'but auto-erotic asphyxiation doesn't happen as often as people think. And when it does, it's usually in a cabinet or cupboard.'

'What about ordinary suicide?' Lottie sniffled.

'Hey . . .' The ex-cop made a gesture. 'It's not impossible. I mean, we all pissed him off. Maybe he found the shame of that too much to live with . . .'

'Do you want to try being serious about this?' Martha said.

'Well, for Christ's sake!' he retorted. 'Did Darius strike you as a man with nothing to live for?'

'What about this client he was supposed to be buying that painting for?' Lottie asked.

'He'd have to have got here pretty quickly,' Nick said. 'Don't you think?'

'Look, if there is a murderer among us,' Freya put in, 'surely the obvious candidate is Simon Matlock? Some of you must be thinking that. I mean, why's he not here? And isn't *he* the one who had a master key to all the bedrooms?'

'But the blood in the projector room,' Lottie said.

'If he's dead, why haven't we found his body lying around, like the others?'

'Oh shit!' Liz said, so loudly that several of them jumped. She'd barely spoken over the last few minutes, staring doomily at the floor. But now she got to her feet. She seemed about to speak, but with a strenuous effort, persuaded herself against it.

'What?' Roy asked.

She watched them all bleakly, but still couldn't say it.

'Liz thought she saw someone earlier this evening,' Nick explained sheepishly. 'Even thought he chased her.'

'Chased you?' Martha looked bewildered. 'Who was it?'

'I don't know.' Liz made a helpless gesture. 'I was outside, near the boathouse.'

'Did you get a look at him?' Roy asked.

'Not really.' She reddened. 'He was tall, I know that . . .'

'Tall as in Simon Matlock tall?' Freya said.

'It *could* have been him,' Liz admitted.

Freya stood quivering, perhaps wondering if an earlier revelation might have saved her stepbrother. Somehow though, she resisted the temptation to apportion blame. Instead, she glanced at the rest of them. 'So, are we saying this for sure . . . that our host here is some kind of lunatic?'

'I didn't say it *was* him,' Liz replied.

'You didn't say anything at all,' Martha said harshly. 'You didn't even warn us—'

'Liz thought she was seeing things,' Nick cut in.

Martha glared at him. 'Can't she answer for herself?'

'Hey!' Liz was jolted out of her despondency. 'Easy, eh?'

'Maybe we should fall out later,' Roy interrupted. 'You know, on the basis that it might help us stay alive.'

'Says the man who didn't even reveal to us that he's a cop,' Martha sneered.

'Ex-cop,' he corrected her.

'Even so, it would've made a difference,' Freya said.

'I don't see how,' he replied. 'I didn't know people were going to get chalked off.'

'It seems odd you didn't mention it, Roy,' Lottie said. 'All we've been doing all weekend is talking about murder cases.'

'Unless you were just a plod, who got nowhere near the real action,' Freya said.

Roy coloured with anger but managed to keep a lid on it.

'For what it's worth,' he said, 'I started on the beat, but I finished up a detective. Only a detective constable, but if you insist on knowing, I was part of the Night Monster taskforce.'

Even Nick was surprised by that. 'You were investigating the Travis Monkton murders?'

'I was only one of sixty, but yeah.' Suddenly, Roy looked tired. 'Perhaps you'll now understand why I kept it quiet.'

'Let me guess,' Freya said, 'because there are some things you still can't say . . . even though you're out of the job, and you might let something go accidentally if people keep peppering you with questions?'

'We're all only human,' he admitted.

'Is the case still open?'

'Not officially.'

'So . . . ?'

'Let's just say that young Jordan was right about one thing,' Roy said. 'There are lots of rumours that there's more to come on Travis Monkton.'

'So, even though you're out, you're still investigating it?' Freya asked him. 'We all saw you dictating notes at Satan's Meadow.'

'As a private citizen, I can do what I want.'

'What's with all this "maybe, maybe not" crap?' Martha said. 'Can't you give us a straight answer?'

'Okay, look . . .' Roy held his hands up. 'There were differences between me and the bosses about where the enquiry should have gone next. I didn't think we had the whole story. That's why we parted ways. And maybe . . . well maybe I'd like to get back in at some point.'

'So, what is the whole story?' Nick asked. 'If it's a personal theory, surely you can tell us that much.'

Roy sighed, hesitated, and then said: 'Maybe there are more victims than we know about. Quite a few more—'

'For God's sake!' Lottie butted in, again sounding on the verge of panic. 'Travis Monkton is in prison. That case is closed as far as we're concerned. But *this* one isn't. What are we going to do?'

Again, they looked at Roy, who shrugged. 'As I see it, there are two possible solutions. We can sit it out here in the hall. Together. And try to stay awake. Or . . .' he glanced at Nick, 'me and you go and have a look at that car again.'

'You mean we *are* going to try and hot-wire it?' Nick said.

'I don't hold much hope,' Roy replied, 'but we've now got a dead body outside and a dead body upstairs, and the best we can do is sit in here and drink Scotch all night? It isn't going to look good. If nothing else, there may be something useful in there, like a mobile.'

He glanced from face to face. No one raised an objection.

'We need to get real, guys,' he said. 'Surviving the night may not be our only challenge here. When this is over, those of us left are going to have an awful lot of explaining to do, and those explanations will need to be convincing.' He looked at Nick again. 'If nothing else, finding a way to get that car going will at least *look* like we tried to do something.'

Nineteen

Liz was quiet when she let the two men out through the front door.

'We'll be fine,' Nick said, seeing how pale she was. 'There're two of us.'

She smiled weakly before closing the door. He wondered if she was concerned that Roy himself might be the killer. If so, given the size difference between them, what would Nick do if the ex-cop turned on him?

Roy meanwhile was preoccupied with other things.

'This bloke your missus says she saw. The one who legged after her. She couldn't . . . I mean, she couldn't have been mistaken?'

'I assumed that at first,' Nick replied, as they walked past Jordan's body and headed along the drive. 'Especially when she said he was the dead spit of Edgar Karnwood.'

It took a second or so for the import of that to strike home. Roy frowned. 'What?'

'I know, I know. Look . . .' Nick lowered his voice even though there was no possibility anyone indoors could hear them. 'I'm betraying a real confidence telling you this. You've got to keep it to yourself.'

'I'm not sure we should be keeping any confidences on a night like this, mate. What did she mean, the dead spit of Edgar Karnwood?'

'Just what I say.'

'Dead spit of . . . I suppose the grandson looks a little like the old fella.'

'Yeah. But . . .' Nick struggled to articulate. 'She thinks it could have been Matlock. And I think Matlock's our prime suspect too. But at first, she really thought it was Karnwood himself.'

'The dead bloke?'

'Well . . . yeah.'

'Is she always this . . .' – Nick expected Roy to say 'scatty' or 'flaky', but the big guy was more diplomatic – 'unsure about stuff?'

'Not usually,' Nick replied. 'But the circs up here are pretty unusual.'

'Why didn't you mention it?'

'Honest answer? Didn't want us to look stupid.'

Roy said nothing to that. They'd now reached the XJ, and stood regarding it with helpless, inexpert eyes.

'Do motors like this ever get stolen these days?' Nick asked.

Roy leaned down, cupping his hands to his face as he tried to scope out the interior. 'Only when the offenders break into houses and swipe the keys.'

'Seriously?'

'When the car manufacturers started adding hi-tech defence mechanisms, it didn't stop the crimewave. It never does. Just redirected it . . . wait a mo . . .' He'd straightened up and now was gazing along the driveway. 'Who the hell is that?'

Over the last few minutes, a slight breeze had picked up, pushing the vapour along the front of the house, breaking it into drifting veils, which afforded occasional moments of extended vision. Both of them were now startled to lay eyes on the figure of an unknown man who appeared to have come sauntering around the farthest corner of the house and was walking along the drive towards the main entrance. He'd just about reached Jordan's body when he realised they were present and had spotted him.

When he halted, it was like a soldier snapping to attention.

'Isn't that Matlock?' Roy said, eyeing the tall figure's dark clothing.

'Might be,' Nick replied, equally surprised.

'Hey!' Roy shouted, a whipcrack in his voice because the figure was now retreating. 'Hey, Matlock! We need to speak to you.'

The figure backtracked faster. When they lurched forward, it turned and ran with huge, heavy strides, heading back along the front of the house, vanishing into the gloom.

'Fuck's sake!' Roy shouted, now at full stride himself. 'That's our perp!'

Nick ran with him. The problem was that neither he nor Roy were particularly fit, the latter with his hefty bulk (while he wasn't obese, he'd clearly enjoyed too many beers and burgers since leaving the job), and Nick, who though a decade his junior, only went to the gym occasionally and under duress from Liz. But they still went at it hammer and tongs. Here, possibly, was the answer to all their problems. If Nick snagged himself a murderer, the first Long, Dark Weekend would go down in history. And he'd have the story of a lifetime.

'Sorry, Liz,' he muttered as they passed the far end of the house, ploughing headlong into the thicker fog. 'Sorry I didn't believe you . . .'

'You can make up for that now,' Roy replied, though like Nick, he was already panting. Somewhere ahead, meanwhile, they heard the thudding of heavy feet on what sounded like wooden decking.

'The jetty!' Nick said. 'Shit, there's a boat along there!'

'A boat?'

'A motorboat. There's two of them, I think.'

'Okay, we've got to nab him before he gets on the water . . .'

Unfortunately, they were too far back for that, though they ran harder and faster, plunging blindly through mist that was suddenly impenetrable.

With a deep belly-rumble, an engine churned to life.

'*Crap!*' Roy growled as they veered left, clattering up the steps on to the jetty and hammering along it. The engine ahead changed timbre as it pulled away from the wooden dock. The ex-cop hissed with frustration as he slowed from a charge to a heavy jog, but Nick powered on ahead. By the time he reached the second boat, wallowing and tilting in the backwash, smoke from the first vessel still hung pungent in the air. Nick climbed down the ladder, the craft rocking wildly. Stumbling to the steering wheel, he shouted back: 'The key's still in!'

Half a second later, Roy had freed the mooring line, clambered down into the boat and lowered the propellor. Nick turned the key and the boat's headlamps came on, the vessel surging forward, initially in a straight line, though once they were past the end of the jetty the turbulent trail of the previous craft was still visible, swerving away towards what Nick thought of as the centre of the tarn.

He swung the wheel left. It was hardly what he'd have called a power boat, but it accelerated steadily until they'd hit what the speedo said was fifty knots. It took him several seconds to get to grips with the fact it wasn't a car and that the contact between steering wheel and rudder was considerably slower. But at least they were still in the chase, their headlights clearly showing the wake left by their quarry. If that wasn't enough, a spotlight mounted on a swivel was attached to the windshield's upper frame.

Roy brought it around and when he toggled a switch, an intensely bright beam shot forward into the murk. Initially, it reflected dazzlingly on them, but then he tilted it downward, training the light on the water, and they were able to accelerate again.

They bounced, jolted and swayed, Nick hanging on to the wheel, Roy clinging with one hand to the gunwale and the other to the top of the shield.

'Bastard might have a vehicle on the far shore!' the ex-cop shouted. 'We could still lose him.'

'He had a vehicle on this side,' Nick replied, flinching in the wind and spray. 'I don't understand why he didn't use that one.'

'If he'd got the XJ going at any stage, that would have given it away that it's Simon Matlock, don't you think?'

Nick shook his head. 'Doesn't make sense though. Suppose it is Matlock. Even if he'd killed us *all*, people would still know that we were all coming here, that he must be the one who'd done it.'

'Didn't you keep it quiet that Black Tarn Lodge was the main event?'

'Yeah, but we've got paperwork at home and booking info on the dashboard to our website. The cops would dig it up soon enough.'

'Whoever it is, whatever his motives, this is our guy. We've got to get hold of him while we've got the chance, so get your foot down.'

All well and good, Nick thought, *but how far is it to the other side?*

This wasn't some massive Scottish loch that would go on and on. It was a reservoir, a tarn. Could they really afford to be bouncing across it at speeds like this when they couldn't see much further ahead than the prow? And were there islands or rocks that might provide obstacles? He hadn't noticed any when looking out over the water earlier, but he hadn't been able to see much because of the mist. He supposed that as long as he stayed in the wake of their quarry, they ought to be safe, but how much did their quarry know about Black Tarn Reservoir?

And on that subject, how much did they know about their quarry?

And what if they actually caught up with him? Whether he was Simon Matlock or not, he was tall. And no beanpole. And if he wasn't Simon Matlock, who was in late middle age – say, if he was significantly younger – that could be a real problem. On top of that, even if he *was* Simon Matlock, he'd already killed twice, so he might still be a handful.

Again, they leapt over turbulence, Nick gripping the wheel with claw-like hands.

It still didn't compute. If nothing else, Simon Matlock had been civilised. Rather mousy, in fact, for a bloke of his size. But what was it Clara had said? Still waters.

'Hey, whoa!' Roy pointed ahead of them. Nick was initially blinded as more spray swept into his eyes. Roy became animated. 'There he is!'

Nick strained to see, and he also spotted their target.

The other boat was about forty yards ahead, dancing and leaping. Roy swivelled the spotlight. With the extra-powerful beam, and the mist having broken into skeins again, they spied a tall figure standing at its controls.

'He must know where he's going, because otherwise he's flying blind,' Roy shouted.

'In that case we're sticking to him like glue.' Nick throttled up, sensing victory.

It wasn't impossible that they'd picked up the better of the two boats by fluke because quite clearly, they *were* catching up. There was now only twenty or so yards between them. The figure at the other vessel's controls was bareheaded but clad all over in black. Matlock had been dressed in evening wear, though that on its own begged the question again: why would he do all this?

They juddered and jolted, the headwind driving spume into their faces. Roy fought to readjust the spotlight, to focus on their opponent. Which was when they had their first real shock. Not so much because it *was* Simon Matlock – suddenly, they could see that clearly – but because he was standing with his back to the controls, staring back at them bug-eyed.

'What the hell!' Roy shouted.

The owner of Black Tarn Lodge stood rigid as he faced them amid what appeared to be a webwork of tautly tied ropes, his hands behind his back. Presumably they too were fastened, possibly to the steering column. Most shocking of all though was the captive's face. It was bloodied around the left temple but divided crosswise by what looked like a thick woollen scarf, which had been pulled tightly over his mouth and tied at the back.

A split second later, a line of rocks emerged from the fog.

'Oh, Christ!' Roy shouted.

Nick swung a desperate left, the boat swerving so tightly that it almost capsized, then cutting a broad sickle through the water, curving wildly away as it somehow, miraculously, avoided the shoreline. Behind them though, Simon Matlock's craft struck it full-on, the impact explosive and devastating.

Nick threw a single glance backward as a searing fireball lit up not just the boulders and trees along the shore, but the entire, foam-covered surface of the tarn. The next thing, a great molten mass was cartwheeling along the waterline, visibly disintegrating but at the same time setting fire to everything it touched . . .

Twenty

They turned a slow circle before heading back along a shoreline now scattered with burning debris. Their sweat-soaked bodies were chilling fast, primarily with shock.

'Jeeeesus,' Roy said. 'And I thought we were catching him because he was running low on fuel. Looks like he was carrying too much.'

Nick couldn't reply. Hissing black fragments bobbed past them.

'Floating fucking bomb,' Roy added.

'Don't . . . don't suppose there's much point going ashore?'

'Don't even know if we can,' the ex-cop said. 'No landing stage, is there?'

Nick took the point. Not that he thought it would have made much difference.

Way above head height, he'd already spotted a grotesque twisted shape hanging suspended in the smouldering branches of a waterside tree, drops of brightly burning fat dribbling down from it.

◆ ◆ ◆

'This is some serious pre-planned shit,' Roy said.

He now had the wheel, while Nick, still numbed, sat alongside him. They had to be halfway back across the reservoir, but the stench of fuel and burning timber followed them. It took Nick a couple more moments to realise that Roy had been talking to him. He glanced sideways. 'Sorry, what?'

'I think our friend was planning that bonfire party back there for all three of us.'

Nick glanced over his shoulder: the flames were subsiding on the far shore, what remained of them soon consumed by swirls of mist. '*We* were supposed to die too?'

'Well, considering the bastard hasn't put a foot wrong so far . . . to inadvertently leave the key in the ignition so we could chase him would have been quite a misstep.'

'We were lured across there?'

'You doubt it?' Roy looked surprised. 'Hellfire, man. You think he'd go to all that trouble . . . abducting Simon Matlock, tying him up in that boat and fixing it so it'd drive all the way over there at top speed, just to get rid of one guy?'

It was a clear-headed appreciation of what had just happened, but even then, Nick struggled with it. Despite his lifelong desire to write horror movies for a living, such a cold, calculated scheme to commit multiple murders was almost beyond his comprehension. 'How did he . . . ? I mean, he must have driven the boat over there himself?'

'Yeah . . .' Roy squinted forward through the mist, steering them towards land by the very faint orbs of light emerging where the Lodge was located. 'But his plan wasn't to burn with the rest of us. He bailed out partway over, obviously. After he'd fixed the accelerator.'

'Into *this* tarn?'

Roy turned the wheel as the jetty hove into view. 'A confident swimmer shouldn't have any more trouble in seven hundred feet of water than in seven.'

'But it's so cold.'

'One thing this nutjob's got, Nick, is willpower. Believe me, that can count for a lot, especially if you've got a change of clothes waiting in the boathouse.'

'A change of . . . ?' Even now the full fiendishness of it was only just dawning on Nick. 'He's really got this thing sorted, hasn't he? So, is he out to get us all, or what?'

The ex-cop mused. 'If it had only been Matlock thus far, I'd say not necessarily. Who knows who he's upset during his life. But me, you, Darius and Jordan as well? Five blokes who've never met until this weekend, and who are never likely to meet again? And if our perp's gig is killing strangers, why stop with five?'

'What're we talking about here, a thrill-killer? Some escaped madman?'

'Could be.'

'But it's so well planned.'

'Sometimes, the best plans can be made on the hoof.' Roy swung the wheel left, guiding them around the angular shape of the jetty, the boat's hull thudding along its various floats. 'There are plenty of successful killers who've made things up as they've gone along. Look at Jack the Ripper. Slaughtered prozzies at random. One night, he almost got rumbled by accident. Still claimed his vic, but quicker than he wanted to, so he then went off and did another one to make up for it. Two in the same night. And all that in a part of London swarming with coppers. Ever heard of John Childs? When he couldn't get rid of his vics anywhere else, he disposed of them in his fireplace . . . in his own front room. Sounds crazy? He still managed to incinerate six people before he got his collar felt.'

He cut the engine as they glided forward, kneeling on the gunwale to catch hold of the mooring line. While Roy tied the boat in place, Nick climbed ponderously up the ladder. But it was only when standing on top of the jetty that he became aware of the figure hurtling towards him. 'Whoa! Who's that?' he shouted.

'Me!' Liz threw herself on to him. 'We heard the explosion. Saw a flash of light. I mean, it was obvious you'd chased someone because we heard both boats leaving. Oh, my God . . .' She hugged him as hard as she ever had, and he responded, though he struggled to feel as elated by the reunion as Liz evidently did.

'It's okay,' he muttered. 'We're fine.'

'Fine!' She pushed herself backward, staring at him with wild, moistened eyes. 'You're fine, you say? And what about me? Do you think I'd have been fine?' She slapped his shoulder. 'And what do you mean by going out there in the first place? You don't know the first bloody thing about boats . . .'

'Liz, listen—'

'What happened out there, anyway?'

'I'm trying to tell—'

'It doesn't matter.' She grabbed him again. 'The main thing is you're okay. We saw this flash . . . heard this boom. We knew you'd gone on the tarn. I ran outside, but I couldn't see anything . . .'

'It's okay. It's really okay.'

Only now did she at last seem to realise that, though he was physically intact, he was pale, sweat-soaked and sooty from all the smoke.

'Okay?' Another hug. 'Yes, you're okay. That's the main thing.'

'See what I mean?' Roy said, climbing up alongside them and ignoring the display of emotion with only the stern indifference a policeman is capable of. He indicated the jetty under their feet, and they saw that it was splashed with water around the top of the ladder, and then all the way back towards land.

Nick regarded it in silence. Their guy had indeed bailed out of his boat once he'd steered it on to the reservoir. His pursuers wouldn't have noticed this; they'd still been a distance behind him at that stage. All he'd then needed to do was swim out of the way and submerge as they passed. Once they'd gone, he could swim leisurely back to the jetty. A couple of hundred yards would have done it.

'What is all this?' Liz said, breaking away, now looking puzzled. 'What do you mean?'

Nick explained what had happened as best he could.

When he'd finished, she looked both astonished and horrified. 'Surely that would have been a terrible risk for the killer to take?'

'This whole thing's a terrible risk,' Roy replied. 'It's not every day you set out to murder a whole bunch of different people all on the same night.'

She glanced from one to the other. 'So, that's what we think this is?'

Nick shrugged. 'I'm not sure what else it can be.'

'It's not inconceivable that Darius and Jordan both died by accident or suicide, or one and the other,' Roy added. 'Not inconceivable, but damn unlikely. And this boat business certifies it. We've got some kind of nut on the prowl, and he's out to get all of us.'

Liz bit her lip, was suddenly tearful again. 'And he's the one who chased me?'

'Almost certainly.'

She looked utterly appalled. 'Why? In God's name, why?'

'I reckon we worry less about that now and more about how we get through the rest of the night,' Nick said. 'According to my watch, it's three-fifteen. That's still over four hours to daylight.'

She filched a scrunched tissue from her jeans pocket, dabbing at her eyes with it. 'We should get back indoors and tell the others.'

'Yeah,' Nick said. 'And this time we tell them everything.'

Liz clearly didn't pick up on his meaning, so as they walked back along the jetty, Roy said casually: 'Nick tells me you thought this guy who chased you looked like Edgar Karnwood?'

'Erm . . .' She glanced round at them, awkward. 'Yes. But a couple of minutes later, I began wondering if I'd been seeing things. I couldn't swear to it, but . . . hell, out here . . . who knows what's going on?'

The ex-cop gazed dead ahead. 'The plot is certainly thickening.'

'I hope the rest of them take it as calmly as you have. I mean that I've been withholding information.'

Nick snorted. 'You were hardly withholding information.'

But Roy seemed less sure. 'Things are getting a tad fractious. Inevitable, I suppose. So, I don't think they're going to be pleased.'

Twenty-One

Though it was now three-twenty in the morning, the house's great hall had a more homely atmosphere than previously. Those who'd stayed indoors had built the fire up high so that it was roaring, its shadows rippling over the picture-clad walls and age-old fittings, and had even brought the cosier items of furniture closer in towards the hearth, so they could all sit together.

There was no cosy atmosphere, though. Their faces were written with angry disbelief.

'Tell me, Liz,' Martha said, 'is there any other info in that pretty little head of yours that you currently consider classified?'

'I . . . sorry?' Liz replied.

'I mean, I respect your right to keep secrets, darling, but perhaps this "need to know" lark is going a bit far when people are dying because of it.'

'Martha,' Nick intervened. 'I don't see how Liz telling you that she thought the guy who chased her was Edgar Karnwood would have helped with our present predicament . . .'

'Oh, don't you? Well, look at it this way, Nick. If we'd known that your other half was prone to seeing the dead walking round, we'd likely never have trusted our safety to you and would have made Matlock drive us all back to civilisation before he did his own disappearing act.'

'Simon Matlock was abducted and now he's dead,' Liz retorted. 'Perhaps show a little respect, eh?'

Martha snorted. 'Given what you and your boyfriend do for a living, Liz, I'll not even bother treating that comment with the contempt it so richly deserves.'

'Look,' Roy said. 'Whoever this is, whatever his motive, the fault for all this lies with him, not with Nick and Liz.'

'Oh, don't worry, Roy,' Martha replied. 'Whoever it is, we'll give *him* a piece of our mind as well. Assuming we even see *him* coming.'

'What I'm worried about is the fact he looked like Edgar Karnwood,' Lottie said, again sounding more terrified than anyone else there. 'What does that mean?'

'It doesn't mean he's a ghost, Lottie,' Roy said tiredly.

'No, I understand that. But no other explanation makes sense either. Unless . . . I don't know, someone who looks a bit like him? A relative maybe?'

'An unhinged twin perhaps?' Martha suggested. 'Newly escaped from his cage in the attic?'

Lottie scowled at her. 'Do you have to be so snarky all the time?'

'What does it matter who or what he is?' Martha retorted. 'All we need to know is that there's a murderer on the loose.'

'It matters, Martha,' Freya replied, 'because if we know what we're up against, we've more chance of dealing with it.'

'Oh, *you're* going to deal with it, are you?' Martha gave a wry smile. 'With all your pretend investigation skills.'

Freya shook her head in disbelief.

'Come on, Martha,' Nick said. 'Back off. Just for once, eh?'

Martha eyed him coolly. 'Is that an instruction or a piece of advice? If you don't mind, Nick, I'll take either or both with a pinch of salt . . . seeing as your main claim to fame is that you're a film writer and yet you've never written a single film that's been made.'

'For Christ's sake!' Liz spat. 'You really are the definition of someone who if they've nothing constructive to add should keep it zipped.'

'At least I'm not trading in cruelty porn,' Martha countered.

'You don't need to, love. You could be deemed an enemy of mankind simply from the way you behave . . .'

'Hey!' Roy said. 'I thought we were going to try and get on. You know, because our survival might depend on it?'

'That rather depends on who's the cause of all this,' Freya said. 'I mean, Martha's being an absolute hag, but that doesn't make her the worst person here. At the same time, we've all been assuming these murders have something to do with Simon Matlock. But suppose they're not. Suppose it's these two?' She indicated Nick and Liz. 'I mean they've been pretty economical with the truth so far.'

'Suppose it's something to do with *you*?' Liz replied sharply.

'Lord help us, Liz!' Lottie said. 'Whoever it is, he killed Freya's brother!'

Freya smirked at Liz. 'Nice try, but no one even knew I was coming up here. I didn't know, myself, until we were almost here.'

'Fair point,' Liz replied, 'but let's not pretend you're some innocent member of the general public, Freya. I mean, are you or aren't you part of a group of people who try to solve murders on behalf of the victims' families?'

Freya frowned. 'I've not tried to hide it.'

'Or is it more the case that you're one of a bunch of busybodies who on several occasions now have got into trouble for harassing so-called suspects—'

'Liz,' Nick cautioned her.

'Don't interrupt me, Nick. If this lot want to chuck accusations around, they should be ready to take some back.' She glared at Freya. 'Don't get me wrong, I'm really sorry about your brother . . . but you can spread slurs about me and Nick all you want. It's still the case that if I'd known you were a member of the Murder Resolution Society, I'd have banned you from this tour. Everything about you people is wrong. Firstly, you're a bunch of amateurs playing at it, but secondly, it's not unfeasible that in your many, varied enquiries, almost certainly without realising it, you got close to a real killer, who's now come here looking for payback.'

Freya's expression narrowed. On reflection, she evidently didn't consider this an impossibility.

'Look . . .' Lottie said. 'Maybe we should all just dial it down a bit, eh? Isn't this what the killer would want? For us all to be falling out?'

'You mean because that'll make it easier for him?' Martha scoffed. 'Because it hasn't been easy enough already?'

'Martha, you're really not helping,' Lottie said.

'And you are, Lottie?' Martha wondered. 'Or should that be Reverend Lottie?'

'Reverend?' Freya said.

Lottie didn't immediately reply, but her cheeks tinged pink.

Martha turned to the others. 'None of you knew about this woman? I can't be the only one who read about it. A few years ago, she was a vicar down in rural Essex. Suffered a complete mental breakdown after a friend of hers, another lady vicar no less, got murdered. She left the cloth after that, didn't you, Rev? And since then, she's been doing God knows what. Question is . . . is she done with her mental breakdown yet? Or has she always been a bit odd? I mean, are we certain the police got the right person for the murder of your pal, Lottie? It couldn't by any chance have been you, could it? And now you're giving full rein to your true inner weirdness?'

'How dare you!' Lottie exploded. 'I've been with other people here all the time. How could you think it might be me?'

'She doesn't think it was you,' Nick said. 'She's just lashing out because that seems to be the only thing she's good at.'

'For the record, I don't think it's likely to be you,' Martha said. 'Appearances can be deceptive, but you really are a puffball of innocent sweetness. Of course, it never entered my head that Miss Scarlet here' – she indicated Freya – 'might be culpable either. Until the Keeper of the Secrets' – now she indicated Liz – 'accused her. Suddenly, I'm not so sure.'

Freya eyed her carefully. 'I was in here when that boat chase happened too.'

Martha shrugged. 'We all were.' She glanced at Nick and Roy. 'Apart from Tweedledumb and Tweedledumber, of course. But that isn't to say one of us isn't working in cahoots with someone else. How often do killers come in pairs, Freya?'

Freya still regarded her with irritation. 'Not as often as fiction might have you believe.'

'But it does happen, yeah?'

'Of course.'

Martha glanced at the others. 'You must admit, it would explain a lot. Miss Scarlet is correct to point out that she didn't know we were coming *here*. None of us tourists did. But once we'd got here, we could easily have summoned our partner-in-crime by telephone.'

'We haven't got our phones,' Liz said.

'We didn't surrender them straight away. But even if we had done, who's to say the culprit didn't keep a spare one hidden?'

'Again, though,' Lottie said with a plea in her voice, 'why? What would be the reason?'

'A couple are right under our noses,' Martha retorted. 'We've already discussed how *you* might've been in on your friend's murder, Lottie. Maybe you got a taste for it, and now you can't be stopped? Or suppose Miss Scarlet's a bit more than just an amateur sleuth. Suppose she's one of these murder fangirls. You know, one of these sad, insecure bitches who write love letters to guys on Death

Row. Maybe her investigations took her into one of these Devil's disciples' orbits, and they hooked up. I mean, who knows where that could have led?'

'But Freya's brother was one of the victims,' Lottie protested.

'You think that means anything?' Martha said. 'Most murders are committed by family members. Isn't that correct, Freya?'

Freya glared at her. 'That's correct.'

'And he wasn't her real brother anyway,' Martha added.

'I think we've had enough of this,' Nick intervened.

'Indeed?' Martha said. 'What do *you* reckon, Roy? You're our resident real detective. Aren't we supposed to be developing hypotheses?'

'There's a difference between that and wild speculation,' Roy said, but he looked troubled by the whole conversation, as if an entire range of possible answers had appeared before him and he was struggling to weigh them all up.

'Well, it isn't speculation that Nick here is a failed screenwriter,' Martha said again. 'Perhaps, though, if he ended up in the middle of a real murder mystery – even if he'd secretly engineered it himself! – he'd finish up with a piece of written work that no movie house could ignore.' She paused to let that sink in. 'Liz would have to be in on it, of course.'

'Bullshit, Martha!' Liz snapped. 'This is going too far.'

'Yeah? Correct me if I'm wrong, but wasn't it only yesterday afternoon when you introduced us to a real-life murderer you happen to be friendly with? How many more are there?'

No one could deny that, of course, all thoughts now switching to Michael Caruso. Nick was particularly stung, because if anyone here had for some twisted reason called in a killer to help them eliminate the tour party, he and Liz had the closest one to hand. In reality, they didn't have that kind of relationship with Caruso – it was more a customer-and-client thing – but the others couldn't be expected to know that.

'And me?' Roy wondered, having noticed that Martha was now eyeing him speculatively.

'Well, you're the ex-policeman, Roy. You must've had the acquaintance of a dozen madmen or more. Some of them might even have been on the wrong side of the law. Perhaps one of them followed you up here looking to get even? Or perhaps they're on your side? Maybe that's why you're a *former* cop? Maybe they're doing you a favour? Maybe if there are a shedload of murders here, and you can give some answers afterwards, the cops will have you back? Haven't you already admitted that's something of an ambition?'

Roy regarded her in pensive silence.

'You're not taking that seriously?' Nick asked him.

'No,' Roy replied. 'But it's not like we're overloaded with alternatives, is it? I mean apart from the obvious one . . . Edgar Karnwood's bloody ghost.'

Twenty-Two

Nick wasn't sure why he'd come back down here. The Lodge's maze-like cellars were an eerie place indeed with most of the lights switched off. In fact, only one light was currently activated, because he appeared to be navigating by a single isolated glow, which led him around bare brick corner after bare brick corner, the rest of the vast basement lying in total, icy blackness.

When he reached the room from which the light emanated, it wasn't, as he'd feared, the profane chapel where Eric Helgoland and his acolytes had carried out their blasphemous rites, but one of those sections of the Costume Vault where so many of Edgar Karnwood's splendid outfits were stored in pristine condition.

He wandered among them again, curious about what had brought him here. And when he realised what it was – a low, gagging, gurgling noise – he halted mid-aisle in front of a drawn curtain, realising that it was coming from the other side. It was louder now though, and uglier.

'I'm coming through,' he said. 'I'm not afraid.'

But when he yanked back the curtain, which he now realised was a shabby bed-curtain, there was no enemy behind it, just a man hanging by his neck.

'Darius!' Nick blurted.

The art dealer, whose face had turned indigo, whose lips and protruding tongue were black, whose entire head had swollen like a balloon, could only regard him through goggling, blood-rimmed eyes. The noose constricting his throat was so tight that the cord could barely be seen, but above him it ascended tautly into shadow.

'Darius!' Nick blurted again. 'Hey, man . . . you're still alive!'

Someone tittered at his rear. He twirled, and saw that, one by one, the silent, costumed figures had stepped down from their plinths and now filled the aisle behind him: Archaeon, the Phantom of the Opera, the fungus-infested astronaut. All of them. At their forefront was the diabolical figure of Karnwood's Mr Hyde, clad in his late-Victorian evening suit, his silk-lined cape, his rakishly tilted topper and that hideous sackcloth hood, the one with the single eyehole torn on the left-hand side. More horrifying than this was the figure at Hyde's feet. Forced down to her knees by the black leather-gloved hand tangled in her piled copper-red tresses. It was Liz, weeping, pleading, the wavy-bladed knife from Helgoland's sacrificial chamber raised above her. And then plunged downward, again and again and again . . .

◆ ◆ ◆

The shattering scream brought Nick to his senses with a jolt. A second scream followed. By this time, he was on his feet. He gazed dazedly around, blinking in the heat from the fire.

'What's going on?' someone else murmured. It was Roy, also now getting up from his chair.

The rest were in a similar drowsy state. All six, having retreated into a sullen, venomous silence after their previous argument, had finally succumbed to fatigue. They'd initially arranged themselves on the furniture facing the fire, which, though the flames had now receded a little, had clearly been a mistake, as the stultifying heat had soon overpowered them.

Nick of course was still shuddering from his nightmare.

'Good Lord,' Lottie said, eyes popping as she too jumped up. 'Were we all out? I thought we'd agreed someone had to stay awake?'

'Relax.' Roy pivoted to scan the far reaches of the hall, which again were thick with dancing shadow. 'Everything's okay. We're all here.'

'Are we indeed?' Martha said. 'No one's noticed Miss Scarlet's absence?'

'Fuck,' the ex-cop said under his breath.

One of the chairs was indeed empty. A third scream sounded. It wasn't as panicky as before, but there was an urgency in it. And this time it was coherent, and clearly Freya's voice: 'Everyone! I need you in the kitchen, quickly!'

Nick made to cross the hall, but Liz grabbed his arm. 'Wait a minute . . . what time is it?'

'Erm . . .' He rubbed the sleep from his eyes and focused on his watch. 'Ten past four.'

'God,' she said. 'We've been asleep nearly an hour. Anything could have been going on.'

Nick nodded in hapless acknowledgement. Liz seemed to have forgotten that he'd agreed to take the first watch, and so he didn't bother mentioning it. In any case, the rest of them were already streaming across the hall. He and Liz went with them, though even as a group they were wary, glancing around and up at the minstrels' gallery, which was deeper in shadow now than the recesses on the ground floor.

The kitchen was accessible from a passage connecting to the dining room, and when they went through there, the banquet that had been set out for them the previous day lay unchanged, half-eaten and congealed, used plates and cutlery scattered along the table. In the kitchen meanwhile, they found Freya standing with arms folded, peering through the window into the foggy darkness of the kitchen yard.

'What's going on?' Roy demanded.

'What's going on is that someone was supposed to be on sentry duty, weren't they?' she replied. 'And yet when I happened to wake up two or three minutes ago, everyone was sparked out.'

They muttered with sheepish uncertainty, apparently too groggy to recollect. Again, Nick said nothing. After Martha's very public revelation that he wasn't much of a writer, this whole thing was in danger of turning into the 'Nick the Ridiculous' show.

'I suppose it was inevitable,' Freya said. 'It's been a long day and we're worn out with stress. So, I thought I'd get a pot of coffee on.' She indicated a percolator bubbling on one of the worktops. 'That can only help, can't it?'

The others mumbled their agreement.

'That's when I saw someone looking in through the window.'

She nodded at the broad pane over the double sink. Again, nothing was visible out there, but the glass wasn't frosted. If someone had come up to the outside, he'd be clear enough.

'I'm afraid I screamed,' she added. 'I'm sorry . . . it was involuntary. But the next thing I knew, he'd gone. Obviously, I didn't go out there after him.'

'Wise decision.' Roy moved to the kitchen back door, to check that it was locked. It was, the key hanging on a hook close by. 'But I think we should go out there now.' He glanced at the others. 'Just to make sure he's not, you know, crouching down beneath the sill . . . something like that.'

'One thing first,' Freya said. Her eyes roved across them. 'Look, I know this is going to sound crazy. But, that face . . . I recognised it. I mean it can't have been the guy I thought it was. But . . . look, it was Edgar Karnwood.' Stunned silence greeted this. 'Yes, you heard it right. The deceased film star. The same guy whose face covers just about every wall in this place. So, no, before anyone asks . . . I couldn't have been mistaken.'

Nick swapped glances, first with Liz, whose eyes were now wide as coins, and then Roy.

'Okay . . .' Roy looked as if he didn't quite know what to think. 'It may be that some people in here owe you an apology, Liz.'

'I certainly do,' Nick said, 'just for doubting you.'

Liz shook her head. 'I hardly feel vindicated. We still don't know what this means.'

'Let's see if we can find out.' Roy lugged the door's bolts back and grabbed the key.

They went outside as a group, scanning the relatively close confines of the kitchen yard. Roy kicked at the woodpile, which in truth was the only place where anyone could have hidden. It fell apart harmlessly. Freya did the same with a stack of garden tools, knocking down a hoe, a rake, a couple of spades, a trowel and an old wood-axe. That left the path round to the front of the house, which Nick and Roy had used earlier, and more ominously, the arched entrance through to the terraced gardens, which was the obvious avenue of escape for anyone who'd been rumbled while trying to enter the house via the kitchen. There was no question that none of them fancied taking that route, even as a group, until daylight at least. They withdrew back inside, Roy barring and locking the door again.

'Well, this is a doozy,' Martha said. 'So now we've got dead maniacs coming after us as well as live ones.'

'Pack it in, Martha, eh?' Liz replied. 'We're all sick of it.'

'I can only tell you what I saw,' Freya asserted.

'You're sure it was him?' Roy asked. '*Edgar Karnwood?*'

'On my honour. I know it sounds crazy, but I absolutely swear it.'

'How old would you have said he was?' Lottie asked.

Martha stared at her. 'That's a serious question?'

'Course it is. If it was a ghost . . . a disembodied spirit, he'd have come back when he was young and handsome, wouldn't he?'

Martha shook her head. 'I don't believe I'm hearing this.'

But Freya took the enquiry more seriously. 'I don't know . . . mid-sixties.'

'Not a zombie then?' Martha said. 'I mean, if he'd been a zombie, he'd have rotted down to his bones by now, wouldn't he?'

'Christ's sake,' Liz muttered.

'Now you mention it, he had a bit of green round his mouth,' Freya replied.

'Green?' Roy said, even more bewildered.

'Just slightly, on his lips. Like a smear. Wasn't exactly decaying, though.'

'Wait a minute!' Nick said. 'Wait a damn minute . . .' Suddenly, incredulously, he had an idea about how he might piece this together. Some of it, at least. He turned to face them. 'How many of you are familiar with the Edgar Karnwood movie, *Metamorphoid*?' They looked collectively nonplussed. But now he felt energised again. Even excited. 'Well, if nothing else, I think we've got an answer to one question.'

Twenty-Three

It was the first time that any of the women had been down to the Costume Vault, though it was no longer a place to be awed by. It was more the case now that the countless costumes and props from so many lurid horror movies seemed vaguely repellent, and none more so than the three-piece 1970s suit, stained all over with what at first glance looked like hardened pea soup.

'This costume was worn by Edgar Karnwood in the final scenes of *Metamorphoid*,' Nick told them. 'As the space scientist being slowly taken over by an alien parasite, he was making a speech to an assembly of VIPs, and yet to conceal his fast-decaying features, he'd donned a very lifelike latex mask of his own face. The horror of the sequence came from the green gunk of his liquifying flesh as it trickled every which way out of his mask and spilled down over his smart suit.'

'*Green?*' Liz said, slowly understanding.

Nick nodded at the faceless mannequin on which the suit was displayed. 'Don't you think it odd that the mask isn't here, seeing as it played such a key role in the film?'

'You're thinking it originally was?' Lottie said. 'But that someone's taken it and is now wearing it?'

'Would explain a lot.'

'Foolproof disguise,' Martha replied. 'The face of a man who's been dead for over a decade.'

'If nothing else, it's kept his own features concealed,' Roy said.

'Also means anyone spotting him might have thought they were seeing things,' Liz added.

'Whatever the reason he chose it,' Roy said, 'at least we now know what we're dealing with.'

Lottie meanwhile shivered. 'Why's it so cold down here?'

'We're in the basement,' Martha replied, as if that answer was surely obvious.

'There are heating pipes. Anyway, it feels more like a draught . . .'

It was a second or two before the import of that struck home. They shuffled out into the corridor, and there was indeed a very slight cold breeze.

'Now what?' Lottie wondered aloud.

'It's coming from this way.' Roy headed right, but warily, as if anticipating a sudden attack from one of the various rooms leading off the brick-built passage.

They proceeded cautiously, turning left, right, left again, only now appreciating what a labyrinth it was down here. Once away from the Costume Vault, the rooms could have been part of any other cellar, all standing in darkness and crammed with boxes, crates and discarded, dust-webbed furniture. Then they rounded another corner, and perhaps forty yards ahead, past more openings on either side, with only dim light in the corridor, the passage came to an abrupt halt at an exterior door, which was currently standing ajar.

Even as they watched it, a couple of dead leaves blew in from outside.

'All right, everyone relax,' Roy said, venturing forward again.

Nick went with him. His male pride wouldn't allow anything else, but he was glad the hulking ex-cop was in front. The four women stayed close too. Each time they passed an entrance, they expected an ambush. But in all cases, there was nothing behind them: just cellar rooms, either empty or filled with unrecognisable junk.

Perhaps only five yards from the end door, it moved inward a little. They stopped, eyes bugging, convinced that someone was lurking just the other side of it. But then the door shifted outward again, more leaves tumbling in, carried on a faltering breeze.

Roy pressed on, the others staying close.

Behind the door, a flight of narrow outdoor steps led up to ground level. Again, they were littered with autumn leaves. There was no sign of anyone out there, either above or below.

'At least we know how he's been getting in and out,' Freya said.

'Is there any way we can close that door again?' Lottie wondered. 'I mean permanently.'

Nick crouched to examine the lock, but the wood had been smashed and the aged metalwork twisted and broken, as if by repeated heavy kicks.

'There *was* a lock on it, but it's been forced.' When he ran his fingers along the door's edge, additional flakes came loose. 'Wasn't even difficult. The timber's perished.'

'Can't we just block it closed?' Liz asked.

'Possibly,' Roy replied.

'What about this?' Freya said.

She was at the entrance to one of the other rooms. Inside it, just about visible in the darkness, was another clutter of old furniture, but also some disused white goods, including what looked like a washing machine.

Roy removed a metal box filled with old tools, which sat on top of it, and then, with assistance from the others, manhandled the old washer out into the passage and along to the exterior door, which they pushed closed and then jammed in place by shoving the hefty mechanism up against it. They followed this by doing the same with a grotty old cooker, and then a dishwasher.

'One man would certainly struggle to move that lot on his own,' the ex-cop said, rubbing his grubby hands together.

'Cool,' Martha replied. 'The only question now is: have we blocked him out or blocked him in?'

Uneasy glances passed between them.

'Either way, I'm pretty sure he'll try to come at us again,' Roy said. 'All we've got to do is be ready.'

'Yeah, well this time we've got coffee, so there are no excuses,' Freya replied. 'I say all of us stay awake from here on and arm ourselves while we're at it.'

Lottie looked baffled. 'There's an armoury here?'

'There's better,' Freya said.

She led them back upstairs, and when they re-entered the main hall, went around it, systematically pointing out the various exotic yet cruel-looking items encased in glass.

'These things?' Nick said. 'These are just props.'

She glanced round at him. 'You saying they're not real? What about this?' She indicated the spotted, five-clawed glove from *Last of the Leopard Men.*

He shrugged. 'I admit, that *looks* as though it could tear you a new one.'

'Let's see if it can.' She took the wood-framed case in both hands and fiddled around its edges.

With a *click*, a catch was released, and the box swung open. Freya slid the clawed glove from the loop of wire holding it in place.

'The claws are real enough,' she said. 'Hooked bone, very sharp.' She fitted her hand inside and flexed her fingers. It was a disturbing sight, a leopard-spotted hand opening and closing, flesh-rending talons on the ends of its digits. But Nick wasn't so sure.

'It looks nasty enough, but you'd have trouble inflicting a lethal wound in a stand-up fight with that. In the movie, it was only ever used by a witchdoctor when the victim was tied down as a human sacrifice.'

Freya tugged the glove loose and tossed it on to the nearest of the hall's coffee tables. She moved along to the next display item, the crusty green bottle bearing the skull-and-crossbones logo.

'Now that may genuinely be dangerous,' Nick said. 'That'll be the hydrochloric acid used in *Revenge of the Phantom*, 1962. Karnwood played a revived Phantom of the Opera, and in one scene, planning to avenge himself on the rival who originally disfigured him, he pours acid over a plaster-cast head of his foe, and it promptly melts. I wouldn't be surprised if *that* was the real thing.'

Freya considered this and opened the box.

'I said I'm not sure that's a good idea,' Nick said.

'Careful, Freya,' Lottie warned her.

'I'll be fine.' Freya tried to work the cork loose.

'What's the point?' Lottie said. 'It's over half a century old. Won't it just be gloop?'

In response, Freya loosened the cork and sniffed at the opening. She wrinkled her nostrils and swirled the bottle around. 'It's sludgy, but there's something in there.'

To test it further, she moved to the nearest coffee table and tilted the bottle.

They watched in silent fascination as a yellow-green liquid drooled out. It had definitely aged. It was very viscous, more like runny marmalade than an actual fluid, but on contact with the tabletop, smoke rose in spirals, the polished wooden surface fizzing and disintegrating.

Freya nodded her approval, but again Nick was unimpressed. 'One-trick weapon,' he said. 'You can only throw it in that bottle, and what if the bottle doesn't break, or you miss?'

She thought for a moment before placing the bottle on the table. 'Think I'll settle for *this*.' Alongside the case in which the acid had been kept was the smaller box in which the crescent-shaped, jewel-hilted dagger was displayed. She took the weapon out. 'This is much more *me*.'

'Jack the Ripper's blade from *Murder Most Foul*,' Nick said. '1971.'

'Surely, it's not real?' Lottie sounded shocked that it might be.

'Don't know.' Freya tested the tip.

'I don't suppose this thing's real either?' Liz asked, opening another box and helping herself to an antique sawn-off shotgun, its walnut stock cut with hunting scenes, its ironwork covered with scroll engravings.

'They used that to kill the monster in *Hound of Hell*,' Nick said. 'Seem to remember that Karnwood, who was playing Holmes, fired two packs of coins at it. But in real life I presume they just fired blanks.'

'These stones are coloured plastic, but the blade's made from steel,' Freya said, still talking about the jewel-hilted dagger. 'It's not as sharp as it looks, but I reckon it could still go through someone . . .'

'Okay, that's enough.' Roy said, coming over from where he'd been checking that the windows were locked. 'All this talk of weapons. What do we think this is, a role-playing game?'

'Most of us think we're under threat,' Freya replied, 'and that we need to protect ourselves.'

'With this stuff?'

She showed him the dagger. 'You saying this couldn't hurt someone?'

'I'll be honest, it's the hurtful potential that's really bothering me.' They stared at him, bewildered. But he pressed on. 'The thing is . . . we don't know anything about this guy.'

'Ah. You mean he might be mentally ill?' Freya said. 'Might be disadvantaged? Well, boo-fucking-hoo. We also know he's a cold-blooded murderer.'

'None of us are really qualified to use weapons . . .'

'Hey, Roy,' she said. 'You're not a copper any more, okay? You don't need to be so excruciatingly politically correct.'

He glowered at her. 'It's not politically correct to worry that a bunch of civies gearing up with weapons are at least as likely to injure themselves and maybe each other as they are the opposition.'

'Seriously?' she asked him. 'You'd rather we weren't able to defend ourselves?'

Roy looked troubled. 'How many of you are seriously qualified to do that?'

'Heaven's sake,' she retorted. 'A trapped rat can defend itself.'

'A trapped rat wouldn't bother discriminating. We need to.'

'Against a mass murderer?'

'How about the person sitting next to you, who may or may not be the murderer, but who you're suddenly not sure about?'

'What're you talking about?' Freya said. '*We're* all in the clear. You lot were all fast asleep when I saw that guy outside the kitchen window.'

'Funnily enough,' Martha intervened, 'when it comes to that, I was just thinking how we're *not* all in the clear.' Everyone glanced round at her, but she now had her eye on Freya. 'We've only got your word for it that you saw anything.'

Freya regarded her with disbelief. Martha surveyed the others. 'None of the rest of us saw this fella.'

They couldn't deny it.

'So, you still suspect *me*?' Freya said. 'I could have killed every one of you while you slept by the fire.'

'I have to agree,' Nick ventured. 'Freya can't be a suspect.'

They exchanged glances, but no one seemed certain of anything any more.

'You just don't seem too upset, Freya,' Martha said. 'I mean, I get it that you like to think you're a super-cool investigator, but even then, you don't seem upset by any of this. Especially since one of the victims was your own brother.'

The rest of them gave thought to this, and even Nick wondered about it. While Freya had clearly been shocked by young Jordan's death, she'd seemed no more distraught overall than, say, Lottie.

'You've put your finger on it once already, Martha,' she replied calmly. 'He wasn't my brother. He was my step-brother, and I've already admitted that he and I didn't get on. The truth is that I was barely even living in the family home by the time Jordan came along.'

'So, was it entirely coincidental that you and he booked on this same tour?' Martha said.

Again, confused glances were exchanged.

'We didn't book it together,' Freya explained. 'But it wasn't a coincidence either.'

'Let me guess,' Liz said. 'That painting again? The one Jordan bought?'

Freya shrugged. 'It's been all over the true crime socials for weeks that Michael Caruso was about to put the pride of his collection, the Travis Monkton portrait, up for sale. There's no secret there. Everyone's heard about it.'

'This again,' Roy said, groaning. 'It's just a bloody painting!'

'I thought you said Jordan was right . . .' Liz began.

'I said he was right that there've been rumours,' Roy replied. 'I didn't say he was right about that painting. And frankly, I had a gander at it too, along with the rest of you, and I . . . hell, I didn't spot anything.'

'That why *you* were on the tour, Roy?' Nick asked him after a second. 'To check the painting out as well?'

Roy looked embarrassed. 'It was a long shot, but I should've known better. More internet bullshit.'

Liz glanced at Freya. 'And do you feel the same? You didn't seem remotely bothered at the art gallery.'

Freya shrugged. 'I won't pretend I wasn't interested to at least see it. And the only way you can get to view Caruso's work is either by coming on one of your tours or by paying a visit to his house on your own, and no one in their right mind is going to do that.'

'And yet Jordan wanted to *buy* it?' Liz said. 'Why?'

'Because he was a gullible Gen Z buffoon,' Freya replied. 'He believed what he read online. And if he bought it, he could really study it. And that way, he could get one over on people like me.'

'That's all it was?' Nick said. 'If he could decode the painting and provide new intel to the law, it would piss off the Murder Resolution Society?'

'Trust me,' she said, 'he'd have considered that money well spent.'

'And because Darius Brant was after the painting as a piece of murderabilia, that made him and Jordan rivals?' Liz mused.

Freya shrugged. 'Later on, yeah. When they both realised they were after the same thing.'

'But you, an actual crime investigator, were only mildly interested?' Martha still sounded sceptical. 'Or did you intend to acquire it by other means? Perhaps murderous means?'

Freya gazed at her with pity. 'If I was here to kill my rivals for the painting, why would I then go on to kill Simon Matlock? Or try to kill Nick and Roy?'

'Muddying the waters maybe?' Martha suggested. 'Concealing your real purpose behind a random massacre committed by some escaped lunatic.'

'Are you actually serious?' Freya glanced at the others. 'Are you people listening to this?'

'Oh, I don't think you're the killer, Freya,' Martha said, 'I know you can't be. But we've only got your guarantee that you were scared by someone outside and not swapping messages with him.'

'Oh, this is the bit where I'm in cahoots with someone again . . .'

But Martha wasn't finished. 'There's something about you that's never quite added up, Freya. This leather-jacketed bad girl thing . . . the Miss Scarlet persona when you came down for dinner. It's all got the air of trying a bit too hard. Are you not up to much in the Murder Resolution Society? Don't they take *you* very seriously either?'

Freya's brown eyes gleamed with thinly suppressed rage.

'Did you need to pull out a real plum to try and impress them?' Martha said. 'Would solving the riddle of the Travis Monkton painting do that for you?'

'You're totally out of order, Martha, and totally off your rocker!' Freya hissed. She glared at the others. 'That goes for the rest of you too, for listening to this claptrap.' Her voice almost broke; she choked with intensity. 'This bloody woman misses no opportunity to jeer at anyone who opens their mouth. She clearly despises all of us. People she doesn't even know. What kind of personality is that? And yet you're letting *her* point the finger at *me*?'

The silence following this was mildly ashamed but also noncommittal. Freya *had* been up and about while they'd been asleep. There'd been *no one* outside when they'd gone to look. And in all honesty, they couldn't just assume that their adversary had no connection to anyone here. Whoever the real killer was, they'd continually been several steps ahead. Was it possible an insider was guiding them?

'Anyone feel they need another coffee,' Freya said, tears of anger glittering in her lashes, '*you can make your fucking own!*'

She tossed the dagger away and stormed out of the hall towards the kitchen. The others glanced awkwardly at each other, before gradually spreading out in their continued appraisal of the so-called 'weaponry'.

Liz led Nick aside. 'What do you think?' she asked quietly.

He shrugged. 'What can I say? Miss Scarlet says she saw Karnwood too. But suppose she's copycatting you? Martha might have a point. Freya never once mentioned that she was his stepsister until Jordan put her on the spot.'

'And Jordan of course was the first to die,' Liz said thoughtfully. 'And then we find out afterwards that there was longstanding animosity between them. Is that relevant, do you think?'

'Who knows? Maybe, but maybe no more so than the animosity Martha herself seems to hold against everyone else here, which we don't have any explanation for at all. Truth is, hon, there could be all sorts going on. Bluffing, double-bluffing. And any one of us could be in league with someone else. We've all had opportunities to whisper directions through an open window or an unlocked door. I mean, he's got to find his way around the estate, just like we have. But he's also got to select and close down targets. Someone relaying intel to him could hardly be a hindrance.'

Liz scrubbed a hand through her hair. 'You think that painting could be the cause of all this?'

'Seems unlikely,' Nick said, 'but it's a kind of common denominator. And consider the alternative. Some madman wanders over the moors until he comes across Black Tarn Lodge, where he sees a bunch of strangers and decides to stalk and murder them. Add to that, he finds a way inside almost straight away. A cellar door that most folk wouldn't even know is there. What're the odds?'

'That painting still up in Jordan's room?' she wondered.

'I suppose so, but look . . .' Nick couldn't deny that he was struggling with this as a potential cause of the carnage. 'You were in Caruso's gallery, Liz. You heard the bids they were tabling. A few thousand? Really? Hardly worth killing for.'

'But what about the info that's supposedly concealed in it?'

Again, Nick felt doubt. 'Those additional Night Monster victims that Roy thinks are still out there? The locations where their bones are buried? Monkton's already doing life. I'm not sure that's worth committing murder for either.'

Liz glanced around at the others, all now drifting in various parts of the hall.

'Damn it,' she breathed, watching closely as Lottie picked up the curved, jewel-hilted dagger that Freya had discarded, while Martha seemed to have settled on a heavy iron poker from the hearth. 'Is there anyone here we can trust at all?'

'Sadly, no,' Nick replied. 'You want my take on this? You want to live . . . you get yourself a weapon too, you watch everyone else like a hawk, and neither of us goes anywhere without the other.'

◆ ◆ ◆

As she stood alone in the kitchen, Freya boiled with rage. When she wiped at her eyes, they were still blurred by tears.

The moment she'd arrived at Piccadilly Station yesterday morning and had seen that Jordan had also booked for the Long, Dark Weekend, her heart had sunk. Something inside had told her to turn around there and then and walk away, but she'd already paid her deposit. It wasn't the lad's fault, she supposed – the poor lad who was no longer even alive – but he'd always had this ability to cause problems. It was true that she'd never really liked him; that he'd never felt like a real brother to her because – well, he wasn't. But deep down, Freya had long known that she should and could have been a better older sister to him. Especially through the potential common interest they'd both had in murder mysteries. She could have reached out to him that way, and made him feel wanted. But the last thing she'd needed was someone hanging around her neck at the Murder Resolution Society who was irredeemably immature. Someone who equated true-life murder investigations with slasher movies, for Christ's sake! It would have been so easy for someone like that to drag her down in the opinions of her fellow members.

And that was the part that really hurt, because in that regard, Martha Lloyd's scathing psychoanalysis hadn't been far off the mark.

Freya would never admit it, but joining the MRS had been a decision specifically taken to direct herself into what she'd hoped would be a more interesting and worthwhile life. Prior to that she'd been nothing. An admin assistant in the Civil Service. In terms of day job, she still occupied that not-so-lofty post. But thanks to the Murder Resolution Society, she'd suddenly – amazingly quickly, in fact – become *someone*.

Not many would know about it of course. The MRS were fairly secretive. But *she* knew. And how much of an improvement that was when it came to that all-important self-worth. She couldn't quantify how differently she now felt about herself. One day an anonymous drone in Britain's shuffling, uninspired workforce, the next an operative, an asset, a secret agent in the war on crime. Perhaps inevitably for a girl like her, who'd spent her youth reading novels much more exciting than real life had ever been, she'd gradually shifted into that persona. Taking out a gym membership and knocking herself into shape; taking make-up lessons, getting her hair done, donning slinkier clothes than she'd ever worn previously.

She didn't mind that Martha had sneerily dubbed her 'Miss Scarlet'. Maybe that was how she thought of herself. It was a cooler pose than she'd ever struck in the normal world. Not that her fellow

MRS members had been overly impressed. Those retired detectives and forensic scientists she'd talked about.

If Freya was serious about investigating unsolved crime, they were all that and more.

They had experience of real investigations, access to private files and personal information via their network of contacts. They had all of them done casework in the past. They'd studied witness statements and intelligence reports, had analysed patterns of crime and collated new evidence. They'd put dossiers together for the attention of various police forces, which on one or two occasions had generated all-new enquiries into clusters of potentially connected homicides. Freya, with no experience, had struggled to keep up with them. In fact, in the early days, she'd suspected they only kept her around because she was a pretty face. But gradually, she'd been learning, making ground, earning her place.

And then Jordan had come along. The annoying kid-brother (who in truth she barely knew), wanting to be a real-life investigator as well, eager to identify and pursue the sorts of real-life killers who'd make Jason Voorhees and Michael Myers seem positively tame.

It was an irony of ironies that, during the course of this Long, Dark Weekend, they'd suddenly encountered one. But even now, Freya was thinking that she could turn it to her advantage. She'd been brutally slighted in there: she, who with the exception of Roy Southerby, was the only one among them to actually dedicate time to curtailing these madmen's rampages, now being accused of murder herself, or complicity in it.

The nerve of it was off the scale. But damn it to goddamn hell, she was going to remain calm and controlled, and she was going to deal with this extreme situation the way she'd always imagined and hoped that she would. And the first part of that required her to completely disregard Roy 'No Longer a Cop' Southerby's advice (let's face it, he must have screwed up royally to get kicked out of the modern-day police!) and secure herself a weapon. And not one of those toys that Edgar Karnwood had used in his innumerable crass movies. A real weapon, something that would put the fear of God into any murderer.

Unconcerned whether anyone heard her or not, she opened the two bolts on the back door, took the key from alongside it, turned it in the lock, and stepped out into the icy mist. For a second, she was utterly disoriented. Any breeze had receded, so visibility had reduced again. But it didn't matter. She marched across the yard in a diagonal line. She knew where she was going, and she was correct. Here lay the tools that she'd kicked over earlier, among them the wood-axe. It was little more than a hatchet, really. A tool rather than a weapon, but at least it wasn't a film prop. She weighed it in her hand, and it felt good: the smooth, hickory handle, the steel head at the end of it, honed to what looked like butcher-shop sharpness.

She hefted it to her shoulder and swung it – and jumped at the sound of a timber *thud*. Whirling around, she saw that the kitchen door had closed.

'The hell?' she breathed.

Of its own accord, or had someone inside closed it without knowing that she was out here?

She was about to shout when she realised that she could see through the window into the well-lit interior, and there was no one there.

That was when the figure sidled into view. She hadn't previously noticed it because it had been standing to one side of the door, plus it was clad in a heavy black coat and, with a dark broad-brimmed hat pulled down, at least half of its pale, rubbery face was concealed.

Without a word, it came towards her.

Twenty-Four

Freya wasn't sure what surprised her more: that the maniac hadn't immediately seen she was armed with an axe, or the way he reacted when he did.

His stance tautened, his shoulders hunching forward as if he were suddenly anxious.

'Yeah, that's it, you'd better be wary,' she said, emboldened. 'There'll be no easy kill for you here.'

The maniac, who was indeed wearing the latex mask that Nick had described, with a slight green mark in the corner of the mouth, didn't appear to be armed himself. This gave him a distinct disadvantage, and he clearly knew that. He'd already stopped advancing while there was still a good ten or so yards between them. Instead, he circled to the right. Freya couldn't immediately understand the strategy. But by instinct, she circled to the left. A split second later, she realised what he was up to: edging his way towards the entry to the side passage. He was going to do a runner round to the front of the building.

She didn't know whether that would be a good thing or bad. Just having sent him packing would be a kind of victory. But not as much as felling him.

But felling him? Seriously? With an axe?

It was all very well her mocking the police for being overly cautious with criminals because they were worried about being prosecuted themselves. But in Britain today the same rampant injustice sought out civilians too. It was while she was thus deliberating that he made a sudden, unexpected move, dashing across the middle of the yard. But not towards the side passage, or her; towards the arched entrance to the terraced gardens.

She cursed. In a blur of motion, he'd gone, the mist swirling in behind him.

It was such an obvious move for him to have made, and for her to have anticipated if she'd only had half an instinct for this sort of thing. He'd never been planning to escape via the side of the house, probably for fear the others would pile out through the front door and cut him off. It was always going to be via the rear. Freya hovered there undecided, the axe-handle slippery in her grasp, peering into that vast, enshrouded expanse of formerly manicured grounds, the layout of which she knew nothing about. But she'd got him on the run. That was all she needed to know.

She grabbed up a trowel, one of the other fallen tools, flinging it hard at the kitchen window, hopeful that any shattering impact would alert the others, and indeed she heard glass exploding as she went scampering through the mist-filled archway in pursuit.

◆ ◆ ◆

In addition to Lottie equipping herself with the jewel-hilted dagger, and Martha choosing the poker, Nick and Liz had also acquired weapons: Nick, the black-lacquered cane with the silver wolf's head with which Edgar Karnwood had inflicted a fatal blow to the skull of his lycanthropic son in 1974's *Werewolf of Paris*; Liz with a Hitler Youth knife, which had played no part in any of

Karnwood's films, but which he'd brought home after his wartime service in 1946.

In all honesty none of them felt much safer, but it seemed more sensible to be armed than not. Roy, who'd had no option but to follow the herd – and had selected the machete with which the great man had dismembered so much red meat in *Malifique* (pork of course, for the close-up shots) – was the first to react when they heard the sound of breaking glass.

'What the hell now?' he said, spinning round.

'It's Freya,' Martha replied, sounding bored. 'Like all wannabes pretending they're something special, she doesn't like being found out.'

Roy glanced at the others. Liz was the first to respond. She shook her head. 'That wasn't someone having a tantrum.'

'I agree,' Nick said.

Again, they went together, hurrying across the hall and down the passage through the dining room to the kitchen, where the main window over the twin sinks had spiderwebbed with cracks and was bulging inward.

It was immediately obvious that whatever had done it had come from outside. But more important, the bolts were now drawn back on the kitchen door, the key still in the lock. Roy opened the door.

'She's gone outside alone,' he said disbelievingly. 'Christ . . . why do people insist on doing stupid things like this?'

'Probably on a "prove herself" kick,' Nick said, glancing at Martha, who pointedly looked away.

They stumbled outside together, tottering to a halt in the deserted yard, at which point they heard a distant cry. It was Freya, but there was no pain or anguish there.

'Roy! Nick!' she was calling. 'Get over here! I've got him on the run!'

'She's not seriously gone into the gardens?' Nick groaned.

He glanced at Roy, who seemed equally bemused. The obvious urge was to follow, and yet every molecule in their bodies was screaming at them to be more sensible, to hold back.

'What time is it?' Roy asked tensely.

'Ten to five,' Nick replied. 'Still a good two and a half hours to daylight.'

From somewhere closer, they heard Freya cry out again. *'I've got him, I've got him . . . quickly, help me!'*

That was too much. If they could end this torment here and now, it was too good a prospect to ignore. All five of them lurched forward together.

'Stay close,' Roy said, as they passed under the arch.

The mist beyond this point seemed as thick as hanging material. It obscured even the perilousness of their footing, the paving stones slimy with moss and rotted, dew-soaked leaves. Within moments of their entering the gardens, they ascended a flight of about ten steps on to a flatter area, where other paved paths led away. On their left a creaky old swing hung from a desiccated branch; on the right, a twisted, nymph-like figure, her faced eroded, stood on a stone plinth, strands of dead vegetation twisted all over her in a parasitic embrace. Somewhere ahead, Freya called out again.

'We're coming, Freya!' Lottie shouted back. 'We're coming! Tell us where you are.'

Another cry. Less coherent this time, and, confusingly, from what sounded like a different direction. That puzzled them, but they pushed forward, coming to a crossroads. Rank vegetation was massed on all sides of it, along with the gutted ruin of a garden shed.

'Are we really sure this is a good idea?' Liz said.

Roy glanced at her. A moment ago, he'd been keen; now he looked undecided.

They pivoted, staring into the murk.

Yet another cry sounded, this one almost unintelligible.

‘That way.’ Lottie pointed left.

‘You sure?’ Martha said doubtfully.

‘It was definitely that way,’ Lottie said.

‘If you’re sure.’ Roy hustled them along.

‘We’re coming, Freya!’ Lottie shouted. ‘Keep calling out, so we know where . . .’

‘And knock that on the head, yeah!’ Roy hissed at her.

She glanced round at him, her pale, round face looking oafish and frog-like in the gloom.

‘Don’t you get it, Lot?’ he said. ‘Every time you make a noise, you’re telling him where we are.’

‘I don’t want Freya to think she’s out here on her own.’

‘Freya came out here on her own purposely. Whatever happens, it’s on her.’

Lottie looked shaken to hear so unpalatable a truth.

‘We do what we can to find her,’ Roy said. ‘But we have to survive too . . .’

His words tailed off as he halted, staring past them. They all turned, seeing nothing.

‘Someone was there,’ he said slowly. ‘Watching us. About ten yards away. Just to the right of the path.’

Again, they stared, and again they saw no one and nothing.

‘Shiiit . . .’ Roy said slowly. Then he burst into action, charging pell-mell into the mist. ‘That was *him*. He’s over here.’

The others went too, and almost immediately, having veered off the main path, found themselves ascending a grassy slope, which was slippery with dew. On the next level they blundered across an overgrown lawn, and then were funnelled down a narrow entry between two ramshackle outbuildings. One possessed a window but the glass had gone, and the frame was filled with cobwebs and daggers of shattered wood. It was one of these latter that caught

Lottie by the knit of her jumper, yanking her backward. She fell on to her bottom.

Nick turned, saw her, and fought his way back past the others to help.

'I thought someone had grabbed me,' she stammered as he hoisted her to her feet.

'Come on,' he said simply. 'We've got to catch up with the rest.'

'Wait . . . I'm still caught.'

Frustrated because even at close quarters he could barely see a thing, and his own fingers were continually pierced by splinters as he fought to free the tangled threads, it took him an age to work her loose. When he did, they looked around, only to find that they were now alone.

'Oh my God,' Lottie breathed.

'This way,' Nick said. 'Hurry.'

They stumbled along the entry, but when they reached the end of it, a wall of blankness greeted them. If nothing else, they were back on a stone pathway of sorts. Again, it was cluttered with dead leaves, as were the meshes of bracken on either side. Nick strode swiftly along, Lottie following. They were travelling blind of course, and when they encountered turns and junctions, blundered this way and that more through instinct than logic.

'For God's sake,' Lottie said. The outline of her face had paled even more. 'Where are we? What are we doing here?'

'I wish I knew,' Nick muttered. He didn't want to say it out loud, but even if they decided right now to turn back, he wasn't sure he'd know the way.

◆ ◆ ◆

Freya knew the others were out here. She'd heard them calling to her. But when their caterwaul had abruptly ceased, she'd started wondering why.

After the initial thrill of the chase, common sense was reasserting itself.

This opponent of theirs was no stone jug. If nothing else, he'd be physically stronger than her. Had he run a little too easily?

She'd thought she was stalking the killer, but might it be the case that he was doing some stalking of his own? And all this time she'd been making it easier for him by shouting.

She clamped her mouth shut and tried to take stock of her surroundings.

She'd ascended two or three flights of steps since the chase began, following paths across ill-kept lawns and along several bowered walks, certain that someone was just ahead of her, running. But now she seemed to have entered a cul-de-sac between a trio of ancient greenhouses. The glass only remained in fang-like shards and their interiors were filled with a dense overgrowth of God knew what, though at this time of year it was visibly mottled and decaying.

Even then, she had the feeling she wasn't alone. Possibly because of the sudden faint rustling she thought she heard inside the nearest of the rotted structures.

Wary that she'd been led into a trap but determined to maintain the impression that she was a fearless crime fighter, she hefted the axe and approached its entrance, even leaning a little way into the vile, dripping leafage within. She heard nothing else at first, until the rustling sounded again and then came swiftly towards her.

She backed away . . . but nothing exploded out in pursuit.

Silence returned. There was no sound at all save for the faint pattering of dew.

Freya turned again, scanning her surroundings, eyes seeking to penetrate the mould-covered ruins of the other greenhouses. She clutched the axe to her chest, drawing as much reassurance from it as she was able. He'd definitely been concerned when he saw that weapon. She had to keep telling herself that. He was a man; nothing more. Which meant that he couldn't see any better in this murk than she could. Even if he knew the terrain, it would mostly be hidden to him; as a male, he'd still have the advantage of superior strength, but that was the only one.

'It's cat and mouse,' she said to herself. 'If nothing else, I can handle *that* . . .'

She walked back along the path, heading out of the cul-de-sac and turning left. This was a new route, which took her past the rear of the largest greenhouse. She glanced back constantly but never saw anyone. Ahead, meanwhile, she appeared to be advancing towards a high wall. There was a gateway in the middle of it, though seemingly with no gate. She halted, wary. The path led through the empty gap, which was surely the most ideal point for an ambush that she'd seen thus far.

At which moment, from somewhere behind, she heard a new sound. An odd, repeating squeak. Metallic, but aged and arthritic, and yet continuous.

She glanced back, seeing nothing, her hair prickling.

What in the seven hells is that?

Corroded metal possibly, turning very slowly? A set of wheels?

She pivoted three hundred and sixty degrees.

Where was it coming from?

The enshrouding fog was completely flummoxing. One minute, she thought the noise was in front of her. Then behind. Was it drawing closer or was she imagining that too?

The noise stopped again and she stood tingling, sweat-soaked despite the chill.

Behind her, the gap in the wall beckoned. She glanced at it, distracted.

The squeaking recommenced again. This time, it was somewhere to her left. Her eyes strained as she looked over there, slowly but surely identifying a humped shape encroaching on her. But then the squeaking stopped, and the shape, if it had ever existed at all, was gone.

Freya half-choked. Only now did she realise that she'd been holding her breath.

The next thing she heard, though, was suddenly very human: the fast approach of heavy feet. She twirled, hefting the axe again – just in time to see the shadowy shape lurching at her. With a scream, she swung the heavy blade over and down, putting every ounce of strength in her gym-toned body behind it.

If the first blow, which clove Roy's features entirely in two, didn't kill him, the second one, delivered to the rear of his skull by the paved path as he landed on it, surely would have. Either way, a second later, the big ex-cop lay motionless, arms outspread.

Initially, Freya was too appalled even to scream.

She tottered backward, hand clamped to mouth. The axe handle still jutted at an upward slant from the bloody, mangled mess of her fellow investigator's face.

She tried to call out for help but could only burble and blubber.

She never even saw the heavy spade that came swinging into view until it was too late.

Twenty-Five

When Freya's eyes flickered open, she had no initial clue where she was. The whole of her face hurt, as if she'd run into a brick wall. Her nose in particular stung so much that she could barely breathe through it. At least she could see, though her vision was dimmed by the ever-present mist. Her thinking was too sluggish to at first piece any of this together, though she could sense that she was on the move, draped on her back over some kind of miniature vehicle, its ancient wheels squeaking repeatedly.

She tried to speak but it came out a mumble, her lips gummed together with copper-flavoured glue. When she tried to force them apart with her tongue, several of her teeth wobbled.

Someone was behind her, she realised. Pushing her.

An ambulance man maybe? One of her colleagues, taking her to safety?

In truth, she knew he was neither of these things. But her limbs weren't obeying her any more, so she couldn't even react, let alone try to get off. Even struggling sent her giddy, in fact dizzy, spiralling her downward into distant black oblivion.

◆ ◆ ◆

'Nick!' Liz shouted.

Nick almost jumped out of his skin. He spun around.

She was working her way through the copse that he and Lottie had blundered into. 'Where is everyone?'

'How the bloody hell would I know?' he said. 'You prats ran off and left us.'

'Do you mind!' she snapped. 'It was Roy. He thought he saw someone, but we couldn't keep up with him.'

'Okay, so where's Martha?'

'I don't know. We got separated too.'

He shook his head. 'Liz, the one thing you try and do in this situation is stick together.'

'It's easier said than done. These gardens are a bloody maze. I've no idea which way is which.'

'How did you and Martha get separated?' Lottie asked.

'It was when I was running after Roy. I thought she was right behind me. But she clearly wasn't.'

'So . . . you just left her?'

'Lottie, I didn't even know I'd lost contact with her.'

Lottie looked at her strangely, and then at Nick, as if finally harbouring suspicions about these two as well.

'Oh, don't start that,' Liz said. 'If we were the killers, we could do *you* right now, couldn't we? Just jump all over you.'

'Thank you very much. That's a nice thought—'

'Let's just stop yapping for a minute,' Nick interrupted. They listened, thinking that for half a second or so, they could hear a distant metallic creaking, though it didn't last long, and after that they heard nothing else. He glanced at Liz again. 'Which way have you come from?'

She pointed to her rear. 'There's another paved path. Leads to a flimsy old wooden thing like a bandstand or summerhouse or something.'

'Summerhouse?' Lottie chuckled tiredly. 'Sounds so pleasant when you're slowly freezing to death.'

'You're not freezing to death, Lottie,' Liz said.

'Speak for yourself, my girl.' For the first time since they'd been here, Lottie had adopted a brusquer, more admonishing tone. 'You're young and fit. I'm old and plump. Just running around out here, my clothes are now wringing wet, and whatever you say, it's bloody cold.'

'Okay, I'm sorry,' Liz replied. 'But it's only two hours to sunrise. You can last that long, yeah?'

'I sincerely hope so.'

'If you can't, don't despair . . .' Nick watched the mist, his thoughts lingering on Simon Matlock, pinioned to the steering wheel of a speedboat as it went careering into a line of rocks, and Darius, face purple, eyes distended. 'There are worse ways to go . . .'

◆ ◆ ◆

Freya didn't regain anything close to consciousness for several minutes more. When she did, she realised that she was slumped in a wheelbarrow. Her face ached terribly, the whole front of her head throbbing, while her back was stiff and cramped, the hard metal edges digging into it. Her slow revival was partly due to the water dripping on to her from a jumble of wet and rotted leaves hanging overhead, but she wasn't fully able to make sense of things until a pair of strong, gloved hands seized her by the collar of her sweatshirt, lugging her backward and up. She landed on her back on what felt like a raised bed of soil.

She was barely able to speak, though any attempt to communicate with her captor was foiled anyway as another of those strong hands grabbed her by the chin, turning her face from side to side. It was too dark to see who and what he was, though the next thing she knew, her left arm had been pulled out and something like a cable tie used to bind its wrist to a metal frame. Only now, as the same was done with her other wrist, did her head clear and her fear start growing exponentially. A yelp burst from her lips, but she hadn't yet rediscovered the ability to kick out with her legs, and her left ankle was similarly fastened in place, followed by her right, leaving her spreadeagled and helpless.

'Pleethe,' she burbled, broken teeth rendering her words unintelligible. 'For Gothe thaake.'

The tall shape of her captor, which she could now just about distinguish, was moving back and forth on her left. Any actual details were indiscernible, but then she heard the *scriiitch* of a match, and a tiny tongue of flame was applied to a candle, which then was placed on a high shelf.

Freya's eyes adjusted quickly to the wavering yellow glow, and she was horrified beyond belief when the hefty figure came and looked down at her again. He was wearing a heavy waterproof coat with a shoulder-cape, and what she could only regard as a Guy Fawkes hat with its brim pulled low and a black feather in its band. Most terrifying of all, of course, were the ultra-realistic latex features of the long-deceased Edgar Karnwood, though in the guttering half-light, the eyes were empty, black sockets.

◆ ◆ ◆

Nick, Liz and Lottie were in the summerhouse when they heard the screech.

From the moment they'd stumbled on to it, the small structure hadn't promised much. It was open aspect: a low timber platform, circular, with a balustrade around it, and a tiled roof over the top, many sections of which had broken away. Its woodwork meanwhile was mouldy and riddled with fungus. Nick was unsure whether there'd ever been a sofa and chairs in here, or even a swing-seat, but still felt it was well-named as a "summerhouse" because it would have been pretty well unusable at any other time of year.

They each now manned a different viewpoint and were gazing out into grey anonymity when they first heard that heart-rending sound.

Nick thought of it as a screech rather than a scream, because a screech it undoubtedly was. It hung on the air for what seemed like eternity, before it was silenced.

They eyeballed each other nervously.

'Which way did that come from?' Liz finally asked.

Nick scanned the vapour behind him. 'This way, I think. I can't be sure, of course, but we can't be sure of anything, can we?'

Liz still looked prepared to investigate.

'Just wait,' Nick said, before she descended the steps to the dew-soaked grass. 'It seems obvious that what we heard just then was the sound of murder.' No one tried to argue. 'So, the question is . . . do you really want to go over there?'

'To intervene in a murder?' Liz replied. 'How can you doubt it?'

'Will we be intervening or will we just be picking up the pieces? Again? Or maybe setting ourselves up as the next target?'

'We're targets anyway,' Liz replied. 'So perhaps if we want to get through this night, we need to be a little more proactive.' She drew the Hitler Youth knife from its black leather scabbard, which she'd belted to her waist. 'It's not like we aren't armed as well.'

Nick chewed his lip. Then laid the silver wolf-headed cane across his shoulder and nodded.

They went down the steps, Lottie tagging worriedly behind, and headed across the grass. Strangely, he felt less uneasy now. Maybe it was down to some deep survival instinct, the same one Liz had just given voice to. They weren't bewildered or confused any more. They *knew* that someone was trying to kill them and were responding accordingly. Other certainties came alongside that. It didn't matter *why* their opponent was doing this. All that mattered now was emerging from this ordeal alive. They could discover the explanations for it later.

They came to another path.

'I don't suppose anyone recognises this?' Nick said.

No one did, but they took the path anyway, following it to the right. Twenty yards on, they halted again. Some distance to the left of them, across what looked like an extensive flower bed, though at present it was all bracken, they saw a dull, yellowish glow.

'Maybe it's the house?' Lottie said. She sounded hopeful about that.

'I'm not so sure,' Nick replied.

'Whichever, a light is a light.' Liz struck off towards it, her antique blade drawn and ready. 'It needs checking.'

They went with her, wading through the sodden bracken, Nick constantly scanning the mist behind. Ahead of them, a box-like outline emerged into view; what looked like a large but ancient greenhouse, many of its panes shattered. The light was clearly coming from inside, but filtered and refracted through a jungle of rank foliage.

Grimly, braced now for contact with the enemy, they advanced again. When they got close to the greenhouse, its wood and metalwork was scabrous, while the vegetation inside clearly hadn't seen a gardener's hand for years. They circled the exterior, listening intently but hearing nothing, constantly spying flickers of light from inside. When they rounded the second corner, they came to a single door standing open. It didn't look like the main entrance, rather a back exit, though this too was decayed and broken.

Nick indicated that he would go first, as his cane would give him extra reach. Liz didn't dispute this, but both women followed directly at his rear. There seemed little point in stealth now as they couldn't advance without the leafage rustling, so he struck out with massive, swiping strokes, chopping his way towards the light, which they quickly realised was a candle because there was a hint of smoke and a smell of wax. They sighted it on a high shelf, though there was little more than a stub.

It was what lay on its left that arrested all their attention.

Freya looked to have been laid flat on a horizontal rack, perhaps a raised flower bed. Her arms and legs were outspread, fastened tightly to the frame's edges with cable ties. But the real damage had been done elsewhere.

Lottie hadn't focused properly before she was already screaming.

Liz grabbed her, clamping a hand to her mouth, but the heavier woman fought free, screaming again and again and again.

Nick felt his gorge rise at the sight of the deep, parallel gouges torn left and right and up and down across the once beautiful features, at the left eyeball that had come entirely loose from its bony orbit, and the soft white throat, which now lay open to the windpipe, ravaged as though by the fangs of a wild animal.

As Liz hustled Lottie away, Nick tottered after them, halting only to vomit, before glancing back over his shoulder and seeing the sacrificial claw from *Last of the Leopard Men*, dangling with bloody tissue as it hung embedded, talons first, in a timber post.

Twenty-Six

Liz, Lottie and Nick fought their way through the rancid vegetation, finally leaving the greenhouse by its front entrance, and finding themselves in something like a cul-de-sac between other similar structures. Lottie was crying hysterically, Liz hanging on to her, as much to try and quieten her as comfort her.

Nick looked over his shoulder again, concerned that the killer might still be inside, lurking somewhere close by but unseen under foliage. Because if he was, would he be able to resist attacking again, when his opponents were so disoriented, so distressed, so horrified?

'Just . . . shut up, yeah?' he said, as the older woman continued to weep and moan. '*Lottie, shut the fuck up!*' That seemed to shock her out of her reverie. 'Give it a fucking rest! We all knew we were going to find someone dead.'

'But . . . we've got to get out of here,' she stuttered. 'We've got to get away . . .'

'That we agree on,' Liz replied, releasing her grip now that her charge was regaining a measure of control. 'Back to the house at least. We're sitting ducks out here.'

Nick mopped the sweat from his brow and raised his cane as he strode along a path leading out of the cul-de-sac, the two women stumbling behind. None of them so much as looked through the grimy windows of the other greenhouses. The matted leafage in there was all-concealing, but it would be too easy to imagine a pair of feral eyes gazing hypnotically back.

◆ ◆ ◆

It was no surprise to Martha that the others had contrived to leave her out here all alone.

What else could one really expect from a bunch of people who, while they might feign an investigative interest in murder, actually delved into it, seeking vicarious thrills? Of course, they weren't seeing it that way now, not when they too had been lined up for inclusion on some madman's butcher's bill. It was a supreme irony that it was all happening here, at this Palace of Pretend, once presided over by one of the most fearsome figures in recent British history, and yet at the same time, a fellow who'd never harmed a hair on anyone's head, much less tortured or murdered them for real. The thrill-seekers had gone to watch his films in their hundreds of thousands, wallowing delightedly in the horror because they knew they could go home afterwards in perfect safety and clear conscience. But this particular group had taken it so much further.

They'd be lucky if they could go home at all.

Not – if Martha was absolutely honest – that this was any consolation to her. Not now that she too was lost and wandering in the mist, constantly certain that someone was shadowing her just beyond the range of her vision.

She spun around several times as she walked, hefting her poker, at the same time painfully aware how pathetic that would look to a practised killer.

'Be sure I'll leave my mark on you,' she said aloud. But of course no one answered.

When she came in sight of a statue, she at first thought it was the nymph, which was located close to the main house's rear yard.

But there was no angled shape of a building looming in the mist behind it, no hint of lighted windows in the murk. And when she approached it more closely, the figure was a faun: humanoid, but with goat's legs and horns. It stood on a low plinth, and doubtless was drawn from the same classical tradition that had inspired whichever past owner had decorated the rest of the grounds with marble figures. Like the other one, it was sorely weathered, heavy with moss, its face rotted into a grotesque parody of humanity.

Peering past it, she didn't see a broad gateway with an arched iron trellis over the top but a much narrower entrance, also open and seemingly giving through to an arboured walk, the footway paved, hedges on either side, leafless boughs interlacing overhead. It didn't promise much, but Martha proceeded along it anyway, if for no other reason than it had to lead somewhere, but also because, at least here, danger could only threaten from in front or behind rather than from all around. Despite this of course, she was terrified, walking stiffly, continually glancing over her shoulder. Even here, in this enclosed space, the gloom had infiltrated, a thick veil of it drawing close behind her, as well as retreating only slowly in front. Every so often she would stop to listen. No sound ever came back to her.

At first, she couldn't understand how she wasn't able to hear the others. Even if they were all close together and speaking in normal tones, wouldn't their voices carry? But then, the academic in her advised that, no, they probably wouldn't, not in these climatic conditions.

At the end of the walk, she sensed that she'd entered a more open space. The hedge that had bordered the arbour on the right continued ahead, unbroken, but on the left, it ceased, the paved path suddenly splitting three ways, one lane continuing as it had, the other two cutting away to the left diagonally. When she traipsed along the middle one, she spotted formal arrangements of thorny stalks on either side of her. Rose beds maybe?

Was this a rose garden? That would explain the arboured walk leading into it, and the hedging along the sides. In other stately homes she had visited, rose gardens were often sectioned off from the rest of the grounds.

'Martha?' the voice said.

She stopped in her tracks, her heart beating so hard that she could feel it in her throat.

She glanced behind, and then to left and right. The wretched, roiling mist hid everything.

Where had the voice come from? Had she heard it at all? Could it have been a figment of her overwrought imagination? It had been muffled and dull, and yet it hadn't sounded as if someone had been calling to her. It had been more like a question.

She turned a full circle, seeing no one. Yes, the murk hid much, but there was no one even close to her. So, she *had* imagined it?

Or had it been one of the others, their voice somehow penetrating the night?

One thing was for sure: she wasn't calling back. Nor – and this felt like a wise precaution too – was she going to seek out the source.

He can't know who I am.

She continued along the path, halting at a point where a recess had been cut into the rose beds and a wooden bench inserted.

He can't know my name.

'Martha?'

It was nearer this time, and clearer, though not so clear that she could work out whose voice it was or even whether it was male or female. Again, she turned, hair prickling, cold sweat seeping down her back. Would it be safer to return the way she'd come?

Return to what? You don't even know which direction it came from.

The obvious temptation was to call out: 'Who are you? What do you want?'

Get real, girl . . . you know what he wants.

She forged on, constantly turning, the poker lofted above her shoulder, hoping against hope that if he was lurking somewhere close by, he'd see that she was armed.

Yes, because that's really going to scare him.

A few yards ahead, the path halted at another hedge and diverted right. Martha had no option but to follow it. She could hardly cut across the centre of the garden, unless she was happy to see her feet and lower legs torn by those ranks of thorny stalks. A few yards further, a wrought-iron gate stood in the hedge on her left. It was narrow, designed to admit one person at a time, and about six feet in height. She half-expected to find it padlocked closed, but it wasn't. She depressed the latch and it creaked open, but again, only the blankness of the mist lay beyond. The obvious thing was still to go through it, and search for the others. But maybe that was too obvious?

She wondered again about the muffled voice she'd thought she'd heard.

You didn't think it, darling. You definitely heard it.

She'd seen no one, but could that be because the voice had come from the other side of the hedge . . . where he was still waiting for her? But then, why would he do that? The gate was unlocked, so why not just come into the garden and attack there? None of this made sense.

Unless you consider that he might be having fun. Let's not pretend otherwise, eh? He's really enjoying himself.

Martha shut the gate and pressed on along the path, her poker pointed forward like a bayonet. At least she now knew the gate was behind her if she needed to beat a sudden retreat.

And then two things happened at once.

About ten yards ahead, another hedge blocked further access, the path turning a right-hand corner, though another bench was located there with what looked like several black bin-liners, all bulging with compost, occupying one end of it. At the same time, she thought she heard a shout. It wasn't from nearby, and it came at her like a whipcrack.

'Shut the fuck up!'

It wasn't the same voice she'd heard before, and there'd been a shrillness to it, a wildness, a panic. One of the others? It had to be.

'Martha?' the other voice said, a lot closer.

She swung back to her front, staring at the bench in the corner, where that pile of bulging bin-liners now unfolded itself upward as it rose on to two feet. He was taller than the average person, all in black, wearing some kind of broad-brimmed hat and a coat with a heavy shoulder-cape. In his gauntleted right fist, a blade glinted.

With a muted shriek, Martha spun back the way she'd come, promptly tripping over her feet and dealing stinging blows to both hands as she landed. Oblivious to the pain, she stumbled back upright and fled on, a pair of heavy feet thudding along the path behind her. She made it to the side-gate in a second or so. It was still closed.

In God's name, you stupid mare! Why didn't you leave it open?

She fiddled with the latch, which suddenly was stiff and slippery in her sweat-slick fingers, those feet coming right up behind her.

With a *clunk*, the latch lifted. Martha yanked the gate open, tottered through and then was hurrying over open, tussocky grass. Those heavy feet were still close – *thud, thud, thud* – coming at terrible speed. She tried to scream, but could scarcely draw in enough oxygen to breathe. And then she tripped again, over something lying in front of her. Falling heavily. This time her impact was cushioned by grass, but her head struck the ground rather than her hands, and Martha knew no more.

Twenty-Seven

'What was that?' Lottie hissed, grabbing both Nick and Liz and bringing them to a halt.

A metallic reverberation had sounded from somewhere ahead.

'Sounded like a gate clanking open,' Liz said. 'Or closed.'

'Hello?' Lottie called out.

Nick was about to hiss at her to be quiet, but on quick reflection, why would he? It could be the killer they'd heard, but that was a chance worth taking if it was Roy or Martha.

'Hello?' Lottie called a second time.

No one replied, but they all knew they'd heard a hard, sharp clatter of metal. Very likely a gate, but not the sound a gate made when you went through it calmly.

They advanced slowly, cautiously, weapons to the fore, and after forty yards, the mist cleared ahead of them, revealing another abhorrent scene.

Two bodies lay on the ground. Martha face down on the grass to the right side of the path. Much more gruesomely, Roy on the path itself, flat on his back, his machete discarded several feet away, his head divided down the middle by the hatchet that was embedded there. The claret puddle spreading sluggishly out on all sides was fantastically huge given that it had issued from one person. Martha, meanwhile, twitched and groaned.

'R-Roy!' Lottie stammered, her pale cheeks glistening with tears as she stood rigid. '*Roy!*'

Liz scurried forward. 'Martha's alive at least.'

Nick stood watching as Liz helped the casualty up and over on to her backside, where she sat blinking and muttering. There was grass and soil in the hair over her left temple. 'My . . . God,' she said only semi-coherently.

'Where are you hurt?' Lottie asked, choking back her tears and going over to assist.

'I hit my head, I think . . .' Then Martha's eyes opened properly, bulging like duck eggs when she set them on Roy, and in particular, on the axe. 'Oh, sweet Jesus . . .' With Lottie's help, she struggled wildly to her feet. '*Sweet Jesus in heaven!*'

'Yeah,' Nick said, hefting his cane to his shoulder. 'Roy seems to have come off considerably worse than you.'

'I don't . . . I don't . . .' Martha could only shake her head in horror, before the meaning of his words struck home. She glared at him. 'Excuse me, what the devil do you mean by that?'

'Good Lord, Nick!' Lottie said. 'You've seen that Martha's been hurt?'

'Yeah, but Roy's been murdered,' he retorted. 'And the murder weapon's still here.'

'Which Martha wasn't carrying,' Lottie pointed out.

'Not when she left our company, maybe.'

'For God's sake, everyone!' Liz put in sharply. 'Roy's lying here dead, and we're squabbling like children.'

Martha pulled free of Lottie's grasp and wobbled over to look at the corpse. Up close, she flinched at the hideousness of it. Nick watched her carefully. She seemed to be genuinely distressed, but it was difficult to be sure on a night like this.

'Martha, let me look at that,' Liz said, indicating her head injury. Reluctantly, Martha bowed, allowing Liz to pick through her hair. Liz did so, then backed away. 'Just a bump on the scalp.'

'Exactly,' Nick said. 'A bump. Nothing more.'

'What happened?' Liz asked her.

Martha looked confused. 'Someone chased me. I thought it was the killer. It must have been.'

'And then you met Roy?' Lottie asked, bewildered.

'Not so much met him as tripped over him. Must've knocked myself out.'

Nick still couldn't keep the scepticism from his voice. 'And for that reason the killer spared you?'

'I don't know.' Martha glared at him again. 'How could I know?'

'Isn't it more likely the killer spared her because he heard us coming?' Lottie asked. 'Heard us calling out?'

Nick couldn't dispute that possibility, but at present he was struggling to get past the fact they'd found Martha here with the dead Roy, he with his head chopped like a grapefruit, she suffering only mild concussion.

'Where did he chase you from?' Liz asked.

Martha glanced leftward. 'A kind of rose garden. Fifty or so yards that way. I came out of it through an iron gate.'

'A gate?' Liz glanced at Nick.

'That doesn't bloody mean anything, and you know it,' he replied, brandishing the cane as though he might take a swipe at someone anyway.

'You seem to be on a hair trigger, Nick.' Martha eyed the cane. 'Something got your blood up?'

Grudgingly, he lowered the weapon. 'I just . . . I . . .'

'Freya's dead too,' Liz explained. 'We just found her in a greenhouse.'

Martha nodded, perhaps having anticipated something like that.

'You don't seem shocked,' Nick said.

'Are we still shockable?' she asked him.

'Look, Martha . . . we've just found you with Roy's body.'

'Maybe I should be suspicious when you say you found Freya?'

'We *did* find her,' Lottie asserted. 'You can't point the finger at us, Martha. We were all three of us together at the time.'

'Maybe there are three killers?'

Lottie looked appalled. 'You surely don't believe that?'

'You were all pretty quick to leave me alone out here,' Martha said accusingly.

'We got split up by accident,' Lottie retorted. 'There was nothing deliberate about it.'

'So you say.' Martha smiled without humour.

'The problem is, Martha,' Nick cut in, 'like Freya said, you patently hate everyone here. If any of us *is* involved in these crimes, you'd be an obvious candidate with or without a motive.'

'You're saying I could have got the drop on a big man like Roy Southerby?'

'In restricted visibility, maybe.'

'*And* Freya? Both of whom were considerably younger than me.'

'Freya was a bored thirty-something. She might have thought she was Mrs Peel but I'm sure she was actually a long way from that—'

'For God's sake!' Liz interrupted. 'Whoever Freya chased out here, Martha was with us at the time. And let's not get too hung up on this idea that one of us has teamed up with a killer.' She glanced at Martha. 'If that was the case, why would she have given herself away by acting like a bitch all weekend?'

'Thanks for that vote of confidence,' Martha replied.

'My pleasure.' Liz made to walk away. 'Why don't we just get back to the house, before we end up murdering each other without needing a serial killer to do it for us?' She glanced at Martha again. 'Which way did you say you'd come from?'

Again, Martha pointed to the left.

Liz nodded and pointed in a different direction. 'Well, we came that way.' She turned about-face. 'Which leaves this way.'

She started walking, the others stumbling to follow, and a short distance later, the paved pathway became a flight of stone steps.

Eyes still fixed on the encircling mist, they went down it.

'If nothing else, you're a piece of work,' Nick told Martha.

'Should I be flattered or offended?' she replied.

'How about neither? What I mean is you're a real conundrum.'

'A conundrum? I see.'

They went down another set of steps.

'Ever since we've been running the Murder Tour, we've been acutely aware it could easily become a fun day out for a bunch of people who are simply weird and get off on grotesque things,' Nick added.

'Never that, surely?' Martha said.

'So, believe it or not, each time we sign people up, we do due diligence on them. We don't want to get into the papers for the wrong reasons.'

'Diligence?' Lottie's voice briefly turned brittle as a tall figure ghosted towards them, only to reveal itself as the statue of the nymph.

'It's not difficult, Lottie,' he replied. 'We go online. Everyone has an online presence these days. Yes, even you. A vicar who took early retirement. We didn't know about your friend, of course. We don't dig too deeply. That would be intrusive.'

'A rule you presumably discarded in my case,' Martha said. 'Because no matter how deeply you dug, you couldn't find anything about me?'

'Which seems suspicious under the circs, I'm sure you'll admit,' Nick said. 'Doubly so given that *you've* clearly researched everyone else here.'

'Surely, what's really suspicious,' Martha said, 'is that, knowing all this, you still let me come along? Or did you maybe disagree on the matter?'

'We discussed it,' Liz admitted as they descended the last set of steps. 'But our final position was what harm could a middle-aged woman do? Just because we didn't know about her, why deprive her?'

'How generous of you.'

'So, perhaps help us out, eh?' Nick said. 'Who are you, Martha? And if you hate the ground the rest of us walk on so much, why are you even here? And don't obfuscate. Try giving us a straight answer.'

'A straight answer?' Briefly, Martha was distracted by the glow of the house lights blossoming through the fog. 'In terms you'll understand? Okay. Fuck you, Nick. You've no right to interrogate me.'

'For heaven's sake, Martha!' Lottie protested. 'Try to help us out.'

'Oh, Lottie . . . sweet Jesus! What in God's name are *you* doing on this tour? I mean, these two are blatant grifters. It's a pathetic reason, but at least it's a reason. I can't begin to wonder what yours might be . . .'

'I thought we agreed to stop obfuscating,' Nick cut in.

'We agreed nothing. So don't bother asking me any more questions.'

'They're only the same questions the police will ask,' Lottie said.

'Fine. Let them. They'll be questioning all of us, in case you hadn't realised. And Messrs Thornwood and O'Hara will have a lot more answers to provide than me.'

Before anyone could reply, they passed through the archway into the kitchen yard. The back door stood ajar, as they'd left it. Lottie and Martha both went gratefully inside. As Nick made to follow, Liz stopped him.

'So, is it Martha?' she asked.

He blew out long and hard. In truth, he didn't think it was, but a range of frantic thoughts had assailed him since they'd found Roy's body. About a maniac killer often being the last person you'd expect. About survival now depending on their finding explanations for every anomaly. About no stone remaining unturned.

'The fact she seems hell-bent on pissing everyone off shouldn't be a red flag on its own,' he said. 'But we've just had two more murders, and she's the only one among us whose recent movements can't be accounted for. And even then, she's refusing to answer questions. You think that's okay?'

'She's hurt,' Liz pointed out.

'It's not hard to do that to yourself if it's part of your cover story.'

'Just keep your cool, all right?'

'There'll be no one here who's cooler than me, I promise.' Nick went in through the kitchen and dining room, and into the main hall, where Lottie was now standing in front of the fire, and Martha, having apparently poured herself a glass of orange juice, was getting comfortable on a chair alongside the sideboard cabinet, its back to the staircase.

She might be 'a bitch', as Liz had called her, but she didn't *look* threatening. She'd even taken the fire poker from her belt and laid it on the sideboard next to her.

'Martha, look.' He walked over and stood in front of her. 'You make a fair point. We're all in this together, and firing accusations here, there and everywhere isn't helping.'

She regarded him coolly, sipping her juice. 'I'm not sure I actually said that.'

'Whether you did or didn't, we need to stick together. So . . .' He offered a hand. 'Will you accept my apology?'

Her nose twitched, as if mere contact with Nick's paw might infect her somehow. But then she sighed, reached out and took it.

At which point, Nick produced a pair of heavy steel handcuffs from the back pocket of his jeans, snapped one bracelet on to her wrist, and shoving her right arm up above her head, clamped the other to a staircase spindle. Before she could even react, he'd grabbed the poker and thrown it further along the sideboard out of her reach.

'What the hell's this?' Martha yelled, yanking on the cuff but without result.

Nick regarded her with a thin smile. 'This? Or rather *these* . . . they're part of the Inspector Aberline outfit. From down in the Costume Vault. Edgar Karnwood wore it in *Murder Most Foul.* I thought they might come in useful when I saw them.'

'Are you out of your mind?' she hissed. 'Unlock these cuffs at once.'

'I can't. The key's downstairs somewhere.'

Martha yanked furiously on the aged cuffs, but they were tight and solid. At first glance, they certainly resembled something a Victorian copper would carry: heavy and brutish, more like manacles. The spindle to which they were attached was equally unyielding, a thick oaken stave fixed seamlessly into both its slanted base and the banister above it.

Liz, having stayed behind to lock the kitchen door and check that the window was mostly still intact, now entered the hall. She stopped in her tracks. 'Nick, what have you done?'

'Nothing controversial,' he replied. 'Martha is now an official suspect. If she won't say anything to divest us of that view, we've got no better option than to keep her locked up.'

'Nick Thornwood!' Martha choked. 'You are a stupid child.'

'Maybe, but I've got the better of you, haven't I? So, come on . . . let's have it. Who are you really? And what are you doing here?'

'This is assault.'

'Least of my problems at present.'

'And probably false imprisonment. And that usually carries a jail sentence.'

Nick shrugged again. 'I've got to live to go to jail. I feel there's more chance that'll happen if you're cuffed.'

The angry silence stretched between them like taut elastic.

Lottie had also now come over. 'Nick, I know you and Roy had got friendly, but come on . . . we can't do this to her.'

Nick shrugged. 'Feel free to go downstairs and look for the key. But you'll be on your own.'

'Nick,' Liz said, 'I know you think Martha showed you up, but this woman has been equally rude to all of us . . .'

'Then stop listening to her and start thinking!' he retorted. '*This woman* is patently no true crime fan, no dark tourist, no gore hound . . . and yet she coughed up four hundred quid to come on the Long, Dark Weekend. It's time she told us why.' He swung back to the captive. 'And if you don't, Martha, you'll be sitting here, chained up, until the police arrive.'

'Or the killer.' She glowered at him. 'Won't look great for you if it's the latter, eh?'

Twenty-Eight

'You're seriously not going to let me out of this thing?' Martha said.

'Not while you're a potential threat to us,' Nick replied. 'And you're exactly that until we know more about you.'

The stare she gave him was heavy with contempt. She turned to Liz and Lottie. 'You know, not everyone lives their life in the glare of the internet. We don't all feel a juvenile need to post every little detail about ourselves online in some vain hope it will bring us to the attention of the entire world.' She fixed on Nick again. 'Has it not yet occurred to you that I could just be a completely normal person who happens to value her privacy?'

'It has, yeah,' he said. 'But that still doesn't explain why you won't tell us about it.'

Martha glanced at Liz. 'You can't talk him out of this nonsense?'

Liz's gaze wavered between the pair of them. 'I'm sorry, Martha. He may have a point. Can't you at least do as he asks?'

Martha switched her attention to Lottie, who visibly shuddered.

'Don't look at me,' the ex-cleric said. 'I'm not going down to that cellar on my own. It's scary enough without some killer wandering around.'

Martha pulled on her steel cuff one more time, to no avail. She sighed. 'Well, you were bound to find out at some point, I suppose. And at least this way I'll be here to see the looks on your faces when you do . . .' She regarded them defiantly. 'To start with, my name's not Martha Lloyd. It's Millie Anderton.' She'd clearly expected some kind of reaction to this, and looked baffled when she didn't receive one. 'That name genuinely doesn't ring a bell?'

Liz glanced at Nick. 'Sounds vaguely familiar.'

'Dear God!' Martha, whose real name was Millie, blurted. 'You really are unbelievable . . . though I suppose it shouldn't surprise me. I mean, a pair of millennial buffoons like you two can't even comprehend that someone might exist who doesn't want to post their life story online for the rest of mankind to salivate over, so someone with so little respect for themselves is unlikely to have any respect for others. But seriously . . . do you really live in a moral vacuum or is there simply nothing at all behind those blank goldfish expressions?'

'Insulting us is hardly going to get you loose from those cuffs,' Nick said.

'Why is that name supposed to be familiar?' Lottie asked.

'Jesus wept!' Millie exploded. 'My husband was Harry Anderton.'

'Oh . . . *shit!*' Liz slapped a hand to her forehead.

'Yes, "oh shit" indeed,' Millie scoffed. 'One of you finally gets it.'

'Harry Anderton . . . who was Travis Monkton's fourth victim?' Nick said, incredulous.

'And the first man Monkton is known to have killed,' Millie said, her eyes as hard as nails. 'For God's sake, you considered that so important that you were telling us all about it on the way to Satan's Meadow.'

'He was slipped some kind of drug while he was sitting in a pub near Inglewhite, wasn't he?'

Millie shrugged wearily, as if simply thinking about it wore her out. 'The police checked the pub's security cameras, but they weren't able to identify the exact moment when it happened. Or who it was who did it. If they had, they might have saved the lives of five additional victims.' She blew out a long, sad breath. 'My poor Harry wasn't even useful in death.'

'I'm still not sure why you hate *us*,' Nick said. 'We had nothing to do with it.'

'Nothing to do with it?' She gaped in disbelief. 'You sound like one of the children I used to deal with as a teacher. The ones who stood around cheering and laughing when there was a fight in the yard. They didn't start it, they weren't joining in, so they genuinely believed it was nothing to do with them . . . even though they were blatantly encouraging it. Don't you understand? This whole Murder Tour thing is an obscenity. You've made money out of my family's prolonged pain and suffering. And now, with these extended weekend tours, you aim to expand the business.'

'Travis Monkton is only one of a number of murderers whose activities we cover . . .'

'Travis Monkton is the star of your show, and don't you dare deny it! Especially this weekend. First, we had Satan's Meadow. Then we had that appalling auction for the painting.'

'Millie . . . these crimes happened,' Liz said. 'We can't ignore them, or pretend that your husband wasn't murdered. I'm sorry about that, though. I genuinely and truly am . . .'

'Yes, you're so sorry that you stood idly by while these vultures – I'm sorry, Lottie, but I include *you* in that – picked over the murder site with devilish glee . . .'

Even Nick was discomforted by that thought. The poor woman having to bite her tongue while the rest of them enjoyed their time at the scene of her husband's torturous death.

'My poor Harry,' Millie said. 'It wasn't as if he was a particularly strong bloke to start with, but to go through all that mental anguish thanks to the financial errors he made. And then to suffer the agonies of hell in the hands of some maniac! And you let these people walk around and take photographs, talking about it excitedly, as if it was one of Edgar Karnwood's films rather than something that really happened.'

'I think we can understand now why you're so upset,' Liz said, adding pointedly: 'Can't we, Nick?'

'Yeah, sure,' he said. 'But I still don't get why you're here. I'd have thought you'd want to be a million miles from the place where your husband died.'

Millie smiled thinly. 'I could hardly expose you if I was miles away, could I?' She regarded them carefully, watching for their reactions. 'You see, I have two purposes on this tour, Mr Thornwood . . . Miss O'Hara: firstly, to experience for myself the sheer nastiness of what you've been doing; hearsay wouldn't cut it. And secondly, to report my findings to the press, thus publicly disgracing you two as the traffickers in human misery you undoubtedly are.' She lugged on her handcuff again, just once, as if to check whether, by some miracle, it had loosened on its own. 'There were limits to this proposed revenge, of course. I never intended to do more than ruin your business. But now it seems someone else has decided to take it several steps further.'

She averted her eyes, as if she'd finally said enough.

'Nick, we have to let her go right now,' Liz said with quiet urgency.

He led her aside. 'You sure about that? She's hardly our friend. In fact, she's just given us a damn good reason why she might be the murderer, or at least in league with him.'

'And would I have told you all that if I was?' Millie shouted over.

They glanced back at her. Her hearing was clearly in tip-top condition.

'I could easily have made up some lie,' she added. 'Told you I was technophobic or dyslexic or anything else that might have given me problems posting my day-to-day life online. The truth is that, with all these other pressures, it's been too difficult keeping my feelings secret. Yes, I have been a mean and nasty bitch with you all. But that was the only way I could vent the ill-feeling that's been bottling up inside me all weekend.'

'Harbouring anger like that can become very self-destructive,' Lottie said.

Millie rolled her eyes. 'Spare me the sermon, Reverend Gray. I already believe in God and heavenly justice. Though sometimes I wonder why. Harry and I didn't exactly have an easy life. A mixed-race couple growing up in the north of England at a time when it was almost unknown. Then our financial troubles . . . he was an awful businessman, I'm afraid, and then the whole thing ending the way it did. But even after all that, nothing I've done here is illegal or even sinful.'

'Nick!' Liz said again. 'We've got to get her out of that cuff.'

Nick's thoughts meanwhile were racing into very uncomfortable territory. 'Suppose there's someone else who feels the same way? But they're less inclined to obey the law?'

She held him with a wide-eyed gaze. 'Exactly.'

It seemed incredible. All night they'd bickered and deliberated over the varied and increasingly unlikely reasons why someone might want to be doing this. And yet one highly possible answer had been sitting right under their noses.

'Nick,' Liz said again. 'We need everyone who can fight to be able to do it.'

Nick swung back to face the prisoner. 'There's no one else you've mentioned this to? Someone who's maybe of a similar mind to you, but perhaps a bit more . . .'

'A bit more insane?' Millie yanked hard on her shackle. 'You think I would? I've already explained to you, I'm very keen on my privacy. Why in God's name would I share something like this with someone who's potentially unstable?'

Nick glanced again at Liz.

'Go and get the key, yeah?' she said.

He moved off towards the cellar door.

'Lottie, you'd better go with him,' she added.

Lottie looked shocked. 'Down to the cellar?'

'I'm afraid so.'

'But the kitchen door was open all the time we were in the gardens. Our man could easily have sneaked back in here.'

'No one should go anywhere alone,' Liz said. 'Surely you can see the wisdom of that?'

Lottie still looked unhappy. 'Can't I stay here with Millie?'

Millie held up her handcuff. 'If you're attacked up here, I won't be able to help you.'

'It'll only take a couple of minutes,' Nick said, hovering near the cellar door.

'If you insist.' Lottie trudged over to him.

'You're still armed?' he asked her.

'Yes.' She examined her jewel-hilted dagger ruefully. 'But much good I'll be. I've never been in a real fight before in my life, never mind a knife fight.'

Twenty-Nine

'Maybe it would be better to leave her chained up,' Lottie said, following Nick down the cellar stairs. 'I mean, it's quarter to six. It'll be daylight in the next hour and a half.'

'An hour and a half can be a long time when you're under attack,' he said over his shoulder.

'Well, if we need to, the rest of us can protect her.'

'And if we're not able to for any reason? And she dies? We'll be complicit.'

'*We'll* be complicit?'

'All right, *I'll* be complicit. Don't worry, I know it was a stupid thing to do.'

'I'm sorry, I wasn't trying to apportion blame . . .'

He continued down. 'Let's just find this key, eh?'

They reached the foot of the stairs and halted to listen.

'Why do I get the feeling you don't sound optimistic about that?' Lottie wondered.

Nick ventured forward. 'Because those cuffs, while they work well enough, are part of a costume from fifty years ago. Who knows if there's still a key? Who knows if there was ever a key?'

'My God,' she said.

'Probably. But no one else.'

◆ ◆ ◆

'I'm sorry Nick did that to you,' Liz said, stepping back again having unsuccessfully examined the handcuff that was fastened to the solid oak spindle. 'That was what my Bournemouth FC-loving dad would refer to as "dumb football".'

'Well, that's the problem in one, isn't it, Liz?' Millie tried to get comfortable in her chair, though with her right hand clamped above and behind her shoulder, it clearly wasn't easy. 'This whole thing's just a game to you people. Even now, with the bodies piling up.'

'That really isn't fair, you know. No one was supposed to get hurt.'

'Oh, I'm sure they weren't. But this Murder Tour thing could only ever have happened in the moral void that is Britain today. There were always going to be consequences.'

Liz regarded her carefully. 'You don't believe there are positives to be gained from informing everyday people about the realities of the world? Educating them on the matter of—'

'Blood, death and torture?' Millie interrupted. 'Don't kid yourself. All you're selling here is graphic real-life horror, packaged up for people who are sick in the head. I mean, Christ almighty . . . Michael Caruso, a real murderer, doing a meet-and-greet on your behalf? How crass is that? I'm sorry, Liz, but you people who revel in atrocities are no better than those who commit them. That said, *you* ought to have a different take by now. You've seen the real face of murder up close. Though in truth, it's probably too late to learn the lessons of it. I sincerely doubt this particular killer will let any of us live.'

◆ ◆ ◆

'Damn, it's not here.'

Nick had gone through every pocket of the Victorian-era detective costume, so neatly suspended from a hanger in one corner of the main compartment down in the Costume Vault. He'd first taken the handcuffs from a low table alongside it. The other items were still there: the truncheon, the whistle on its chain, the leather-clad notebook.

But there was no sign of a key.

A few yards away, despite everything else, Lottie still seemed fascinated by the range of flamboyant outfits on show here. In particular something that looked as if it should be worn by a latter-day musketeer. A firelock pistol was shoved into one side of its belt and a basket-hilted sabre into the other, while a series of framed stills on the wall next to it, depicting bound peasant women being led to the gallows, indicated that this was a relic from 1969's *The Witch Hunters*. The only thing missing in this case was the witch-hunter-in-chief's hat. After so many years in storage, many of these exhibits were bound to be incomplete.

'So, what do we do?' she asked.

At first, Nick was unsure, but then he had a thought. 'I could have a rummage in that toolbox we saw on the washing machine near the back door. See if we can find a saw or something.'

'Cut through the spindle on the staircase, you mean?'

'Feels like our best option.'

Lottie nodded unhappily. That section of the cellars down by the back door was mostly disused and only partially lit. She went to the doorway, gazing into the shadows at the corridor's far end.

'You wait here, if you want,' he said. 'Where all the lights are working. Won't take me a minute. I'll bring the toolbox back with me.'

'No thank you. I could be waiting on my own for ages. I'll come too.'

Nick appraised her. She was beyond frightened by now. All of them were. They'd passed through fear into that numb, nerveless state that any animal under constant threat gradually adjusts to; still on a hair trigger, ready to respond with fight or flight, but thinking fast and clearly.

'Stick close behind me, yeah?'

'Don't you worry, young man.'

Young man, he thought as they shuffled along the passage. Not so much a term of endearment or even recognition; more a challenge. As in: *You're the youngest, the fit one, the strong one. If someone comes for me, they'll have to get through you first.*

Nick felt fresh sweat on his brow. He'd never been much of a fighter. He knew that he *could* fight if his life depended on it. It was that animal instinct again. Any creature could fight. The question was could he fight well? Or at least well enough.

Up ahead, the shadows waited.

◆ ◆ ◆

'Can I get you something to eat?' Liz said. 'There's plenty left in the dining room.'

Millie gave her a disbelieving stare. 'You can eat at a time like this?'

'A glass of water maybe?'

'I'm fine, thank you.' Again, all Liz could do was stand there and wait. Millie watched her with interest. 'If we do survive this, how are you and Nick going to explain yourselves to the authorities? I mean, even if there hadn't been a maniac out here . . . marooning us in the middle of nowhere, swanning around in a location you hadn't examined, with no means of contacting the outside world . . .'

'We didn't know our phones were going to be stolen,' Liz countered. 'We didn't know we'd have no access to Simon Matlock's vehicle.'

'Dear me, Elizabeth. First of all . . . when you're playing with people's lives, you need to consider every possibility. But I suspect that wouldn't have worked with a dark-tourism gig. I mean, everyone being safe from the outset? Kind of defeats the object?'

'Millie, we're not the only people providing this kind of service.'

'Service?'

'It's not even new. Legions of people visit the Auschwitz-Birkenau site in Poland and the genocide museums in Cambodia.'

'For God's sake, Liz. Those are internationally funded heritage sites, not just commercial enterprises.'

'Chambers of horrors then. Dungeons and torture rooms preserved in medieval castles. Hell, up until the Russian invasion of Ukraine, Western tourists paid big bucks to visit Chernobyl. You consider it weird and distasteful, but whatever curious itch people have, there are plenty of companies aside from ours who'll accept money to scratch it.'

'The problem comes, Liz, when you're doing it at the expense of those still living.'

'I told you no one was supposed to get—'

'That doesn't matter! I *was* hurt.' Millie's voice almost cracked. 'Ultimately though, I'm still going to have the last laugh. Even if I die tonight, even if we all die, the outrage that is your Murder Tour will be fully exposed, because whatever happens, news about *this* weekend is going to travel far and wide.'

◆ ◆ ◆

There was perhaps thirty yards of passage between Nick and Lottie when sudden blackness engulfed them. The reality was there hadn't been much light in this part of the basement to begin with, the little there was seeping around several corners at their rear. Needless to say, they'd come the wrong way repeatedly, each time their chosen route leading to a bare stone wall – in one case with a high letterbox-shaped window in the upper part of it, the window thick with cobwebs and blotted out on the other side by autumn leaves. The poor lighting was the main reason Lottie was now lagging behind, though it was also partly on Nick's instruction. He was equally uneasy, mainly due to the various dark entrances they had to pass.

But when *all* the lights went out it was a moment of pure terror.

Lottie screamed, and threw herself to the left-hand wall, hoping to flatten herself against the bricks, though it wasn't clear to her how that might provide protection. As it was, she toppled through one of those unlit doorways and found herself in the tomb-like atmosphere of an empty cellar room. She spun around, helpless, and then spied a faint hint of light. It was another letterbox window, perhaps twenty yards away, and again high up, though in this case with no shrouding of leaves on the other side. The faint hint of ambient light that encircled the house from the lamps at the front strained through it, providing a modicum of luminescence.

She steadied herself and was about to call out for Nick, who couldn't be far away, when suddenly, because she'd changed position slightly, the head and shoulders of a tall man shifted into view in the room, directly in front of that flat rectangle of milk-pale light.

Lottie's lips locked; her breath caught in her chest. Nick's name froze in her throat.

The figure didn't move. Just regarded her in stony, studied silence.

Thirty

Was it possible that he didn't know she was here?

Lottie disregarded that hopeful consideration almost as soon as it occurred to her.

Of course he knew. He'd known where she'd been all along. Good Lord, he'd been waiting in here while they were blundering around the corridors, getting lost. There was no point pretending otherwise.

'Why . . . why are you doing this?' she said softly. 'What have we ever done to you?'

Still there was no reply and no movement.

'There's no need for this. We're not your enemies. We're sorry if we've stumbled into something that's got nothing to do with us. But I assure you, there's no reason why you can't allow us to leave. None of us who are left have seen your face.'

Good God, woman. Meaningless babble. Simpering cowardice. Weren't you once a warrior of God, a fighter for right against wrong?

'Please,' she said. 'I'm sure if you try hard enough you can forgive whatever transgression you imagine we've . . .'

Her words slowly failed her.

Neither sympathy nor empathy nor pity of any sort existed within that motionless, implacable silhouette.

There was only hatred. And homicidal rage.

'Nick!' Lottie whimpered, darting to the right. She was certain that was where the entrance led back into the corridor, only to rebound from the bare brick wall. Her nose, clearly broken, immediately began gushing blood.

She gasped and choked, but threw herself back, finding the wall again, slapping up and down with the flats of her hands. Their adversary was right behind her, she was sure. Then her left hand encountered open space . . .

'Nick!' she squealed, toppling through the gap, only to be grabbed, an arm encircling her body.

'No!' she screamed. 'Please, no!'

'Christ's sake, Lottie . . . what the hell are you doing?' Nick hissed.

'Nick . . . Nick, oh my God, Nick. He's in there. He's in that room.'

◆ ◆ ◆

'I'm just saying that you didn't need to hit Nick with such a low blow,' Liz said. 'I mean about his scriptwriting.'

Millie smirked. 'Or lack of it.'

'And in front of everyone else.'

'No further disrespect intended, Liz, but I think your partner's non-existent movie career is the last thing anyone will remember about tonight.'

Liz regarded her carefully. She knew Nick would be vexed that she was defending him like this, because he'd be ashamed that she felt he needed it. But that was the difference between them. Liz had always been blunter and more forceful in her dealings with people, whereas Nick tried to let slights and mistreatment wash over him, and not atypically, never even succeeded at that.

'You researched him till you found out where he was most vulnerable, didn't you?' she said.

'I made it my business to find out all about you people. It was easy enough. Looked you all up online on the first night, when I knew who I was on the trip with. But Nick was the easiest. I only had to go on IMDb . . . where he barely figures at all.'

'And you went straight for it. The first time, he rode it out, so you went for it a second time.'

'Gosh!' The woman in the chair feigned horror. 'I'm so sorry if I've ruined the false narrative he's been running that he's some kind of success story.'

'Ruining things for people is what you do, isn't it, Millie? Or at least, it's what you seem to do now. You've hardly spoken kindly about your own husband.'

For the first time, the normally belligerent Millie wasn't ready with a sharp response.

'I guess that was quite important to you, having religious beliefs,' Liz added. 'That Harry was your *husband* rather than your partner. But that still doesn't give you the right to speak badly of him just because he didn't give you a gold-plated lifestyle.'

Millie was visibly stung. 'How dare you!'

'Sorry,' Liz said, 'but I've got to get my response ready for when the press come calling. How does this sound: "Tragic widow wasn't best pleased with us. But from what I heard and saw, she's been hard to please all her life" . . .'

Before further insults could be exchanged, there was an echoing *clunk* of woodwork from the far end of the hall. They turned and looked, assuming the others were returning from the cellar, only to suddenly notice that the plinth near the front door, where the Madame Tussauds mannequin had previously perched, was now empty. That was when they sensed movement in the hall's north-west corner, where what looked like the mannequin had just come up through the cellar door.

◆ ◆ ◆

Nick only needed a fleeting glimpse of the head and shoulders framed in the window to take a full, two-handed swing with his wolf-headed cane. The impact was ferocious, the *crack* echoing all around the room.

Immediately, a heavy shape fell full-length to the floor.

And then . . . nothing. Silence.

Nick ventured forward and, though blinded by near-complete darkness, struck downward over and over. The first blow bounced from the concrete, sending an agonising jolt through his shoulders and down his spine, but the second one hit the target solidly, as did the third and fourth. Of course, body shots were never going to be enough.

He needed to put this bastard down permanently, and so stalked along the length of the fallen form, striking at it with massive, overarching blows, driving the silver wolf-head deep into the torso of his prey, and then suddenly landing one on the prone figure's head, which yielded with another sharp *crack*.

'Hell!' Nick breathed, stepping backward, pinpricked all over with sweat.

Had he . . . ?

It had sounded great in his mind. *We need to put this bastard down.*

But there was nothing like the breaking of human bone to put paid to bravado.

'Nick,' Lottie said from behind. 'Nick, are you all right?'

'Hell's bells,' he muttered. 'I didn't mean to . . .'

There was no doubt that he was a little bit angrier at present than was healthy. Strange how scorn and belittlement could fire you up even more than a killer trying to annihilate you.

'Lottie . . . help me.'

'What is it?'

Still gripping the cane with one hand, he hunkered down alongside the unmoving figure, patting at it with the other. There was no life there. In fact, as he patted a little further, he began wondering if there ever had been.

'Shit,' he said. 'We need some damn light in here.'

'I don't know what's happened to the lights.'

'This is fucking ridiculous.'

'Is he alive?' She sounded too frightened to come any closer.

He glanced to his left, where the weak light slanting through the letterbox window had created a faint square of luminescence on the concrete floor. It was only about four feet away.

'Lottie, get over here with that dagger,' he said. 'If he makes any sudden moves, stick him.'

She edged forward, dagger held out where he could just about see it. 'Is he alive or dead?'

'Believe it or not, I think neither.'

'Neither?'

Having felt all along the torso, it was apparent to Nick that whoever he'd just felled hadn't been wearing any clothing. In addition, the figure was made of hard, smooth plastic. He took a firm grip, hooking a hand into one of its armpits; the shoulder appeared to have been fitted with a rotating joint. Lugging the body along the floor, it moved easily, the head coming quickly into the glow from the window.

Lottie sucked in a tight, shocked breath.

Edgar Karnwood gazed back at them, though his face had broken in half, because quite clearly that part of the fallen figure was made from wax.

◆ ◆ ◆

The women looked on agog. Unable to blink. Numbed by astonished horror.

The nightmarish figure didn't bother looking their way. Not until it had closed the cellar door, turned the key in the lock, and then slipped it into the pocket of its 1950s double-breasted jacket. Only then did it turn and face them. Through raw instinct alone, Liz was tempted to start backing away, to run for her life. But how could she abandon the manacled Millie? The killer – now that she stared him in the face, even in the wavering firelight, she could identify his rumpled, rubbery mask – had chosen the perfect place to position himself. How long he'd stood on the plinth for, she wasn't sure, but talk about hiding in plain sight, talk about making himself party to all their thoughts and plans.

He wasn't visibly in possession of a weapon, but that didn't prevent his slow, inexorable advance along the hall towards them.

Immediately, she yanked the Hitler Youth knife from its scabbard, brandishing it defiantly. 'I'll gut you like a fish!' she shouted.

He came on, nevertheless.

'All right . . .' She slid the knife back into its leather. 'How about *this*?' She scampered to the sideboard, grabbing up the ornate sawn-off shotgun from the Sherlock Holmes movie and levelling it on him. She glanced at Millie, hoping to signal with her eyes that the woman needed to back her up in the preposterous claim she was about to make, but the captive sat rigid, watching the approaching figure with terror.

'This thing's loaded!' Liz said loudly, training the antique on the abomination's chest. 'That may seem unlikely, but I guarantee it's true. They only used blanks in the film, but we found a box of cartridges in the kitchen for use in a modern shotgun. I've used guns before and I know they'll work just as well.'

None of this was true, of course. But to her surprise, the figure came to a halt, regarding her through the empty black pits where its eyes should be.

He had to know she was kidding him. He simply *had* to.

And yet maybe it was a chance he couldn't take?

She watched, the roots of her hair prickling, as he reached into his hip pocket. For the first time Liz noticed that he was wearing leather gloves. Good God, had he been wearing those while posing as the waxwork? How blind were they to have missed such a clue?

She stepped forward, lifting the shotgun to shoulder height, still aiming it.

'I mean it!' she shouted. 'Get your hands where I can see them, or I'll fire.'

This order was ignored. When his hand reappeared from his pocket, it was clutching a small, compact pistol made from black steel. A Walther? Liz didn't know much about guns, but she'd seen plenty of James Bond movies.

Maybe that's a prop too?

But if so, he was now pointing it directly at her, as if intending to fire.

And fire, he did.

Thirty-One

Nick and Lottie had been confused to find the hall mannequin lying stripped and abandoned in the cellars. When they also stumbled over a pile of dark clothing, including a shoulder-caped coat and the missing witch-hunter's hat, they started piecing it together. But clearly there was no time for a powwow. Still enveloped in darkness, they struggled back to the stairs. Once away from those basement windows, the blackness deepened. But then what was unmistakably a gunshot echoed down to them, the noise ricocheting around the subterranean passages.

When two more shots rang out, louder still, they could pinpoint the direction.

'*Liiiz!*' Nick choked, all but falling his way up the staircase, clambering on all fours.

'I'm sure she'll be all right,' Lottie said in a voice carrying no conviction at all. 'I'm sure she will.'

When they reached the top, there were flickers of blue sparks from the electrical installation on the wall, along with several torn, dangling cables. Immediately, they realised what had happened to the downstairs lights. They also found the door locked.

'You bastard!' Nick bellowed through the heavy oak planking. 'I'm going to slit you open like a fish for this . . . gonna kick your corpse all over this fucking house!'

◆ ◆ ◆

The bullet would have hit Liz square in the midriff had it not been for the shotgun in her grasp, the impact on the weapon sending it spinning out of her hands. The bullet went wide too, heading who knew where.

Liz didn't wait to see. She broke and fled across the hall, diving over the furniture in front of the hearth. The masked figure turned after her, taking aim again, firing twice, punching two holes in the back of the armchair behind which she now cowered. A mass of foam upholstery spewed out on to her. She whimpered but kept low.

Fleetingly, their assailant appeared torn between shooting at Liz again, which he initially seemed inclined to do as he edged in her direction, or moving on to Millie, who only drew his attention belatedly by again yanking madly on the handcuff. Even then, he was distracted further by a sudden hammering on the other side of the cellar door, and a wild, muffled shouting. The figure thus swung to the door instead, took aim and fired two further shots.

A pair of neat holes were punched into the woodwork, at roughly chest height.

◆ ◆ ◆

If Nick hadn't still been on his knees, he'd have died in that instant, the two slugs smashing through the door above his head burying themselves in the grimy wooden ceiling that sloped down the staircase behind them.

Lottie yelped, grabbing Nick's belt and pulling him downward.

He went voluntarily. Perhaps ten treads down, they halted, lying side by side, staring up with dirty, sweat-soaked faces.

'Hope the others managed to get to cover,' Lottie breathed.

'Millie won't have been able to, will she?' Nick said, voice shaking.

'Look' – she put a hand on his trembling shoulder – 'we heard shooting, but that doesn't mean he's killed anyone.'

'Do you think he'll have held back? Does he strike you as that kind of guy, Lottie?'

'Oh, God . . .'

'Why don't you call on Him properly? You're a vicar.'

'I was, but I failed at it.'

'So, you don't have the Big Guy on speed-dial?'

'It doesn't work like . . . wait a minute!' She jerked upright on her knees. 'The outside door! He's locked us down here but mustn't have realised that we found the outside door.'

Nick snorted. 'Or he's confident that two of us alone can't move a pile of white goods that it took four or five of us ten minutes to build into a barricade.'

'Then his confidence is misplaced.' She grabbed his arm. 'Come on. Let's not let the Lord's mysterious ways go to waste.'

◆ ◆ ◆

With his two main targets on opposite sides of the hall, the killer again seemed undecided about which to go for next. In truth, it gave neither of them a glimmer of hope. He was equidistant between them and could easily have hit either one from where he stood.

Liz crouched behind the armchair, which was little protection, half the stuffing knocked out of it already. One possibility remained: some forty yards to her right, on the hall's east side, the door to the Movie Room corridor was still open. She leapt to her feet and bolted towards it, but she hadn't taken more than a couple of strides when he spun and fired again.

She'd sensed that he was about to, and so dived and rolled, just saving herself, the round striking a locked door east of the fireplace. The shot was fortuitous, penetrating the door just below its handle, blowing out the locking mechanism, the door swinging open on darkness. Liz glanced up from the floor and seeing that he'd now ejected what was clearly a spent magazine, and was swiftly reloading, got up and hurtled at the new exit he'd made for her, barging clean through it. Again, speed was everything, because just as she slammed the door behind her, another hole blasted through the middle of it, the slug whipping past her with inches to spare.

◆ ◆ ◆

To Millie, still seated and handcuffed to the staircase spindle, the events of the last few moments had happened in near-slow motion, her eyes goggling as she watched their tormentor making his way down the hall towards them, veering partway towards Liz, then starting to shoot. All of which, with her so helpless to intervene, had seemed to take an age.

She hadn't wasted it, or at least she'd tried not to, yanking and yanking at the solid steel bracelet, standing up and planting a foot on the timbers beneath the banister, tugging and tugging, regardless that the metal bit deeply into her wrist, the skin and tissue tearing away in chunks, blood running freely.

All the while her eyes were glued on *him*, all manner of thoughts rushing through her head, few of them making sense in this moment of extreme terror.

For example, he was tall, certainly tall enough to have effectively posed as the wax facsimile, but not as tall as the original Edgar Karnwood, the cuffs of his 1950s jacket hanging far over his gloved hands, the cuffs of his trousers having been rucked up around his ankles so as not to impede his walking. Okay, so this wasn't the real guy. But God almighty, it was hardly a consolation.

At least he kept hold of the pistol, even after Liz had fled the scene. It seemed incredible to Millie that she was actually pleased about that, but what alternative was there? She'd seen the deaths some of the others had suffered, but with this thing, this powerful handgun, it would all be over in the blink of an eye. Except that, as he now perambulated back towards her, he didn't seem to be pointing it anywhere.

Certainly not at her.

In fact, Millie felt a renewed sense of horror as she saw that he'd applied the gun's safety catch and now was slipping it back into his pocket.

◆ ◆ ◆

Aside from the minuscule light spilling through the jagged holes where the bullets had come through, Liz was in pitch-blackness and feeling frantically up the wall alongside the door. Finding a light switch, she flicked it on and spun to survey her new surroundings.

It was only small, but perhaps the most decorative room she'd so far seen in the Lodge: lavishly carpeted; tapestries depicting archaic images of rural life; another age-old, fire-blackened hearth, though this one was not currently lit. There was even an array of antique instruments: a lute, a timbrel, a lyre. Presumably, this room had been kept locked for the weekend because it wasn't deemed to be of relevance to horror addicts, or maybe because its contents were simply too valuable.

It didn't matter. She quickly laid hands on an enormous writing bureau standing just to the left, shoving and manhandling it sideways until it stood against the door. Only half satisfied with that, she crossed the room to a heavy brocade curtain and pulled the material back.

A diamond-paned window gave out on to a mist-covered lawn.

It would be no problem smashing her way out of here. The glass looked old, and there were plenty of smaller sticks of furniture she could use as missiles or clubs.

Except that . . . fleeing the house entirely when she had friends inside it who were still in peril was hardly the way she wanted to leave this place.

Of course, she couldn't help anyone if she died in this room.

In the far left-hand corner stood another internal door. She hurried over to open it, finding only a narrow, unlit space, a cubbyhole, one wall of it lined with books, though when she stepped aside, light flooded in from behind her, showing another door at the back of it. On the right meanwhile a stairway twisted steeply upward.

Three potential avenues of escape then, and yet it nagged at her still: what a betrayal it would be to run.

She went back into the Music Room, shivering, drenched in cold sweat. No further shouts had sounded from the hall since she'd come in here. What did that signify?

Liz glanced down at the Hitler Youth knife. Vicious piece of steel though it was, it wouldn't be much use against a firearm. She scanned the room for something more effective. Nothing came to view, but there were antique cupboards in here, chests of drawers. Anything could be contained therein, though probably not a weapon. When her eyes alighted on an ancient blunderbuss fastened to the side of an overhead beam, she almost reached up for it . . . but didn't quite.

She'd already threatened him with one redundant firearm. Granted, he'd taken heed of it, but only fleetingly. How would he react to a weapon for which she didn't even possess a match, let alone a fuse and a horn of gunpowder?

At which point, a gurgling squawk of a scream sounded from the hall.

Liz twirled to face the door again, more sweat breaking on her brow.

The scream persisted for what seemed like an age, followed by a lingering, sepulchral silence that was even more terrible because it meant only one thing.

He'd finished with Millie and was now coming for her.

Thirty-Two

Breathing hard again, Liz ran back through the interior door, trying the next door on the other side of the cubbyhole. Locked. She scampered up the staircase, hitting another light switch. One floor above was a narrow corridor lined with peeled, fading wallpaper, minus carpets. She hurried along it, but there were only three or four doors. All narrow, all locked. Except for one at the end, which, when she opened it, revealed the empty shell of a bathroom, pipes where the washbasin should have been.

She backed into the corridor. Another part of the house awaiting renovation. That was why this area had been locked.

She then heard an echoing *thud* from below.

The sweat froze down her back.

How long would that writing bureau hold?

Another *thud*. Louder, angrier.

Liz hared back down the staircase. As she arrived in the cubbyhole at the bottom, there was another brutal impact and this time a splintering of wood.

Desperate, she tried the other interior door again, only to notice that it hadn't been locked by a key, but by a bolt at the top, which, with some effort, she was able to pull back.

She went through into another spacious area, again slapping at the nearest wall, activating a switch. Several overhead lights came on, set at regular intervals along a lengthy gallery. There were windows to the right of her, running the length of it, located above padded seating. Handsome paintings adorned the other wall, and arranged every few yards down the middle, dining tables set with chairs. There was nowhere obvious to hide, though another door stood at the far end, this one open.

An explosive impact now sounded from the Music Room.

Liz slammed the door behind her and raced forward, weaving around the tables and knocking chairs over. Each time she passed under a light, she leapt, smashing its bulb with the Hitler knife, returning the gallery, section by section, to the ultra-dimness that was all the mist swirling beyond the windows permitted.

When she'd extinguished the last one, she halted and looked back, breathing hard. As she did, the distant door opened, light penetrating through from the Music Room, the tall, besuited figure of her opponent silhouetted there. Thanks to his mask it was possible that he could see even less than she could. But he came forward anyway. She fled on through the next door into what at first seemed like a continuation of the gallery, though rather than bricks and mortar, this extension was entirely a thing of glass and steel. It also rose to loftier heights, containing some kind of upper level.

A genuine Victorian-style conservatory, she realised. She didn't even need to find a light in here because with so much glass, just enough moonlight was distilling through the fog to display the interior.

Again, it ran lengthways along the side of the house, but at ground level had been divided into two aisles by a central row of lush, tropical plants growing to chest height.

Liz stumbled along the right-hand aisle. With a *clatter*, the door swung open behind her.

Having just reached a break in the line of greenery, she ducked into it and squatted down.

Her foe didn't immediately advance, and another of those terrible silences filled the conservatory. Liz glanced at the floor, noting that it mainly comprised steel gridwork. No doubt there was some mechanism beneath, which periodically enabled the entry of warm air or steam. The problem was that it would echo when she walked. She wouldn't be able to creep without it creaking and groaning.

Though that worked in her favour too.

Her skin prickled as she heard her opponent venture forward, by the sounds of it along the left-hand aisle. He was coming slowly, stealthily, but thanks to the steel underfoot, she could hear him.

For all that she'd been forewarned of his advance, Liz knew that she couldn't just make a run for it. Thanks to the moonlit interior, she'd easily be spotted if she attempted to dart down to the far end in search of an exit door. It was a distance of maybe forty yards, which was too far. And yet by his clanking footfalls, he was already close. More promising, about five yards away on the right, a spiral stairway ascended to the next level. She glanced upward again. The steel landing overhead was little more than a single walkway. It didn't span the width of the structure, so it wasn't an upstairs as such, but it still ran the entire length of it. Almost certainly there'd only be plants up there. It seemed improbable there'd be any means of exit – unless there were panels in the roof, which she could open.

The approaching footfalls halted.

Liz risked a peek through the foliage.

He was standing still about thirty yards off, clearly listening.

Again, sweat streamed down the inside of her clothes. If she remained here, and he continued forward, he'd find her. There was no debate. She glanced again at the spiral staircase. And bolted for it, jumping to her feet and running, hammering her way up the reverberating treads, at any second expecting a bullet to come caroming through the steelwork, puncturing her flesh, tearing its way through bone and vital organs.

But that didn't happen, and again she wondered how much her foe could actually see from beneath his prosthetic face.

The next thing, she'd reached that upper level.

As she'd suspected, it was no more than a single walkway running end to end along the conservatory. On the left, a railing prevented anyone from falling off it, while on the right stood a succession of low tables with earthenware plant-pots on them. The ceiling was indeed made from sloped glass panels, some of which looked to have hinges and catches.

They were still out of reach, but the solution was obvious. Liz humped one plant pot after another off the nearest table. They were heavy, but fear was fuelling her strength. At which point, she heard footsteps approaching below. And there he was, standing at the foot of the staircase, for the most part a featureless shape, though his rubbery face, turned up towards her, was paler than the rest of him. Slowly, like an automaton, he raised his right hand. It was holding the pistol.

Frantic, she hurled one of the pots. It spun down through the air, scattering soil, and exploded on the steel footway alongside him. He jumped aside, stumbling back and falling on the central row of plants. It was almost the first human reaction she'd seen from him.

So, he could be hurt. Could even be killed.

She'd known that all along, of course, but to see it proved was a boost to her morale. Unfortunately, now that he'd spotted where she was, she wasn't going to have time to clamber on to tables and fiddle with locks on overhead panels. Instead, she grabbed up another pot. As she did, his footfalls ascended the spiral stair.

She didn't aim, simply dropped the pot down the interior of the spiral. It blew apart, scattering more soil and razor-sharp fragments.

She followed it with another and another, literally bombarding the staircase he hoped to ascend to her by. She was winging it, relying on luck, but the fifth or sixth one made good contact. There was a hefty, meaty smack as of soil-packed stone striking flesh and bone. A pained grunt responded, and she heard the sound of a body falling, tumbling head over heels. She didn't venture down to see what damage she'd done, just fled hell for leather along the upper walk, hoping to God that it would connect with some kind of fire escape at the far end.

When she got there, she tottered to a halt.

The walkway widened here into a square platform. In the middle of it she saw what looked like a heavy wrought-iron garden table, along with several wrought-iron chairs. A perfect spot to dine al fresco one late summer evening. But there was no exit.

She glanced back along the walk. With no sign of anyone approaching, she moved to the barrier, to peer down into the main body of the conservatory. And that was when she saw him again. Advancing at ground level. Not exactly limping but moving more slowly than before. It was evident that she'd done some harm to him, but not very much. She retreated across the dining area, turning and peering down through the glazed dead end. It was impossible to know what awaited her down there or how far down it was, but she knew she had no option. Grabbing up the first of the wrought-iron chairs, she swung it in a circle and sent it colliding with all her might against the plate glass. It rebounded on to the platform alongside her. The glass didn't so much as chip.

Liz stared at it aghast. This wasn't an original Victorian structure, then. It had been refurbished with modern safety glass. Frantic, she grabbed the chair and swung it again. It made the same shuddering noise and had the same zero impact.

Liz went rigid, muscles and joints locking.

What did she do? How in God's name could she get out of this?

Then she noticed the narrow gap between the platform and the window. Only a foot or so, again with a barrier there to prevent anyone slipping down it. She would need to climb over that barrier in order to jump out, but with the glass remaining intact, there was no hope even of that. From ground level meanwhile, she heard a distinct metallic click.

She dropped to her knees.

Fifteen feet below, perhaps twenty yards back along the lower level, flame spat.

With a resounding *bang*, a slug, which would have ended her life, punched instead through the reinforced window, leaving a circular hole dead centre, about four inches wide, the entire rest of the massive pane riddled with fractures.

Liz grabbed up the garden chair again and hurled it with everything she had. This time, the window exploded outward.

From below, she heard a hissed curse and the sound of heavy feet receding as her opponent ran back towards the foot of the spiral stair. Again, Liz was left with no choice. She clambered on to the other side of the barrier, the icy, mist-laden air embracing her. She still saw nothing of what waited below. It didn't matter. Some distance behind, the footfalls changed tone as they ascended the spiral.

She jumped.

Thirty-Three

Liz arced downward for what seemed the longest time. She was descending from at least fifteen feet of course, and even if she landed on soft grass, was likely to break both her ankles. Instead, though, she hit the top of an outhouse. It was made from timber, but its roof was tarpaper. The tarpaper was braced underneath, but she'd only come down from six or seven feet when she struck it, and though it hurt, the impact juddering through her entire body, no obvious damage was done.

She lay sprawled, gasping, her tailbone stinging abominably, before she realised what a stroke of luck she'd just had. And then she heard a pair of feet clanking along the upper walk inside the conservatory. She blinked upward through the fog, thinking that she could just about discern the huge, jagged aperture where she'd exited. He only needed to appear there, lean out with his pistol, and it was still over. Rolling on to her front, she lowered herself over the edge, swung by her hands for a second, then dropped the remaining couple of feet. Landing on grass, she hobbled quickly away, not knowing which direction she was headed in, just determined to expand the distance between herself and the conservatory.

When she'd lost sight of all the main buildings, she halted and hunkered down to listen, heart pounding, every scrap of her clothing saturated with sweat. But no shots had been fired after her, no challenges called. She couldn't even hear those clanking feet any more.

Thankful for once for the extreme restriction in visibility, she rose up and lumbered on, the bruises she'd inflicted on herself finally making themselves known. But she hadn't gone a dozen yards before she was on gravel. She halted again, standing stock still. Gravel would crunch, and she couldn't afford to give her position away. Not to a gunman. Or had she already done that?

Was that a footstep she'd just heard? About ten yards to the left?

Liz pivoted round, her sweat running in rivers again.

As before, she sank to a crouch. Instinctively, she reached for the Hitler Youth knife at her waist, only to find that it had come loose when she'd fallen, the sheath now hanging empty. She cursed under her breath. On all sides meanwhile, she imagined she could hear things.

Rustlings, patterings.

Was that a whisper?

She froze in place, ears pinned back.

It couldn't be him. How could he have come outside so quickly?

An exit door, you berk!

But he was alone, wasn't he? Who could he be whispering to?

How about himself? He's that much of a nutter.

Liz knew that she couldn't stay here.

Slowly, stealthily she raised herself up again, muscles coiling for a quick dash. Only for her eyes to alight on a misted figure about fifteen yards to the right.

At least, she thought it was a figure. It was motionless, but man-shaped.

Her heart began trip-hammering. She didn't know how much more of this she could take. It almost seemed pointless to keep resisting. Wherever they went, he was waiting for them. She straightened to full height, too weary and now too agonised

– the blows to her back and hips had been ferocious – to even contemplate running again. She was about to call out a challenge of her own when a hand slapped across her mouth from behind.

Liz squealed, only for Nick to hiss into her ear that she had to be quiet.

Through blind instinct, she continued to struggle. He battled to control her, though even Nick – easy-living Nick, who hadn't been in a fight or even done sports in more years than either of them could remember – seemed to have toughened up during the course of this night. He tightened his grip around her, hauling her away to the right. The figure she'd seen standing there hurried forward. It was Lottie, her silver coat glimmering.

'Liz, be quiet!' she murmured. 'Please. He'll hear us.'

Liz went limp, allowing the pair of them to hustle her off the gravel and away along a narrow passage between two outbuildings.

'You've no clue how glad I am to find you alive,' Nick breathed, kissing her cheek and even her eyes. She mumbled in response, but only when they emerged again into open space, now crossing another lawn towards a tall, square-shouldered outline, did he take his hand away, allowing her to gasp for air.

'In here.' Lottie stumbled ahead to what was now evidently a potting shed. She opened the door and Nick thrust their captive through. Lottie, bringing up the rear, closed the door behind them, but very quietly, its *click* barely audible.

'My God,' Liz moaned. 'He's got a gun . . .'

'Yeah, we noticed.' Nick set her down on a crate. He grabbed the wolf-headed cane, which he'd obviously left here when they'd first chosen it as a hideout. 'Just make sure you keep your voice down, yeah? This thing's like one-plank thick. He could fire twenty shots through it from so far away that we wouldn't even have heard him coming. But, Christ!' He threw himself on to her again, hugging her tightly. 'I am so bloody glad you're alive . . .'

‘I get it,’ Liz gasped, kissing his cheek but easing him off her. ‘I get it, but we’ve got to stay alive to stay in love, yeah?’

‘Yeah,’ he conceded. ‘Yeah . . . course.’ He backed away across the interior.

‘What happened to you?’ Lottie asked. ‘Where’s Millie?’

Liz hung her head, sweat dripping, and had to admit that, though she didn’t know about Millie, she’d heard the woman scream. She then explained as best she could about her own narrow escape. Nick responded by detailing his and Lottie’s eventual exit from the house via the cellar’s outer door, adding that the report of another gunshot, this one sounding as though it was outside, though in actual fact it was probably the one fired inside the conservatory, had forced them to lie low rather than try to find a way back in.

‘Nick,’ Liz said, when he’d finished. Only the chalk-pale shapes of their faces were visible. ‘Nick . . . this guy’s an out-and-out killer. I mean he is absolutely determined to get us all. And he’s good at it.’

‘He’s certainly had good luck,’ Nick replied.

‘No.’ She shook her head. ‘He’s found effective cover in the mist. But whoever he is, he’s still got stalk-and-slash down to a fine art.’

‘What’re you saying? That he’s done it before?’

‘Either that or he’s been putting in a hell of a lot of practice. The way he played with us out in the gardens. That stunt with the mannequin . . .’ She shook her head. ‘What I’m saying is this isn’t just some amateur. You know . . . someone, like Millie, who’s pissed off because of what we’ve been doing here. I think this person would probably rejoice in the whole concept of the Murder Tour. For a moment or two back there, I considered Michael Caruso. But I don’t think even he qualifies. He did it once and never again.’

‘We keep saying this,’ Lottie said, dabbing blood from her nose with a twist of cotton wool. ‘But does it matter who he is? I mean, he could be Count Dracula or the Wolfman . . . but either way, we can't just stay in hiding. Not while Millie's chained up in there. We have to help her.'

Liz glanced at Nick. 'What time is it?' she asked.

Nick checked his watch. 'Just short of twenty past six. There's an hour left to sunrise. But it's mid-November, remember. It'll be more twilight than daylight. And even normal daylight wouldn't necessarily burn this mist away. Not straight off.'

Liz hung her head. She felt as though a steamroller had passed over her. Not only that, the mere thought of returning to face that maniac again made her nauseous. But Lottie was ultimately right. Millie had tried to hurt them, had planned to destroy their fledgling business. But on nights like this, if you weren't one of the people, you were one of the beasts.

'If we're going back inside,' she said, 'we need to find a way. The obvious entry is the point where you two came out, but there's no reason to assume the internal cellar door won't still be locked.'

'We've already said a couple of times that there'll be other ways in and out,' Lottie replied.

'Maybe, but we don't know where they are,' Nick said. 'And we'll likely make a racket checking. The truth is we're probably not even safe here. Our guy will almost certainly be searching the estate.' He eyed them both. 'Hey, maybe we just look to ourselves? There's still one motorboat left. We could grab it, motor out to the middle of the reservoir, cut the engine and float there till morning. He wouldn't be able to get to us then.'

'Even with only an hour left to sun-up, we'd likely freeze to death out there,' Liz said.

'We'll freeze to death in here too,' Lottie cut in. 'Which is all the more reason why we should go and try to help Millie. If nothing else, the activity will warm us up.'

'Lottie,' Liz said, 'you do remember that I said I heard Millie scream?'

'Yes, but you also said you didn't see what happened to her, so she could still be alive.'

Liz regarded her with interest. 'Where've *you* got this second wind of courage from, all of a sudden?'

'I don't . . . well . . .' Lottie relapsed into an awkward silence but then seemed to steel herself. 'I don't suppose it can hurt to admit it. You're already aware that, a few years ago, a friend of mine was murdered. And that it was horribly brutal. So brutal that . . . well, I wasn't even there, but when I heard the details, I almost gave up on life, let my entire vocation lapse.'

'Lots of people lose their faith in God,' Nick said.

'It wasn't that,' she replied. 'I still believe. But . . . I just realised how uncourageous a person I was. Michaela and I had had it fairly easy, you see. We'd both occupied rural parishes down in Suffolk. Leafy part of the world, village communities. The worst we usually had to deal with was parishioners bickering over the fairy cakes during the after-service tea party on Sunday mornings. Oh, I was fine with it. Toddling along quite happily when Michaela was suddenly killed. She was only in the next parish. Lord, I can't describe how shocked I was. I mean, even though the police caught the culprits. I've always been terrified by violence, you see. And then to have it brought home to me so abruptly . . . not just about violence itself, but about the people who do it. How they can live side by side with us, and we don't even notice them until it's too late. About the awful forces that can be unleashed when the worst of man comes to the surface. I'm sorry, I suppose that sounds very melodramatic.'

'Don't worry,' Liz said. 'After tonight, nothing will.'

'At first, I thought I'd seek a reassignment . . . you know, to an inner-city parish, where I could try and face that fear.' Lottie spoke quietly but intently, reliving it rather than just recalling it. 'But the one or two parishes I went to look at where there were vacancies . . . I mean, it's no surprise there were vacancies.' She shook her head. 'The tragedy in the lives of so many of the people I'd be expected to counsel. There was drunkenness, drug addiction, spousal abuse . . . All the seeds were there. That's when I knew I couldn't face it. That I just wasn't up to the job.'

'And now the time's come to prove that you are?' Liz said.

Lottie stiffened, as if the mere question made her uncomfortable. 'Let's just say that this time I'm not going to run away . . . or try and kid myself that I'm someone I'm not. Plaster myself with make-up and trinkets . . . use props like this' – she felt in her mac pocket, digging out the small bottle of Chanel No 5 – 'to pretend that I'm some woman of the world who's above concerning herself about others.'

'And that's why you came on the tour?' Nick said. 'You thought it would teach you something about violent crime?'

'And about violent criminals,' she said. 'Michaela's death was indescribable. Apparently, they tied her down on the altar table first. That's one of the reasons I was so reluctant to watch *Malifique*. I thought it would bring it all home to me a bit too quickly. You see, ever since Michaela died, I've been haunted by dreams about her killers, seeing them as demons rather than men. As monsters, ogres, creatures that no sane person wouldn't flee from. But deep down, I've always known that's not the truth. They're just men. They don't look like monsters. Most of the time, they probably don't even behave like them. It's a terrible conundrum, of course. But I thought that if I could look closely at some particularly lurid cases and perhaps familiarise myself with the causes . . .'

'I don't suppose we helped you much there,' Nick said. 'We tend to go for the sensational.'

'It doesn't matter now,' she replied. 'I know that violence and murder happen. And I know that's what we're facing here. And as I say, this time I'm not just going to head for the hills. Not while one of our number is at the mercy of a madman.'

There was a lengthy silence while they absorbed this, Liz and Nick weighing the pros and cons.

'You say you heard Millie scream, Liz?' Lottie asked.

Liz nodded.

'Was it a scream of terror, or . . . or a death scream?'

Liz struggled to reply.

'There's a difference?' Nick asked.

'Oh yes,' Lottie said. 'When Michaela was murdered, the killers tape-recorded what happened. I never heard the tape, but obviously the investigating detectives did. Apparently, her screams were unimaginable. One of the police, a rough man, but kind-hearted too, I thought . . . a Detective Sergeant Heckenburg . . . he spared me the details, but he promised me they were going to catch them, and that when they did, if that tape was played in court, there'd be no hope for those responsible. They'd never see the light of day again.

'The thing now is that I can't help but think of Michaela as a martyr, and myself as the acolyte who didn't learn the lesson the first time . . . but who's determined to learn it this time.' She glanced at them again. 'I suppose what I'm saying is that, even if you don't come with me, I'm still going to make my way over there and try to get into that house. Someone has to see if Millie is all right. I can't just leave her.'

'You won't need to.' Liz got to her feet, flinching at the ache in her stiffening bruises. 'We'll be coming with you.'

Thirty-Four

Nick made the case that, before anything else, going around the front of the building and simply looking through the windows to try and work out exactly where Millie was, and whether she was dead or alive, should be their first course of action.

It seemed eminently sensible, though all of them were aware that the killer could be waiting for them when they got there with his gun ready. As Liz said, though, nothing they did from here on was likely to be risk-free, adding that the madman could easily be waiting for them outside the shed. Thus, when they finally set out, they went in single file, crossing the lawn with eyes darting everywhere, trooping back along the passage between the outbuildings. From here, they circumnavigated the gravelled area before halting again to take stock. With only silent vapour greeting them, they pressed on, but rather than following the exterior of the house closely as they'd done on previous occasions, they gave the conservatory and the gallery a wide berth. It was still a nerve-wracking experience, and despite the cold, which again bit into them, they were damp with sweat when they finally came round the front south-west corner on to the drive itself. Here, they waited, watching.

Though dawn wasn't far off, the mist lay over the reservoir impenetrably, and in fact came right up to the front of the house, where, thanks to the exterior lights, it hung in a phosphorescent pall.

They listened for several moments but there wasn't a sound.

'You know,' Lottie said quietly, 'if he's aware that we've escaped, or that some of us have, won't he try to get away himself? He can't afford to just assume we won't make it back to civilisation and raise the authorities.'

'This would be his only way out of here, if he does.' Nick put his hand on the stationary Jaguar XJ. 'Even the boat would only get him to the other side of the tarn.'

'He's still here,' Liz said. 'I'm sure of it. He hasn't got the job done yet.'

Despite this, they advanced along the drive, passing the front of the house.

Some forty yards beyond the car, they came to the first ground-floor window that looked into the main hall. Nick approached first, peeking through it from the side. When no one opened fire on him, the others came up too. The blaze in the hearth having died down again, the interior was half-filled with shadow. The chair where Millie had been sitting was on the far side, diagonally opposite from where they were now. They could just about make her out. She was still seated, still cuffed to the spindle behind her, head lying to one side.

'Is she hurt?' Lottie whispered.

'Hard to say.' Nick squashed his nose against the glass. 'But to be fair, she doesn't look to be in terrible shape.'

'I don't suppose there was any need to kill her. I mean, she's already immobilised.' Lottie sounded hopeful rather than optimistic. No one bothered replying.

They moved on, closing slowly on the motionless form that once was Jordan Pugmire.

'Easy,' Nick cautioned them.

No one needed telling twice. They'd all seen enough news articles about the irregular warfare in Afghanistan, the Middle East and Ukraine, to know that it wasn't beyond a cunning adversary to position himself as a fallen warrior, and when his comrades approached, jump up and blast away from point-blank range. But it wasn't like that. Even with the mist, they recognised the youngster from ten or fifteen yards. They saw something else too, and this stopped them in their tracks.

At the top of the steps, the front door stood ajar.

They regarded it stiffly.

'Let's not pretend this is a good thing,' Liz finally said.

Lottie glanced at her. 'Why not? It's easy access.'

'Too easy. He *wants* us to go in.'

'I agree,' Nick said.

They waited, undecided about what to do next.

'Does he really need to spring an elaborate trap?' Lottie eventually asked, hugging herself as the chill cut into them again. 'He's got a gun. He could just come out here and shoot us.'

They pondered this. It wasn't impossible that, in all this chaos, the door had been left open by accident.

'Again, I'm wondering if he's just run off?' Lottie said.

Nick shook his head. 'The car, I told you . . .'

'Maybe he hasn't got the keys. Maybe they're somewhere on the other shore. Burned up with Simon Matlock, or perhaps even at the bottom of the tarn.'

'What's he going to do, walk?' Nick replied. 'And walk where? It's miles and miles to the nearest village?'

'There's a bus stop,' Lottie said. 'Don't you remember? At the bottom of the hill, the one we passed on the way up here. I don't know how regularly rural bus services run, but I imagine they're on the road fairly early in the day.'

Fleetingly, Liz wanted to laugh. The thought that the wreaker of all this havoc, the mass slayer and torturer of Black Tarn Lodge – who knew what they'd end up calling him, the Moorland Ripper? The Beast of Bowland? – might now be calmly waiting at a bus stop was almost comical.

'Either way . . .' Lottie straightened up again. 'I said I'd come back here for Millie. And now there's an open door, I can't ignore it.'

Nick and Liz glanced at each other. It seemed like madness, but in truth there wasn't much alternative. Their feet were now numb, their fingers deadened. Britain rarely suffered the extremes of winter weather you saw in Alpine regions or the Arctic north, but people *did* die here from exposure and cold. And now they understood how.

'Okay.' Nick hefted his wolf-headed cane. 'But we've got to be ready for anything.'

Liz no longer had a weapon, of course, and it wasn't much consolation to her when she saw Lottie brandishing her jewel-hilted dagger; the ex-vicar looked about as threatening as a schoolkid with a plastic fork. But if nothing else, Liz supposed she could grab a stool or bottle, or something, once she was inside. Whatever, she wasn't going down without a fight. Not when they'd come this far. They ventured through the door, Nick leading.

The vast hall lay quiet, only the dancing red shadows providing movement. As they advanced, their eyes again sought out the minstrels' gallery. It was extra dark up there. Someone could easily be crouching out of sight, taking aim at them.

But if that was the case, no shots were fired.

The empty plinth where the Edgar Karnwood waxwork had welcomed so many august persons to the Lodge over so many triumphant years was an ugly reminder of how they'd come to this situation. They halted, unable to avoid staring at it.

'Shall I bar the door behind us?' Lottie asked. 'If he's actually outside hunting us, we might be able to turn the tables on him completely.'

'Probably best not to,' Liz replied. There was no necessity for her to explain why. The potential need to make a quick escape was on all their minds.

They progressed onward, veering across the hall towards the staircase, and the chair next to the sideboard cabinet, where Millie still sat motionless, her head turned away.

'Millie?' Lottie said, as they drew closer. 'Millie, it's us.'

Still, the seated woman didn't move.

The fear running through them intensified as they approached. At first glance, everything seemed to be fine. There were no visible wounds on Millie's body, apart from her right wrist, where she'd flayed a bracelet of flesh away in her efforts to get free.

Nick cleared his throat. 'Millie?'

Still no response.

Liz glanced over her shoulder. Was that movement she'd spied in the far corner?

She looked more closely, but no . . . just another wavering shadow.

'Millie?' Nick reached down, taking her by the right elbow, shaking her, shifting her position. Her head lolled round, and she looked straight at them.

Lottie shrieked . . .

Thirty-Five

'Why . . . why, why?' Lottie demanded tearfully. 'Why would he do something so hideously, horribly cruel?'

Nick shook his head. 'I'm damned if we can tell you.'

'Why not just put a bullet through her skull, end it quickly?'

'Maybe he's got no bullets left.'

'He had enough left to shoot up the conservatory,' Liz said.

'It's utterly inhuman,' Lottie wept.

Nick said nothing else, but clung tight to his cane, while Liz had equipped herself with the jagged hilt of a whisky bottle, which she'd broken on a section of paved flooring. They'd posted themselves a few yards away from Millie's seat and were now standing, keeping watch in different directions across the hall, eyes scanning for the slightest hint of activity. Lottie meanwhile had stumbled to the sculptured newel post at the foot of the stairs, where she was still leaning, her face blotchy and wet.

Millie watched them silently from where she sat, her eyes wide open, two glassy baubles in a face that was mostly unblemished, though her mouth was an expanded, blackened hole, still smouldering from within. The jar of acid from Edgar Karnwood's *Revenge of the Phantom* sat on the sideboard next to her, empty.

'He's a sadist, that's all.' Lottie punched the newel post so hard that she split her knuckles. 'Purely and simply. He enjoys killing, and he enjoys inflicting horrific suffering while he does.'

'Concisely put,' Liz agreed.

'And we only know one person like that, don't we?' Lottie straightened up and looked round at them.

'I think we know plenty, to be honest,' Nick replied. 'Or maybe we've just been doing the Murder Tour too long.'

'I mean we only know one who's alive today. Who might even be here with us now.'

Liz wasn't really listening. Her thoughts were a chaotic scramble: she was at least as upset as Lottie, but she was frightened too. She'd only just escaped this guy's clutches herself. What would he have done to her, if he'd winged her with his pistol and she'd been helpless to resist him? And then there was Millie . . .

Dear Lord, we handcuffed her to that stair-rod. She couldn't possibly have escaped. We served her to him on a platter . . .

'I'm talking about Travis Monkton,' Lottie said loudly. She sniffled, palming the tears away. 'I mean, who else is capable of this? Who else revels in prolonging the deaths of his victims apart from the goddamned Night Monster himself?'

Nick glanced at her distractedly. 'Monkton's in Gull Rock. You've heard about that place?'

'Of course I have,' Lottie snapped. 'Who hasn't?'

Gull Rock. Official title HMP Brancaster. The farthest place from anywhere in the United Kingdom, or so it seemed for anyone unfortunate enough to have to make the long, dreary drive towards it. Britain's own version of a supermax. The final destination for England and Wales's irredeemably and unrepentantly wicked.

'It's escape-proof,' Nick said.

'I bet the law enforcement agencies of the world wish they each had an extra officer for every time they've heard that,' Lottie replied.

Nick was about to shake his head, to rebuff the idea further, but then he caught Liz looking at him. 'You're not telling me you're thinking the same thing?' he asked her.

'Nick . . .' Liz tried to resist the idea herself, but it wasn't easy. 'These murders would be very Travis Monkton. Every kind of tool and method you can think of has been used so far. They've involved torture, mutilation. Like Lottie says, this has been a sadist's banquet.'

'Liz, come on. If Monkton had escaped from Gull Rock, it would have been all over the news for days.'

'Suppose it's just happened?' Lottie put in. 'We've been out of contact for quite a few hours now.'

'Not long enough for him to have got all the way from the Norfolk coast to the wilds of northern Lancashire. It's just not possible.'

'Isn't it equally impossible that he's got nothing to do with this?' Liz said. 'I mean, we're involved in a Murder Tour, and we make a big deal out of Travis Monkton's murder den. We even go to an art gallery of the unhinged and one of us buys a painting of the guy. And then, by pure chance, we walk into a killer who's exactly like him? Good Lord, Nick!'

Nick's certainty that they were wrong slowly but visibly started to fade.

'Didn't Roy say something?' he muttered. 'About him having disagreements with his police bosses over their handling of the Travis Monkton enquiry?'

'My God!' Lottie blurted. 'You don't think they got the wrong man, and the real Night Monster's still up here in the Forest of Bowland?'

'I'm no expert on the Monkton case,' Nick replied, 'but as far as I'm aware, he was totally bang to rights. Didn't he confess at the end?'

'Yes, he did,' Liz said. When it came to organising the Murder Tour, Nick was their wellspring of true crime knowledge, but given how prominent a role Travis Monkton played in it, she'd undertaken some research herself. 'After he was arrested, all kinds of corroborating evidence emerged. The judge had no hesitation in giving him a full-life tariff.'

They brooded on this. Ultimately of course, it was imponderable. With none of the relevant research materials to hand, they could only rely on recollection.

Nick shook his head. 'Lottie was right before . . . it doesn't matter who it is. Even if we could find out, what difference would it make?'

'But before, I was more concerned about Millie,' Lottie said. 'There's nothing we can do for her now. But if we can work out who murdered her – put an actual name to the culprit – it might give us some indication of his weakness.'

'Weakness?' Nick eyed her dubiously. 'You mean like kryptonite? We're not talking some super-villain here.'

'You could have fooled me,' she retorted. 'What's the half-time score? Killer six, Victims nil. And all in the space of a few hours.'

'She might have a point, Nick,' Liz said. 'We're not leaving here anytime soon. Even when the sun's up, it'll be ages before our ride comes. And in the meantime, he's not going to stop. Unless someone stops him.'

Nick snorted. 'Even if he does have a weakness, or an oddity we can exploit, how are we going to find out about it?'

'To start with,' Lottie said, 'young Jordan insisted there were clues about the Travis Monkton mystery in that painting.'

Nick knuckled his forehead. 'I appreciate that we're clutching at straws here, but let's not get carried away. Why did the Murder Resolution lot refuse young Jordan in the first place? Nothing to do with him being a sick puppy, by any chance?'

Lottie gave him a look. 'According to Millie, we're all of us sick puppies.'

'Nick, we can't just be dismissive of this,' Liz cut in. 'If it's a lead, it's a lead. That painting of Travis Monkton . . . if Jordan said there were clues there, it might be relevant to something important. Hell, I know it sounds unlikely, and yes, we *are* grabbing at straws. But look at the facts. No other Murder Tour we've run has hit problems of any sort. Then, on this one, when Michael Caruso announces that he's putting his Travis Monkton up for sale, all hell breaks loose. You said it yourself, called it "a common denominator". Both Jordan and Darius came on this tour to try and get hold of it. Freya and Roy came along just to have a look at it . . . They'd also heard about the secret messages it supposedly contained. And then, in the space of one night, all four of them are dead. Coincidence? Seriously?'

'Matlock?' he argued. 'Millie?'

'Wrong place, wrong time maybe.'

'That clearly applies to all of us,' Lottie said.

The threesome gazed at each other for helpless seconds. They were exasperated of course, and haggard and wearied and terrified all at the same time. But it was clear they couldn't just stand around here and wait for the next attack. Some kind of direct action needed to be taken, even if it was the longest of long shots.

'The painting's still in Jordan's bedroom?' Nick said.

'Far as we know,' Liz replied.

Lottie went straight for the stairs. 'What are we waiting for?'

They ascended together, Nick at the front, Liz watching the rear, Lottie in the middle, all three now pointedly ignoring the images of Edgar Karnwood's diabolical ancestors in *House of Torment*. As they progressed along the minstrels' gallery, they scanned the ground floor below. Again, the only movement was the ultra-faint dance of shadow and flame. When they turned into the corridor where Jordan's bedroom was located, it was no real relief. Deep darkness lurked at the farthest end, and it was easy to imagine a gunman concealed there. To add to the stress of that, they then found the bedroom door was locked.

'Great,' Nick said. 'We're going to have to go back outside and search that poor little bastard's pockets for his key.'

Disgruntled, but again wary of every shadow they encountered, they returned along the gallery and down the stairs. At the bottom, everything remained as they'd left it, the hall lit now by only the low-key lamps and the dimmest remaining embers on the hearth. They crossed over to the main door, which still stood partly open, and went out on to the top step.

Given the way things had been turning for them, Liz had half-expected Jordan's body to be gone, moved and hidden when they most needed it. But it lay as before. Probably locked up now by rigor mortis. Briefly wondering how unbelievable it was that, suddenly, they just accepted this sort of thing without batting an eyelid, she and Lottie stood in the doorway and watched while Nick descended the steps, crossed the drive and squatted down, rifling gingerly through the dead man's pockets.

Only for all three of them to suddenly jerk to attention, alerted by an approaching rumble.

Nick jumped up, swinging round to face the reservoir. Liz understood. It sounded as if their sole remaining motorboat was heading straight towards them. But then, as the chugging intensified, their attention was diverted to the drive – just as a huge pair of dragon-like eyes emerged through the vapour.

Only slowing to a halt a few yards short of the youngster's body.

Dragon-like eyes. Or alternatively, the headlamps of a large, heavy vehicle.

Thirty-Six

'Oh my God . . . are we glad to see you!' Liz shrieked delightedly, charging down the steps. Even now, with Clara having jumped out of the bus on to the drive, she couldn't believe it and threw herself on top of the startled bus driver.

'What happened to *him*?' Clara said. She was wearing jeans and a shabby jumper, her hair, normally neat and tight in a sensible bun, now hanging in tousled disarray. Though she was clearly less concerned about her own appearance than about the prone figure lying in front of her bus. 'What the heck's going on?'

'What's going on with *you*?' Nick responded, grabbing her arm. 'What're you doing here?'

Clara gazed at them, bewildered. 'What do you mean? You sent for me.'

'What?'

'I got a text from Liz's phone about two hours ago. Said there was an emergency and you needed me to come straight back.'

Nick and Liz glanced at each other.

'Well . . . there *is* an emergency,' Liz stuttered. 'But *I* didn't send you a message.'

Clara shook her head. 'It was a text from your phone. It said: *Sorry, Clara. Problem here, so plan has changed. Please come and get us straight away.*'

Again, the other two glanced at each other. Lottie now came down the steps as well, looking equally bemused.

'I rang you back,' Clara said, 'but no one answered.'

'You know what that means?' Nick said slowly. 'He wants Clara too.'

Again, the driver glanced from one to the other, registering their mutual dismay. 'What do you mean, he wants me too?' She pointed at Jordan. 'And what's with this kid? He isn't . . . surely, he's not . . . ?'

She hesitated to say more, but the renewed reference to the casualty reminded Liz that they weren't safe in the open. She took Clara's elbow. 'Come inside, and we'll tell you everything.'

Still full of questions, Clara went in with them. Once they were all back indoors, Nick pulled the door to.

'What's going on?' Clara demanded. She was starting to look grouchy as well as tired. 'Are you seriously telling me you guys didn't send that message?'

Liz palmed the air. 'No, but first things first. The kid, as you call him, Jordan Pugmire—'

'He looks dead to me,' Clara interrupted.

'He is,' Nick confirmed. 'He fell.'

'Fell?' Clara glanced again from one to the other, finally noting their bedraggled state, and then the dried blood in and around Lottie's nostrils. 'And where are the others?'

'It's a long story,' Nick replied. 'Basically, something's happened during this Murder Tour. Someone we encountered. On the road or maybe at one of the various murder sites . . . I don't know. Whatever it is, that someone now wants us silenced. *All* of us.'

Liz didn't totally buy that – they'd barely met anyone anywhere during the tour – but it was as good a hypothesis as any.

'Guys, we still need to get that painting,' Lottie interrupted them. 'Jordan said there were clues in it. Suppose they're clues to the murderer's identity, and we come back here with the police later today, and all the bodies are still here but the painting's gone?'

Clara still looked nonplussed. 'Bodies?'

Liz glanced at Nick. 'You got the key?'

He dangled the key to Jordan's bedroom.

She nodded, relieved. 'Clara, we're going back upstairs. We need to retrieve something from one of the bedrooms. First though' – she opened the front door again – 'we have to move that body.'

'Should you do that?' Clara asked. 'If it's a fatal accident. Aren't you supposed to . . . ?'

'We've no choice. While me and Nick are upstairs, you and Lottie can get back on the bus and drive down to the turning area at the end of the drive, so you can pull a three-point. Young Jordan's in a bad enough state as it is without you driving over him to get there.'

'Okay, but—'

'Then drive back here and wait for us at the door. But keep the bus locked and stay low.'

'Stay low?' If Clara had seemed groggy and sallow-faced on first arriving here, she now looked wide awake. 'Liz, it really sounds as if there's more about all this I should know.'

'In a nutshell,' Nick said, 'there's a gunman on the premises picking us off. He might take potshots at you.'

'I see. Well . . .' Clara sighted Millie slumped in her chair on the other side of the hall, and paled even more. 'Well . . .' She swallowed. 'I suppose it was bound to happen at some point. Some of the madmen we've learned about on this tour. We were always likely to meet one who wasn't finished yet.'

◆ ◆ ◆

Upstairs, Liz and Nick halted on the minstrels' gallery, again scanning the open space below. As before, nothing moved. It seemed remarkable after everything that had happened that there were only minor instances of damage here and there.

Nick shook his head. 'None of this seems real.'

'Don't even go there,' Liz retorted. 'It'll likely take us so long to get back here with the cops that he'll have had ages to tidy up after himself. Our story may well sound like a pack of lies, but six people will still have died, and we'll have to account for it.'

They moved on to Jordan's room. Inside, the light was on, but the bed unused. The kid's untidily packed rucksack sat open.

'Poor little fella hadn't even unpacked,' Nick said.

'Never mind that now. *This* is what we're here for.' Liz crossed to where the painting, neatly boxed again, stood propped up on the writing desk. She opened it, and took it out. They glanced over it, but it was exactly the same image they'd seen before. Nothing jumped out as being crucial to their situation.

They packaged it again and headed back out to the stairs, Liz carrying the box, the pair of them intensely alert. With deliverance so close at hand, it seemed a near-certainty they'd be attacked again before they could leave. But in fact, they descended the staircase unmolested. The only problem then was that, when they stopped at the bottom, there wasn't a sound from outside.

Shouldn't they have heard the bus's engine again?

Shit, no . . . Liz thought.

Warily, they approached the entrance. The door stood ajar. Nick eased it open a little more. The bus waited outside, as planned, pointed in the homeward direction. But its engine and headlamps had been turned off. Likewise, there were no lights inside.

'Now what?' Nick breathed.

They went down the steps to the vehicle's front door. It was closed, and when Nick rattled the handle, locked. Liz glanced through the glass, which was grubby and dusty, concealing much of the interior. She was about to suggest they get back inside quickly, when a set of pale features slammed into view, only inches from her face. She jumped with fright.

But it was Clara. She'd been keeping low as they'd told her.

Lottie's face also then appeared, peeking down from one of the windows at them.

Clara stood up, hit a switch on the dashboard and with a pneumatic hiss, the front and rear doors, which worked in tandem, folded themselves open. Still with the painting under her arm, Liz went in through the front, Nick close behind.

'Any chance we can have the lights on, Clara?' he asked. 'So we can check this out?'

'Not a great idea,' Clara replied, hitting the door-control switch again, both doors hissing closed. She took charge of the steering wheel. 'Not when the visibility up here's so bad already.' She hit the ignition and flicked on the headlamps. The high beams reflected straight back from the turgid curtain of mist. 'Try this.' She felt in her glovebox, bringing out an electric torch. 'This work?'

'That'll do,' Liz said.

They trooped down the aisle, Liz finally finding a seat that suited her, Nick sliding into the one behind, Lottie, suddenly looking utterly exhausted, sitting down opposite. The vehicle lurched forward, Clara driving slowly and jerkily through the reduced visibility.

They couldn't help but lean over to appraise the immense structure of the Lodge as it slid past them. There was a palpable sense of relief, but even with the little Liz could see of it, it wouldn't have surprised her to spot a sniper in one of the windows, dead set on taking them all out.

'I hardly dare ask this,' Clara said over her shoulder, 'but all the others are dead, yeah?'

'Didn't Lottie tell you?' Nick replied.

'Said something about it.'

'Well . . . yeah, I'm afraid they are.'

'You're absolutely sure? Because it's not going to look great if someone's badly injured and we just drive away and leave them.'

That was Clara all over, Liz thought. Level-headed and pragmatic as ever.

'They're all dead, Clara,' she confirmed, handing Nick the torch. 'I guarantee it.'

Clara shook her head sadly as she worked the gears, putting her foot down. To their left, through fleeting breaks in the mist, they spied the glass-smooth surface of the reservoir, then the jetty with a single motorboat alongside it. And then they were among trees, and tilting forward as the hillside road commenced its descent.

'At least we're not likely to meet someone coming the other way,' Lottie said.

'I don't care if we do,' Nick replied. 'I'm just glad we're moving.'

'Are we going straight to the police?' Lottie asked.

'Don't see as we've any choice,' he said. 'As soon as bloody possible, in fact.'

'He'll still get away, though, won't he?' she said dolefully. 'I mean he'll be long gone by the time the police get there. We'll be the only suspects.'

'Not necessarily,' Liz replied. 'Let's see what this painting tells us.'

She'd now extricated the artwork from its box. Shoving the cardboard aside, she stood the framed image upright, resting it on her knees and propping it back against the seat in front. Nick leaned over her to look, switching the torch on.

As before, there was nothing glaringly obvious.

Not as far as they could see.

'Just a guy in a prison cell,' Nick said, shrugging. 'Granted, he looks uncannily real. Caruso's got talent. But I can't see where the clues are supposed to be.'

'The shadow on the wall behind him looks a bit weird,' Liz observed, puzzled but uncertain what it was that struck her about it as odd.

'Shadows can be all things to all men,' Nick said. 'They can make you look fatter, thinner. Especially if Caruso was just painting what he saw. Who knows what the light source was. Or what angle it came from.'

'Any writing?' Lottie asked.

'Some.' Liz ran her fingertip along the painting's bottom edge. Caruso's scribbled signature was present, along with another of those pretentious Latin inscriptions, but that was all.

And anyway, her vision was now blurring. Doubtless, this was down to fatigue. They'd been awake and running around madly for nearly twenty hours. Masses of twists and sprains were making themselves felt. In addition, the relief that they were finally safe, or at least on their way to safety, was making them all light-headed.

'Maybe we should just give this thing to the cops?' Nick yawned. 'They'll have experts.'

'Art experts?' Liz said doubtfully.

'Whoever they are, if nothing else they'll be more awake than we are.'

Liz agreed. She too yawned, but she was exasperated as well. After everything they'd been through, after they'd literally been to war simply to stay alive, she really didn't want to now find herself in custody as a suspect. It might even be worse than that. They were all in a dingy and bedraggled state, a good sign that they'd been engaged in violent scuffles. It could even be that they ended up getting charged.

But ultimately, Nick was right. Still, nothing in this painting struck her as significant.

Or maybe they were just too exhausted to see it. She wondered how long it would be before they reached any kind of civilisation. Would they have time for a nap and then be able to cast fresher eyes on it? She glanced from the window, noting that they'd already descended out of the mist. In fact, the bus was travelling at a decent speed. There was nothing out there she recognised, though. Nothing she could even see in the early morning darkness.

'Where are you taking us to, Clara?' she called down the aisle.

'Nearest place is called Slaidburn,' Clara replied over her shoulder.

'That's just a village though, isn't it?' Liz said. 'I'm not sure there's any point going there at this hour.'

'We might be better off heading for Lancaster,' Nick said.

'No roads west from here, Nick,' Clara replied. 'But at Slaidburn, we can join the B6478. That'll take us over that way. I think.'

'You *think*?'

Clara glanced round, looking irate. 'Cut me some slack, eh? I was a bit fuddled on my way up here. Snoozing in bed when I got messaged, remember? Think I came a different way from the way we came before . . . I'm not quite sure, but it led to the right place in the end.'

Nick raised a hand of apology and leaned forward to look at Liz.

'Don't you think it weird?' he said, briefly seeming troubled. 'That he just let us go in the end?'

Liz thought about it. 'Maybe Clara's arrival was one opponent too many.'

'Or maybe he saw it as an opportunity. To escape, I mean. Don't suppose it's possible he might have stowed away in the baggage hold?'

'No one's in the baggage compartment, Nick,' Clara said, overhearing them. 'I'd have noticed. A light activates on the dashboard when it opens.'

'How about on the roof?'

'The roof?' She cracked a laugh. 'Good luck to him. There's nothing up there to hang on to. And once we get on a straight road, I'm hitting the gas.'

'Suits me.' Nick yawned again. 'The sooner we get *somewhere*, the better.'

He sat back, and rather painfully rearranged his position, as if he were planning to sleep.

Liz, however, was too wired for that. She didn't want to burn out what remained of her vision on that wretched portrait, though, so instead of checking it out again, she left it on her seat while she stepped out into the aisle and commenced stretching. As she did, the bus seemed to decelerate. She glanced out of the right-hand window, assuming they'd be approaching a junction, only to find herself staring into what looked like a void. There were no trees there, but no fields either. There wasn't even any hillside.

Glancing out on the left, she saw the same thing. It looked like mid-air.

She worked her way down the aisle. 'Clara?'

'It's okay, Liz, don't worry,' Clara replied. 'This is a quicker route.'

In front of them, Liz was now astonished to see the headlights spearing along a narrow green track, which ran straight as an arrow but had five-foot-high brick walls on either side.

'Is this . . . ?' She couldn't contain her astonishment. 'The viaduct? Are we crossing the viaduct?'

'Yeah, but like I say. It's not dangerous. I did it before. Save us half an hour easily.'

Not dangerous? Liz thought. *How old is it?*

She was now standing alongside the driver. The route in front of them, the old viaduct track-bed, was thick with untamed vegetation. The bridge itself had to have been standing close to two hundred years. Hadn't Nick said that it had ceased to function in the 1920s? Chunks of brickwork had even fallen from the walls on either side. Hopefully, that level of erosion didn't extend to the great pillars teetering down below.

'Didn't you say you got lost coming back?' Liz asked.

'Not lost,' Clara replied.

'But you struggled to find your way?'

'That's why I ended up taking this route.'

Liz supposed that made sense, though she was less sure where the confidently aired metric about it 'saving them half an hour' had come from.

She glanced down and for the first time, spied a smear down the right side of Clara's face. It hadn't been visible previously but now she'd tucked her hair back in order to drive.

In the glow from the dashboard, it was red.

Just like the small damp blotch, also on that side of Clara's head, just above the hairline.

Slowly, more through instinct than logic, Liz found herself backing down the aisle, only for the soles of her boots to start scraping and crunching. It sounded like grit.

Or perhaps soil? From an earthenware plant-pot maybe?

Clara floored her brake. The bus, though travelling slowly, ground to a halt so abruptly that a whole range of items spewed down from the luggage rack.

Loosely tied rolls of used, damp clothing, but also a bagful of electronic devices.

So forceful was the stop that Liz was thrown on to the seat to her left. One of the devices landed on it too, directly in front of her face. An iPhone. Hammered into scrap.

She snatched at it, though momentarily couldn't comprehend what she was seeing.

There was more consternation further down the bus. When she glanced back, both Nick and Lottie had been thrown hard against the seats in front of them, winding themselves. More startling to them, though, was the large, oblong shoebox-type object that had also come thumping down from the luggage rack and now lay open in the aisle between them. Though it wasn't so much the box that had shocked them, as what hung halfway out of it.

Liz rose slowly to her feet, while Nick stumbled down on to his knees.

'What . . . the hell is this?' he stuttered, laughing . . . but not laughing really. Confused.

'I'd be careful with that,' Clara said, watching through the rear-view mirror. 'Those fingers are packed with artistic talent. Wouldn't do to damage them.'

Liz glanced at her blankly, before swinging back to Nick.

'What the fuck?' he said, astounded.

At first, he'd taken it for a prosthetic, or perhaps a fragment of a department store mannequin. But when he shone the torch down on it, it became clear that it was a genuine human arm. Or a partial one. The jointed wrist was the main giveaway. It had been severed at the elbow, though whoever was responsible had sealed off the stump with what looked like a heavy-duty, waterproof dressing.

'Dear God,' Lottie said, rising slowly to her feet.

'What the fuck!' Nick gazed along the aisle. 'Clara, what the . . . ?'

Clara, though, had now stood up and turned, her right arm levelled. 'Stay where you are. All of you. Except for you, Liz . . . you can back up a bit.'

Liz retreated down the aisle a distance of three or so seats. For a crazy half-second she still thought their driver was kidding around, covering them with her index finger – until her eyes had adjusted sufficiently for her to see the weapon. It was familiar to her, of course. She'd been shot at with it several times already.

'Sideways, Liz.' Clara was eerily calm as she waggled the firearm to indicate that Liz could now slide into one of the seats. 'You already know this is no water pistol.'

Liz complied but was rapidly succumbing to shock. Only when her hands were raised did she think to glance back along the aisle. The other two were in a similar posture.

'If you need further proof, how likely is it that that madman Caruso would let me saw his arm off while he was still alive?' Clara said. Oddly, bewilderingly even, her voice sounded different. Still northern, but less Manchester, less working-class. 'A bullet to the back of the head was the easiest solution.'

'So . . . you've . . . ?' Nick still looked baffled as he shone the torch down on the lopped-off limb. 'You've killed Caruso?'

Clara cocked her head sideways. 'You know, Nicky, given that you have this yearning to write horror movies, it's always amazed me how slow on the uptake you are. I mean, you even went to uni. What did you get . . . a third?'

'I . . .' Nick's eyes fixed on the Walther. 'A second.'

'Ah. Drinking man's degree. Gives you some cred. But presumably that's why your Latin's so sketchy.' She arched an eyebrow. '*Non bona similitudo?*'

He frowned all the more. 'I'm . . . not following.'

'*Non bona similitudo*,' Liz said. 'The inscription on the Monkton painting.'

'*Non bona similitudo*?' Lottie said slowly. '"Not . . . not a good likeness."'

'There, you see.' Clara smiled at her. 'All that religious study served a purpose after all.'

Lottie shook her head. 'I overheard Darius saying something about it. When he was trying to persuade Jordan to sell the painting to him. He said that was the reason Caruso was initially reluctant to part with it.'

'Really?' Clara arched an amused eyebrow. 'Well, that's what people assumed the inscription meant. That it wasn't a good likeness of Travis Monkton. But what if it actually meant that it wasn't a good likeness of the Night Monster? Perhaps purposely so?'

'Clara, what are you saying?' Liz whispered.

Clara sighed. 'I thought *you'd* be a little more observant, Liz. You don't remember all that newspaper outrage . . . when Monkton was waiting to be sentenced. Standing in the dock, impassive. Not a hint of remorse. "The blue-eyed devil", as the red-tops called him. "Blue-eyed devil", Liz? Dear me . . . you're almost as bad as Nick.' She kept the weapon levelled as she reached behind to the dashboard and, flicking a switch, turned on the bus's interior light. 'Why don't you show us all, Nicky? And I'm talking about the painting, not your todger.'

Slowly, Nick picked up the framed image and turned it around. Liz stared at it.

'The eyes have it, Liz,' Clara said. 'Blue-eyed devil indeed, eh?'

'Except that his eyes aren't blue,' Liz replied, her heart sinking like a stone as the terrible realisation seeped through her. 'Not in this picture. They're green and brown.'

'Rather like mine,' Clara said. She held up the back of her left hand. 'Seen this V-shaped scar anywhere before?'

They didn't need to glance at the painting again to recognise a very faint and yet distinctly similar mark on the back of Travis Monkton's left hand.

And now I know what's wrong with that shadow on the prison wall, Liz told herself. *It has rounded hips, a narrower waist, even a bustline.*

'Not a good likeness,' Lottie said again, with slow, awful understanding.

'You're . . .' Nick stammered. 'Clara, you're saying *you* were the Night Monster?'

Clara's face split into a fierce, feral grin. 'Not "was", Nicky. *Am.*'

'The rest of you get down!' he bellowed, throwing the painting aside and hurling the torch as he launched himself at speed along the aisle.

'Nick, *no!*' Liz screamed.

Clara swayed sideways, the torch passing harmlessly, before snapping off two quick rounds. The double flash-bang was deafening, the two slugs ripping side by side into Nick's chest, flinging him violently sideways and back, dropping him down between the next two seats.

Liz and Lottie had instinctively ducked, but now looked slowly up, eyes goggling.

'So like Nick,' Clara sighed. 'He knows I've got a loaded gun. And he charges anyway. What an absolute plank.'

Thirty-Seven

'Don't even think about moving, Liz!' Clara said, pointing the Walther.

Liz was back on her feet already. 'Clara, you . . . *bitch!*'

'I said don't move, and while you're at it, shut up!'

'You murdering bitch!'

'I said shut the fuck up, Liz!'

But of course, Liz couldn't. She was reeling, her eyes locked on the footwell where Nick lay motionless, tears fogging her vision. 'You just . . . you didn't need to . . . *you goddamn bitch!*'

Clara snarled and pointed the weapon directly at her head.

'I'll kill you for this . . .' Liz lurched into the aisle.

'Liz, no!' Lottie screeched behind her.

Liz halted again, sodden eyes riveted on their nemesis at the front of the vehicle.

'That's it,' Clara said. 'Much more sensible. You stay where you are too, Rev.'

Lottie indicated Nick. 'Clara, at the very least, I need to check on—'

'He's just taken two shots to the heart, darling,' Clara snickered. 'I think he's beyond the help of Saint Francis of Assisi now, never mind a defrocked, demotivated fat girl like you.'

'I . . . I wasn't defrocked, I . . .'

'No one cares, okay!' Clara snapped. 'Literally, no one gives a fuck about your failed and futile vocation! So shut up from now on unless I tell you to speak!'

Silence descended, Liz standing rigid about three seats down from the front, Lottie further back, but both now compliant, their eyes nailed fearfully on their captor.

'That's it,' Clara said. 'That's better. But what a pair we have here. Who'd have imagined that you two would make it to the end? The pretty girl who threw it all away on a loser of losers, and the poor man's Vicar of Dibley.'

'You bitch!' Liz hissed. 'You shot my fucking boyfriend.'

Clara smirked. 'He got off lightly, I'm sure you'll agree.'

'You're saying you're the Night Monster?' Lottie asked, still in a tone of incredulity. 'That can't be true. The police . . .'

'The police aren't what they were, I can tell you that.' Clara shook her head. 'Thankfully, for the likes of me, it's all about money these days. They had their man and weren't interested in Roy Southerby's theory that someone else was involved.' She snorted at Liz's reaction. 'You didn't believe that guff about more bodies being buried, did you? Or that Roy had come here to set eyes on the painting? No, Liz . . . I listened to his Dictaphone after I took it from Matlock. Roy was here to set eyes on those who *wanted* the painting. Could've been any one of you, couldn't it?' She smirked again. 'Pity for him it wasn't.'

'Clara . . . this is insane nonsense,' Lottie stuttered. 'It *has* to be.'

'Why's that, Reverend Gray? Because women aren't supposed to do this sort of thing? You never heard of Elizabeth Bathory? Bathed in the blood of young girls? Queen Bloody Mary? Liked to eat roast chicken while watching Protestants burn at the stake? Jeez, you must've heard of Rose West?'

'Course I have. What're you trying to prove?'

Clara shrugged. 'That it's an equal opportunities game. Why should the boys have all the fun?'

'It took a boy, though, didn't it?' Liz said coolly, fighting to get herself together because she knew she had to. 'I mean, to facilitate these crimes. You're not telling me Travis Monkton was nothing more than a fall guy?'

'Oh, he was involved,' Clara conceded. 'But only in terms of the abductions. He had no belly for the rest of it.' Her smirk became a full-blown vicious smile. 'That was all me.'

'So how come he ended up taking all the blame?'

'Isn't it obvious? The abductor always ran the greatest risk of detection.'

'And Monkton was happy with that?'

'You have to love adoring acolytes, don't you?'

'You and Monkton are as mad as each other!' Lottie blurted.

'Well, they do say like attracts like.' Clara shrugged. 'But I think that's oversimplifying it. You see, the internet was in its infancy then. Largely unpoliced. There were lots of secretive, niche-interest groups, which the rest of society would have considered beyond the pale.'

'Seriously?' Lottie said. 'Torture, murder?'

'And worse, Rev. Hey, you need to start flaunting yourself in your jewellery and make-up again. Get out a bit more. You'd be amazed what's lurking behind the polite veil of everyday society.' She glanced again at Liz, who was watching her coldly. 'What's up, Liz, cat got your tongue? Too busy thinking about Travis prowling the highways and byways, looking for easy targets? And me in that dingy concrete bunker, waiting with all my tools, wearing only my leather gauntlets and thigh-boots and my heavy-duty leather apron?'

'And when your wait was over, Lapdog Monkton just sat outside in his car?' Liz said, sensing that Clara was very proud indeed to be admitting that she was Britain's most feared serial killer, and determined to undermine it. 'I sincerely doubt that.'

Clara eyed her narrowly. 'Your doubt is misplaced, Liz. And don't worry about Travis. He always got his reward later. His needs were far more easily satisfied than mine.'

'I hope he enjoyed it, given the risks he took for you.'

'Sometimes we took them together,' Clara said. 'It's not so easy snatching strangers off the streets. Not when you're operating alone. Harry Anderton, for example. Millie's husband. Our first male . . . we weren't at all sure how that was going to go down, so I did my bit. Slipped poor dull Harry a Mickey Finn when he wasn't looking . . . It's amazing how a blonde wig, a bit of tarty make-up and a push-up bra can distract a fella.'

'Good Lord!' Lottie protested. 'You make it sound like sport.'

Clara rolled her eyes. 'You never heard it said the chase is as much fun as the catch?'

'Clara, how did you get like this?'

'Well, the lurid circumstances of my early life would make an interesting sermon for you, Rev, but I'm not as garrulous as the rest of you. I mean, I've been shadowing you people pretty closely these last few hours. Not all the time, I should say . . . but I've still learned all there is to know about you.'

'And it hasn't just been this last night, has it?' Liz said. 'All year we've had you working for us as a part-time bus driver, but in actual fact you were stalking us even then, weren't you?'

Clara feigned regret. 'I was left with no choice. That David Hockney wannabe, Michael Caruso, was starting to get ideas above his station.'

'He knew you were the real Night Monster?' Lottie asked.

'Not as such, but he knew that Travis Monkton wasn't. They were banged up eleven hours a day in the same concrete shoebox. They were bound to start talking.'

'And Travis wasn't supposed to, was he,' Liz said. It wasn't really a question. 'He'd been your infatuated follower. He was supposed to take the whole blame for ever more.'

Clara still watched them along the barrel of her pistol, but now looked thoughtful.

'I must admit, I thought he'd keep his stony silence longer than he did. But then he had a minor breakdown. I guess the weight of facing the rest of his days in Gull Rock was too much for him. It's too much for a lot of them, apparently. That place is no picnic.'

'He named you to Caruso?' Liz asked, fascinated to know, despite their situation.

Clara smiled. 'Seeing as he never knew my real name, that wasn't possible. You see, no one exchanges personal info in that dark, strange world where Travis Monkton and I first encountered each other. Just as I've never divulged my real name or address to you, Liz.'

Liz frowned. 'You're not Clara Kershaw?'

'It's a nice name. It served. But no. That's not even the name that Travis knew me by.' The killer chuckled again. 'What that foolish lunk did do, though, was let it slip that he'd been serving a higher power. Plus a few other minor details: the fact I was a woman, my odd, witchy eyes, the telltale scar on my hand. I doubt he thought it would do any harm, though what he didn't expect was for Michael Caruso to get released after serving only seventeen years of a thirty-year sentence, on the grounds of prison overcrowding. All of a sudden, out of the blue, Caruso had his life back. He'd even inherited money from an aged relative and was able to set up his own art gallery. A portrait gallery of the criminally insane, eh? Wonderful idea, if it hadn't been such a threat to me.'

'Let me guess,' Liz said. 'Blackmail came next?'

'Of course. Caruso passed it on to Monkton that he'd adjusted the portrait, now incorporating certain key details that reflected the true Night Monster.'

'The eyes and the scar?'

'And the female shadow and even an all-new Latin inscription, which basically said "this is not the Night Monster". Whoever the real killer was would need to visit the gallery and buy it off him. For an exorbitant price, of course . . . if they didn't want it to go on open sale. We haggled for nearly a full year without once meeting.'

'The year you were working for us?' Liz said.

Clara smiled. 'Really getting to grips with this, now, aren't you, Liz? He never knew who I was. We interacted only through Monkton, but that was play-acting on my part. I'm not the sort of person who pays criminals to keep quiet about me. Instead, I go after those criminals if they don't.'

'That's why you offered your services to us?'

Clara shrugged. 'Your Murder Tour visited Caruso's art gallery on a regular basis. I mean what better way for me to keep an eye on things and at the same time remain incognito?'

'Just out of interest, where did you get the bus?' Liz asked. 'I mean we could hardly reject you when you turned up at the job interview with your own vehicle.'

'I bought it. Wasn't even expensive. A second-hand old banger.'

'But why go to all that trouble?' Lottie said, voice querulous. 'If you enjoyed killing so much, why not just kill Michael Caruso when he first tried to blackmail you?'

'He'd already thought of that. Had sent a message that the painting was in a safe place, and that if anything happened to him it would appear all over the internet . . . and I don't need to tell you that it wouldn't have taken long for someone to spot the likeness to me then. The giveaway feminine shadow. My odd eyes *and* a scarred hand? So, like I say, I haggled. And drove the tour bus, watching, scoping his place out. In the end of course, it got serious. I had to go into the gallery with the rest of you and see for myself, because by this time Caruso had ceased negotiating, and the word on the true crime socials was that he planned to sell his Monkton at market value. Anyone could have got hold of it, and I had to know who.'

'Which is why only his arm seems to be left of him?' Lottie asked.

'Tragic waste really,' Clara said. 'Did a real number on that girl who lived next door to him. Talented boy. But in the end, there's no honour among murderers. So yes, ladies . . . I paid him a visit yesterday evening, while you were all settling into the Lodge. And it's a good thing. Turns out he wasn't just selling the original. He'd made copies.' She reached down to the side of her driving seat and pulled up a bulging folder. 'Signed prints, would you believe!' She tossed them on to the seat. 'I mean, what was to stop him making more? On which subject, you can slide that original along the aisle towards me, Lottie, if you wouldn't mind.'

Eyes still fixed on the firearm, Lottie picked up the framed painting and walked it down the aisle, pushing it ahead of her until she was level with Liz.

'That's close enough,' Clara said. 'You can throw it from there.' She tittered. 'I don't mind if it gets damaged.'

Lottie did so, and Clara caught it one-handed, giving it another quick once-over. 'Excellent. Can go with the rest of the bonfire fuel.' She placed that on the driver's seat as well.

'And us?' Lottie asked. 'Is that our destiny too?'

Clara eyed them, again with an air of pretend sorrow. 'I'm afraid everyone here has become a nuisance, Rev. Not intentionally, I admit. But who knows what conclusions you people might have come to? And this was especially concerning for me when I found out that one of you was part of an investigation team called the Murder Resolution Society. Later on, of course, I also heard that one of you was an ex-cop, who wouldn't let go of the Night Monster case. I mean, hell . . . once the ball had started rolling, it *had* to roll all the way. But don't worry, it's all going to get tied up neatly at the end. You see' – her voice hit a lower register, as if she were confiding a secret – 'it's Michael Caruso who killed you. He followed you up here from his gallery for reasons only a complete psycho like him would understand. He found his way around the property by using the same schematic from the Black Tarn Lodge website that I used. In fact . . .' She slipped a phone from her jeans pocket and held it up. 'I used it on *his* phone. And after that, after Caruso killed you all, he vanished. Never to be seen again.'

'You missed out the most important part,' Liz cut in. 'The bit where you *really* did all this because you enjoyed it.'

'What I've just told you, Liz, is the truth,' Clara said. 'But I won't pretend there wasn't a significant element of pleasure too.'

'Okay, Clara,' Lottie said, nodding to herself as if reaching some decision. 'I think you've had your fun.'

'A lot of fun, Lottie.'

Lottie edged forward. 'But now it's over, so why don't we start by lowering the gun?'

'Stay where you are.' Clara raised the weapon to eye level. 'I saw you waving that curved blade around earlier. It didn't look like you knew one end of it from the other, but anyone can kill if they get close enough.'

'You think they'll buy that ridiculous story?' Liz asked her.

'It'll be a complicated crime scene, I admit,' Clara said. 'But once the police find Michael Caruso's fingerprints in and around the property, and even on some of the murder weapons, this gun included, you seriously think they won't settle on the one person involved in all this who they know for sure has murderous tendencies?'

Lottie, meanwhile, had edged forward again. 'All very good, Clara, but the truth is that you don't really want to do this.'

'Lottie, what are you doing?' Liz asked her.

'You think so?' Clara replied.

'Whatever situation you got trapped in with Travis Monkton,' Lottie said, 'he's gone now, he's in prison. You don't have to be his slave.'

'His slave?'

Lottie advanced a little further. 'I've seen how abusive relationships work.'

'My dear Lottie, you must be one of these people who believes Myra Hindley wasn't an evil cow in her own right.'

Lottie halted to consider it. 'I think people can be brainwashed.'

'Brainwashed?'

'Terrorised, even.' The ex-cleric pressed on again. 'You were probably so brutalised by your relationship with Monkton that you didn't even know what you were doing.'

'Lottie!' Liz said warningly.

'It's my dagger you're worried about? Here, see.' Lottie lifted the jewel-hilted weapon with her fingertips, before dropping it. 'It can't hurt you now.' She advanced again.

'Lottie?' Liz advanced as well. 'There's putting your demons behind you by being brave, and then there's being plain old stupid.'

'No, let her come,' Clara snickered. 'Such innocence should be nurtured, not discouraged.'

Lottie was only a couple of feet in front of her now. 'Clara, put the gun down.'

'For God's sake!' Liz said, halting tensely.

'You don't need it. See . . .' Lottie was finally face to face with their tormentor. 'I've nothing in my own hands. Except *this*.'

It was a small bottle of Chanel No 5.

The jet of perfume hit Clara squarely in the eyes.

Gasping at the sudden, shocking pain, clamping one hand to her face, the madwoman lost her balance, enabling Lottie to barrel forward, shoving her backward, and dive for the dashboard, hitting the door-control as hard as she could, at the same time shrieking: *'Liz, get out! Run for your life!'*

Liz was so startled that she stood rigid, only belatedly turning and stumbling back down the aisle towards the back of the bus, where the rear exit was opening.

Lottie and Clara meanwhile grappled wildly with each other, Lottie going for her opponent's gun arm, but already being clubbed repeatedly by the weapon.

'Interfering cow!' Clara snarled, still rubbing at her eyes. 'You've just killed yourself.'

'*Liz, run!*' Lottie squawked, only for Clara to grab her by a straggle of hair and send her tumbling head over heels down the steps to the bus's front door, which was also now open.

And out through it.

The former track-bed was so narrow that there was almost no room on either side of the stationary vehicle. So, Lottie didn't so much strike the broken parapet of the viaduct's boundary wall as go clean over the top.

Liz still hadn't left the bus, but stood in the rear doorway, staring back, horrified. Only when Clara straightened up and aimed the gun in her direction did she throw herself out into open air.

Thirty-Eight

Liz's first problem was that she had no choice but to step straight on to the top of the parapet wall. The next problem was the flimsiness of that wall. Almost immediately, more bricks and crumbling mortar dislodged, falling from beneath her into the lightless abyss. Squealing, she threw herself back on to the side of the bus, ripples of movement passing all along the wall in either direction, the weathered structure cracking and sagging outward, more and more bricks falling free.

She leapt high, clinging to the raised edge along the vehicle's roof just as her own section of wall gave way, an avalanche of rotted stonework cascading into the darkness below. For a couple of seconds Liz hung by her fingertips, spreadeagled against the side of the vehicle. But she knew that death was still coming. She could hear it barging down the aisle towards the bus's rear exit. It might even be able to see enough to start shooting at her right now.

Re-energised by terror, she hauled herself skyward, jamming the toes of her boots into the narrow windowsill, levering herself upward, shoving her elbows on to the flat of the roof, the surge of adrenaline driving her on and on. The next thing, she was up on top of the bus, heaving for breath. And almost going dizzy as that mist-filled abyss spread out before her.

'Lottie!' The word escaped her as a sob, before she tottered around and stumbled across to the other side of the roof, where again she glimpsed a terrifying drop into vast, misty nothingness.

She backed up again, still dizzy, thinking to lay herself flat on the roof, only for common sense to scream that it would be equal lunacy. The killer below would now be wondering where her opponent lay, looking to punch bullets upward through the metal.

Her only option was to get off the damn thing. But then the vehicle began to rumble and judder. The engine had been switched on.

With a reverberating clunk, a gear was engaged. The bus lurched forward, but came to an almost immediate, violent halt. Liz tottered where she stood, arms windmilling. It jolted forward again, gears clanking as it accelerated. Another furious brake was coming, she could tell, stumbling to the roof's middle, dropping to a crouch. And indeed, the next stop was so sharp, the brakes biting so hard, that she was flung frontward, tumbling, and in so doing, almost tipping over the left-side edge, wildly grabbing at anything she could, her hands finding only bare metal, and yet, somehow, her desperate fingers acted like suction cups, locking her in place.

Empty darkness lay immediately to the left, one of her legs hanging over it.

Gasping, she rolled back into the centre of the roof. The vehicle rumbled forward again, only to pull another abrupt halt. The same thing happened again, and again, and again. Liz bounced over and over. She was almost now at the front of the bus.

Fall down in front of it and this maniac will simply drive over you.

That left only one option. The rear. She scuttled a short distance backward, but even if she jumped down behind the bus and tried to run back along the viaduct, wouldn't the fiend behind the wheel simply throw it into reverse, catch up with her again, run her down?

Some option.

Liz flattened herself on the roof, clutching the bare metal with such force that she imagined she'd leave skin behind if thrown forward. Thus, when it crashed to its next standstill, she rode it out. Ahead, she now saw that they were almost at the far side of the valley. How long before they were back on the road? And then that lunatic, Clara, would accelerate and accelerate . . .

There was no choice. And the time was now.

Absolutely now.

Liz got to her feet and ran back as hard as she could along the top of the bus. The booming impacts of her footfalls must have been audible. Or maybe not, as the massive vehicle ground and growled its way through ever deeper tangles of vegetation. With luck, that same mesh of desiccated mulch would provide a cushion for her.

She reached the back of the bus and, without thinking, jumped.

It was her second big leap of faith that night, and this time she descended ten or so feet, landing with such impact that it knocked the wind from her, pain flaring angrily through the monstrous bruising already covering her body. Even after hitting the ground, she cartwheeled forward through dead but thorny thickets, tearing both her clothes and her skin.

Biting down on the agony, she swayed upright and recommenced running.

The track-bed spooled out before her, straight as a ribbon, whole sections of its parapet walls having long ago collapsed, giving fleeting glimpses of oblivion. It was a distance of maybe six hundred yards to the far side, and she wasn't sure she'd make it, not with her left hip and left knee a double dose of torture, the knee joint in particular grinding as though packed with broken glass. Behind her meanwhile she heard a furious clanking of gears, the engine gunning itself back to life.

Already, Clara was reversing after her.

Liz charged headlong, the breath ripping through her chest like a saw, snagged and plucked repeatedly by the hanks of thorns and bracken, but this time the vehicle was having problems too. Glancing back, she saw that it wasn't gaining as it should. It was still coming, but perhaps even a skilled driver like Clara was inexperienced in reversing at speed along a narrow strip of track with plummeting depths to either side.

Encouraged, Liz ran on, now sticking to the broad wheel ruts the vehicle had already left behind, much of the vegetation lying flattened inside them. Her speed thus increased. Halfway over, she was still accelerating, extra adrenaline blinding her to all pain. She glanced back again. The reversing bus remained far behind. A couple of times when it tried to speed up, it lost traction, and collided with one or other of the parapet walls, sending more rubble showering downward. Those must have been terrifying moments even for a certified loon like Clara. Liz on the other hand was almost across.

Directly ahead, she spied a wide gap in the dense hedgerow, what had once been a heavy steel gate, something you'd normally see on a farm, having been thrown open to allow admittance on to the viaduct. Beyond it, though, she also saw mist, a great veil of it creeping downhill from the higher, wooded terrain.

On the other side of the gate, she stopped. Panting hard, trying to get her bearings, seeing only a hedged cart track meandering away in front of her. It didn't promise much, but to the immediate left there was another leafless hedge with a gap in it, and beyond that what looked like a field. She slid through, still resisting the pain and breaking into a sprint as she crossed open land. Even then, the going wasn't easy, the field sloped, uneven with stubble and heaped with hay. But the mist now flooding down from the woods was as thick and milky as it had been up at the reservoir.

Liz didn't think she'd ever been as glad of obscured visibility.

◆ ◆ ◆

Clara was still raging with anger, literally foaming at the mouth.

She'd never liked Liz O'Hara from the moment they'd begun working together. With her understated good looks, her clipped attitude and cool air, Liz was every inch the self-empowered office girl, her massive ambition matched only by her massive lack of talent. It had always given Clara secret pleasure that Liz, though well-enough educated and oh so superior in her manner, was still destined for nothing special. Certainly not for as long as she was welded at the hip to a loser like Nick 'all ideas and no know-how' Thornwood. It had become especially scrumptious when she'd realised that she was going to have to kill them both, though conversely, it was all the more irritating now that Liz was still eluding her.

'Of all the people,' she spat, reversing through the gate on to the north side of the valley. That hoity-toity bitch had to be the one.

She hit the brake, jumped up and ran down the aisle, halting by the open rear door and listening. No sound. Nothing. But Liz couldn't be far away. Not in her battered, bruised condition. Not that it would be easy finding her now that fresh vapour was trailing down across the landscape. Though clearly the woman would have headed *that* way, into the fields, to make use of the spreading murk.

'I love a bitch who thinks she's clever,' Clara snorted.

She went back along the aisle, searching the various footwells, but finally locating the electric torch lying half under a seat. She snatched it up and weighed the Walther PP in her hand. She'd only fired four shots since reloading it earlier. That meant there were six remaining. That would be more than enough, but just to make sure, she headed back to the front and, opening the glovebox, took out two extra clips and shoved them into her jeans.

She'd have liked to find a more imaginative way to dispense with Liz, but an element of damage limitation was creeping in. It wasn't far off seven o'clock in the morning. If she was to get the rest of the bodies back up to the Lodge, contaminate the premises with Caruso's prints, and then reunite the sad bastard's arm with the rest of him, seven hundred feet down at the bottom of the tarn, she had to start acting on it soon. So, gun it would need to be.

She dismounted from the bus and advanced through the stile on to the field, the mist already swirling past her, piles of hacked hay hampering her, making her kick to get through it. A couple of times, she clicked the torch on, but the intense beam did little to penetrate the gloom, and most likely would act as a warning that she was coming. She switched it off again as she prowled forward, sticking it in her belt. All the time, she kept the gun levelled, even when she stopped to listen.

Perhaps on the fourth or fifth occasion, she heard the sound of feet on the move.

Her fist tightened on the weapon's handgrip.

The infamous Walther PP semi-automatic: 007's preferred means of despatching his foes. It was disappointingly quick in its execution, but like all items designed to destroy human tissue, it excited Clara merely being close to it.

More important now, of course, was that she'd definitely just heard feet thudding away. But the damn vapour, drifting past in ever-thickening veils, was obscuring everything. Until suddenly, for half a second, it wasn't.

It broke, and Clara glimpsed her prey hovering about thirty yards to the left.

She swung that way, knocking the Walther's safety off.

Liz came into view again. Just about distinguishable.

'Got you dead, O'Hara,' she said under her breath. She wanted to shout it, but didn't dare. Liz was standing and listening, clearly unaware that she'd been detected. Which was all the opportunity Clara needed to get much, much closer. Ten yards away, she stopped, lifting the Walther to eye level in a textbook, two-handed grip – and was struck from behind by something with the force of a charging bull.

The impact caught Clara directly between her shoulders and sent her staggering forward, pile-driving the breath out of her. Her knees buckled and she flung her arms wide, losing hold of the gun, which went spinning into obscurity.

Shaken and hurt, she still had the wherewithal to stay upright and look back, startled to see that a third party had entered the scenario. A third party who now lay writhing in the hay, apparently more severely injured than she was herself.

'Nick?' she said with slow disbelief. 'Nick, how the hell did you . . . ?'

But the explanation immediately presented itself, because Nick's tattered anorak now hung open, and beneath it she saw a snugly fitted undershirt made from some thick, durable material, dark in colour. Body armour, because the two rounds she'd hit him with were clearly visible there. Side by side, semi-embedded in the vest, but also flattened out.

Nick cringed as he struggled to get to his feet, the pain defeating all his efforts. Which of course, it would. The bulletproof garment might well have absorbed the lead itself, but from that range, the punches delivered to his midriff would have been bone-breaking. Highly likely, Nick had a fractured sternum to contend with.

'Well, well . . .' Clara chuckled. 'How typical of you, Nicky. You couldn't even ambush me from behind, and in fog, without fucking yourself up.'

She wasted no further time on him, spinning back round, expecting Liz to be coming at her as well. But she wasn't. She hadn't even moved. Clara drew the torch and speared its beam forward. It was more than a minor shock to find that it wasn't Liz she was looking at, but some idiotic farmer's idea of a scarecrow, a hideous effigy indeed, but only held upright by an iron post.

She swung back to where Nick lay groaning.

'Some things never change, eh, Nicky?' she said. 'See what you've just thrown your life away for?' She came and stood over him. 'Anyway . . .' She reached under her sweater and pulled out the wavy-bladed dagger from the Eric Helgoland chapel. 'At least you've given me an opportunity to use this . . . and the means by which to sort Liz out as well. Least, I hope you have. I mean, it'd be a bit embarrassing if even her boyfriend's agonised screams fail to lure her back to us. Let's put it to the test, eh . . . ?'

'You don't need to,' Liz said, leaping up from under the pile of hay next to her. 'I'm already here.'

She levelled the pitchfork and charged.

Astounded, Clara slashed with the blade, but couldn't reach her target, because three steel points had already penetrated her middle, and were ripping deeply into the organs beneath. She gargled and squawked as she toppled backward, but Liz advanced relentlessly, the eyes glazed in her dirty, battered face, pushing and pushing until the pair of them came to the limp, lifeless form of the scarecrow, where Clara halted, mouth foaming blood, still waving the knife, still hitting nothing. Certainly not Liz, who shoved with the pitchfork nevertheless, driving its three steel prongs all the way through her and deep into the ragged mannequin behind.

When she finally let go and backed away, gasping, the pitchfork handle stayed level, while the killer remained on her feet, though her eyes were two fading lamps, one brown, one green, which briefly fixed on her, before going out.

Nick, who'd managed to get up, hunched forward, hugging his ribs, but staring in horrified fascination at the grisly totem.

Liz swung to face him. She stood there rigid. 'So . . . you're alive!' It was almost an accusation, but tears of relief glimmered in her lashes. 'I mean obviously you're alive, but . . .'

He opened his anorak. 'Karnwood's Bond movie, remember? Once I knew we were facing a gun, I offered this vest to Lottie. She tried it but it didn't fit . . .'

Liz stumbled towards him, trying to clasp him softly, but still setting him writhing and gurgling in pain.

'I'm sorry, I'm sorry,' she said, laughing as well as crying as she helped him down to his knees.

'It's okay,' he grunted. 'It's just . . . those shots were like hammer blows.'

'Thank God for James bloody Bond movies, eh?'

'The only one of Karnwood's that wasn't a horror,' he muttered. 'Gotta be a lesson there.'

A minute or so passed as he recovered, then, slowly and carefully, she assisted him back to his feet. The sense of warmth that washed over her induced a fresh flood of emotion, tears streaming down her cheeks, shock, relief and horror all rolled into one.

For Nick's part, they were primarily tears of pain. Lots of stuff was broken in there, he was certain of it. Though mainly bones. To start with, his legs were so weak that he could barely stand. Gingerly, still cringing, he looped one arm over Liz's shoulder.

'Lord, you're heavy,' she muttered.

Nick could only grunt, his knees threatening to give way.

'Need a hand?' someone asked.

Despite encumbering each other, the twosome spun around, wild-eyed. To see a squat, tubby shape limping towards them through the scattered hay. New terror gripped them fleetingly, until they realised – to their astonishment, and joy – that it was Lottie.

Her hair was loose and filled with dust, her face and the entire front of her flashy silver coat smeared green by moss. They laughed in disbelief.

For all that it pained him, Nick shook his head. 'How did you, I mean . . . how?'

'Seems Clara wasn't quite as good a killer as she thought,' Lottie said, taking in the bullet-embedded vest under his anorak. 'In my case, it was an iron buttress about five feet down. It jutted out a couple of feet or so. I hit it hard and it hurt, I can tell you that.' She rubbed at her backside, wincing slightly. 'But at least it saved my life.'

'Bloody miracle,' Nick muttered.

'And you got here just in time.' Liz nodded to one of the field's corners, where in the milky light of the breaking dawn, a double-decker bus had pulled up at the crossroads.

'That's a bloody miracle too,' Nick grunted.

'I've always said there are strange powers in this world.' Lottie looped an arm under his other shoulder, so that, slowly and carefully, they could walk him towards it. 'And not all of them are evil.'

Perhaps not all, Nick thought, glancing over his shoulder. *But enough.*

The pinned and twisted form of Clara Kershaw slowly receded behind them. Still standing upright, her head hanging motionless, the grinning, demonic face of the scarecrow peeking over her shoulder.

Acknowledgements

Huge thanks go to my agent, Kate Burke, my editor-in-chief, Maisie Lawrence, my editor, Ian Pindar, my copyeditor, Sadie Mayne, and my proofreader, Gill Harvey. You guys are all gems. I couldn't have done this without you.

Did you enjoy uncovering the dark secrets revealed by a trip to Black Tarn Lodge? If so, then you'll absolutely love *The Island* by Paul Finch.

A dream holiday. You'd die to be there.

You are offered the getaway of a lifetime on a remote island with a group of strangers. Things have been difficult recently, so you jump at the chance to swim under the summer sun, explore the peaceful woodlands and return to an elegant hotel for a glorious dinner.

Then one of your group disappears. His body washes up in the picture-postcard harbour, and it's clearly no accident. Can you get out alive?

A totally addictive and incredibly twisty thriller – available now or keep reading for an exclusive extract from Chapters 5, 6 and 7!

Five

'You look uncomfortable, Jack,' Wayland said. 'You got some idea that, any minute now, the press pack is going to jump out and start snapping us? And then tomorrow they're going to run a story that says: *Look at this . . . McGurn and Crayford caught in company with Harry Wayland. They were bent after all. What further proof do we need?* Well . . . newsflash, kids. They *don't* need any further proof. They know damn well you're bent.'

Wayland was nearly sixty with iron-grey unruly hair and thick sideburns. His once wolfish looks were leathery and seamed, battered both by age and considerable experience. But he'd taken off his leather jacket and underneath that was wearing a white T-shirt. His physique, while lean, was sinewy. He looked strong and fit.

'Just to be clear, Harry,' Jack replied, 'we weren't actually convicted of anything.'

'You used up your entire lifetime's supply of luck when that decision was reached. And you know it. The sole reason CPS didn't prosecute you is because the only witness they had was a drug-addled chemist called Ronald Jesperson, who'd been helping you check the quality of the gear but who still grassed you up as soon as he was facing other charges. But Jesperson was in such a state by then that putting someone like him on the witness stand would have been comedy value only.'

'Okay, we were lucky.' Claudia shrugged. 'Doesn't feel like it, I can tell you.'

'You don't need to tell me anything, Claudia. I know.'

They'd found a quiet corner for themselves in The Waterwheel's downstairs bar. Neither Jack nor Claudia had been personally acquainted with Harry Wayland, formerly DCI Wayland of the Major Incident Team, but there was no Greater Manchester Police officer, past or present, who didn't know about him.

It was Harry Wayland who'd led the enquiry that eventually brought Jimmy Cornwallis, aka 'the Dogman', to book. A self-styled urban guerrilla and infamous serial killer, Cornwallis, who chose his own nickname, inspired by his own 'dogged nature', was a shell-shocked ex-para with strong right-wing leanings, who on returning to Britain from the army, found it a crime-ridden mess, and undertook to clean things up by stalking and killing the prostitutes, pimps and drug-dealers infesting many of those north-west English towns he considered his home. A very dangerous individual indeed, he'd clocked up thirty victims, using a variety of crude weapons – knives, clubs, neck-wires – before being cornered by Wayland, who'd shot and killed him while he was resisting arrest.

However, despite Harry Wayland's high-level police skills, he was also corrupt. It later transpired that many of the murder enquiries he undertook – Wayland was regarded as a homicide expert – he diverted when it looked as though they were leading towards his underworld paymasters. This often resulted in the conviction and imprisonment of innocent men. They may have been criminals, undesirable specimens, but none were guilty of the murders for which they were jailed.

Wayland had taken down some of the worst of the worst, but he had also gone to great pains to jail the innocent, often for life, purely for money, the real killers left to roam the Earth with impunity.

Perhaps inevitably in Wayland's case, the Professional Standards people had fought hard for a jail term. Despite his previously stellar career, he served seven years of a ten-stretch. Just surviving that, as a former copper who'd sent villains down whether they deserved it or not, was impressive. And yet here he was now with a nonchalant air and philosophical attitude. He sat back, swilling from a bottle of lager.

'Society's changed gears these last few years,' he said. 'We're deep into a new age of pious intolerance. The eighties, which was when I started . . . fuck, feels like a lifetime ago. There are no likeable rogues anymore. We don't have loose cannons or Jack the Lads. All we have now are the thoroughly despicable, the low lifes who are beyond redemption, the out and out reprobates who need exposing, vilifying, rooting out. I'm talking coppers, of course, not normal folk. Look at a secretary the wrong way these days, and you're on a charge. Lay a finger on some shit-house who's been battering old ladies and you're out of a job.'

'There's no point trying to convince us we didn't do something wrong,' Claudia said. 'We know we did.'

Wayland glanced at Jack. 'She always this contrite?'

Jack shrugged. 'Doesn't pay to be anything else.'

'Doesn't pay to be remorseful either. Listen up, fellas . . .' Wayland leaned forward. No one else was earwigging, but he lowered his voice anyway. 'This shit's going to drag on. There's no respite for the likes of us, no forgiveness. And you know who's behind that. The metropolitan elite.' He spat the words, as if they were poisonous to him. 'That's right . . . those cosy middle-class wankers whose lifestyles we protected by taking so many villains off the street. None of that counts for anything now, you see. All the collars you felt, all the risks you ran, all that stress . . . all that falling out with your missus, every night, Jack, because each time you came home and your head wouldn't stop pounding after the teenage OD victims you'd pulled out of the drains that afternoon, or the little 'uns you'd found beaten to crap and dumped in a pond by their drunken mum's dog turd of a boyfriend, Claudia—'

'I thought you just said we were *part* of the problem?' Jack interrupted.

Wayland sat back again. 'You are. Or were. We all were. Doesn't mean *we* didn't get fucked over too.'

'Strangely enough,' Jack said, 'none of this is cheering us up.'

Wayland swilled more lager. 'I know something that might.'

He laid a business card on the table. It was beige and printed only on one side. It read:

DAMNED RANKERS

Underneath it, there was a telephone number.

'Damned Rankers?' Claudia said.

Wayland smiled. 'You think your world has ended. But I'm telling you it hasn't.'

Jack looked the card over. 'What is this?'

'In short . . . a support group. For discredited ex-officers.'

Claudia arched an eyebrow. 'Never heard of it.'

'Course you haven't. It's all done on the hush-hush. Imagine the fuss if the metro luvvies found out.'

'A support group?' she said. 'And you're part of it?'

He crooked a half-smile. 'I'm its official rep.'

'A support group for dirty cops?' Jack said.

'You look as if that's some kind of joke.'

'Isn't it?'

Wayland finished his bottle. 'Look, you did wrong. But you've paid for it. You've lost your careers, your reputations. Is it right you keep on paying for it just because the metro elite says you should?'

'Harry . . . cut the conspiracy crap,' Claudia said. 'We committed serious criminal offences. Like you said, it's a miracle we didn't do time.'

He eyed her. 'Perhaps if you *had* . . . like me and a few others, you wouldn't be so dismissive.'

'A few others? How many are there?'

'Enough.' He got to his feet, but a minute later, had returned to the table with a bottle of lager for himself and pints for Jack and Claudia.

'It's seriously called Damned Rankers?' Jack said.

'Catchy, eh?'

'Catchier than Bent Bastards, I suppose.'

'Or Damaged Goods,' Claudia said.

Wayland shook his head. 'You two are a right pair.' He glanced at Claudia, '*You're* acting like you'd voluntarily go inside,' then at Jack, 'and you're giving it the tough-guy routine, pretending you don't give a shit, which is a sure sign you do. It's bollocks. Your lives need to go on.' He tapped the card. 'And this is the key.'

Claudia picked up the card. 'What is Damned Rankers?'

'What I've told you. The circumstances you'll now have to live the rest of your lives in are not unique. But they are unusual. And no one knows about that better than the handful of others in the same place.'

'Who are these others?'

'Uh-uh. No private info until I know if you're in or out.'

Claudia put the card down. 'And if we're in, what benefits are there?'

'We offer friendship, advice, guidance. Sometimes a bit more.'

'A bit more?' Jack said.

'Well . . .' Wayland lowered his voice again. 'I imagine you two have got quite a bit stashed away. You didn't do the things you did for nothing. But you're not going to find decent jobs easily from now on, so at some point, that money will run out.'

'Financial assistance?'

'Maybe.' Wayland swilled from his bottle again. 'You know, most people I've approached have snatched my hand off by now. But seeing as you're playing hard to get, I'll humour you a little longer.' He looked thoughtful. 'Damned Rankers was the brainchild of a very private British-born billionaire, one of whose younger relatives was a student at uni down south. One night – no dates, sorry – she was attacked on her way home from a party, raped and strangled. The investigation made ground quickly. They closed in on a good suspect, a real weirdo who'd been causing nothing but trouble for women and girls in his neighbourhood for years, but who was reputed to have possession of a loaded pistol. A specialist firearms team moved in to arrest him in the early hours. The team leader went in first, called out a warning but almost immediately had cause to open fire. One shot went into the suspect's chest, the other into his head—'

'Damon Banks,' Jack interrupted.

Wayland shrugged. 'Maybe.'

'Give it a rest with the maybes, Harry. It was Damon Banks.' Jack glanced at Claudia. 'Tactical Firearms inspector, Sussex. He attempted to arrest Kenneth Renfrew, a Brighton resident who was also a registered sex offender and a suspect in three murders of local women. The arrest went haywire when Renfrew supposedly reached for a weapon on his bedside table and Banks shot him dead. In fact, alarmed by the intrusion, Renfrew had been reaching for the bedside light. A subsequent search of the property revealed strong evidence linking him to the murders, but no sign of a firearm, loaded or otherwise.'

Claudia nodded. 'I remember now . . . 2010-ish? Banks was charged with murder and convicted. He even lost his appeal, which infuriated the Federation and *Sun* and *Daily Mail* readers all over the country.' She looked at Wayland. 'I believe he's still in custody, still contesting his life sentence.'

'And let me guess,' Jack said, 'his campaign is now being bankrolled by this reclusive billionaire.'

Wayland shrugged. 'No stone will be left unturned in the quest to get Banks out. A highly decorated officer, who made one mistake . . . the only outcome of which was the removal from this world of a worthless toerag to whom females of any age were nothing more than playthings.'

'And now this billionaire, whose identity I suspect we could learn for ourselves if we dug deep enough . . .'

'I wouldn't count on that.'

'Whatever . . . he's now expanded his campaign to assisting other officers whom he considers have also got the shit end of the stick?'

'Harry . . .' Claudia shook her head. 'What does this new boss of yours not understand about *our* particular position? In contrast, for example, to Damon Banks?'

'In your case . . . and *mine,* there's no miscarriage of justice to be overturned. So . . . to us, all he offers is support. Friends help each other. There's nothing illegal about it. It's not even iffy. Look, he's doing a good thing. Getting ex-cops who went off the rails back into society, making them useful to their fellow men again.'

Jack and Claudia sat, pondering.

'Ultimately,' Jack said, 'it's all going to boil down to a bunch of us in hardbacked chairs in a draughty church hall, isn't it?'

Wayland smiled. 'Or first-class holiday accommodation in the Scilly Isles.'

Claudia looked puzzled. 'Come again?'

'Our next official get-together is mid-June. A week-long break, all costs and expenses paid, at Porth West, a new but exclusive resort on St Dunstan in the Isles of Scilly.'

'A holiday?' Jack said.

'You think you don't deserve one?'

Jack and Claudia glanced at each other. This was the last thing they'd expected. Jack shook his head. 'Sorry, Harry. Count me out.'

Wayland shrugged again. 'Up to you, but this could be the biggest miscalculation you've made since putting your life and career in the hands of Ronald Jesperson.' He turned to Claudia. 'How about you?'

'I'll be honest . . .' She flushed a little. 'I was thinking of starting again. Moving away.'

'We can help with that. The guy in charge has limitless funds. We can help you sort your mortgage out, get a new job, open a new bank account. All that stuff.'

'It's tempting. I won't deny it. But I don't know, Harry . . . I just want to be through with all this. Put it behind me.'

'You don't want any connection to your old life?'

'Correct.'

'We can arrange that too. We can sort a name change for you . . . hell, if it comes to it, we even know a few good plastic surgeons who'll give you a discount.'

'I thought this wasn't something iffy,' Jack cut in.

Wayland eyed him with irritation. 'It isn't. Jack, will you get it into your head, the guy who's paying for this thing is worth more than everyone else you know put together, times five thousand. You don't reach that level of economic superiority if you don't know how to play a few angles. But that doesn't mean you're a crim. Quite the opposite. You make the system work, you don't try and buck it. But listen, it's up to you.' He emptied his bottle and stood up.

'Where do we get in touch with you if we change our minds?' Claudia said.

'You've got the card.' He sidled round the table. 'But don't leave it long. That number will change.'

'Why?' Jack asked.

'Try using your noggin. The new puritans and their virtue-signalling mates in the media find out about this, it'll be the kind of coverage our benefactor doesn't need.'

'Perhaps *we* should sell them to the press?' Jack said, after Wayland had left. 'Our last big payday.'

Claudia looked round, accusation in her face. 'Why would you want to do that?'

'Come on, Claudi.' He fingered the card. 'This thing's got dodgy written all over it.'

She jumped to her feet. 'Well, *you* ought to know.'

'Wait up, what's the matter?'

She was halfway to the bar, but now came back. 'You're really going to turn your nose up at the one chance we might get to live something approaching a normal life again?'

'How will this give us a normal life? A new social circle, maybe, the odd interest-free loan.'

'Jesus, Jack! Even that'd be better than what we're facing now.'

'Claudia, you're your own person,' he said when she returned with fresh drinks. He slid the card towards her. 'You must do what you think's best. But one thing I don't reckon either of us needs at this moment is a week in the Isles of Scilly.'

She looked at him. 'Do you know anything about the Isles of Scilly?'

'Well, I mean . . . they're . . .'

'They're supposed to be really nice.'

'And is *nice* what we need?'

'Well, if *not nice* is what you need . . . do nothing. Stick around here.' Sulky again, she sank some lager. 'And suck it up.'

Six

It was just before ten and those still present at the wake in The Waterwheel were mostly the worse for wear. And it wasn't pleasant.

Claudia stood in the porch alongside her sister to say goodbye to all those on their way home. Not knowing how to react, many decided to blank her. She responded by blanking them back. But one or two caustic comments were made.

'Look at you . . . like butter wouldn't melt.'

'To think how proud we all were of you.'

'You know our Maggie's eldest girl died from an overdose?'

'No one's surprised, Claudia. We all thought it a bit weird that you got into the cops. You're a slip of a lass. You wouldn't know one end of a truncheon from the other. Unless it's the end where the batteries go, eh?'

She replied to that last one by calling the loutish younger nephew of one of her maiden aunts 'a fucking dickhead!' and told him to step outside where she'd show him 'the end of the pavement'. At which point, Jack steered her back into the bar. Minutes later, Judy came in and reiterated that they were a total disgrace. She never wanted to see either of them again and hoped they'd both get what was due to them.

'You see?' Claudia slurred, as she and Jack traipsed back through the town centre. 'See now why I want to disappear to the other end of the country?'

'You don't need to go that far,' he replied. 'Just shut them out. Shouldn't be hard. I mean, no disrespect to your family, Claudi, but if half of that lot had a brain cell, it'd top itself through sheer loneliness.'

'I've got to get away from here, Jack. Everything about this place reminds me, you know.'

They trudged on, the pub and bar district falling behind them. There were few pedestrians around now, and fewer cars, the only sound the fast clicking of Claudia's heels.

'I'm thinking of ringing the number on that card,' she said.

He shrugged. 'Your call.'

'And what will you do?'

'I don't know. I was seventeen years a cop. There's nothing else I want to do even if I could.'

'If you're working round to talking about doing yourself in again, I'm not buying.'

He'd alluded to this one time only, several weeks earlier, while muttering that he finally understood why certain folk considered ending it all a viable option.

'I wasn't totally serious about that.'

'You're not forty yet. There are loads of things you could do.'

'I'll find something, don't worry. But it'll be at a time and place of my own choosing.'

'Your problem, Jack, is you were always a control freak . . . always had to be in charge of everything.'

He was determined not to get vexed with her. She'd had a rough day, she was drunk, plus she was the only friend he had left. 'You never objected to my management style back in the day.'

Claudia became thoughtful as she wobbled along. 'You took *me* into your confidence more than anyone else. So, maybe I didn't have reason to . . . maybe that's where it all went wrong.'

'There was only you I ever trusted.'

'Pity. Because you had a good team under you.'

He snorted. 'Dropped us right in it when the time came, didn't they?'

'They didn't exactly drop us in it.'

Jack didn't reply. It was difficult not to harbour some level of resentment against their former colleagues, but what Claudia said was essentially true. Despite Ronald Jesperson's statement, there'd been no hard proof against either of them, though examination of their financial records had revealed anomalies – increased earnings failing to marry up with official salaries, overtime, and so forth – and when pressure was put on the rest of his team, a couple of younger members had cracked and admitted that drug hauls seized during raids always seemed lighter when being logged into evidence than they'd appeared to be on seizure. It hadn't been sufficient for the CPS to open full proceedings, but it had been more than enough for the pair of them to be dragged in front of a misconduct hearing.

'They could have been more vocal in their suspicions than they were,' Claudia added.

'Why mention any suspicions at all?'

'Because they didn't want to go down themselves, did they? They hadn't done anything wrong and had careers to think about. You surely don't blame them?'

Jack grunted. 'Look . . . I know I'm the one who fouled up.'

'Wasn't just you.'

'That's kind, but if it hadn't been for me, you'd still be on a fast track to the top floor. Look, I know I act like some kind of loner who can tough anything out . . . But . . .'

At which moment, with a screech of tyres, a silver-grey Saab veered across the road towards them – for half a second, they were rabbits in headlights – before mounting the kerb and blocking further access along the pavement.

The Saab's two front doors clattered open, and Charlie Quincannon and Lennie Hargreaves emerged, the former grinning as he stood facing them, the latter circling round the vehicle on to the pavement, cutting off any potential backward flight. Both wore dark waterproofs, zipped up tight, and dark gloves. A spanner slid into view from Charlie Quincannon's left sleeve. Hargreaves meanwhile hefted a ball bat to his shoulder.

Jack and Claudia backed towards the nearest shopfront.

'How you doing, piglets?' Hargreaves shouted. 'Or should that be ex-piglets?'

'Bacon sarnies, I'd say,' Charlie chuckled.

Sweat beaded on Jack's brow as he risked a glance behind them. There was a recessed doorway, but no escape. The shop was closed and locked, the recess grilled off.

He glanced back. 'Take it easy, eh?'

'Take it easy?' Charlie smacked the spanner into his gloved hand.

'Not got your shotgun with you?' Hargreaves said. 'That's a shame.'

The shop window now stood at their backs, preventing any further retreat.

Oddly though, despite there only being three or four yards between them, it now became a stand-off rather than the blitz assault Jack had expected.

'Told you we'd catch up with you,' Charlie said.

'You think you'll get away with this?' Jack replied.

'Let me see . . . two ex-coppers, bent as fuck, who no one likes anymore, with no influence whatsoever. And then us two . . .'

'Who no one likes either,' Claudia said.

Charlie gave her a grouchy look. 'Maybe, but we've still got lots of influence. Besides, we go to jail, so what? Nice little holiday with a few of our mates.'

'You two are nobodies,' she retorted, drawing more courage from her semi-drunkenness. 'Gofers at best. You don't even qualify as muscle . . .'

'Easy, eh?' Jack murmured.

'All that may be true,' another voice said. 'But it's not just *them* you're dealing with.'

A third party had climbed from the Saab's back seat. He was a great sagging block of a man, an ungainly mass squashed into a three-piece suit. His head was round and hairless, a pair of circular metal-framed glasses perched on his stubby nose.

'Tell you what, though . . .' He ambled on to the pavement, hands in his trouser pockets. 'You've got a mouth on you, girl. I was thinking of letting you walk . . . But now I've changed my mind.'

'We're civies now, Pete,' Jack said.

The new guy looked startled. 'So, you just get a pass?'

'Look . . . it was a game we all played. You knew the rules.'

'The problem is *you* didn't play by them.'

'I think you're just embarrassed because your firm's a joke,' Claudia said. 'Because we just dismantled you instead of doing business with you.'

'Christ's sake, Claudi!' Jack hissed. Most likely it was the combo of booze and everything else bad that had happened to her in recent months. But hell, why stir the pot?

Peter Quincannon eyed her long and hard. 'You didn't get this one as well trained as you should have, ex-DI McGurn. She's gonna cop it now. Alongside you.'

'Dirty Peter!' someone else said, sounding delighted. 'How the hell are you?'

All five of them turned, surprised, as Harry Wayland stepped out from the unlit alley alongside the shop, phone held upright. 'Still coming the big boss, Pete? Talking like you're Crowley's own Bugsy Siegel?'

Peter Quincannon regarded him with confusion, then recognition, then distaste. 'Three in one go. Fuck me. Must be my lucky day.'

'Or maybe not.' Wayland indicated his phone. 'I've been filming you for the last two minutes. Caught every word you and your goons have just said. I've even looped in a couple of mates I've still got in the job. So, if anything happens to these two people, or me – not just tonight, but basically ever again – they'll know exactly whose door to knock on.'

Peter Quincannon snorted with amusement, but it didn't reach his myopic little eyes. 'You think it's that simple?'

'I know it is.' Harry strode up to them, still filming. 'I also know the only way you're going to get your lard-arse out of this one is to take it far from here. Very far. Right now. And take your comic relief with you.'

Charlie Quincannon looked almost too startled to respond. 'You don't . . . you don't talk to us like that.'

'Talk to who? *Him?*' Wayland pointed at the older Quincannon. '*Dirty* Peter?'

'All right, Wayland!' the older gangster warned.

'Bet you've never heard about the stuff he got up to when he was younger, eh?' Wayland laughed. He tapped his phone. 'We're still on the live feed, by the way.'

'I said *ENOUGH!*' Peter Quincannon barked.

Harry's smile faded. 'In that case, pack up your circus and go home.' His voice was quieter, softer, but with an undercurrent of edged steel. 'There's nothing for you here, Pete . . . and there never will be.'

The stand-off dragged on for several taut seconds, the gangster trembling with impotent rage. 'Get in the car,' he finally told his underlings.

'Fuck's sake, Dad!' Charlie complained.

'Get in the fucking car! And *you*!' The gangland patriarch rounded on Hargreaves. 'Both you fucks, move it! *NOW!*'

He glared at the three ex-cops one more time, before climbing in himself, the vehicle rocketing out on to the road, tyres smoking as it pulled a fast three-point and tore away.

Slowly, the trio on the pavement let out their breaths.

'You've still got mates in the job?' Claudia asked.

'Like hell.' Wayland showed them his phone. It wasn't even recording. 'But I've still got those two most crucial police skills of all. Bullshit and bluster.'

'God's sake, Harry!' Jack said. 'What the hell are you playing at?'

Wayland eyed him. 'I think the words you're looking for, Jack, are thanks very much for saving our undeserving backsides from a right royal kicking.'

'Why are you following us round?'

'Well, no one else had your backs. Clearly.'

'You knew we were in trouble?' Claudia asked.

Wayland gave her a pitying stare. 'Really must have lost your edge if *you* didn't.' He turned to Jack. '*You* knew, didn't you?'

Jack yanked at his collar. 'Bollocks . . . I don't know.'

'What're we talking about?' Claudia glanced from one to the other.

'Those two clowns,' Jack admitted. 'Charlie Quincannon and Lennie Hargreaves. They had a go at me last night.'

Her eyebrows lifted. 'And you never mentioned it?'

'Don't worry about it,' Wayland cut in. 'They won't be coming back. Dirty Peter's lucky he only got a year when you busted his firm. He won't do anything else that might screw his life over.'

'He was pretty pissed off about their Paddy,' Jack said.

'Yeah, but not so much that he didn't let him take the full rap. Besides, he's got sons all over the north-west. Most from underage mums, I'm guessing.'

'How did you know they came to visit me last night?'

Wayland shrugged. 'Didn't. Saw them obbing the funeral today. They were keeping their distance, though not so much that I didn't spot them straight off.'

'Well, *I'm* grateful even if Jack isn't,' Claudia said.

Wayland zipped his top. 'All part of the service.'

'We haven't signed up for any service,' Jack replied.

'Bet you're thinking about it now, though, eh? Look . . . this is a perfect example of what Damned Rankers can offer. All alone, we don't have a hope. But together, we can go places.'

'You on some kind of bonus for everyone you recruit?' Claudia wondered.

Wayland laughed. 'The one bonus I get is helping out people in the same predicament as me. But listen . . . don't take my word for it. Take our benefactor's.'

Jack frowned. 'This mystery billionaire?'

'Since we met in the bar earlier, I've learned that he's going to make a personal appearance. On St Dunstan, no less.'

'This guy's actually going to be there?' Jack said.

'Wants to get to know you all personally. See for himself what's needed to help you out.'

Jack and Claudia exchanged bewildered glances. This whole thing was happening so fast. Could it be that somewhere in this world that hated them they might have a friend after all? A powerful friend.

Wayland grinned. 'You think you've got no one left in your corner, kids. But you are so, so wrong.'

Seven

'Well, this was always going to be the most uncomfortable part of the week,' the woman in the puffer jacket and jeans said. 'So, let's get it over with. I'm Cheryl Baxter.'

Jack and Claudia introduced themselves in return, shaking her hand, though it felt awkward. But at least she'd come over to them. The three other people waiting on the small stone quayside at Porth Conger were keeping themselves to themselves. Cheryl Baxter was probably in her late forties. Her short, light-blonde hair fell into natural ringlets; she was bright-eyed, pert-nosed and full-lipped. She'd attempted to be pleasant, but hadn't given much away.

In the past whenever Jack and Claudia had met cops they didn't know, at a Federation bash or whatever, they could ask them which force they hailed from, but that was a no-no today. Better to let these people volunteer any personal information in their own time.

However, Jack couldn't help wondering about Cheryl Baxter, who had now crossed back over the quay and was speaking with one of the others, a young girl of Indian heritage. From Baxter's accent, he suspected she hailed from a Yorkshire force. But wherever it was, she didn't seem the type to have got up to no good. There was something too wholesome about her.

'Penny for your thoughts?' Claudia asked quietly.

He nudged at his travel bag with his foot, to ensure it was still close (though there was nobody around to steal it). 'Can't believe you got me here.'

'*I* didn't get you here. It was the promise of meeting our new benefactor.'

'What are we really expecting?'

'A million quid each.'

He arched an eyebrow. 'Yeah, right.'

'I'm joking.'

'You don't say.'

She got huffy. 'If nothing else, we're going on holiday. You're allowed to smile.'

'Going on holiday.' He shook his head. 'Like this whole deal isn't weird enough.'

With a hefty *clank*, the boat waiting at the dock lowered its gangway. There was a gate fixed at the end, so it wasn't time to board just yet, but a surly-looking crewman was visible on deck, preparing everything. The other passengers, Cheryl Baxter among them, grabbed their luggage and shuffled towards it.

'I mean, how will it look,' Jack said in a low voice, 'if we do end up monetising this situation?'

'Monetising?'

'Making a bob or two. From being corrupt police officers.'

'You mean a bob or two more than we did when we actually *were* corrupt police officers?'

Now the gate had been lifted and the gangway opened. It was only narrow and one by one their fellow travellers were balancing their way up it.

'Nobody's seriously thinking about monetising anything,' Claudia said. 'This guy just wants to help us out.'

She picked her pack up, but Jack hung back.

'Damon Banks shot and killed a sex murderer,' he said. 'Which right-thinking member of society wouldn't have tacitly approved? But *we* were on the take. How are these things similar?'

She looked frustrated. And cross. 'We've got ourselves a supporter. That's all you need to know. Now, if you're not going to enjoy yourself, fine. But don't throw a wet blanket on it for me.' She headed to the gangplank. With some degree of reluctance, Jack followed.

◆ ◆ ◆

The trip from St Agnes to St Dunstan had a holiday atmosphere. The sky a cloudless blue, the sea calm. The midsummer sun rode high, but there was a stiff Atlantic breeze, so they were glad of their jumpers and waterproofs.

It was a fifty-minute voyage, but this wasn't the luxury superyacht they'd half expected. It was a private charter, paid for in advance, but it had the appearance of a converted fishing boat, its storm-battered hull and the metal barrier along its gunwales in need of a paint job. The skipper and his single crewman, unsavoury individuals, installed themselves in the pilot's cabin at the vessel's stern and didn't reappear for the remainder of the journey. The rest of the main deck, about fifty or sixty square feet in total, was open to the elements, and any other bits of equipment, its antennae or boom mast, or any additional housing that had once been there, had long gone, replaced by passenger benches, some located around the bulwarks, some in the middle, facing frontward.

That said, it was spacious enough with only the six of them on board, excluding the crew.

Jack and Claudia had settled themselves on the portside bench when Cheryl Baxter came over with the young Indian girl, whose name was Varada Rathour. She seemed too mousy and petite to have been a serving police officer, at least for long enough to fall into the sort of bad habits that had landed everyone else here. She was in her early twenties, pretty, with smooth schoolgirl features, dark eyes and shoulder-length black hair currently being tossed in the sea breeze.

No doubt Cheryl Baxter had meant well when she'd brought her over, but the poor girl seemed embarrassed.

Glad it's not just me, Jack thought.

All they had in common with these people were the extreme betrayals of trust they were each responsible for. Some kind of kinship, that was.

'Been to the Scilly Isles before, Varada?' Claudia asked.

'I've never even been to Cornwall before.'

'Are we still in Cornwall?' Jack said.

'The Duchy of Cornwall,' Cheryl Baxter replied.

'There's not much on the islands themselves,' Claudia said. 'Mainly tourists. I've been checking it out on YouTube. But in summer they're supposed to be beautiful.'

After that, the stilted conversation dried up.

Sod it, Jack thought. They were going to have to break the ice at some point.

'What force were you with, Varada?' he asked.

'Oh . . . *oh*!' Her eyes widened. 'I wasn't a police officer.'

'You weren't?' he replied, unsurprised.

'I was civilian staff . . . Operational Support. TacOps, as we called it.'

'That's Lancashire, isn't it?' Claudia said.

'Yes, Lancashire Constabulary.' Rathour looked apologetic. 'That's where I *was*. I'm not there now, obviously.'

Jack glanced along the bench to Cheryl Baxter, who'd stiffened a little at the turn in the conversation. 'West Yorkshire,' she said curtly.

'We were GMP,' he replied.

'All northern forces,' Claudia observed.

Wasn't it a little odd that everyone they'd met so far came from the same region?

'I don't think *he* was.' Baxter nodded over to the starboard gunwale, where one of the other passengers stood alone. 'I tried to speak to him earlier, but he'd only mutter. I think his name is Jonas Pugh.'

Pugh was a nervous, twitchy sort in his mid-fifties with an unruly mop of red-grey hair and a thick matching moustache. He stood by the barrier, swigging from a hip flask, seemingly unconcerned whether anyone noticed.

'Did he say where he was from?' Claudia asked.

'No, but he has a slight Welsh accent.' Baxter nodded to where the final other passenger was seated alone. 'I don't know about him. We exchanged pleasantries but that's about all.'

Sensing that he was under discussion, this second object of interest glanced around, made eye contact and with a bland smile, stood up and ambled over.

'Sorry, I've not introduced myself.' He offered his hand. 'Alan Rothermere.'

Jack was the last to shake with him. 'Jack McGurn.'

Rothermere nodded and smiled again.

There was something about this chap that put Jack on guard. It was that copper's sixth sense. Sometimes you just knew when you were in the presence of a bad egg, and yet there was nothing especially unlikeable about Alan Rothermere. He was somewhere in his late forties, with fair hair, greying around the edges. About five-nine and chubby, he wore a gabardine overcoat over a V-necked sweater and a shirt and tie. Everything about him was prim and proper.

He didn't stay to make small talk but went back to his seat, dug into his holdall, extracted a paperback and commenced reading.

It bemused Jack that he'd taken such an immediate dislike to the guy. Was it because he knew that Rothermere could only be here because he'd done something wrong? It was the same with everyone else on the boat.

He stole another glance at Pugh, who was drinking again. Was *that* the problem in his case? Pugh glanced casually over and Jack averted his gaze.

What about Cheryl Baxter? Varada Rathour? Jack checked Rothermere out again, furtively. The guy continued reading, smiling to himself. He looked as innocent as they came. Your regular Mr Average. An inoffensive, upstanding citizen.

Which again, he obviously wasn't.

About the Author

Photo © C. Finch

Paul Finch is a number-one e-book bestseller and a top-ten *Sunday Times* bestseller. He first worked as a policeman in the north-west of England and then as a journalist.

His writing career commenced with episodes of the hit television drama *The Bill*, and since then, he has written extensively in the horror, fantasy, historical epic and sci-fi genres, including for *Doctor Who*. He is a two-time winner of the British Fantasy Award and a recipient of the International Horror Guild Award. However, Paul is probably best known for his dark crime thriller novels, including the Heckenburg and Clayburn series, and for his first novel with Thomas & Mercer, *The Island*. In his capacity as thriller writer, he has twice been shortlisted for the Crime Writers' Association Dagger Awards.

The Lodge is Paul's second novel for Thomas & Mercer, and, while firmly in murder-mystery territory, it draws on his love of Gothic fiction and classic horror movies. It also leans into the worlds of true crime, which he reads regularly, and so-called 'dark tourism', which he is both fascinated by and worried about in equal measure.

Paul lives in Lancashire with his wife and business partner, Cathy.

Follow the Author on Amazon

If you enjoyed this book, follow Paul Finch on Amazon to be notified when the author releases a new book!
To do this, please follow these instructions:

Desktop:

1) Search for the author's name on Amazon or in the Amazon App.
2) Click on the author's name to arrive on their Amazon page.
3) Click the 'Follow' button.

Mobile and Tablet:

1) Search for the author's name on Amazon or in the Amazon App.
2) Click on one of the author's books.
3) Click on the author's name to arrive on their Amazon page.
4) Click the 'Follow' button.

Kindle eReader and Kindle App:

If you enjoyed this book on a Kindle eReader or in the Kindle App, you will find the author 'Follow' button after the last page.